Manche X
Manchee, William
Ca$h call : a Stan Turner mystery
/

34028067101346
TOM $12.95   ocm53831911
05/22/08

Comments on the Stan Turner Mysteries

Publisher's Weekly - Dallas lawyer Stan Turner attracts his usual share of trouble and more in William Manchee's *Second Chair*, the third in a series. Turner must fend off a lawsuit from his CPA's widow, who blames him and his wife for her husband's death, as well as defend a college student accused of murdering her newborn child. Appealing characters and lively dialogue, especially in the courtroom, make this an easy, entertaining read.

The Book Reader - The courtroom scenes are superb, intoxicating, the descriptions filled with power. The climax is shrewd and fits the modern American temperament of winning at all costs. Manchee, an attorney, spins a good plot, playing out the scenes slowly so that the reader is caught in the what-comes-next trap. Richly textured with wonderful atmosphere, the novel shows Manchee as a smooth, polished master of the mystery form.

MyShelf.Com - Stan Turner is a very pleasant guy and the kind of lawyer that we would all love to have in our corner. All of the characters are believable and fit into the plot. William Manchee has done it again with *Second Chair*. . . . I have had the honor of reading *Death Pact* to review, and I will say that it is the best book that I have ever read so far; *Second Chair* is a close second to *Death Pact*. William Manchee can spin a tale that totally keeps you holding on and wanting more. You can bet that I will read anything that this talented author puts out. Kudos to William Manchee for a 5 star read again!

The Richardson News - Manchee's fictional lawyer always wins the war, but he does lose battles, which makes him a believable character. Manchee's story is a page turner. He manages to keep the reader's interest with a serpentine plot and realistic dialogue.

Norman Transcript - Like *Undaunted* and *Brash Endeavor*, *Second Chair* takes the reader for the ride of their life. Manchee's command of the justice system, added to his experience in court and with clients, makes for a good read.

Scribes World - Manchee weaves a fast paced, tightly wound narrative filled with intrigue, deception and circumstance which are not always as they seem. *Undaunted, A Stan Turner Mystery* proves Manchee's understanding of the justice system . . . . This novel has it all. love, duplicitous murder, a serial killer, The Corps, suicide, and a bigoted white supremacist all race the reader through the pages of this gripping work.

CA$H CALL

To my partner

Pat Hubbard

CA$H CALL

A Stan Turner Mystery

Book IV

by

WILLIAM MANCHEE

Top Publications, Ltd.
Dallas, Texas

CA$H CALL

A Stan Turner Mystery

A Top Publications Paperback

First Edition

Top Publications, Ltd.
12221 Merit Drive, Suite 750
Dallas, Texas 75251

All Rights Reserved
Copyright 2002
William Manchee

ISBN#: 0-9666366-8-6

Library of Congress Control Number 2001127211

No part of this book may be published or utilized in any form or by any means, electronic or mechanical, including photocopying, recording or information storage and retrieval systems without the express written permission of the publisher.

The characters and events in this novel are fictional and created out of the imagination of the author. Certain real locations and institutions are mentioned, but the characters and events depicted are entirely fictional.

Printed in the United States of America

Contents

Christine	1
Don Blaylock	23
Evil Forces	31
Wrongful Death	39
Hot Checks	47
DWI	51
Murder by Tire Iron	63
The Golden Dragon Partnership	69
The Embezzlement	79
The Accident	85
Winning the Lawyer's Lottery	99
Shattered Lives	107
Poetry	115
Margie's Recollections	133
Richard Banks	153
The Alibis	175

Mid-America Life	187
The Wedding	199
Deposition	203
Laura Bell	213
The Last Straw	219
Reluctant Witness	223
The Lineup	229
The Miracle	251
Docket Call	265
Turner & Waters, L.L.P.	279
State vs. Cochran	285
A Low Blow	301
The Verdict	309
A Million Fish	317
A Perfect Snow	325

CHAPTER ONE

Christine

Everyone needs an escape from the relentless pressure that we all face in today's feverish world. Whenever I felt overburdened with my client's problems, or with my own, I would get my three boys together and we'd all go fishing. I don't know why it worked so well, but it did wonders for my sanity. As soon as the kids were in the car, and I got behind the wheel of our big Chevy custom van, all thoughts of my law practice and the reality of my life evaporated like the morning dew on a hot August day.

Though I wasn't the greatest fisherman on the planet, it wasn't for lack of trying. I had fished all my life, but just couldn't quite master the art. All of the tips from the pros at the tackle shops, in the fishing magazines, and on TV hadn't helped. A couple of times I even hired a guide just to see how it was supposed to be done. Visual observation usually worked for me as I was a quick study. But in the case of fishing, there was more to it than met the eye.

In the end it didn't really matter, because we always had a great time whether we caught anything or not. It was cheap therapy—well, not all that cheap actually when you consider the gas, lodging, license, bait, tackle, food, and boat rental fees—not to mention the dozens of expensive lures that the kids loved to snag on the bottom of the lake.

It was unfortunate that Rebekah hated fishing because that meant she and Marcia missed out on these great adventures. It was particularly hard on Marcia because she hated it when her brothers did things that she couldn't do. She would plead relentlessly with her mother for permission to go and sulk for days when Rebekah refused. Of course, I had no problem with bringing Marcia along, but Rebekah wanted her little princess to be ladylike, not a tomboy. With three older brothers that was definitely a losing battle.

It was on a Friday in August 1983 when the need for one of these therapy sessions became abundantly clear. Cash flow had dried to a trickle, receivables were climbing and aging to the point that the Turner Law Firm's demise appeared imminent. It wasn't that I didn't have business—business was booming to the extent I could hardly keep up. Apparently the word had leaked out that I worked for free or was a sucker for a sad story. Usually I didn't let this bother me, but with the recent death of my CPA and the suicide of his wife, I was generally depressed and was often tempted to curl up with a bottle of Jack Daniels. But when you have a wife and four kids depending on you, that's not a viable option.

As the day slowly waned, I stared out my office window at the cars traveling up and down LBJ Freeway. That wasn't unusual. It actually helped me calm down when I got too stressed out. Sometimes the tranquility of the moment would even lead to *inspiration*—something I usually needed desperately. My daydreaming was suddenly interrupted by my secretary Jodie's deliberate voice over the intercom. "Paul Jones on line two."

The name sent a shudder down my spine. I knew what he wanted: money, the root of all evil. It should have been obvious to him that I didn't have any or American Express would have already been paid. He knew that, so why the phone call? *Should I take it? Or, should I have Jodie tell him I was out. Better yet. I'll take it and tell him to take a hike. That would feel good . . . but it would only piss him off and he'd just start calling more often.* I walked over to the phone and picked it up. We exchanged frigid greetings.

"Your payment's late again—forty-five days," he informed me.

"I know. I'll get something out to you soon."

"What seems to be the trouble? Our records show you pay this account consistently late."

"I know, cash flow's a little tight."

"Well if you know you can't pay the bill, then why do you use the card?"

My blood pressure began to rise. It really ticked me off when a bill collector asked a good question. He was right. I shouldn't have used the damn card. Every month it was a chore scraping up enough money to pay it. But did he really expect me to discuss responsible household budgeting with him? No, he was trying to embarrass and humiliate me.

"You're right. Just as soon I get the bill paid, I'm going to cut it up and throw it into the garbage. Then you'll never have to call me again."

There was a moment of silence. "Well, that's not really necessary. Just send us a payment."

"Listen, I've had this card for three years, and everything's been paid, hasn't it?"

"Yeah, but it's always late."

"It may be late, but you always get the payment, plus your ten percent late fee. You should be happy I always pay late. You get all that extra money."

"Ah, well. I'll mark our records that you're going to have a check in the mail by—"

"By the weekend . . . hopefully."

"Okay, and try next month to pay this bill on time."

I let out a silent scream. He just had to throw in one more insulting remark. If we had been face to face I would have punched him out. "I'll do my best," I said and slammed down the phone.

I pulled out my checkbook and frowned at the negative balance. No matter how hard I worked, there was never enough money. As I was putting the checkbook away, Jodie walked in and said, "Maybe one of your deadbeat clients will pay their bill today, and you can send AMEX something."

Jodie, up to then, had always been understanding and sympathetic, but it didn't lessen my embarrassment. She probably regretted the day she came to work for me. Her check had bounced more than once, but she always redeposited it without mentioning it to me. Each time I got the notice from the bank I nearly died. It was kind of surprising to me she still showed up every morning with a cheerful smile. She was a wonderful secretary, and I feared one day she'd get tired of my financial instability and quit.

I smiled and replied semi-confidently, "Oh yeah, somebody's bound to pay sooner or later."

Jodie frowned, put her hands on her hips, and said, "Why don't you get tough with them, cut them off if they don't pay—sue them if you have to?"

I looked up at her somewhat surprised. It was the first time she had ever been so outspoken. She was a beautiful young girl and particularly sexy when angered. My pulse quickened. "Law practice isn't just about money, Jodie. Most of my clients want to pay me, but they can't always do it."

"I think a lot of them could pay you if they really wanted to."

"You think so?"

She nodded. "Yeah, it's just not a high priority to them. They know you won't do anything if they don't pay."

"You don't have much faith in human nature, I guess."

"No, I don't. Robert Taylor is a perfect example."

"Robert Taylor?" I said. "How's that?"

"Did you know he just got back from a cruise to the Cayman Islands?"

"What?"

That bit of information blew my mind. Robert Taylor had come to me with hat in hand. He had been sued and wanted me to defend him. When I asked him for a retainer he moaned and whimpered about how broke he was. He promised he'd pay my bills promptly every month as soon as he received them. Gullible me agreed. "But he owes me three grand."

"I rest my case."

"How do you know he went to the Caymans?"

"When I called him about his bill, his secretary told me."

"That dirty bastard."

I turned, gazed out the window still in shock. I looked back at her. "Okay, I guess you're right. Get him on the line."

"Really?"

I nodded. Jodie eagerly left the room. *That son of a bitch has been lying to me through his teeth.* After a moment Jodie's voice came out over the intercom, "Robert Taylor on two."

I hesitated a moment thinking about what I should say, then picked up the phone and said, "Robert?"

"Yes, Stan. What's up? Don't tell me they filed another motion for summary judgment."

"No, I was just curious about your trip to the Cayman Islands. You didn't tell me you were going on vacation."

"Oh, yeah. Didn't I mention that to you?"

"No. Did you have a good time?"

"Sure, it's always beautiful there."

"Really, *I've* never been there myself."

"You haven't? You ought to go some time."

"I'd like to, but I have this problem with clients who don't pay their damn bills."

"Listen, Stan. I know what you're thinking, but we had planned this vacation long before I got sued. Gloria would have killed me if I canceled it."

"Uh huh. You begged me to take the case without a retainer. You swore to me you would pay all your bills on time. You said I had nothing to worry about."

"I know."

"And then instead of paying my bill, you take a lavish vacation. I should have let them take a damn default judgment against you!"

"Come on, Stan. It's not like that. I'm serious. Gloria would have divorced me if I canceled the trip. You know what a pain in the ass she can be."

"Well, you better start sending me some serious money or I'm going to withdraw from the case."

"Don't do that, Stan. I'll pay you. Don't worry."

"It's not a matter of worrying, Robert. I've got bills to pay—lots of them."

"I'll send you something Monday, all right? Just give me a little time."

"Okay . . . but don't let me down or you'll be looking for a new attorney."

"I won't."

I sat back in my chair and took a deep breath. It felt good to let off a little steam once in awhile, particularly during periods of depression. I couldn't help feeling a little guilty though, coming down on him the way I had. Jodie walked in, smiled and asked, "So, is he bringing over a check?"

"On Monday."

"Monday! Why not today?"

"He doesn't have it today."

"He would have had it if he had not gone on vacation."

"True, but his marriage is in trouble. He would have been in deep shit had he canceled his vacation."

"You're not buying that story are you?"

"Hey. . . . I've met his wife, she *is* a pain in the ass."

"He's just using you. Can't you see that?"

"No, I believe him."

Jodie shook her head. "You're so good to your clients. I just hate to see them take advantage of you. I wish they would just pay their damn bills when we send them. We shouldn't have to beg them to pay us."

"Maybe they need the money worse than we do."

"Yeah, you can tell AMEX that the next time they call."

"I couldn't sue a client anyway. Most of them are my friends. It wouldn't be right."

"Why not? You sue people all the time for your clients."

"That's different. That's them suing, not me. I'm just doing my job. . . . Besides there are too many of them. I wouldn't have time to practice law. I'd be spending half my time in court suing my own clients."

"Okay. . . I give up. So what are you going to do about your dire financial situation?" Jodie asked.

I looked at her and smiled. Her anger had turned to sadness and depression. I sighed. Why was I such a terrible businessman? I didn't know what I was going to do. Then the telephone rang. Jodie turned and left to answer the phone. She yelled back to me, "It's Robert Taylor again."

I frowned. What did he want now? Had he been holding out on me? Did he suddenly find some money to pay me with? I prayed that was the case but somehow knew it wasn't. I lifted the receiver.

"Robert?"

"Listen, Stan. I was just thinking. Do you ever get paid *in kind*?"

My heart sunk. When clients started talking about paying me *in kind* that usually meant I wasn't going to get paid at all. I looked over at the six pieces of ancient Peruvian pottery that sat prominently on the top of one of my bookcases. It was payment *in kind* from a missionary who'd been down in Central America several years saving souls. I'd defended him here in a civil suit stemming from a car wreck he got into while he was home visiting family. He swore on a stack of Bibles it was worth fifteen thousand easy.

"What did you have in mind?" I asked.

"I've got this great boat that I never have time to use. It's just sitting out in the back yard and I know your boys love to fish. . . . How about we swap the boat for my bill?"

"What kind of boat?"

When I hung up the phone, I felt exhilarated. In the past, whenever we went fishing we were forced to fish off the bank, on a dirty old fishing barge, or out of a John boat. This was not real fishing and I longed for the day I could get a Bass Tracker®. Robert's boat wasn't a bass boat per se, but it was a nice combo ski and fishing boat that would be quite satisfactory. Jodie walked in and was shocked to see me smiling from ear to ear.

"He's bringing in money?" She asked.

"No," I replied gleefully.

"Then what are you so happy about?"

"He's bringing me a boat."

"A boat . . . oh my God. Tell me you didn't—"

"I'm going fishing. I hear the striper are hitting top waters at Texoma."

Jodie looked at me incredulously. "But what about our cash flow problem?"

I shrugged. "Why don't you try to find me an expert on Peruvian civilizations. Maybe I can figure out how to unload that ancient pottery I've got in my office."

"Good luck."

"Call the SMU library. I bet someone over there might have some ideas."

"Fine."

"I don't have any more appointments today, do I?"

"No."

"Good. Rebekah has a nursing seminar she's got to go to tomorrow, so it's a perfect time to go fishing."

"Oh, what a wonderful solution, Stan. . . . So, since you obviously won't have the money to pay me on the fifteenth, I think I'll take off too."

Jodie sarcasm stung a bit, but not enough to diminish my excitement which was waxing by the second as I thought of gliding across Lake Texoma in my new boat. Well, it wasn't new exactly. Robert had said it was a 1975 model, but eight years for a boat wasn't that old.

"Good idea. You've been looking a little stressed out here lately. You could use the afternoon off."

"Fine. I'm out of here then."

Jodie turned and started to leave. I looked at her and said, "Don't worry about getting paid. You're my number one priority. I couldn't practice law without you. You know that, don't you?"

Jodie took a deep breath. She turned, looked back at me and said, "I know, but what if you just run totally out of money? Then what?"

I didn't have a good answer for her, nor was I about to let something as trivial as *money* dampen the ecstasy I was feeling on my first day as a boat owner. I smiled and said, "Have a nice weekend, Jodie. I'll see you on Monday."

Jodie shook her head, turned, and walked out the front door. I cut the lights, locked the door, and headed to Robert's place to get my new boat. On the way there all I could think about was where we'd start looking for those stripers.

Rebekah's mouth dropped when I walked in the door at three in the afternoon. She glanced at the clock and then back at me. It suddenly dawned on me that Rebekah wasn't going to be pleased with my new acquisition. She looked at me warily. I wondered if there was anything I could do or say to lessen her inevitable displeasure over what I had done. Nothing coming to mind, I decided just to plunge onward and hope for the best.

"Stan, what are you doing here?"

"You won't believe what I brought home."

"Really? What is it?"

Marcia came running in yelling, "Daddy. Daddy. You're home early." She jumped into my arms as she loved to do when I came home. I flung her around a couple times and gave her a bear hug.

"Yes, amazing, isn't it?"

I smiled and looked into her bright brown eyes. She

looked just like her mother did when she was a girl. In fact, if you put pictures of them at eight years old side by side, it was hard to tell them apart.

After putting Marcia down, I said, "Go find your brothers. I've got a surprise for everyone."

"Oh. A surprise. Daddy's got a surprise!" she yelled as she ran off. Rebekah's look of apprehension was intensifying by the minute as she waited to find out what was going on. I smiled at her, but she didn't respond. A minute later Reggi, Mark, and Peter ran into the room with Marcia hot on their heels.

"Okay, come on outside," I said. "It's in the driveway."

They all rushed out the front door and stopped in their tracks when they saw it. I looked at Rebekah and held my breath. Reggi broke everyone's stunned silence, "Whoa! What a cool boat."

"Stan, you bought a boat?" Rebekah groaned.

The boys climbed eagerly into the boat. Marcia tried to follow them but wasn't tall enough to make it over the side. I grabbed her under the arms and lifted her inside.

"No, I didn't buy it exactly. A client gave it to me."

"Why would he do that?" Rebekah questioned.

Mark pushed a button on the dash and there was a loud, "Hoooonk! Hoooonk!" The kids laughed in delight. I couldn't help but laugh too, but Rebekah wasn't smiling.

"It's an inboard/outboard. It cruises at thirty-five miles per hour. We can use it for skiing or fishing."

"Okay, what's going on? Clients just don't give you expensive boats."

"It was a trade."

"Oh, for chrissakes. You took this boat instead of money?"

"Well, you know Robert Taylor. He has owed me three grand for over six months. I've been pressing him for the cash but he just doesn't have it. So, I figured at least with the trade we'd have something the family could use."

Rebekah shook her head. "I can't believe you. We are destitute and you're letting your client unload a worthless piece of junk on you."

"What are you talking about? It's a beautiful boat and we're going to have some great fun with it."

"Can we take it out, Dad?" Reggi asked.

"Yes, that's the plan. We can take it to Texoma tomorrow while your mother is busy with her seminar."

"What about Marcia?" Rebekah said. "I don't want her out in the boat."

"She'll be okay. Don't worry."

"Four kids are too many for you to watch. Marcia can stay with my mother. I'm sure she won't mind watching her."

"No. Mommy! I want to go fishing," Marcia moaned.

"No argument. You are *not* going fishing. Little girls don't fish. Maybe Grandma will take you to a movie."

Marcia started bawling. "I don't want to go to—"

Rebekah glared at her then turned to me. "See the trouble you caused with your foolishness."

"Listen. I don't need a bunch of crap from you. I'm taking my boys fishing. It's no big deal, so calm down."

"Who's Christine?" Rebekah said pointing to the *Christine* painted on the side of the boat.

"What?" I said. "Oh that. I think Christine was Robert's ex-wife."

"Wonderful. My husband is running around with a boat named after his deadbeat client's ex-wife."

I laughed. "Okay. We'll change the name if it bothers you. How about *Rebekah One?*"

"Don't do me any favors," Rebekah said, as she shook her head, turned and stormed back into the house.

I know it didn't make much sense to accept the boat in payment of Robert's bill, but I frequently made decisions based on gut feelings rather than logic. I had learned early in life to trust my instincts and so far that had been a good strategy. The moment Robert mentioned the boat, I knew it had to be. I also feared Rebekah would react the way she did—not because of the money so much, but because being an emergency room nurse she had seen some very serious injuries resulting from boating accidents. She would be scared to death every minute we were out on the lake. But I just couldn't let her fears keep us from enjoying life to the fullest. We would be careful, extra careful for her sake.

The following morning at five we were eating breakfast and getting ready to take off. The fishing was usually best between six and ten in the morning, and it took an hour to get from our house to Lake Texoma. Rebekah had finally resigned herself to our male madness and worked diligently to make us a nice picnic lunch. At five-thirty she hugged the boys goodbye, gave me a peck on the lips, then waved goodbye with Marcia at her side.

"Goodbye, Daddy. Bring me home a big one!" Marcia yelled as we pulled away.

We drove north on Highway 75 to Sherman and then cut over to Lake Texoma via Pottsboro. Just out of Pottsboro we stopped at a convenience store to stock up on lures and buy some snacks. After dropping a half dozen lures, four candy bars, and a six pack of Coke on the counter, I asked the clerk if he knew where the stripers were schooling.

He said, "Just go north out of Little Mineral and when you get to end of the point, go west about a mile. You should be able to see the boats tracking the striper school."

"Great. Thanks for the info."

"No problem. You need a license?"

I thought a moment, then opened my billfold to check. Sure enough there was a Texas license. I checked the expiration date and was glad to see it hadn't expired.

"No, mine's still good," I said.

The sun was just peeking over the eastern horizon when I finally put *Christine* in the water for her maiden voyage. It was tricky getting her into the lake. Previously we had always launched from a dock. Backing the boat into the lake wasn't as easy as it looked. The kids held their breath as we eased our way down the boat ramp.

"Don't go too far, Dad," Reggi said. "You might kill the engine."

"I know. Tell me when you think the boat is in far enough to float."

"Now!" Reggi screamed. I put the car in park, set the brake and got out. The tricky part was getting into the boat without getting soaked. I stepped up onto the trailer, edged my way over to the boat and climbed in. Reggi unhooked the cable that held the boat in place on the trailer. I cranked the engine and put it reverse. All eyes were on me while I backed off the trailer. Upon clearing the trailer I pushed the throttle forward and eased the boat over to the dock. After parking the car we all climbed in the boat and were ready to go.

The kids were all smiles as we idled out of the harbor. I didn't know what to expect as I pushed the throttle forward. The boat took off with a thunderous roar jolting us backward. Everyone started laughing hysterically. Soon we were sailing across the lake at full throttle experiencing exhilaration I had never thought possible. As I looked back at my delirious crew I knew trading for the boat had been a good decision.

It took us about thirty minutes to locate the armada of boats who were stalking the school of stripers. We idled into the pack and got ready to fish. Reggi could handle his own rod and reel, but my two youngest needed constant help and monitoring. As a result, on most of these trips I did very little fishing of my own. Usually, I was kept busy untangling bird nests or tying on new lures. After everyone got their line in the water, we waited . . . and waited . . . and waited.

"I got one!" Mark screamed, as his pole bent, and his reel began to wail. "It's a big one." He pulled back and tried to reel it in when suddenly the line went limp. "Oh, crap! I lost it."

"Oh, no. That's too bad," I said. "I thought maybe we wouldn't get skunked today."

Mark reeled in his line. He had lost his lure as well as the fish. Peter and Reggi watched their poles anxiously, but there were no more strikes. After a while it became obvious the striper had moved on, and the armada began to disperse. We followed a couple of guide boats for a while but they soon split up and we lost them. We found several other groups of boats and joined them, but we saw very little action. It was almost noon when I suggested we go to the islands and take a swim.

There were a string of islands about midway between the Texas and Oklahoma sides of the lake. They had nice sandy beaches, picnic tables, and big shady trees. A lot of people camped there, and at night you could see their campfires across the lake. It was hot, and the boys were exhausted, so I got no argument.

As we neared the shore, I cut the engine to an idle and we gently pushed up onto the beach. After I tied the boat to a rock so it wouldn't drift away, we took our shirts and sneakers off and hit the water. A brisk southerly wind created some nice waves that the kids used to pretend they were surfing. Fortunately, Rebekah had insisted each of the kids take swimming lessons when they were toddlers, so they were all like fish in the water.

The water was cool and very pleasant on this hot summer day. It was totally enjoyable, and my only regret was that Rebekah and Marcia were not there to enjoy it with us. After a half hour I got out of the water and watched the kids play from the shore. The sun was hot so I applied a thick layer of suntan lotion, hoping to avoid looking like a lobster on Monday. After another half hour had passed, Reggi came in to shore with a serious look on his face.

"Let's go do some more fishing, Dad," he said. "I'm tired of swimming."

"I doubt we'll catch any striper this time of day," I

replied.

"I bet there are some nice bass in those coves we passed."

"Maybe. I guess it wouldn't hurt to check it out."

"Great! Let's go."

"Call your brothers in."

Reggi turned and yelled, "Mark . . . Peter! Get your butts over here. We're going bass fishing!"

After they had put their clothes back on, they got back in the boat, and we shoved off. I idled backward a ways and then turned the boat around and gave it full throttle. The kids looked at each other with broad smiles. Normally I had a good sense of direction. Even on a big lake like Texoma I had never had a problem getting where I wanted to go. But suddenly I looked around and didn't know where I was.

"Daddy," Reggi yelled, pointing toward the shore. "Look at that cove over there. I bet it's full of bass."

"Yeah, Dad," Mark chimed in. "Let's go over there."

I scratched my head, wondering where the hell we were. Finally I shook my head and said, "Okay," and headed the boat toward the cove.

It was a beautiful little cove about a half mile deep. I slowed the engine to an idle and glided along the shore. When we were about a hundred yards out, I saw a bass jump, so I cut the engine and dropped the anchor. The boat slowed, and when the anchor hit bottom we turned 180° and then came to a stop.

"This looks as good a spot as any," I said.

Everyone jumped into action as the hunt began. "Daddy, fix my lure. It's tangled," Peter said.

"All right. Bring it over here."

While I was fixing Peter's lure, Reggi made a long cast toward the shore.

"Nice," I said.

He smiled and started slowly reeling the lure back toward the boat. Mark cast his lure to the rear of the boat.

Half way to its expected destination it snagged and dropped straight down about ten yards from the boat. The lure lay dead in the water.

"Crap!" he said. Then suddenly the lure disappeared, and his pole bent like a palm tree in a hurricane. "I got one!" he yelled.

"Good. Don't let it get away this time," I said.

"Damn," Reggi said. "Mark always catches the first fish."

He was right. Mark, for some reason, always caught the first fish and, often, the only fish. Reggi was shaking his head in disgust when there was a jerk on his line. His eyes lit up.

"I got one! . . . Oh, man! It's an elephant!"

By this time Mark had his catch on board. It was jumping around like water on a hot griddle. As hard as he tried, he couldn't get a grip on it to pull off the hook. "Help me, Daddy!" he screamed.

"Daddy! Get my line in the water," Peter moaned. "I wanna catch one!"

"Okay," I said, finishing up my knot. "You're set."

Peter tried to cast but snagged the side of the boat instead. "Help me!" he said.

"Give it here," I said. He handed me his pole, and I cast the lure fifty feet and watched it hit the water. I gave it back to him. "Here, now reel it in slow."

As I grabbed Mark's fish to take out the hook, Reggi brought his aboard.

"Wow! It must be five pounds."

"It's a big one, all right," I said as I extricated the hook from Mark's fish with a pair of needlenose pliers. To my rear I heard a splash. I turned to see a bass jump eighteen inches out of the water.

"Daddy! Look. I've got one," Peter yelled.

"Whoa! I guess so."

The pole was suddenly jerked out of Peter's hand and

he fell hard against the side of the boat still holding the line in his hand.

"Peter! Hang on. Don't let it go," I said, grabbing his foot so he wouldn't go overboard. After crawling over him, I reached out and grabbed the pole just before it sank out of sight. I got up and started reeling it in. "Stand up." Peter rubbed his stomach and then struggled to his feet. . . . "Now here," I said, handing him the pole. "Hang onto it this time."

Peter took the pole and began reeling in the fish. It was slow as the fish was stronger than he was. I watched in amazement at our sudden fortune—but not for long.

"I've got another one!" Mark yelled.

"Me, too," Reggi screamed.

"Jesus! We must be in a school," I said. "Where's my pole? I want some of this action."

"Daddy, take off my fish. I want to catch another one," Mark said.

"Take it off yourself. It's my turn to catch one."

Thirty-two fish later, the waters calmed and we stood with our lines in the water, dumbstruck—numb from excitement beyond our wildest fantasies. I took a deep breath and shook my head.

"Well, I think we caught them all," I said.

"No, I bet there are more," Reggi said.

I looked at my watch and saw it was almost four. Since I wasn't sure exactly where we were, I decided it was time to head on home. We certainly didn't need any more fish and it might take a while to get my bearings and find Little Mineral.

"Okay, men. It's time to head back."

"Nooo!" Peter moaned.

"Not yet, Daddy," Mark echoed.

"No argument," I said sternly. "It's getting late."

Reluctantly, the boys reeled in their lines and settled in for the ride home. As I was about to crank up the engine, I saw a boat coming at us fast. When it got about fifty feet from us, it slowed down to an idle and came up along side. It was an Oklahoma Fish & Game patrol boat with two officers aboard. My stomach tightened. *What is this about?*

"Hi, there," the older of the two men said.

"Hi," I replied politely.

The two officers scanned the fish scattered about our boat.

"Quite a catch you got there."

"Yeah, we came up on a school, I guess. I've never seen anything like it."

"You gotta license, I guess?"

"Oh, sure. I checked it before we came out."

"Good. Let me take a look at it."

"Sure," I said, as I reached for my wallet. I pulled out the license and handed it to the officer.

He studied it a second. "This is a Texas license."

I nodded. "Right."

"I hope you have an Oklahoma one."

"An Oklahoma license? Why?"

"You're in Oklahoma waters."

I looked around at the landscape. "I am? I thought for sure I was on the Texas side. I didn't mean to come into Oklahoma waters."

"Well you did, and unless you've got an Oklahoma license we've got a problem."

Suddenly I remembered I had purchased an Oklahoma license when I was up at Lake Murray a few months before. "Wait. Maybe I do have an Oklahoma license."

"Daddy, what's wrong?" Mark asked.

"Nothing, Mark. Just a little misunderstanding."

"I gotta pee," Peter said.

"Hold it a minute. I'll be done here soon ," I said as I fumbled through my wallet. "Here it is, an Oklahoma Fishing License." I handed it to the officer.

"Nice try, but this expired forty-five days ago."

"What? That can't be. Aren't they good for a year?"

"This was a 30-day license."

"Oh no. I am *so* sorry. I never intended to come into Oklahoma waters. I promise to buy an Oklahoma license next time."

I was trying to plead ignorance even though I knew in my heart it wouldn't work. How could I have been so stupid not to realize I needed an Oklahoma license? It just never occurred to me. I thought of all the times I had gone fishing without a license. Who would have thought I'd run into a Fish & Game Warden? I couldn't remember the last time I'd even seen one.

The officer frowned. "I'm afraid we can't let this go. What I can do is sell you an Oklahoma license."

Relief blew over me like a cool ocean breeze. "Great, no problem. How much is it? Twelve bucks?"

"That's what it is *on shore*, but out here it's two hundred dollars."

"Two hundred dollars!"

"Yeah, I'm afraid I'm gonna have to collect two hundred dollars or take you into custody."

"Take me into custody? You're going to arrest me over a fishing license?"

"I'm afraid so."

"Can't you take a check or a credit card?"

"No. . . . Just cash."

I knew I didn't have two hundred dollars—not even close. And I knew if I got arrested over a fishing license Rebekah would divorce me for sure. What concerned me the most, though, was what they would do with the kids while I was in the tank. Something like this could traumatize a child for life. It was ridiculous to think I could be taken to jail for not having a fishing license, but then I remembered watching in dismay one day at the county jail when a DPS officer brought in a guy in cuffs who had neglected to wear his glasses while he was driving. They treated him like he had just raped a coed. I struggled to breathe.

"Listen, I am an attorney. Just give me a ticket, and I'll pay the fine just as soon as I get back home. You can trust me. I'm an officer of the court."

"It's not that I don't trust you. It's just regulations. You don't have a fishing license, so we've got to bring you in."

"What about my boys?"

"We'll have to bring them in too, I reckon."

"Daddy, are they going to arrest us?" Reggi asked.

"No, just me."

"Step into the boat," the officer instructed as he took out a pair of handcuffs.

"You can't arrest my Daddy," Peter screamed as he swung his pole at the officer nearly hitting him in the head. The officer grabbed the pole and yanked it away from Peter.

"What's your name, boy!"

"Peter Turner," he said meekly.

"Hasn't your Daddy told you never to resist—Turner?" He looked at me. "Stan Turner?"

"Right," I said wondering why *that* mattered.

"You're not the Stan Turner who defended that college girl over in Sherman, are you?"

"Yeah, Sarah Winters. Did you hear about that?"

He smiled and shook his head. "Did I hear about it? It's all I heard about for three months. . . . Well, I'll be. It's a pleasure to meet a man of your stature, Mr. Turner. . . . I'm so sorry about this little misunderstanding. You know what I'm gonna do?"

"What?"

"I'm gonna buy you a fishing license. It will be my pleasure."

"Gee. That's really nice of you."

"You know that took a mighty lot of courage to chase after that devil worshiper the way you did. You're a *real* hero in these parts."

"Well, thank you, but—."

"Can we escort you back into Texas waters?"

"Oh no. That's not necessary. But if you would point me toward Little Mineral, I would appreciate it."

He nodded and pointed out across the lake.

"Thanks," I said as I cranked up the engine and got the hell out of there. We waved as we sped off. Twenty minutes later we pulled into Little Mineral. It took us an hour to clean all the fish, load them into the cooler and ice them down. Finally we got in the car and started home. I was still rattled from the encounter with the game warden. The kids had been very quiet ever since it happened so I figured I better do some explaining.

I said, "Well, I guess next time I better get a Texoma license. I never even dreamed we'd end up in Oklahoma waters. We always stay on the south side of the islands."

"I knew we were in Oklahoma," Reggi said.

"You did? . . . Why didn't you say something?" I asked.

"I didn't know it made any difference."

"Well, usually it doesn't. How many times do you get stopped by the Fish and Game Warden, huh?"

"We don't have to go to jail?" Mark said, sounding disappointed.

I laughed. "No, thank God. Can you imagine what your mother would have done, had she been forced to come bail us out of jail?"

"She'd be really pissed," Reggi said.

"Yeah, she'd be nuclear pissed. I can guarantee we'd never go fishing again."

"I'm glad we didn't get arrested then," Reggi said. "This was the greatest fishing trip I've ever had. I can't wait for the next one."

I smiled. "Then listen up, men. When we get home don't mention the game warden. We never saw a game warden, did we?"

"What game warden?" Reggi said with a smile.

"I didn't see any game warden," Mark echoed.

"I saw one," Peter said.

Reggi took off his fishing cap and whacked Peter over the head.

"Ouch, Daddy. Reggi hit me!"

"You didn't see a game warden, did you?" Reggi persisted.

I said. "Okay, cut it out."

Reggi continued to glare at Peter. Peter sunk down in his seat, "*Okay,* I didn't see one."

CHAPTER TWO

Don Blaylock

In law school we were admonished never to get too close to a client because of the difficulty in maintaining objectivity. It was perhaps sage advice, but extremely impractical for two reasons. First of all, clients over time would invariably become friends, and they would be extremely put out if they were suddenly cast aside as a client. Secondly, since I worked eighty hours a week practicing law, I didn't have much time for socializing. If my clients couldn't be my friends, I wouldn't have any.

This was the case with Don Blaylock. It was a hot August day when I first met Don. I remember the heat because it was the 17th consecutive day that the thermometer had topped the one hundred degree mark in North Texas—not ideal weather for sitting out in the sun for two hours playing a Little League baseball game.

I was the coach of the Pirates, and Rebekah and I had just arrived at the ballpark with Mark and Reggi. She had been very concerned about the boys playing in such hot weather, so she made me stop by K-Mart and buy a plastic tarpaulin to put over the dugout. Reggi and I had filled the big Igloo cooler with water and were carrying it to the dugout when I first noticed Coach Blaylock getting out of his blue and grey Chevrolet custom van.

He stood about six feet tall, obviously worked out, and wore his jet black hair combed straight back. He was almost thirty-six years old and blessed with bright blue eyes. It was the first time our teams had played each other so I hadn't had the opportunity to meet him yet—but his reputation had proceeded him. His team would be tough to beat.

As game time approached I walked over to the Red Sox dugout to exchange lineups. Coach Blaylock and his assistant coach were giving some last minute instructions to their players. We exchanged greetings and shook hands. He introduced me to his eldest son and assistant coach, Rob, and also his younger son, Greg. After we exchanged lineups, we visited a minute.

"Can you believe this heat?" I said.

"Oh, I know, isn't it terrible? We're going to have to keep a close eye on everybody out there today. We don't need anybody getting heat stroke."

"That's for sure," I replied as I wiped the sweat from my brow. I glanced at the lineup card he'd given me.

"I see your younger son here is a pitcher."

"He's working on it," Don said with a smile.

Greg gave his father a dirty look and said, "What do you mean *working on it?* I've got a 3-0 record."

Don smiled. "Greg's been pitching very well this season, but he still has a lot to learn. When he gets to the big leagues, the hitters will be merciless."

"Well, I guess he has a good teacher. Didn't I hear that you played for the Mets?"

"For one of their farm teams. Unfortunately I separated my shoulder in a collision at home plate my rookie year and never had an opportunity to go to the majors."

"Oh, no. What a rotten break."

"Oh well, luckily while I was playing college ball for USC, I got my marketing degree."

I sighed. "I always wanted to play professional baseball too but, much to my despair, I never quite had the talent for it. I still love the game though."

"I know what you mean. Maybe our sons will have better luck than we did."

"Hopefully. . . . Well, I better get back to the dugout.

Nice meeting all of you."

"Likewise. See you later."

It was a good game: a pitcher's duel with the Red Sox narrowly beating us. Greg Blaylock knocked in the one and only run, which proved decisive. After the game was over, the teams lined up on the baseline and then proceeded to shake each other's hands. I went over to Don to congratulate him as was the custom in the league.

"I think you son has mastered the art of pitching," I said.

"Yeah, Greg is getting more consistent each outing. He could use a little more speed, but that will come with time. I've got him on a weight lifting program to improve his upper body strength."

"His fastball looked pretty sharp to me. In fact your entire team looked pretty impressive."

"Our team is coming together, but your guys didn't look so bad. I understand the Pirates were the champions last year."

I nodded proudly. "Yeah, we were. I'm not sure exactly how we did it, but it was nice."

"Congratulations."

"Thanks."

"So . . . when did you all come to Mesquite?"

"My company transferred me here in February but Pam and the kids didn't move until school was out in June."

"Huh. Where are you all from?" I asked.

"California—San Jose."

"The Silicon Valley, huh?"

"Right, I'm a salesman for Thermotech Industries. Last year we opened an office in Garland, and I was promoted to sales manager for the new office."

As we were talking, a cute blond wearing tight yellow shorts and a sleeveless white blouse walked up. Her legs were slim and nicely tanned. She was holding a cold drink and periodically wiping her brow with a wet towel in a vain effort to cope with the heat. She smiled at me and said, "Hi."

"Oh, Pam," Don said. "I'd like you to meet Stan Turner. Stan, this is my wife, Pam."

I smiled as I shook her soft, delicate hand. She was so pretty I couldn't help but feel a tinge of excitement. "Oh, nice to meet you, Pam. I was just complimenting your husband on what a fine young pitcher you have in the family."

"Thank you. Don't tell him that though, he already has quite the ego," she noted.

"Excuse me a minute," Don said, as he walked back toward the dugout. "I've got to go talk to one of my players before he leaves."

"Go ahead," I said and then turned back to Pam. "Right, I know how that is. Reggi's the same way. But I guess it's good for them to have high self-esteem."

"I suppose. Didn't you have *two* boys out there playing today?"

"Right, Reggi and Mark, they're our two oldest. Reggi is 14, and Mark is 12. The other two kids are at grandma's house. Rebekah didn't want them sitting out in this heat."

"Oh, a big family. You must sit through a lot of ball games."

"Yeah, it helps having two on the same team. We'd have twice as many games to go to otherwise."

"Yes, I wish Rob and Greg had been a little closer in age so they could have played together," Pam said.

"Is Rob playing now?" I asked.

"Yes, he pitches for the high school varsity squad, and he plays American Legion ball during the summer," Pam replied.

"That must keep you all busy."

"Yes, it does," Pam said. "How old are your younger children?"

"Peter is ten, and Marcia is eight."

"Oh, they're all two years apart," Pam said.

"Right—eight, ten, twelve, and fourteen."

As we continued to talk, I saw Rebekah walking toward us. A tinge of guilt nagged at me for finding Pam so alluring. Beautiful women were, without a doubt, my nemesis and being caught talking to one was sure to make Rebekah jealous. I smiled, motioned for her to come over and introduced her. She studied Pam carefully.

"We've just been discussing your children," Pam said.

Rebekah raised her eyebrows. "Oh, yes. We've got a lot of them."

"So I heard. . . . We only have three—Greg who you saw out on the mound today, his older brother Rob, and his little sister, Donna. She's the same age as your daughter, I guess. I can't imagine having four children. I can barely keep up with three."

"It's a challenge. Stan gave me a taxicab for Christmas last year."

"What?" Pam said, frowning.

"A taxicab," Rebekah repeated. "He said I might as well make a little money between trips for the kids," Rebekah explained with a straight face.

"She's kidding of course," I interjected. "But it's not such a bad idea actually."

Pam laughed. "Well, luckily Rob is almost sixteen and will be driving soon. I can't wait. It will be nice to be able to send him on errands and to have some help carting Greg and Donna around."

"That *will* be nice," Rebekah replied.

Pam looked at her watch. She smiled and said, "Well, speaking of carting kids around, I've got to get Donna to ballet lessons."

"Oh, yeah. Go ahead," Rebekah said. "We'll be seeing you out here again, I'm sure. It was nice meeting you."

"Yes, we'll have to get together sometime."

"Great."

After we said goodbye to Pam and waved to Don, we piled the boys in the van and headed home. The boys were tired as the heat had really drained their energy. Rebekah wasn't talking much either which usually meant something was eating at her. I had a good idea what it was, so I figured I better deal with it.

After we got home and were alone I said, "So, the Blaylocks seem pretty nice."

"Yeah, and you better keep your eyeballs in their sockets the next time you see Pam."

"What? I didn't—"

"I saw the way you looked at her."

I laughed, now feeling *very* guilty again. "I was just enjoying the view, don't worry."

"Yeah, uh huh," she said as she gave me a dirty look. "Why were you talking to her anyway?"

"I was talking to Don when she arrived and joined in the conversation."

"I didn't see Don," Rebakah said.

I gritted my teeth. "Well, he left to—"

"They're a little stuck up, don't you think?"

"Huh? . . . Why do you say that?"

"Well, she obviously thinks her son is God's gift to baseball."

I nodded and said, "Judging from his fast ball, she *may* be right."

"He's not any better than Reggi or Mark."

"Well. I'm not so sure about that. Athletic ability doesn't run in either of our families. Just be thankful God gave our kids *my* brains and *your* good looks."

She smiled. "Well I don't know where they got their good looks, but they definitely have your brains."

"I think they're smarter than me, actually. Marcia beat me in a game of checkers yesterday."

Rebekah didn't respond. I could see her mind was elsewhere. She looked at me thoughtfully and said, "I don't think they were too impressed with us."

"Who?"

"The Blaylocks."

I gave Rebekah an exasperated look. She was always so paranoid. "Why do you say that?"

"I don't know. They seem a little aloof. I'm sure Don thinks the Red Sox have the championship locked up—particularly after they beat you today."

"You think so?" I said surprised and concerned about her observation.

"Uh huh, but he shouldn't take anything for granted. Nobody thought you'd win the championship last year."

"That's for sure," I said, nodding. "We might just whip their ass the next time around."

"You bet."

I chuckled. "And then again—maybe not."

We both laughed.

In the coming months we got to know the Blaylocks pretty well. Not only did we see them at baseball games, but it turned out Pam and Rebekah were both members of Junior League, and Donna and Marcia both attended the same dance academy. When they discovered this, Pam and Rebekah started to car pool and often took the girls out to lunch. As we got to know them better I must admit Rebekah and I were a little bit jealous. Don and Pam seemed to have the perfect life—a loving relationship, beautiful children, plenty of money, and lots of friends. Unfortunately, their good fortune didn't last.

CHAPTER THREE

Evil Forces

It's unsettling to realize that while you are stretched out on the sofa watching *Dallas* or *M*A*S*H*, evil forces could be conspiring against you. That while you sit in the warmth and security of your own home, an avalanche of adversity could be perilously close to being unleashed in your direction. No matter who you are or where you live, no one is exempt from such ill fate—nor was Don Blaylock.

The call came in after midnight. Rebekah passed me the telephone. I sat up on one elbow.

"Hello."

"Stan, this is Don Blaylock. I'm sorry to bother you at this hour, but I need your advice immediately."

"It's okay, Don. What's up?"

"Rob and his friend Jesse are in jail."

"In jail? What happened?"

"Rob and Jesse went to a bar with a couple of girls, I guess. Rob drank too much and was having trouble driving home. Some cop saw him and stopped him for suspicion of DWI."

"Oh, God. . . . So, where are they?"

"Dallas City Jail."

"Okay. They usually keep them there a few hours before they transport them to the county jail—so we have some time."

"What should I do?" Don asked.

"Go on over to the jail. I'll meet you there in thirty

minutes. We'll have to run a writ. Did you call the other boy's parents?"

"No, I'm not at home. I'm at Baylor Hospital."

"What are you doing there?"

"The cop let the girls drive Rob's car home. They got into an accident near Fair Park."

I sat up and threw off the covers. "Oh, geez! Are they all right?"

"I think so."

"Well, you can tell me more about that later. Call the other boy's parents, I can't help him unless they retain me."

"All right, I'll see you in a few minutes."

I got up and put on jeans, a T-shirt, and sneakers. One of the fringe benefits of running writs was there was no dress code. After jumping into my yellow Corvette, a gift from a satisfied client, I headed down I-30 toward Dallas. As I passed the Fair Park exit I noticed a scorched, late model Mercedes being loaded onto a flat bed tow truck. *Glad I wasn't in that baby when it went up in flames.* I took the Business 75 exit, traveled a few blocks, turned down Main Street and pulled up in front of the Dallas City Jail. I got out of my car and looked around warily. Downtown at night was dangerous, but since this was City Hall, I guessed it would be safe. I walked up the long steps to the lobby and took the elevator to the second floor.

The reception area was crowded with all sorts of people wandering around nervously or sitting impatiently. There were a few street people, several drunks, a number of Hispanic women, a tall well-dressed black man and a beautiful blond woman in a cocktail dress. I figured each had an interesting story. Scanning the room, I spotted Don sitting on a bench looking rather forlorn. I walked over quickly and greeted him.

"Stan, thanks for coming," he said.

"No sweat. Have you talked to the jailer?"

"Yes, but they said we needed some kind of writ of

habeas corpus or something."

"Right. What's the charge? Did they say?"

"DWI."

"What about the friend? What's his name?"

"Jesse Ramirez. He's been charged with public intoxication."

"Okay, I'm going to go see my bondsman. I'll come back here to have the boys sign their bonds, and then I'll run the writ. Did you get a hold of Jesse's parents?"

"Yes, I talked to his mother. His father is out of town. She asked if you would get Jesse out of jail too."

"Okay, good."

Don shook his head. "What am I doing here, Stan? What did I do wrong with Rob? I've warned him over and over not to drink and drive. What possessed him to get behind the wheel when he was drunk?"

"God knows. Teenagers these days just don't have much common sense."

Don got up and angrily clenched his fist. "Just wait until I see him. He's going to wish he were never born."

I sighed. "Calm down. You're going to get through this. I'm sure Rob has an explanation. He seems like a good kid."

"Maybe you're right. I bet it was Jesse. I never liked that kid. It must have been *his* idea to go to Greenville Avenue. Rob will never associate with that punk again, you can damn well be sure of that!"

It took me twenty minutes to run to the bondsman's office and get the bond. As I was driving I wondered why Rob would have done something so stupid. Would Reggi be as irresponsible when he started driving? *Jesus, I hope not.* I wondered what I could do to make sure I never had to make this trip to get Reggi out of jail. When I got back, Don was pacing up and down the hallway. I intercepted him and told him I had the bonds and was going to go see Rob and Jesse so they could sign them. After giving the bonds to the jailer to get signed I sat down next to Don and said,"Well, now we wait."

"How long will it take?"

"It depends."

"On what?"

"On whether they can find Rob and Jesse any time soon. It's crowded back there."

"Wonderful."

"So, has Rob ever given you trouble before?"

"No, never, I really don't understand this."

"Huh, well maybe it's just a fluke. Sometimes kids just get unlucky. I remember when I was in college I got three tickets in one week. It was all bullshit stuff. I think the police pick on young kids, don't you?"

"I suppose, but nothing like this has ever happened to me. I never expected to have to bail Rob out of jail. He's always been such a good kid."

"Times have changed. It's tough to be growing up these days with drug dealers and gangs on campus."

I commiserated with Don for over an hour. He told me all about how he and Pam had met, fell in love, and got married. He related how his marriage hadn't been all peaches and cream, how they had struggled for years financially and finally got a break when the promotion came. He told me he thought Rob might have the talent to be a major league pitcher. Then he filled me in on the accident.

"A Mercedes on I-30?" I said.

"Right."

"Huh. I saw them hauling it away on my way in. Was anybody hurt?"

Don shook his head. "I think the girls are going to be okay, but the driver of the Mercedes wasn't so lucky."

"Really? How bad are his injuries?"

"Pretty bad. . . . He died, I understand."

"The car is in your name, I presume?"

"Right. I couldn't put it in Rob's name until he's

eighteen."

"How much insurance do you have?"

"You know, I'm not even sure." Don said.

Finally the jailer signaled that he had the bonds signed. I took them and advised Don I would be back in thirty minutes. Then I went to my car and headed for the sheriff's office. Hearing about the accident had jolted me. I tried not to seem alarmed as Don related the story. He had so much on his mind already. But I knew if someone had died, there would surely be a wrongful death suit filed. When I returned to the jail, Don was staring out a window into the darkness. I walked up, put my hand on his shoulder and said, "Okay, I think we're getting close."

Don turned around and gave a sigh of relief. "Thank God!"

After taking the writs to the jailer, I came back and sat next to Don and said, "Just another thirty minutes and we're out of here."

"Another thirty minutes?!" Don complained.

"Yeah, I don't know what they do back there, but they don't do it in a hurry, that's for sure."

Forty-five minutes later, we could see Rob and Jesse through a glass window getting their belongings returned. A minute later they stepped into the waiting room. Don rushed over to Rob.

"Are you all right, son?"

"Yeah, I'm fine."

"Come on, let's get out of this wretched place," Don said.

We all left the jail waiting room and walked down the stairs into the cool night air. When we got to the sidewalk, I asked, "So, where are you going now?"

"I've got to go back to the hospital. Pam is there with Jennifer and Linda."

I didn't feel like going to the hospital. My mind didn't function too well in the middle of the night. All I wanted to do was go home and go to bed, but I knew I had better go and learn as much about what had happened as I could. On the way to the hospital I couldn't keep my mind off Reggi. He hadn't got his driver's license yet, but that day was fast approaching. It was pretty scary to think he'd be out on the road soon.

The hospital parking garage was deserted as I pulled in just after four. I parked my car and then caught an elevator to the main lobby. Before I went up to Jennifer's room, I called Rebekah to tell her I would be a while longer. I knew she would be worried and wouldn't sleep until she had heard from me. She sounded grateful to get the call. A few minutes later I entered Jennifer's room. Pam, Don, and the boys were already there. Don and Rob were arguing.

"I thought you were going to stay home and watch the Ranger's game," Don said.

"That was the plan, but things happened. Jennifer and Linda came over and they wanted to go out. What was I supposed to do?"

"I can understand you going out, but the drinking? Why did you have to get drunk?"

"I didn't mean to, I just didn't pay close enough attention to how many drinks I was having."

"Do you realize how this is going to screw up your life?" Don scolded. "How many times have we discussed drinking and driving. What do we have to do to get through to you!?"

"Nothing! I just screwed up. I'm sorry."

Don looked at me. "Well, I sure hope Stan can do something to help you out of this mess."

I flashed a reassuring smile and said, "I think there is a good chance I can. The important thing now is to remain positive and work together to get through this. Beating each other up won't help."

Don nodded and turned away. Rob looked at his mother. She shook her head.

"They may kick you off the baseball team," Pam said.

Rob frowned. "What? No way."

"Yes, don't you remember Roger Hamilton. They found drugs in his locker and he got kicked off the team."

"Oh shit. They can't do that. I've got to finish the season."

"You should have thought of that before you got in your car drunk," Don replied.

"Damn it!" Rob said. "I can't believe this."

"Watch your language young man," Don said as he glared at Rob.

"What else could go wrong? Jesus!" Rob said.

So much for my peacekeeping efforts.

"Pam Blaylock, please come to the nurses' station," the intercom blared.

Pam left the room and rushed over to the nurses' station. We all followed her, curious as to the purpose of the summons. A nervous middle-aged lady was standing talking to the nurse. The nurse saw Pam and said, "Oh, Mrs. Blaylock, this is Jennifer's mom, Martha Rich."

"Oh, hi, this is my husband, Don, my son Rob, Stan Turner, our lawyer, and Rob's friend, Jesse."

"I know Jesse. Hi, Jesse," she said.

"Have you seen Jennifer yet?" Pam asked.

Martha said, "I just left her. I wanted to thank you for staying with her. She told me how wonderful you were."

Pam shrugged. "Oh, I didn't do anything really, just sat and talked with her. Are they going to discharge her soon?"

"No, they're going to admit her," Martha said.

"Why, I thought she was okay?"

Martha hesitated, then said, "They think she is, they just want to keep an eye on her . . . you know . . . since . . . since they say she's pregnant."

Rob's face turned white, "Did you say pregnant?"

Mrs. Rich turned and looked at Rob directly in the eyes. "That's right, Rob, I said pregnant."

CHAPTER FOUR

Wrongful Death

Several weeks later, I was attending a Small Business Section meeting of the Dallas Chamber of Commerce. As the program started I noticed Don Blaylock across the room. During introductions I caught his eye and nodded. After the meeting he came over to say hello.

"Hi Stan, I didn't know you were in the Chamber."

"Yeah, I've been a member for the last couple of years."

"Have you heard anything on Rob's DWI?" he asked.

"No, the DA hasn't contacted me yet. They're pretty swamped most of the time so it takes awhile."

He nodded. "You've got a good chamber here in Dallas. They seem very well organized and quite aggressive."

"I've heard they're one of the best. . . . Hey, congratulations on the championship. I didn't get to the game, but I heard Greg was spectacular."

"He pitched pretty well."

"So does Rob help Greg with his pitching?"

"Yes, they are very close. They practice together everyday."

"That's great. So, what's Rob going to do next summer after he graduates?"

"He's going to baseball camp in Florida."

"Oh really?"

"Yeah, this camp is run by a couple former American League coaches and is supposed to be really great for anyone interested in making it to the majors."

"Hmm, that sounds like fun. I bet Rob is excited about it."

"Yeah, he and one of his friends are going together, so they should have a good time and learn a lot."

"I can imagine," I said.

Don gave me a hard look. "Listen, Stan. I'm glad I ran into you today. I need you talk to you about a little investment we got into that's gone south."

"Really. What kind of an investment?"

"A Chinese restaurant franchise. . . . It's a little complicated to discuss right now. Can we get together later?"

"Of course."

"I can stop by the office if you want, or you may just want to stop by the house on your way home. That way we'll have a bottle of Jack Daniels to help us get through the meeting."

"That bad, huh?" I said, now very curious as to what had happened.

"Yeah, I'm afraid so."

We agreed on an appointment the following Thursday night at Don's place. I didn't mind house calls once in awhile if they weren't too far out of my way. The atmosphere was usually more relaxed, and the clients more open in the comfort of their homes.

When I got back to the office, Jodie advised me that Stuart Miller had been trying to reach me. Stuart Miller was a VP at World Port, a commodities exporter. His brother Lyle was the president. They had gotten into financial trouble and hired me to defend a dozen or so lawsuits that had been filed against them. We didn't really have a defense to most of the suits, but they needed time to raise capital to stay in business. Fortunately, none of the creditors had prosecuted their suits very vigorously, so it was almost a year before any of the cases came to trial. By that time they had found an investor and had the funds to settle up with everyone. They were very grateful and promised me a lot more business. I picked up the phone and returned the call. He told me an employee had been killed.

"Oh, no. Did I know him?" I asked.

"No, I don't think so," Stuart replied.

"Gee, that's terrible. I'm so sorry."

"Yeah, he was a good employee. Everybody liked him."

"How did it happen?"

"We're not sure, but apparently he was crossing Lemmon Avenue and was hit by a drunk driver."

"Oh, you're kidding?" I said.

"No."

"God . . . that's terrible! Did they arrest the driver?"

"Yes, and they've charged him with DWI and involuntary manslaughter."

"Good! Maybe they'll nail his ass."

"Hopefully."

"So, is there anything I can do?"

"Maybe. . . . He was from India and his family has only just recently immigrated to America. They don't know any attorneys, so they asked me to recommend someone."

I sat up in my chair and grabbed a yellow pad from my credenza. "Well, thank you for thinking of me. What was your employee's name?"

"Anant Ravi. He was a computer engineer. We sponsored his immigration here."

I began taking notes on the yellow pad and then asked, "How old a man was he?"

"Thirty-nine."

"So, tell me about the driver? What kind of car did he drive?"

"It was a 1982 Porsche, I believe."

I raised my eyebrows and replied, "Hmm. A high roller, huh?"

"Yeah, probably some rich kid out partying. Anyway, will you take the case?"

"Me? . . . Well, I'm not a personal injury attorney. But I don't see why this should be any different than any other lawsuit. I'll have to investigate the facts, of course. But, yeah, I think I could probably handle it."

"Good, I'll tell the family."

"Thanks, Stuart. I really appreciate you thinking of me."

"No problem, you've always done good work for us so I know you'll do a good job handling this for Anant's family."

"You can count on it. Thanks a lot."

I put down the phone and sat silently for a moment in shock. A wrongful death case could conceivably bring a multi-million dollar settlement. Suddenly I felt excited. I smiled, jumped up, and rushed into the reception area where Jodie was busy at work. She looked up and was startled by the look on my face.

"Guess what?!" I said.

"What?"

"Our financial troubles may be over."

"Huh?"

"Stuart Miller just referred a wrongful death case to us."

"You're kidding?"

"No, I'm not. His employee, some poor guy named Anant, was killed by a drunk rich kid over the weekend. The family didn't know an attorney so they asked Stuart for a recommendation."

"Really? Have you ever done a case like that before?"

"No, but I've never won the lottery before either."

Jodie frowned and said, "Don't you have to hire a dozen expert witnesses and spend a truckload of money to prosecute a case like that?"

I tried to repress a smile. "You're right. It could be expensive if we have to try it, but if they don't deny liability, we could settle it quickly."

Jodie shrugged, smiled, and said, "Well, I hope it works out. You certainly deserve it."

"We all deserve it. You'll get a nice bonus too, if I hit it big."

"Good. How about a new BMW?"

I smiled. "Hey, you never know. I might just do that."

Jodie shook her head skeptically. "Right."

"I think I'll go home and tell Rebekah about our good fortune. She's been a little depressed about money lately, so this might cheer her up."

"What about your appointments?"

"Reschedule them, would you? None of them are critical. I really want to go tell Rebekah."

Jodie shook her head and said, "Okay, get out of here."

*****

Thirty minutes later I rushed into my house. Rebekah was ironing in front of the TV, and Marcia was at the kitchen table doing a crossword puzzle. Rebekah looked up and smiled.

"Stan! What's wrong? What are you doing home?"

"Daddy!" Marcia exclaimed and then jumped up and ran to me.

"Hi, baby doll," I said as I picked her up and held her in my arms.

Rebekah smiled and came over to me. "So, what's up?"

"I had to come home and tell you the good news."

"What good news?"

Marcia wiggled out of my lap and said, "Daddy, can I play with your typewriter?"

I looked at her and smiled. "Okay, love. Go ahead, but be careful."

I took a seat at the kitchen table. Rebekah sat down and waited for my response.

"Do you remember Adam Cartwright? We were in law school together."

"You mean, Congressman Cartwright?"

"Uh huh."

"Yeah. What about him?"

"Well, you know how he was able to go into politics, don't you?"

"Didn't he win a big case and make a million bucks or something?"

"Exactly. It was a wrongful death case. He settled it for $3.3 million. His cut was $1.1 million."

"Okay, go on."

"So, Adam worked a while and then said *screw this rat race* and retired. He had all the money he would ever need, so he didn't need to work anymore."

"How nice."

"But just so he wouldn't be bored, he went into politics."

"Right."

"Honey, I just got a wrongful death case. It could be a big one."

"Really?" Rebekah said.

"Yes."

"Who is it? How did you get it?"

"One of my corporate clients, Stuart Miller, referred it to me. It looks like a great case. The guy was drunk so there shouldn't be a liability issue. That's usually the biggest hurdle in these kind of cases. The only question left is: how much are his damages?"

"Yeah, but can the guy pay a big judgment?"

"He must have money, he was driving a late model Porsche. Most people like that have lots of insurance."

"I hope you're right, honey . . . but I'll believe it when I see it."

"You're not excited by the possibility?"

"No. You know when it comes to money, things never work out for us. I'm afraid to get excited."

"I don't know, honey. Our luck may have just changed."

"I hope so. God knows I'm tired of living from hand to mouth, but I'm not going to count on it. I don't want to be disappointed again."

"Again?"

"Yes, don't you remember Interactive Technologies?"

"Right, but this is totally different."

I had forgotten about Interactive Technologies. That was another client who couldn't pay his bill. He talked me into taking stock for my services. It was a publicly traded company selling over the counter, so I thought it was legit. It seemed like a good deal at the time. The stock was selling at $30 a share when he gave it to me, but it was lettered stock so I couldn't sell it for two years. I was so sure we were going to get rich off this stock, I took the family out to dinner to celebrate our good fortune. Of course, the stock dropped to three cents a share the day before I was eligible to sell it. Apparently my client dumped all his shares knowing that the stock would plummet once everyone he had paid off in kind could sell. He had timed it perfectly.

"I'm not saying it was your fault, but when it comes to the big score, we're jinxed," Rebekah said.

"I don't know, honey. I really feel good about this deal."

"I hope you're right, but I think I'll celebrate when the money is in the bank and the check has cleared, if you don't mind."

"Suit yourself," I said. "I came home because I thought you'd be excited."

Rebekah smiled. "I *am* excited, cautiously excited. Now, how about a sandwich?"

"Sure, what have you got?"

"Peanut butter and jelly?"

We both laughed and then embraced. Rebekah laid her head on my shoulder. I bit her neck. She giggled.

I said, "You should have married that guy that had a crush on you in high school. What's his name?"

"Joey Littleton."

"Right. You'd be living in a Hollywood mansion by now."

Joey Littleton was a renowned screenwriter who had gone to high school with Rebekah. They dated a little, but Rebekah never liked him that much. He, on the other hand, loved her and was crushed when she wouldn't marry him.

While we were struggling to survive during law school, Joey Littleton sold his first screenplay for over six figures. The movie went on to be produced and was a big hit. Although she denied it, I think a time or two Rebekah wondered if she hadn't made a mistake in turning Joey down.

She nodded affirmatively. "God knows he asked me enough times . . . but, I didn't love him."

I pulled away and looked her in the eyes, "And I thank God for that everyday."

CHAPTER FIVE

Hot Checks

The first big cold front of the fall had blown through and it had been raining hard all day. Rebekah had called and said they'd canceled the soccer game that night. I was kind of glad because I had lots of work to do and leaving early for a soccer game would put me even farther behind. As I was working on a real estate contract that a client was pushing me to finish, I heard Jodie on the intercom telling me Don was on line two. I picked up the phone. "Hi Don."

"Stan, oh man, I'm so glad I caught you. Pam's been arrested. She was at our restaurant in Greenville and two constables arrested her. One of her friends just called me."

"What? You've got to be joking."

"I wish I were, but I'm not. I'm leaving right now to go to the Greenville city jail. Can you come?"

"I'm on my way. See you there."

As I rushed out the door, I told Jodie to call the contract client and tell him it was going to be another day before their work was done. She gave me an exasperated look and shook her head. Despite a steady rain it only took me forty-five minutes to get to Greenville. When I made it into the police station with a dripping umbrella in hand, I saw Don sitting on a bench. I went over to him.

"What's the word?" I said.

"Nothing yet, I was told to sit and wait here."

As we were talking, a policeman with a clipboard appeared and said, "Don Blaylock?"

Don motioned to the officer and replied, "Yes, that's

me." We walked over to where the officer was standing.

He nodded and said, "We've got your wife in custody. She's charged with three counts of passing worthless checks. You can pay the checks and the fine or post a bond."

"Passing worthless checks? That's ridiculous," Don said.

"The checks are in the file if you'd care to see them."

"I sure would," Don said indignantly.

The officer went back into the clerk's office and retrieved the file. He put it down on the counter and flipped through it. He pulled out three checks and showed them to us. Don studied them and then shook his head.

"I don't understand this. Pam would never write a check if the money wasn't there."

"She might have made a mistake in her checkbook," I suggested, "but she should have received letters from the creditors and from the DA warning her to pay the checks or she'd be charged and a warrant issued."

"She'd never ignore warnings like that. She'd go ballistic if she got that kind of letter."

"Well, we can figure out what happened later. Right now I'll put up an attorney's bond so we can get her out."

I went over to the front desk and filled out a bond form. I signed it and gave it to the jailer. Thirty minutes later Pam walked out of the jail, her eyes swollen and her skin pale. She immediately broke down when she saw Don. They embraced. It took her a few minutes to regain her composure. Then she released Don and ran her fingers through her hair.

"I've never been so humiliated in my life," she moaned.

"I'm so sorry, honey!" Don said. "I don't understand how you could have bounced those three checks. You're so careful."

"I had plenty of money in the account. The bank must have made a mistake."

"Let's go to the bank right now and straighten this out," I suggested.

Pam let out a shriek. "Oh, Don! Melinda Williams and Nancy Brown were at the restaurant when they arrested me. What are they going to think? I'm sure the whole Junior League knows I was arrested by now. Oh God! How could this have happened?"

Don took Pam back into his arms and held her tightly. She cried hard for several minutes. I felt really sorry for her. I remembered what a wreck Rebekah had been the time she was arrested. If it hadn't been for the kids needing her so much, she might not have recovered at all.

"I don't know, honey. But we're going to get to the bottom of this just as soon as we get to the bank." He let her go, took her hand and gently pulled her toward the door. "Come on, honey, let's go."

Several minutes later we were at the customer service window of the bank going through an interim bank statement with a clerk. After several minutes of searching through the canceled checks Pam let out a gasp, "Luther wrote a $5,000 management fee check after we fired him."

"What?" Don said. He grabbed the check away from Pam and stared at it.

"Who's Luther?" I asked.

"He's the asshole who got us in this mess. Goddamn him!"

Don got up and waved the check angrily. "That son of a bitch! I'm going to kill him!"

Don marched out of the bank heading toward his car. I rushed after him fearful of what he was about to do. I didn't know who Luther was or what he had done, but I obviously had to delay Don long enough for him to cool down.

"Don, wait. What are you going to do, punch him out?"

He didn't stop. "No, I'm going kill the dirty bastard! I'm going to strangle him with my bare hands!"

I grabbed his arm and tried to get him to stop. "Calm down now. Let's talk about this. Tell me what's going on. I'm sure there is a better way to deal with this. It won't do Pam and your kids any good if you end up going to jail for assaulting him."

Don turned and glared at me. "That asshole caused my wife to go to jail. He's gone too far, I'm not letting him get away with this!"

"Nobody expects you to, but let's talk about an appropriate response. Beating him up isn't the answer."

Don pulled away and started again for his car. "I'm not going to beat him up. I'm going to kill him."

I dashed in front of him and blocked him from getting into his car. I said, "Take Pam home. I'll come by your house tomorrow afternoon."

Pam put her arm on his shoulder. She said, "Stan's right, honey. Let's go home."

I nodded, "Go home. I'm tied up tomorrow morning, but I'll stop by your place tomorrow afternoon. You can tell me then what this is all about and we can figure out how to deal with Luther."

Don glared at me, barely able to contain his anger. Finally he let out a muffled growl and replied, "It's a good thing for Luther you were here . . . otherwise I'd of killed that little weasel!"

As Don was simmering down I became aware of a crowd of bystanders around us, including a couple policemen coming out of the bank. I shook my head, smiled and motioned for Pam to get into the car. As Don and Pam drove off I looked at the crowd and said, "Show's over, folks. Have a nice day."

CHAPTER SIX

DWI

When I got back from Greenville, Rob was waiting for me. I had forgotten that I had scheduled an appointment with him to get started on the defense of his DWI charge. It wasn't going to be an easy case since he probably *was* intoxicated when he was driving home that night with his friends. Sometimes, however, the police screw up and create defenses that otherwise wouldn't exist. I wasn't optimistic that this would be the case, but I had a duty to Rob to explore every possibility. Luckily, this was Rob's first offense and courts were often lenient the first time around. Jodie showed him into my office.

"Did you hear about your Mom?"

"No, what about her?"

"Well, I just left her and your Dad. She's okay, but she's very upset over her arrest."

"Arrest? No way!"

I explained the situation to Rob. He wanted to rush home and make sure she was okay, but I told him she needed her rest right now and he really couldn't do anything for her at that moment.

"Anyway, she's going to be okay. Right now we need to talk about your situation. . . . So, how are you holding up?"

"I'm okay, I guess," Rob replied.

"Well, I got a notice from the court that we've got to appear to make a plea two weeks from Thursday. You'll have to appear with me."

"How do think I should plead?" Rob asked.

"I don't know. You haven't told me what happened

yet. I need to know the whole story if I'm going to properly represent you—not just what you'd like me to hear. Will you do that?"

"Everything?"

I nodded. "Yes, everything. Let me judge what *is* or *isn't* important."

He frowned, then took a deep breath. "Okay, where should I start?"

"Why don't you start by telling me about you and Jennifer? I need to know everything about your relationship with her since, I gather, she got you into this mess."

"It wasn't all her fault."

"I didn't figure it was."

"Well, we met a few months ago. I knew the first day I saw her that I wanted to get to know her better. She's a cheerleader, you know, and very popular so I knew getting a date wouldn't be easy. But I had to try. After getting nowhere the first few attempts, she finally agreed to go to a party with me. I was excited and nervous about the date. I knew that if I didn't impress her, there wouldn't be a second one. Unfortunately, we got off to a bad start."

"How is that?" I asked.

"It was a Friday night and when I jumped into my car to go pick her up, the battery was dead. I couldn't believe it. I was so pissed. Luckily, mom was home, so I jumped the car with hers. Then, when I was finally ready to go, Dad drove up. I almost died, as I knew he would further delay my departure with his usual barrage of questions. All I could think about was how angry Jennifer would be.

"I couldn't just brush my dad off, because then he would get suspicious. He asked me where I was going. I lied and told him I was going to a movie with Jesse."

"Why didn't you just tell him the truth?" I asked.

"Oh, I couldn't do that because he would have never let me go to an unsupervised party."

I smiled and nodded. "Right."

"Then he wanted to know what I was going to see. Since I had no clue, I just told him I didn't know yet. He didn't like that answer much, but finally shrugged and let me go. Once out the door, I got into my car and took off."

"What kind of a car do you drive?" I asked.

"A Ford Mustang GT."

"Nice car," I said as I jotted down the information on my yellow pad. "Go on."

"I drove straight to Jennifer's house, which luckily was only five minutes away. As I was driving over there, all I could think about was how mad Jennifer was going to be. I figured the entire night was going to be a disaster. When I got there she was waiting and, much to my surprise, seemed very happy to see me."

I said, "That must of been a relief."

"Damn straight," Rob said. "Jennifer is totally awesome and I really liked her. I wanted that date, trust me."

"Do you have a picture of her?"

Rob smiled and went for his wallet. He pulled out a wallet-size yearbook picture. She looked about 5'4", 115 lbs, with blue eyes and natural blond hair which she wore in a pony tail.

Rob looked intently at the photo and said, "When I got there, she looked really sexy. Her skirt was very short and her blouse left a *lot* exposed, if know what I mean. When she got in the car, she scooted up next to me and put her left hand on my thigh like we had been dating for months. I was so distracted I could hardly drive."

"I bet."

"I told her she looked great and then put the car in gear and took off with a burst of power that I hoped would impress her. Then, I apologized for being late. She seemed quite satisfied with my explanation and assured me the rest of the evening would be much better."

One of nice things about practicing law is rarely does it get boring. Rob's story was getting good and I was thoroughly enjoying it. I couldn't help but think back to my junior year in high school. Somehow, I had gotten a date with a fun-loving senior. Like Rob, I was naive and got much more than I had expected. I grinned and told him to continue.

"As I was driving we talked about my car, school and our parents. Then, I suddenly realized I had no idea where I was going. Jennifer thought that was so funny. When she stopped laughing, she told me how to get Linda's house.

"About ten minutes later we arrived. The street was lined with cars so we were forced to park about a block away. As we walked up, the door opened and Jesse staggered out and welcomed us. He was obviously drunk which surprised me."

"Why did that surprise you?" I asked.

"Well, I was hoping the party wasn't going to be a big beer bash. I was in training, you know—being on the baseball team and everything. Drinking was strictly forbidden. I figured it wouldn't hurt to have a beer or two, but I didn't want to be under a lot of pressure to drink. I definitely didn't want to get drunk and come home smelling like a brewery. My dad would flip out if that happened."

"Right."

"So, we went inside and it only got worse."

"Really? How?"

"Of course, Linda's parents weren't home so everyone was doing as they pleased. The smoke was thick and the music was deafening. Not that I don't like music, but I value my eardrums."

"Was there hard liquor?" I asked.

"Yes, and the usual contests to see who could drink it the fastest."

"Hmm."

"What surprised me the most was when Jennifer lit up a cigarette."

"Oh really? You didn't know she smoked?"

"No, and I was disappointed, although I didn't tell her

that. . . . She tried to get me to light one up, but I definitely wasn't going to smoke while in training."

"Are your teammates as scrupulous as you at following the rules?"

"Most of them are. The coach hammers us with the rules and has no tolerance for anyone who breaks them."

"Good for him," I said. "So then what happened?"

"Jennifer wanted to dance, so we went into the den where the music was playing. I don't like fast dancing but since Jennifer does, I got stuck dancing most of the evening. Around eleven thirty I began to get concerned about the time. Midnight was fast approaching and I knew my father would not go to bed until I was home. It was embarrassing to have to bring up the idea of calling it a night, but I had no choice."

"Jennifer wasn't tired?" I asked.

"No, she has incredible energy. She is a cheerleader and in very good shape. She wasn't ready to leave and began pouting when I suggested it."

I shook my head. "So what did you do?"

"I hated to have to argue about going home, but I knew my dad would be up waiting for me. I was about to put my foot down when she smiled, gave me a seductive wink and led me into Linda's bedroom."

"Oh, really?" I said smiling.

"As you can imagine, all thoughts of my father vanished."

"Right. So—"

"So, she started taking off her clothes and then, you know—we had sex—incredible sex."

"I see. . . . So, when did you get home?"

"We fell asleep, and Jesse didn't wake us up until after two. I was so upset when I discovered how late it was. I knew my father was going to ground me for life.

"Did he?"

"No, I left my window open as a precaution in case I

got home late. Dad often dozes, so I can say I came in while he was sleeping. It doesn't always work but it did this time."

"Lucky you."

"Really."

"So, did you use any protection when you had sex?"

"No, I just assumed Jennifer was on the pill."

"Was she?"

"She said she was, but now I know different."

Rob was naive. He was obviously no match for Jennifer. He reminded me of myself when I was his age. My parents had sheltered me so much when I was young, I wasn't prepared for the real world. Consequently, I had to endure some pretty painful lessons about life as I got older.

"So that was our first date," Rob said.

"So, do you think Jennifer got pregnant that night?" I asked.

"I don't know. We dated for several months and had sex a lot. It could have happened any one of those times."

"I know she said she was on the pill, but weren't you still worried about getting her pregnant?" I asked.

"No, I figured her pills would work."

Rob seemed like a decent kid. His naivety was actually refreshing. Kids nowadays were exposed to so much violence, pornography, and immorality everywhere they turned, that there wasn't much evil to which they hadn't been exposed. Jennifer, on the other hand, knew exactly what she was doing. I wondered what her intentions had been—just sex, a child, a ticket away from her mother, or had she just fallen in love with Rob? I hoped it was as simple as the latter.

I rubbed my chin. "Hmm. So tell me about the night of the accident."

"Sure," Rob said.

"It was a Saturday night. Mom and dad had left with some friends to go to the Majestic Theater. I had invited everyone over to the house to watch a Ranger game. It was supposed to be a nice quiet evening. I wouldn't dare give a party at the house as my parents and the neighbors are tight. They'd report any suspicious activity. Jesse arrived first, and then the girls showed up a little later with two grocery sacks full of beer.

"Linda wore light blue shorts, white sneakers, and a red halter top. She's a brunette, tall, and lean with a nice tan. I guess I gazed at her a little too long. Jennifer noticed and got pissed off."

I laughed. "It doesn't take much to make a woman jealous," I advised.

"Tell me about it," Rob said. "She wouldn't even let me touch her. It took her nearly thirty minutes to get over it."

"But she got over it?"

"Yeah, I took her into my bedroom and made love to her."

"Just like that?"

"Hey, she is something else. I can't get enough of her."

"How long did that take?"

"Probably an hour or so. . . . When we came back into the living room, I sat in a big over-stuffed chair with Jennifer on my lap. We watched the game for awhile but Jennifer got bored and wanted to go out. That's when I found out she hated the Rangers."

"She hates the Rangers?"

Rob nodded. "Right. She's a Yankee fan, if you can believe that."

"Oh, God," I said. "Why?"

"I don't know," Rob replied. "I never thought to ask."

"So, you went out?"

"Yes, she had heard about a warehouse off of Greenville Avenue that was supposed to be rockin' that night—no cops and no IDs required. I wasn't crazy about the idea, but when Jennifer gets an idea in her brain, there is no distracting her. You might as well just do it and get it over with.

"That didn't bother you?"

"Sure it did, but it was something I just had to put up with."

"So why did you take your car? Didn't Jesse have one?"

"His car is a piece of junk. There's no way we could have taken his car."

"So, you found the warehouse okay?"

"Right. We drove to I-30, went west toward Dallas and then north on Central. About twenty minutes later we were cruising down Greenville Avenue. Just past Northwest Highway we turned into an alley and went east a few blocks to a parking lot where we left the car. We had to walk several blocks to the warehouse."

"There wasn't parking nearer the warehouse?"

"No, I guess they didn't want a bunch of cars around the warehouse that might attract attention."

"Huh. What did it look like inside?"

"It was basically a big room with a stage in the middle. It was very crowded and the music was loud. We found a small table and some stools to sit on. There were two pickup trucks at opposite ends of the warehouse with several kegs of beer in each. Jesse went to one of them and brought back four beers."

"So, weren't you worried about getting caught drinking? You said your coach had no tolerance for breaking the rules."

"Yes, I was very uneasy at first, but as the night wore on and Jesse kept bringing us more beer I quit thinking about it."

"Hmm. How long did you stay?"

"Jennifer loved the dancing so we stayed quite awhile. Finally, I insisted we go home. Luckily, Jesse and Linda were so bombed they didn't object."

"Weren't you worried about driving home after drinking so many beers?"

"To tell the truth, I didn't think I was that drunk. We had been eating pretzels and stuff and I had been dancing so much I figured I had worked the liquor out of my system."

I laughed. "Really?"

Rob shrugged. "I know it sounds stupid now, but I really thought I was okay."

"But you weren't?"

"No. After we left I was having trouble staying in my lane. It wasn't long before I saw red and blue flashing lights in my rear view mirror."

"Wouldn't you know," I said.

"I pulled over, and the cop came up to my window and asked me to get out of the car. He gave me one of those sobriety tests, you know, where you have to walk a straight line?"

"How did you do?"

"Not good."

"Did he give you a Miranda warning before he arrested you?"

"Yeah, right. He read me my rights."

"So, why did he arrest Jesse?"

"Oh, because he got really upset when the cop put the cuffs on me. Jesse yelled at the cop and I think he actually pushed him."

"Really?"

"Yes. . . . Anyway, the cop got really mad and threw Jesse up against the car and cuffed him too."

I shook my head. "Wonderful. . . . So, the cop let Jennifer drive your car home?"

"Right. He gave her a sobriety test and she passed it. I don't know how, but somehow she did."

"She must not have been drinking as much as you, huh?"

"I guess. I wasn't really paying that much attention."

"So, then they took you to the Dallas City Jail?"

"Uh huh."

"They probably videotaped you when they booked you. How do you think you looked? Was it obvious you were drunk?" I said.

"Probably," Rob admitted.

"Did they take any blood?"

"Yeah, they said if I didn't give them blood, I'd lose my license."

"That's true, but it could be all they need to convict you."

Rob closed his eyes and took a deep breath. "So, now what? Am I screwed?"

Jodie walked in looking upset. "I'm sorry to bother you in a conference, but Don is on the line and he's very upset." Rob grimaced. I picked up the line.

"Don?"

"You won't believe this! This has been the worst day of my life. Oh, Jesus. I don't know what I'm going to do."

"What happened now?"

"The IRS levied our bank account."

"What?"

"Herb Winters, our loan officer at the bank, called right after Pam went to bed. He said the IRS had levied our bank account and that all the outstanding checks were going to bounce."

"Oh, my God, " I said. "How much did you have in there?"

"They got $21,000 and change."

I looked at Rob and shook my head. I whispered. "The IRS seized $21,000 from your dad's account"

"Oh, shit!" Rob said, sinking back into his chair.

"I called Jim and apprised him of the situation," Don said.

"Who's Jim?"

"He's a neighbor I brought into the deal. He in turn recruited three of his friends. So there are five of us all together.

"Oh. I see."

"He reluctantly agreed to kick in enough to cover his share of the NSF checks. He said he would try to get the other partners to do the same, but couldn't guarantee anything as everyone was getting low on cash."

"I can imagine."

Don continued. "Later on when I went back to the restaurant to close up, I was shocked to see the lights out and a letter addressed to the Golden Dragon Partnership taped to the door."

"What did it say?" I asked.

"I've got it here. . . . I'll read it to you."

Golden Dragon Partners

Dear Sir or Madam,

Please be advised that we have taken possession of these premises pursuant to Article 21.1 of your lease agreement for non-payment of rent. Currently, there is due the sum of $8,231.00. We regret this action but your continued delinquency and unwillingness to communicate gives us no other choice.

Please do not attempt to gain access to the premises. Notice is hereby given that the landlord is asserting its landlord's lien against all property within these premises. Removal of any items is prohibited by law.

Should you have any questions, call Embassy Management Co. 972-555-2117.

Sincerely, Bob Wilkinson

I said, "God, I am so sorry, Don. Luther Bell is turning out to be a monster."

"I guess we're out of business whether we like it or not."

Not knowing how to respond to Don's remark, I kept my mouth shut. Oftentimes things looked bleaker than they actually were, and I didn't know enough about what had happened to render an opinion.

"I'm going to kill that bastard!" Don said. "He's gonna wish he was never born."

CHAPTER SEVEN

Murder by Tire Iron

I entered the crowded courtroom and sat down in the row of seats directly behind the counsel tables. Court was already in session and the judge was listening to an attorney present his case. It was nine-fifteen and I was actually fifteen minutes early for my hearing. I often arrived early for hearings, as the consequences of being late were quite severe. Judge Babcock was an elderly judge and had grown impatient over the years with lackadaisical attorneys. It was not unusual for him to humiliate a tardy attorney in front of his colleagues, and, if the offense was severe enough, to cut his fee. I listened intently to the attorney's argument to the Court in hopes I might learn something of value. More than once, something I had picked up accidentally in court saved my ass in my own practice.

I had determined from the attorney's argument that it was a Chapter 11 case involving a general partnership called Bassett Products. Apparently, the trustee assigned to the case was asking the Court to impose liability on the general partners.

"Your Honor, as the Court is aware under Section 723 of Title 11, United States Code, general partners are personally liable to the estate for the debts of the partnership. Therefore, the trustee will be bringing adversary proceedings against all of the eleven partners," the attorney noted.

"When do you anticipate bringing these actions?" the

judge asked.

"We're working on them right now, Your Honor. I would estimate they will be filed within the next ninety days."

"Very well, I'll calendar this case for a status conference in 120 days," the judge said.

"Thank you, Your Honor."

The mention of general partnership liability reminded me of one of my business law professors at SMU, Preston Parks. He often warned us against advising clients to use them because they provided no liability protection for the partners. Each partner was jointly and severally liable for the acts of the others. The professor was critical of attorneys who set clients up with general partnerships when a corporation or limited partnership could be used. I wondered who the idiot was who set up Bassett Products. He obviously didn't take business law from Professor Parks.

Another problem with general partnerships, I recalled, was the requirement that partners provide additional capital as needed. In a corporation once you paid for your stock, nobody could make you cough up additional money. In a general partnership, however, when you got a cash call you had to open up your wallet and fork over more dough. This is what was happening to the poor bastards who invested in Bassett Products. The Trustee, who now controlled the partnership, was making one last cash call and anyone who didn't pay voluntarily was about to be sued.

After my hearing, I headed for the IRS Northwest field office. Representing as many small business owners as I did necessitated frequent dealings with the IRS. My meeting was with a Harold Clemmons, a Revenue Officer. We were meeting to discuss a client, an airline stewardess, who hadn't filed a tax return in ten years. She got scared and came to see me when her parents were arrested by the FBI for failing to file their returns. I guess tax evasion is hereditary.

The purpose of the visit was to negotiate a payout of the $43,000 she owed in back taxes. Prior to coming to see me, she had never filed a tax return although she had been working for five years. Fortunately, I got all of *her* returns filed *before* the IRS Criminal Fraud Division came looking for her. Harold could still refer the case to them for prosecution, but I had dealt with him in the past and worked with him on a committee for the Chamber of Commerce. He had always been reasonable. I convinced him that she had been brainwashed by her parents, but now understood her duty to pay taxes. Now, the only problem was figuring out how to pay the tax bill which would be growing at an astronomical rate with all accruing penalties and interest.

After a long meeting with the Revenue Officer, we agreed on a five year payout at $1,283 per month plus interest. I wasn't sure my client would be able to make the payment, but it was the best I could negotiate. A better move would have been a Chapter 13 since interest wouldn't accrue while she was making payments, but she wouldn't go for it. I got up to leave.

I said, as I slipped the file back in my briefcase, "Good, then I guess that's it."

Clemmons sat back in his chair and smiled. "I guess so. . . . So, what do you think about Luther Bell?" Clemmons asked.

"Luther Bell?" I repeated, recalling the events of the previous day.

"You remember Luther Bell don't you?"

"I'm afraid so," I replied.

"He was murdered last night."

"Murdered?" I said, feeling a cold chill sweep over me. Don had threatened to kill Luther Bell, not once, but twice the previous day. Had he made good on his promise?

"I heard it on the radio a few minutes ago. Apparently he was beaten to death with a tire iron."

"Did they say who did it?"

"Some investors, I think. Do you know Don Blaylock?"

My mouth fell open. "Yeah, he's a client."

"Well he's a suspect along with another investor—Jim somebody. I don't know him."

"Jesus, I've got a meeting with Don in a little while."

Clemmons shook his head. "It looks like you're gonna have your hands full with this one."

I nodded and took off in a daze. *Should I have done something last night to calm Don down? Maybe I should have gone over to his house to make sure he didn't do anything rash.* When I got back to my office I got on the phone with a friend at the DA's office to see what I could find out about the murder. She told me what she had heard. After hanging up, I called Rebekah.

"Honey, I'm glad I caught you at home. Did you hear about Luther Bell?"

"I saw something about it on the news. Who is he?"

"An insurance agent. You know, the one who keeps calling to get an appointment to sell us insurance."

"Oh, that guy. . . Jesus. I can't believe someone killed him. I know he was a pest but—."

"Apparently Don Blaylock did some business with him."

"Oh, really. So, what happened?"

"Someone surprised him in his garage last night between 9:30 and 10 p.m. Apparently the assailant hit Luther over the head with a tire iron knocking him unconscious and then beat him repeatedly until he was dead. I guess it was dark and Luther never saw it coming."

"You don't think Don had anything to do with it, do you?"

"I don't know, but he *did* threaten to kill him."

I told her about Pam's arrest and Don's threats against Luther.

"Oh, my God."

"I guess they've given the case to their top

investigator, Detective Harold "Bingo" Besch. I've never met him but I've heard he's tough."

"Should I call Pam?"

"No, I'm meeting with them in a little while. We haven't discussed the murder yet. You can call her tomorrow after I know more about what's going on."

"Okay," Rebekah said. "Poor Don and Pam. They were on top of the world and now they've fallen into a snake pit. I hope they didn't have anything to do with Luther's murder."

"Me too."

CHAPTER EIGHT

The Golden Dragon Partnership

As I was contemplating Don's situation, I couldn't help but worry about the possibility of another murder trial. My stomach began to tighten. I took a deep breath and tried to relax. Rebekah would have a stroke if I even contemplated defending Don. But I was jumping the gun. Don couldn't possibly have murdered anyone. He was the most clean-cut, honest man I knew. It couldn't have been him, even if he was awfully pissed at Luther Bell. And Pam—no way could she have killed anyone. As I drove up to the Blaylock's house, a constable's car was just leaving. Don was standing on the front porch reading a citation. I figured he had been sued over the car wreck. I was right.

"How bad is it?" I asked when I reached him.

"$2.7 million!"

"Oh God! I was afraid we might be looking at some hefty damages when I saw Jennifer had killed a doctor."

We went inside. I said hello to Pam and took a seat in an overstuffed chair. Don brought in a bottle of Jack Daniels. He asked me if I wanted a drink, but I declined. Liquor invariably made me sleepy and dulled my cognitive powers, and I knew I needed to be wide awake and alert for this interview. Pam brought me a cup of coffee.

"How can they sue me? I wasn't even in the car," Don moaned.

"They can sue anybody, but that doesn't mean they can

win. It will be difficult for them to prove you were at fault. You may own the car, but for you to be liable they would have to show you were negligent in letting Jennifer drive. Since you didn't even know she was driving, I can't see a jury holding you responsible for what happened."

"What should I do?"

"Call your insurance agent and tell him you've been sued. The insurance company should defend the suit. They'll hire an attorney to defend both you and Jennifer."

"But Stan, we only have a $300,000 policy," Pam said. "That's not nearly enough."

"I know, but a lot of times plaintiffs will settle for less. Nobody wants to go through a big trial and wait years to get paid—particularly when liability is questionable."

"I'm so worried," Pam said. "Rob may go to jail, Jennifer's pregnant, and now Don's been sued for millions of dollars. What else can go wrong?"

"I could be arrested for murder," Don replied.

"You were with me. They can't pin that on you," Pam said.

"Nobody will believe you. They will just think you are trying to protect me. Besides, we could have done it together."

"Wait a minute," I interjected. "If you want me to help you, I need you to back up and fill me in on what this is all about. I heard about the murder and I know you are both suspects, but I don't know the whole story about your investment with Luther Bell."

"*His* investment," Pam noted pointing a finger at Don.

Don frowned, then turned to me and said in a dejected tone, "Okay, I'm sorry. Let me see if I can explain all of this to you."

"Good," I replied.

"Should we wait for Jim?" Pam asked.

"No, he called and said he couldn't make it," Don replied.

"Jim is one of the partners, right?" I asked.

"Right. He is a group manager for a local electronics firm, PCS. His wife's name is Wanda. She's a housewife and volunteer at the children's unit at Doctors' Hospital. They have just one child, Paul. You've met him. He's our catcher on the Red Sox."

"Oh, yeah. I remember him. I haven't met his father though."

"Anyway," Don said. "Like I mentioned to you before, Pam and I invested in a restaurant recently."

"Right, a restaurant. . . . Hmm," I replied. I had put a number of restaurants into bankruptcy, so I had an appreciation for what an incredibly difficult business Pam and Don had gotten themselves into. I settled back into my chair expecting the worst.

"Well, as you know, Luther Bell was our managing partner. He's the one who got us in the restaurant in the first place."

"Yes, I met Luther at a Chamber meeting once and he's called me a couple of times trying to sell me insurance."

"Right, that's where I met him too. Anyway, Pam and I had accumulated a little money and were looking for an aggressive investment."

"Aggressive?" I asked. "Why?"

"It suddenly occurred to us that we only had a few years before Rob started college. We hadn't saved anything so our strategy was to set aside as much money as we could and invest it aggressively so we might come close to having enough for Rob's college expenses."

"Oh, I see. I've got the same problem. Rebekah and I haven't saved a dime yet for our children's college fund. We just figured Rebekah would go back to work when Reggi started school and she'd just sign her checks over to the University of Texas each payday."

Pam smiled. "I'm not a nurse, so I couldn't make near enough."

"I'm just kidding. I'm afraid my kids will have to do what I did—work and get well acquainted with the school's financial aid officer.... Anyway, I'm sorry for interrupting. Go on."

Don nodded and continued, "So, when Luther called and said he was a financial consultant, I just naturally mentioned that we were looking for an aggressive investment. At first he suggested a universal life product with an 11% return but I told him we were looking for something that would return 18% or better.

"That stumped him for a minute. But then he told us he was looking at a Golden Dragon franchise out of California. I was familiar with this restaurant chain and knew it was quite successful on the west coast. A franchise deal was attractive to me because I had seen several of my friends make great returns on franchise investments. One of them had bought a couple Whataburgers and another one a Swensens. They both were bragging all the time about the money they were making. I figured with a little luck my $10,000 could grow to maybe $50,000 which would pay a big chunk of Rob's education. Luther promised to call me later when he had more information about it. I told him I would mention the deal to Jim and some other potential investors.

"A few days later, Luther called and said that he had a prospectus and some financial projections for us. He sent them over by courier for us to look at. I called Jim Cochran, and he and Wanda came over to check them out.

"We spent the afternoon looking them over and all agreed they looked spectacular. We were very excited about the venture."

"You were excited about it," Pam said. "Wanda and I thought the numbers looked too good to be true."

"Yes, but you went along with the deal."

"Only because you said you were sure they were accurate."

"How was I supposed to know that Luther had

tampered with them?"

"Okay," I interjected. "So you told Luther you wanted in on the deal?"

"Yes, Jim and a couple of guys at his office wanted to invest too. So I told Luther to go ahead and get the paperwork filled out."

As we were talking, their daughter, Donna, came in with a big golden retriever close behind. The big dog immediately came over to me and started sniffing my shoes.

"Hi, Donna," I said. "Is this your dog?"

"Yes, this is Rip. . . . Where's Marcia?"

"Oh, she's at home. I came straight from the office so I couldn't bring her along."

She exaggerated a frown. "Next time bring her."

"Okay, I will."

"How's my little monkey," Don said. "Come here. I haven't seen you all day."

Donna turned to her father and said indignantly. "I'm not a monkey."

"Don raised his eyebrows and then asked, "You're not? How come Mom said she had to pull you down from a tree today?"

"I was trying to get Cindy's cat down. Rip chased her up a tree."

"I didn't see any cat," Pam said.

"When I got up there, she ran away."

"Well, you're lucky you didn't fall off the tree and break a leg," Don said.

"Kids are fun, aren't they?" I said.

"They're a pain in the ass if you ask me," Don said as he grabbed Donna, threw her over his lap and began to spank her gently.

"Daddy, don't spank me!"

"Why not?"

Donna wiggled off his lap and glared at him.

"That hurt," she complained as she forced a frown and

rubbed her bottom.

"Oh, I barely touched you. I was just kidding around. It didn't really hurt, did it?"

Donna smiled and said, "No."

"Then come over here and give Daddy a big hug."

Donna's face stiffened as she inched her way toward her father. When she got within an arms length he grabbed her and pulled her into his arms. She giggled as she wrapped her arms around him and gave him a big hug.

Don groaned like she was crushing him. She laughed in delight. Don said, "What about Stan, does he get a hug?" She ran over to me, put her arms around me and hugged me as hard as she could. I laughed.

"Oh, thank you, Donna. I think you are stronger than Marcia. That was a great hug."

Pam smiled. "Okay, Donna, go play until bedtime. We're discussing important business with Stan. Take Rip with you."

Donna patted Rip on his back and started running toward the door. "Come on, Rip," she said.

"Bye," Mr. Turner, "Donna said as she and Rip ran off down the hall.

"Isn't it great to have a daughter?" I said. "It only took you guys three tries. It took us four. Rebekah wanted to give up. She was sure we'd have another boy, but I knew it would be a girl. I even bought pink bubble gum cigars to give out and wouldn't let her bring anything blue to the hospital."

Pam laughed. "It's a good thing Donna came when she did, because I wouldn't have tried a fourth time."

"It *is* great to have a pretty little thing like her prancing around the house," Don mused.

"It is. I wouldn't trade Marcia for anything," I said.

I was glad Donna had made an appearance as the mood at the Blaylock house had gone up a few notches. I hated to have to plunge back into the grit and grime of reality but that was why I was there. I said, "Okay, so where were we?"

Don continued, "Well. Several weeks later, Luther had the deal put together, and we were summoned to the bank where the venture was to be financed. We met with the bank officer handling the loan, Herb Winters, and gave him our financial statements. He explained the loan to us and said he'd have an answer from the bank in a couple of days. After the meeting, Luther gave us copies of the partnership agreement. He said it was a standard agreement. Jim wanted to take it home but Luther insisted we read it and sign it then. We glanced over it but obviously didn't have time to read it verbatim. Jim asked if the agreement required additional capital contributions. Luther said in emergencies it did, but he didn't expect that to ever happen.

"The next day, Luther showed us the restaurant sites. We agreed on a location that previously had housed another restaurant, as Luther said it would be less expensive to finish out. A couple weeks later, the deal closed, and Luther invited us to a closing party at Anthony's in Northpark to celebrate."

I cringed when Don told me there had been a closing party. It reminded me of Kurt Harrison and the Panhandle Building fiasco that nearly cost me my law license when I first started practice. Harrison had been a high roller who was more concerned with appearances than reality. Luther apparently shared many of these same traits, which was a bad omen. We got up and stretched our legs. I called Rebekah and told her I'd be home by 10:00 p.m. She asked how bad it was. I told her it was too early to tell but that I'd fill her in when I got home. Pam put Donna to bed. Greg managed to tear himself away from his Dungeons and Dragons game to say hello. I chatted with Rob a minute when he stopped by to change clothes and then Don continued the saga.

"Luther told us the closing party was at eight. We arrived a few minutes late and the party had already started.

It was a formal affair so Pam wore a black cocktail dress with a pearl necklace and matching earrings. She looked ravishing and turned a lot of heads when she walked in."

I said, "I bet."

Pam blushed. "Don looked pretty dashing himself in his tux."

"Thank you, dear," Don said, flashing a smile. "Anyway, I told the waitress that we were looking for the Luther Bell group and she led us into a private dining area where the others were enjoying cocktails. Luther saw us come in and immediately came over to greet us. After complimenting me on my taste in women, he pointed us to the bar."

"I don't know if you've ever been to Anthony's, Stan, but the place is quite spectacular, and the service is first class," Pam said.

"No, I guess I'll have to check it out," I said.

"It's wonderful. . . .So thirty minutes later we were served a five course dinner consisting of lobster bisque, garden salad, shrimp scampi, and roast beef, along with plenty of fine wine. They served raspberry cheesecake for dessert. When the meal was completed, Luther got up and thanked us for investing in the Golden Dragon and promised we would all make a lot of money."

"Eight weeks later the Golden Dragon Restaurant officially opened. The mayor of Greenville presided over the ribbon-cutting ceremony which drew a pretty big crowd of local businessmen, civic leaders, the press, friends, and family. The restaurant officially opened for business at eleven-thirty the morning of November 13, 1983. We were all relieved that the restaurant was now opened for business and optimistic that it would be a big money maker.

"Unfortunately, it wasn't long before relief and optimism turned to pessimism and despair. That's when the cash calls started. The first one was twenty-five thousand dollars—half again our initial investment. Pam and I were crushed and felt horrible that we had gotten Jim and the others into the venture. But despite this first cash call we were still cautiously optimistic that things would work out okay in the end."

CHAPTER NINE

The Embezzlement

Looking at my watch as I listened to Don's story, I saw it was already ten. It was time to go. I had promised Rebekah I'd be home, but the story wasn't over. The worst was yet to come and I had to hear it all—every tragic detail of the rise and demise of Don and Pam Blaylock. They had become my friends and I felt sicker and sicker as the night waned.

Don cleared his throat. I looked over at him and smiled. He continued his story.

"After Luther had gone through the franchise training school, he admitted to us he still didn't have the experience necessary to operate the restaurant. As a result, the partners all agreed to hire an experienced assistant manager who could handle most of the day to day management chores. Carl Stillwater responded to Luther's advertisement placed in the *Dallas Morning News*. His résumé stated that he had managed a Dairy Queen in Ardmore, Oklahoma for three years, then an IHOP for a year after that. I asked Luther why Stillwater wanted to leave his current job and was told he was tired of Oklahoma and felt Texas had more opportunity.

"Luther and Stillwater got along famously from the first day they met. Stillwater was knowledgeable, confident and dependable. As time went on, Luther spent less and less time at the restaurant and eventually turned the job over almost completely to Stillwater. We found out later that Luther had managed to obtain a new brokerage contract with another insurance company and was selling insurance again.

"Jim was really pissed off when he found out about it. After the first cash call he insisted on reviewing the books. This annoyed Luther. He complained he had better things to do than dig up all the partnership records and sit around while Jim pawed through them. He stalled for several weeks but finally succumbed to Jim's pressure to review the books.

"It didn't take Jim long to see that someone was embezzling from the business. There were a lot of voided tickets which he at first attributed to sloppiness but then he discovered something really odd. Several checks had been sent to the same vendor all in the same month. Curious about this, he started inspecting the endorsements. They were all deposited in the same bank account—East Texas Collection Agency.

"Jim and I immediately reported the situation to the local police. They assigned the case to a Detective Johnson. After looking at the evidence Jim had provided, he started a criminal investigation. A few days later he staked out the First National Bank of Quinlin where the checks were being deposited into the account of the East Texas Collection Agency. He said it was probably a sham corporation, and by calling it a collection agency, the bank wouldn't be suspicious of checks being deposited that were made payable to a number of different companies.

"During the stakeout he observed a late model Ford Ranger pick-up waiting at the window. The teller signaled him that this person was depositing checks into the East Texas Collection Agency account. He started his engine and eased over behind it. A woman was driving and she seemed upset at how long it was taking to get her transaction processed. She looked in the rear view mirror and must have noticed Detective Johnson behind her. Apparently realizing he was a cop, she panicked and took off. Detective Johnson and a DPS officer chased her about twenty miles down the road before catching her. It turned out she was Ruby

Stillwater, Carl Stillwater's daughter.

"We were shocked that Stillwater had been cheating us. We were relieved to find out Luther wasn't involved, and were feeling a little embarrassed for suspecting him. Later that day they arrested Stillwater at the restaurant. He didn't put up a fight. We spent the evening figuring out how much he had embezzled from us. The final number was $34,225.06.

"Jim had blamed Luther for the embezzlement and told him so. They got into an argument and nearly came to blows. Jim wanted to get a new manager, and Pam and I thought that would be a wise idea too.

"Luther was very upset at the time. He said he had a contract and the partners couldn't fire him. Jim disagreed and said they could fire him for cause. Jim and I agreed to have a partners meeting and discuss it formally. Luther was pissed, but said he'd come. Jim told him to bring a complete set of financial reports so the partners could see exactly where they stood.

"Our accountant was Abe Dumas. He officed down the street and turned out to be incompetent. Luther had reportedly hired him because he was convenient and cheap.

"The partners' meeting was at Jim's house. It was a stormy night with torrential rain, frequent bursts of lightning, and loud thunder. Luther arrived ten minutes late, which irritated all of us even more. Wanda was serving drinks and coffee when Luther knocked on the front door. He wore an expensive blue suit, a silver silk tie, and carried a briefcase. He looked very impressive. After leaving his umbrella on the front porch, Pam led him back to where everyone was waiting. She offered him a drink, which he accepted. The only seat available was a piano stool where he finally sat. We exchanged cool greetings and then got down to business.

"Luther passed out the financial statements and everyone studied them. I was shocked when I saw the debts the partners owed to the IRS, the State Comptroller, and the landlord—not to mention the regular vendors. Luther blamed everything on the embezzlement and said they needed another cash call. Jim became livid at this and moved that Luther be fired. Pam seconded the motion and it carried. Luther seemed stunned at first. He just sat there in deep thought while the partners discussed finding a new manager.

"After a while, Jim came up with the idea that Pam could manage the business. Pam was against it at first but finally agreed on an interim basis. When I asked Luther to meet with Pam to help with the transition he became hysterical and stormed out of the house. He rushed to his car in the midst of the downpour and drove off.

"The next morning at eight thirty. Pam and I arrived at the Golden Dragon Restaurant. The restaurant wasn't scheduled to open until eleven but employees started arriving at nine. Pam went in the office and started organizing the accounts payable while I surveyed the inventory on hand. By nine-thirty, most of the employees had arrived, so I called them all together and told them Pam would be their manager from that day forward.

"With the employees settled down, Pam and I went to the bank and took Luther off the checking account. Then we paid a visit to Abe Dumas. It was almost noon, and Abe was behind his desk thumbing through a magazine. An old guy with only one leg, he looked more like a bum than a CPA. We told him that Luther was gone and that he was working for us now. He seemed surprised but didn't object. We asked him about the money we owed to the IRS and State Comptroller. He told us not to worry about it until we got a "Notice of Intention to Levy." Then it would be serious and we'd have to deal with it. He said that usually took six months.

"Pam took over and dealt with all the angry creditors as best she could, not realizing Luther had laid a trap for her."

Looking at my watch, I saw it was nearly midnight. I

was exhausted and was having trouble concentrating. It was time to leave.

"Well, that's quite a story," I said. "I'm glad Luther didn't invite me in on your deal. He probably would have sold me too."

"I was going to call you, Stan," Don said, "but you are always claiming poverty so I didn't bother."

"That's true. I've got about twenty-five dollars in my savings account, I think."

"Yeah, I bet."

I laughed. *If he only knew.* "It's getting late, and I promised Rebekah I'd get home two hours ago."

"Thank you for coming, Stan," Pam said. "I feel so much better now that we've told you everything. There is hope, isn't there?"

I forced a smile. "Sure, don't worry. Everything will work out okay. It always does. . . . I am concerned though. When I called the DA's office they indicated that you and Pam were prime suspects in Luther's murder. I suppose Jim and Wanda would be too. It's important that you don't talk to the police or anyone from the DA's office. As a matter of fact, don't talk to anyone because whatever you say can come back to haunt you. I want to be there if you are questioned. Tell Jim and Wanda to keep their mouths shut too."

"We will and we won't talk to anyone," Don said. "Neither of us killed Luther, Stan. They can't pin this on us."

"I know that, but the DA doesn't. Unless you have an iron-clad alibi you can bet he *will* try to pin it on you. . . . So, do you have an alibi?"

Don and Pam looked at each other and then back at me with solemn faces.

I said, "That's what I was afraid of."

By the end of the evening, the burden of the Blaylock's problems shifted from their shoulders to mine. Now they expected me to right their capsized vessel and send them on their way. As I drove home, I was overwhelmed by the burden they had dumped on me and looked out into the night wondering how I could possibly rescue them from their dire predicaments.

CHAPTER TEN

The Accident

The following day, Jennifer was scheduled to meet with me. I wanted to get all the details of the accident so I could evaluate her liability exposure. I also wanted to know what she and Rob did the night of Luther's murder. I was on the telephone when Jodie came to my door and signaled that Jennifer had arrived. After I hung up the phone, I hit the intercom button and told Jodie I was ready to see her.

In a moment the door opened and she strolled in confidently. I stood up. She was definitely a looker. I realized immediately how Rob must have been mesmerized by her beauty. I certainly was. She didn't look like a teenager either. If I had met her in a bar I would have guessed twenty-two. She took a seat in a side chair in front of my desk.

"Thanks for coming in, Jennifer. I really appreciate it."

"It's no problem. I hope there is something I can do to help. I feel so terrible about what happened. The Blaylocks must hate me."

"They don't *hate* you. They are obviously upset over what happened. But they realize Rob was just as much to blame as you."

"No he wasn't. He didn't even want to go to the warehouse. It was all my fault. I wanted to go dancing. Why did I have to insist on it? It was a stupid idea," Jennifer said.

"You had no idea this would happen," I replied.

"Why didn't *I* drive? I knew Rob was drunk. If I had just taken the keys from him, we wouldn't have been in the accident. Damn it! They'll never forgive me."

"I'm not so sure about that," I said.

"I hope they don't throw him off the baseball team. That would devastate him.

"And his father," I added.

"Oh. . . . Rob's going to hate me," Jennifer sobbed. "God, I can't believe this mess I've gotten myself into."

"Well, it's water under the bridge now, so let's just figure out the best way to deal with it. . . . Why don't you just tell me what happened?"

Jennifer wiped her tears away with a tissue. Then she began her story. "After the cop had taken Rob and Jesse away we headed toward downtown on Central Expressway. We took I-45 to the eastbound on-ramp to I-30 and eased our way into the flow of traffic. Traffic was light so everyone was traveling fast. As we were about to pass the Fair Park on-ramp, a red Chrysler LeBaron convertible full of kids suddenly veered in front of us going barely fifty miles per hour. Unfortunately, I had momentarily taken my eyes off the road to get another tissue since I'd been crying. I didn't see them until it was too late.

"I turned sharply to the left trying to avoid the Chrysler and ended up veering into the center lane in front of a silver Mercedes. The Mercedes swerved to the left but couldn't avoid hitting us. The collision forced the Mercedes further to the left until it collided with the concrete median, flipped over several times, and burst into flames. I slammed on the brakes and we came to a screeching halt. The Chrysler continued on down the highway. I could see the occupants looking back at the us. The driver never even slowed down.

"Linda had struck the front windshield and was knocked unconscious. I wasn't seriously hurt, but emotionally I was a wreck. I jumped out of the car and watched the burning Mercedes in horror. Suddenly, the car exploded and the concussion from the blast knocked me down. I tried to stand, but halfway up, everything went black."

"God, that must have been terrible," I said trying to

fathom the horror Jennifer must have felt at that moment. *How quickly our lives can go up in smoke.*

"It was," she said. "I haven't had a decent night's sleep since it happened. I keep seeing the Mercedes burning. Sometimes I can hear the doctor screaming, smell his flesh burning—it's just unbearable."

"You didn't actually hear the doctor scream, did you? Or smell burning flesh?"

"No, I don't think so. It's just my imagination, I guess."

"Well, you may need some counseling to get through this. I can refer you to someone, if you like."

"No, I'll be all right."

"So that's it?"

"That's all I remember."

I shook my head. "Okay. Now that I have the facts I'll figure out what defenses are available to us. This will be a tough case, but I think there are a few possibilities."

"Like what?" Jennifer asked eagerly.

"Unavoidable accident for one. Assuming you weren't speeding, there was nothing you could have physically done to avoid the accident under the circumstances. Secondly, the negligence of the third vehicle's driver was the actual cause of the accident. You had the right of way."

"You think that will be enough?"

"Not necessarily, but at least it's something."

Jennifer nodded dejectedly.

I said, "Listen, let's change the subject a minute."

She looked up and replied, "Okay."

I pushed the intercom button on the phone and picked up the receiver. "Jodie come in here please." Turning to Jennifer, I said, "If you don't mind I'm going to let Jodie take notes for me."

"Sure, whatever."

Jodie came in and took a seat on the sofa behind Jennifer. I really didn't need her to take notes. My real purpose for having her in the room was to get her opinion as to whether Jennifer was being candid or not.

"I've got to ask you about the night of Luther's murder. You were with Rob, right?"

"Yes. We went to the Mesquite Library."

"About what time was that?"

"Eight or so."

"And how long did you stay there?"

"About an hour."

"Then where did you go?"

She looked straight through me like she was in deep thought. Finally she blinked and replied, "Home."

I studied her, sensing she was hiding something.

"Are you sure?"

She looked away and swallowed hard. Suddenly she began to cry. I got up, picked up the box of tissues and took them to her. I sat down in the side chair next to hers. She took a tissue and blew her nose. I put my hand on her arm to try to console her but it didn't do any good. She turned and looked at me. She was crying harder now. "I don't know, Mr. Turner. Sometimes I wonder if I'll make it another day."

I didn't understand her sudden emotional crash so I said, "What's wrong? Is there something you're not telling me?"

"Well, I should have told you this before, but—"

"It's okay, just tell me now."

"After we went to the library Rob wanted to go home and check on his mother. When we got there she was in her bedroom staring at the wall. He tried to talk to her but she wouldn't respond. It was like she was in a trance or something. Rob was so upset he took his father's .38 out of his drawer, stormed out of the house yelling that he was going to kill Luther Bell. I followed him trying to calm him down, but he was way too upset for that.

"On the way there, Rob put the gun in his lap. While he was making a turn, I grabbed it away from him. I didn't want him shooting Luther. We fought for the gun and nearly ran off the road, but I managed to unload it and throw the bullets out of the window. Rob was pissed but kept on driving. I guess he was going to kill Luther with his bare hands.

"When he got to Luther's condo we parked in the driveway. The garage door was open. We both jumped out. I ran over to Rob to try to stop him. We struggled some more and then we saw Luther lying on the ground in a pool of blood."

I asked, "What did you do then?"

"I was scared—scared someone would think we had killed Luther so I pushed Rob back toward the car and told him to get in. We had to get out of there fast before someone saw us. When we got home I put the gun back in the drawer while Rob kept his father busy. Pam was asleep and didn't even know I was in the room."

I said, "You're sure Luther was dead when you got there?"

"Yes, absolutely. Rob didn't kill him."

Jennifer looked at me intently. She didn't blink. I felt like she was telling the truth, but I wasn't positive.

"If anyone saw you two, you're in serious trouble."

She closed her eyes and exhaled. "I know, but I don't think anyone did."

"Did you touch anything?"

"No, I don't think so. We just looked at Luther lying there on his side with his eyes wide open. It was dark, but there was no doubt he was dead."

I shook my head. "Okay, if Detective Besch tries to question you, don't talk to him."

"I won't."

We stood up and started walking to the door.

Jennifer said, "Thank you, Mr. Turner. You've been so wonderful. I'm sorry I cried like a baby."

I laughed. "Oh, don't worry about it. It's good to let your emotions out."

After Jodie escorted Jennifer to the door, she came back to talk about what had happened. I suggested she pour us both a cup of coffee. She did and then sat down to brainstorm.

"So, what do you think? Is she telling the truth?" I asked.

Jodie replied, "I'm not a hundred percent sure, but I think so. She seemed sincere."

"I don't know. She may be protecting Rob. She's a pretty smooth talker."

"So what are you going to do?"

"I don't know. I should tell Detective Besch about it, but I'm afraid he'll stop looking for the real killer and just try to pin it on Rob. I'll have to tell him eventually, but I need more time."

"What if he finds out on his own and figures out you were holding out on him?"

"Then we're screwed. He'll figure Rob is guilty and that's why he didn't come clean."

"What are you going to do now?" Jodie asked.

"Find out more about Luther Bell—see if he had any other enemies. I think I'll start with his former employer."

She nodded. "Oh, by the way. I found you that expert on Peruvian civilizations."

"Really?"

"Yes, Melanie Dixon. She works at the Dallas Museum of Natural History down at Fair Park. I told her about the pieces you had, and she's very anxious to see them."

"Wow. You *are* Miss Efficiency."

She smiled. "You've got an appointment tomorrow at 3:00 p.m. I packed them all up carefully and put them in a box."

I laughed. "You really *are* worried about getting paid."

"Somebody around here needs to be concerned about it."

I shook my head. "How did you get saddled with a

bum like me?"

"You're not a bum. You're just so wrapped up in everybody else's problems you don't have time to take care of your own."

"Hmm. You ever thought about being a shrink?"

She rolled her eyes and said, "Get out of here."

*****

Walking into the offices of Mid-America Life brought back memories of my law school days when I sold insurance to make ends meet. In retrospect, it was a valuable experience, although at the time I hated it. The constant rejection a salesman had to endure in any business was brutal, but selling life insurance was the worst of all sales jobs. Fortunately, those days were behind me. I took a deep breath and walked up to the receptionist.

"Hi, I'm Stan Turner and I'm here to see Mr. Walsh."

"Oh, yes. He's expecting you. I'll tell him you're here."

After a few moments, I was escorted into Mr. Walsh's office. He was a portly gentleman with thin white hair. Stacks of papers, booklets, brochures and other paperwork cluttered his desk. He sat back and relit an old cigar.

"So, Turner, didn't you used to work for Cosmopolitan Life?"

Walsh's inquiry shocked me. I hadn't expected him to know me.

"Yeah, a few years back."

"I knew your boss, Helms. He and I were at New York Life together fifteen years ago."

"Really?"

"He told me he had some aspiring attorney working for him. I told him you'd never get through law school while you were selling insurance full time. I guess you proved me wrong."

"Well, I had a lot of incentive to graduate—a wife and four kids."

"You should have stayed in the business. With a law degree you'd be a dynamite salesman."

"No, I don't think so. I learned early on that I wasn't cut out to be in sales."

He nodded and put his cigar in the ash tray. "So, what can I do for you?"

"You had a salesman—Luther Bell."

"Yes, I did. A hell of a salesman. Too bad about him gettin' his brains splattered all over his garage."

"I represent Don Blaylock and Jim Cochran. They are suspects in Luther's murder. I was hoping you might give me some insight into Mr. Bell's life. I'm particularly interested in how he got into franchising. It seems a little strange he'd be doing that while he was working for you."

"Well, Luther knew his days were numbered here at Mid-America so he decided to get a head start on his new franchise venture. I'm sure he was hoping to hang on here until he could draw a salary from the Golden Dragon partnership.

"I knew something was up," Walsh said, "because Luther's production was way down. In fact, he and I had a little disagreement about it."

I looked at Walsh in eager anticipation. He leaned back in his chair and took a long drag on his cigar. His eyes became fixed as he reached back in his memory to tell the story.

"I was frustrated and angry over the lack of production from my staff. My sales force was pitiful compared to what it had been in the past. For years I had great producers who made my agency number one in the nation. They were eager, hard working soldiers who pounded the pavement day after day calling on prospects, tirelessly working their prospect lists, undaunted by rejection, never taking *no* for an answer. Now the company had saddled me with college graduates, MBAs—desk men who thought people bought insurance because they *needed it* or, God forbid, that it was a *good investment.*

"My wife was counting on me winning a trip to Hawaii. You see, the company runs a contest each year and those who meet certain production targets get an all-expense-paid vacation. This was the first time Hawaii was the destination. We had gone to Atlanta, San Francisco, and Disneyworld, but this was *Hawaii.* Helen had been after me for years to take her there and now all I had to do was get my men to sell fifty thousand dollars more in premiums and we'd be on our way at the expense of Mid-America Life. I was determined to somehow motivate them.

"So, I gathered them together for a sales meeting and told them exactly what we needed to win the contest. I showed them pictures of Hawaii, gave them brochures describing everything they'd be able to see and do and really tried to fire them up.

"I told them to review their prospect lists and come up with twenty-five names that they could contact that month. Beside each name, I told them to write one paragraph explaining how they were going to approach that prospect, what objections they expected to get, and how they would handle them. Finally, I asked them for a weekly progress report on how they were doing.

"Everyone seemed to respond pretty well except Luther. At the time I was puzzled by it. Selling came naturally for Luther. He was young and handsome, liked people and loved to talk. He was a dreamer, always with some new plan to make a million bucks, and he loved to tell anybody who'd listen about those lofty ambitions.

"Luther had attended Penn State but flunked out his sophomore year. He quickly realized two things—first, that being a college graduate was of great importance to his success in life, and secondly, that no one ever checked his résumés. Consequently, he soon convinced himself and everyone else that he was a graduate of Penn State with a degree in finance."

"How do you know that?" I asked.

"I *did* check his résumé, and they told me he had flunked out."

"Why did you hire him then?"

"Because a college degree wasn't a prerequisite to this job so it didn't matter. I heard him tell other agents he had graduated and I also know he told some of his clients he was a graduate of Penn State."

"That didn't bother you?"

"No, a salesman's got to puff a little. It's no big deal."

"Hmm. Okay," I said. "Go on."

Walsh continued, "Luther tried to sneak away right after the meeting but I told my secretary to make sure he stopped by my office before he left. She gave him the message as he was going out the door. He wasn't happy.

"When he came into my office I told him how disappointed I was with his production and, in particular, his high lapse rate. I told him I wanted to see him go to Hawaii and that I was counting on him."

"How did he respond to that?" I asked.

"He was hostile and belligerent. He questioned my records. I assured him they were quite accurate. I told him he was a good salesman and could be successful if he really worked at it. He became agitated, twisted nervously in his chair and then glanced at his watch as if he were late for something.

"Frustrated with his lack of commitment, I instructed him to have a prospect list on my desk by the following day at five o'clock. Again, I mentioned how nice it would be for him to go to Hawaii. His reply was he didn't much care if he went to Hawaii or not."

"Why was that?"

"His wife, Laura Bell, had filed for divorce but they were still fighting over child support. A final hearing was months off.

"I told him how sorry I was and how much I liked

Laura and his daughter. But nothing I said seemed to matter. He just didn't give a shit so I got mad. I told him if he didn't get his act together, I was going to put him on straight commission. When he heard that, he turned red and stormed out of the room. I heard his tires squealing as he raced out of the parking lot."

"So, Luther was married?" I asked. I knew he was, obviously, but I just wanted to keep Walsh talking.

"Yes, he and Laura were separated. They had one child together, little Betsy. He brought her here to the office a couple times. It's a shame she won't have a father to watch her grow up."

"Why were they separated?"

"Infidelity. Luther couldn't keep his snake in his pants, if you know what I mean."

"I see."

"Laura forgave him once, but the second time she told him to take a hike. In fact, when he didn't leave the house quickly enough, she pulled a gun on him."

"Really?"

"Uh huh. He came in here right after it happened. I've never seen him so upset. When I asked what was wrong he spilled his guts."

"It had been a perfect day for a picnic and Laura and Luther had taken advantage of the pleasant weather to take Betsy to the Dallas Zoo. On the way home they had stopped at a Pizza Inn for dinner and by the time they got back to their apartment it was nearly eight-thirty. Laura insisted Betsy go right to bed. She had planned an amorous evening with Luther and had wine chilling in the refrigerator. Betsy put up a fuss but finally went to bed after negotiating a bedtime story from her father.

"When Luther returned to the living room, Laura was waiting in her negligée. After drinking some wine they started a little foreplay. It was getting pretty hot until Laura noticed a bite mark on Luther's back. She knew immediately

Luther had been cheating on her. It wasn't a big surprise. She had suspected it, but this was clear and convincing evidence of his deceit.

"Luther denied it at first, but finally admitted he had picked up a woman at a bar and taken her back to his motel room in Tyler. He told Laura it didn't mean anything, and that he loved her and Betsy. He begged for her forgiveness, but Laura wasn't in a forgiving mood. She told him to get out.

"He refused to leave, so Laura went into her bedroom and retrieved a gun she had purchased at a pawn shop. She came out of the bedroom with it pointed at Luther. He was shocked and obviously shaken when he saw the gun pointed at him. He tried to reason with Laura and get her to put down the gun, but when he realized she might pull the trigger he made a hasty retreat."

As Walsh talked, I couldn't get the image of Laura holding a gun in Luther's face out of my mind. Obviously she had to be a prime suspect now too. I wondered if the police knew about the incident with the gun. Walsh was gracious enough to give me Laura's address and telephone number which I jotted down. He seemed to enjoy the story telling so I pressed him for more information.

"So, what about the franchise? What do you know about it?"

"He tried to keep it a secret, but I heard it was some kind of restaurant. I know he was spending most of his time working on it. He didn't meet his production quota, so I had to make good on my threats to put him on straight commission."

I knew all about straight commission. When I worked for Cosmopolitan Life they put me on a $2,000 a month salary for a year until my account grew enough to support me. Had I been forced to work on straight commission, I would have made zero for the first few months and wouldn't have got up to the $2,000 a month level for years. It was common for agents to get a guaranteed salary in the beginning, but eventually they were expected to go on straight commission. If, after several years, they weren't cutting the mustard, management would often put them on straight commission to force them to quit. They didn't want to fire them because their unemployment rate would go up.

"So, obviously that didn't work," I said.

"Yeah, everything came to a head a couple weeks later. It was at our regular sales meeting. I had a big chart up with a thermometer drawn to illustrate the progress of the agency toward the production goal needed to win the trip to Hawaii. Luther stared at the chart but was clearly off in another world—probably at his new restaurant. When I was done with my pep talk, I went over to talk to him.

"I asked him if he had some apps for me. He just shrugged, which really made me mad. I called him a loser and told him if he would spend less time in bars and stay away from loose women, he might find time to sell some insurance.

"That pissed him off so he started yelling at me. He said some pretty nasty things that I couldn't just let slip by. I was about to fire him when he announced he was quitting. He went directly to his desk, cleaned out a couple of drawers full of his personal belongings and that was the last time I saw him."

I said, "So how long had Luther been selling life insurance?"

"About four or five years. He was a fine salesman, but he was lazy and was always looking for the easy score. Hard work is what makes a life insurance salesman successful. I keep telling my men that, but they don't want to hear it."

"You mentioned Luther was out with a lot with loose women. Did you know any of them?"

"I heard he spent a lot of time at the Sunset Strip. It's a topless bar off Stemmons Freeway at Walnut Hill Lane. A lot of the guys go there. He mentioned a club near his house too . . . the Rendezvous Restaurant and Club, I think. It's just a singles' hangout on Greenville. I never met any of his girlfriends, and he didn't talk about them because he knew I liked Laura."

"Well, you've been very helpful. I can't think of anything else to ask you right now, but I'm sure I'll think of something later. Can I call you, if I do?"

"Sure, glad to help. I feel really badly about Luther's death. It's really a shame."

Somehow I didn't believe Walsh really felt all that badly about Luther's death. From what I had just heard it must have been a great relief for Walsh to be rid of him. I thought about what I had learned from Walsh. The thing that stood out was Luther's active sex life. This interested me. Ex-wives, girlfriends, illicit lovers, topless dancers—surely amongst them there would be a murder suspect or two.

CHAPTER ELEVEN

Winning the Lawyer's Lottery

Keyur Ravi came to my office with his uncle, Amit. He was of slight build, had curly black hair, and wore glasses. His uncle was an inch shorter and obviously liked to eat well. After Jodie got them some tea, she led them into the conference room where I met them. I was a little nervous because I knew this could be a very lucrative case and I really wanted to handle it. I was sure they had been contacted by numerous PI attorneys, as this type of accident usually drew a flock of them.

"I was very sorry to learn of your father's death, Key," I said. "It must have been a terrible shock."

"Yes, I've been very sad lately," Key said.

"I can imagine. Were you and your father close?"

Key didn't respond.

"The divorce, you know, it made it very difficult," Amit interjected.

"Of course. Divorces are kind of unusual in your culture, aren't they?" I asked.

"Yes, it was a terrible thing. Very destructive for the family," Amit said.

"So, how did the funeral go?"

"It went very well, thank you," Amit said. "Your friend, Mr. Stuart, was so helpful in making all the arrangements. He has been so nice, we are eternally grateful."

"Yes, Stuart's a great guy. Is there any other family?"

"No, Anant was divorced," Amit said, "Our mother is

dead, and our father is back in Bombay. I'm the only living sibling, you know. Our sister died very young."

"Well, under the Texas Wrongful Death Act the victim's father would have a cause of action as well as any children."

"He's an old feeble man who has no use for money," Amit replied.

"Well, maybe so, but he does have a right to be a plaintiff in the suit. If he doesn't want the money maybe he would assign his cause of action to you or someone else in the family."

"I'll try to talk to him and see what he wants to do."

"Let me know and I'll prepare the paperwork for him to sign."

"Okay then, so how do we proceed now?" Amit asked. "We've already had three lawyers call us on the telephone wanting to represent Key. Yesterday, two came by our house offering to handle his case."

I shook my head. "Ambulance chasers. They must have been monitoring the police radio or saw Anant brought into the emergency room. I've got a contingent fee contract right here for Key to sign."

I handed Key and Amit the contracts and explained, "Essentially the contract says that we will prosecute the case through trial if necessary, but you don't pay us anything unless we recover money for you. If we recover money after we file a lawsuit then we get one-third of the recovery and you get two-thirds. You're responsible for all costs of court. However, we will advance those funds for you if you cannot afford to pay them yourself. If the case is appealed then we get forty percent and you get sixty."

"What if we don't have to file a suit?" Amit asked.

"Well, then we get twenty-five percent and you all get seventy-five, but that's unlikely in a wrongful death case."

"How much money do you think I'll get?" Key asked.

"Well, that's hard to say. Each case is different. A lot depends on the amount and kind of insurance that the defendant has. If the insurance is not enough to cover your damages, then the value and extent of the defendant's assets become important."

"What do you mean? I don't understand. I thought when you got a judgment that was how much you got," Amit said.

"No, unfortunately that is not the case. You may get a million dollar judgment but if the defendant only has a hundred thousand dollars insurance and no non-exempt assets then you'll only actually get a hundred thousand dollars."

"How much insurance does the defendant have?"

"We don't know yet, we haven't seen a police report and haven't talked to the defendant yet. However, he was driving a late model Porsche and comes from a wealthy family so that's a good sign."

Amit handed the contract back to me and said, "This will be fine. If Mr. Stuart says we should trust you then we will trust you, right Key?"

Key looked at Amit and nodded, "I just want the man who killed my father to be punished. I don't care so much about the money."

I smiled. That was a familiar refrain from clients but it was a lie. It was all about money. A good personal injury case was like winning the lottery and clients knew it. If it wasn't about money, Key wouldn't have been in my office. He would have been at the DA's office making sure the bastard who killed his father got prosecuted.

"Well, the district attorney will be handling the criminal case. The only punishment we can ask for is punitive damages if we can prove gross negligence or intentional misconduct."

Key signed the contract and handed it to me. I smiled and said, "Thank you. We'll get right on this and keep you posted. In a couple weeks, I'm going to need to spend some time with you, Key, to learn all about your relationship with your father. We've got to show the jury how you've been damaged by his loss. I'll call you and make an appointment."

*****

Driving down to Fair Park brought back memories of the Texas State Fair. Every year the kids got a day off from school to go to the Fair, so Rebekah and I always took them. They loved the rides, and Rebekah and I loved the food and exhibits. As I pulled into the parking lot of the Dallas Museum of Natural History, I felt a little embarrassed. What if my Peruvian pottery was nothing but junk? My client probably laughed all the way home after unloading it on me. I considered turning around and going back to the office, but then I'd have to face Jodie.

After parking my car and taking the box out of the trunk, I went inside and asked the first person I saw where I could find Melanie. They showed me to her office and I knocked.

"Come in."

I opened the door slowly and looked in. Melanie was behind a small table desk. One of those desks without drawers that look very impressive but are totally impractical. The first thing I noticed were her long, slender legs stretched out beneath the desk. They were so magnificent I was immediately mesmerized. When I looked up she was smiling. I'd been caught.

"Nice desk," I said.

She rolled her eyes and replied, "Right. . . . You must be Stan Turner?"

"That's me."

"So let's see what you have there."

I put the box on the desk, and she opened it. She stuck her hand inside and pulled out a piece wrapped in tissue paper. She opened it carefully and began studying it.

"Well, Mr. Turner. This is quite a nice piece. Your secretary said you got it from a missionary?"

I told her the sad story while she unwrapped the rest

of the pottery.

"So, is this stuff worth anything?" I asked hopefully.

"Yes, I should think so."

"How much?"

"Well, that's hard to say. There isn't a formal market for these relics. There are people out there who *do* buy them, but you've got to find them and take bids. It's not an easy task."

"Oh," I said.

"But, if you would like, I'll contact a few people and see what the market looks like."

"Would you? That would be great. Is this something you've done before?"

"Yes, from time to time. I usually get a fifteen percent commission if I find a buyer."

"That seems fair."

"Good. I'll get a contract together and call you when it's ready to sign."

I gave her my card and left elated at the prospect of unloading the pottery. But on the way home it wasn't the pottery that was on my mind. It was Melanie and those long luscious legs.

*****

Before Pam, Don and Jim came to my office to continue their story, I decided to call Howard Hurst, head of the Franchise Division of the Golden Dragon Restaurants headquartered in Monterey, California. In the paperwork that Don had given me, I had found the Franchise Agreement that Hurst had signed on behalf of the franchisor. I figured he might have some insight into what had transpired. I got lucky and caught him in the office.

Hurst said, "The first time I actually talked to Luther was just after he had received our franchise package. He was confused about how to proceed with the franchise and called to get some direction."

"What was he confused about?"

"He wanted to know when the $50,000 franchise fee had to be paid, how the equipment financing worked, and the approval process for the location."

"So were you able to answer his questions?" I asked.

"Sure, I explained everything in detail and he seemed satisfied."

"Do you think after your explanations that he actually did understand how everything worked?"

"Well, I was concerned about several items."

"What were they?" I asked.

"Legal, accounting, and management."

"Could you explain?"

"He said he didn't intend to consult an attorney. I figured that was his business, but we generally like our franchisees to have legal counsel to be sure they fully understand their duties and responsibilities. Secondly, he told me he intended to do his own accounting. That is an invitation for disaster. Accounting is very tricky and time consuming. I doubt he had the ability to do it properly or, if he did, he definitely wouldn't have the time. Which leads me to the final problem."

"What's that?"

"He thought he could manage the restaurant himself."

"And you had concerns about that?"

"I would say so. He had no experience and no idea how difficult it was to run a restaurant."

"So with all these misgivings, why approve the franchise?"

"He promised that if he felt he was in over his head, he would get help. I know he did hire a manager and an accountant fairly soon after the restaurant opened."

"Did you have any other conversations with him?"

"A couple days later, I got the completed application back with some proposed sites in Greenville. Luther had retained a broker who had helped him find the locations. I called Luther after our people had looked over the sites and asked him some questions. He explained that he knew the area well since his father used to be a preacher there. Apparently he studied theology and his family hoped he'd follow in his father's footsteps. That didn't happen, I guess, because he liked women and liquor too much."

"Really. He said that?" I asked.

"Uh huh. He seemed kind of proud of it actually."

I shrugged. "Somehow that doesn't surprise me."

CHAPTER TWELVE

Shattered Lives

When Jim, Don and Pam came to my office to tell me the rest of the Golden Dragon saga, the picture was starting to come into focus. Luther Bell had been way over his head but not smart enough to realize it. It appeared he genuinely thought the restaurant was going to be a cash cow that would provide him substantial income. He would take his management fee and skim additional money at every opportunity. Unfortunately, the hiring of Carl Stillwater along with numerous other management miscalculations eliminated any such possibility. Jim, Pam, and Don took a seat across from me, and Jodie brought them coffee. I got up and refilled my cup.

We chatted a few minutes and then Pam continued the story. "After a couple days I realized I hadn't been getting much mail. I called the post office and was advised the mail had been forwarded to Luther Bell's home. That really upset me, so I went immediately to the post office and demanded the change of address be canceled. The local postmaster advised me that in the case of a dispute over the rightful owner of mail it would be held pending agreement of the parties or a court order directing where it should be delivered.

"I called Don to tell him what had happened, but he was out of the office. Desperate to do something, I called Jim hoping he would be at work. He was and I filled him in on the situation. He got very angry and said he was going over to

Luther's place immediately to straighten things out. He can tell you what happened."

Pam paused and we all looked at Jim. I took a sip of my coffee in anticipation of the rest of the story. Jodie came in and refilled everyone's cup. Jim looked like he was in a trance, so I said, "So, what happened, Jim." He looked at me, took a deep breath and then continued the story.

"After getting Pam's call, I was so infuriated I immediately left the building and headed for Luther's condominium. It was late in the afternoon when I knocked on Luther's door. Margie Mason, Luther's girlfriend, answered and claimed Luther wasn't home.

"I was frustrated because I knew Luther was home. His Cadillac was parked out front. Margie was just covering for him. I said, 'Give him a message for me, would you?'"

"Margie asked, 'What's that?'"

"I replied, 'Tell him that he better release the Golden Dragon's P.O. box by noon tomorrow or his dentist is going to have lots of reconstructive work to do on his mouth!'"

"Margie didn't respond. After a few seconds I turned and walked away. Margie closed the door and locked the deadbolt. The following day Luther released the P.O. box, but unfortunately it was too late for Pam as you know."

In my short legal career I had seen some strange things, but nothing quite so bizarre as the Golden Dragon fiasco. There was no doubt each and every one of the partners had a more than ample motive to kill Luther Bell. I wondered if one of them actually *was* guilty.

"So what do you think, Stan?" Jim asked.

"I don't know what to think. Luther had a lot of enemies besides you guys. His ex-wife is a good suspect. She actually drew a gun on him one time." I told them that story.

He pissed off his manager over at Mid-America Life and they had some words. I'll just have to do some more digging to find out who hated him enough to kill him."

"Do you think they will arrest any of us?" Pam asked.

I shrugged. "They could arrest any one of you. You all had strong motives to kill Luther and I haven't heard a good alibi yet. If any of you *do* get arrested, keep your mouth *shut*, okay?"

They all nodded. I watched them carefully for body language that might indicate one of them was guilty, but all I saw was despair. They had been sailing through life, tasting and relishing the American dream, but now they had encountered a storm—no, not just a storm, a hurricane, and they were washed up on the rocks. Now the question was: could they survive the storm or would their lives be broken into pieces and scattered across the beach?

After the meeting, I noticed I had a telephone message from Melanie. I quickly dialed the number and a receptionist put me through.

"The contract is ready," Melanie said.

"Oh, great. . . . Mail it to me and I'll sign it and send it right back."

"I was thinking since I go by your place on the way home, maybe we could meet somewhere. I've talked to a few prospective buyers and I'd like to report on what I've found out. You could sign the contract then."

"Okay, where and when?"

"Six o'clock at Bennigan's near Valley View Mall."

"Sure, that's not far. I'll see you later then."

"Great. Bye."

Looking at my watch, I saw it was nearly three o'clock. I wondered why Melanie wanted to meet in person. What could be so important that a face to face meeting was needed? Not that I minded seeing her again, but it would cause complications. If I was sociable and had a few drinks, I couldn't go right home because Rebekah would smell the booze and ask questions. I'd have to try to explain why I had met Melanie for Happy Hour. Then it might get ugly. I picked up the phone and started to call Melanie to cancel the meeting but Jodie yelled that Tex was on line two. Since a call from Tex meant he had a new client to refer, I quickly punched two and took the call. At five o'clock, I remembered I hadn't canceled my meeting with Melanie so I picked up the phone and called her. There was no answer.

The bar at Bennigan's was packed. I looked around for Melanie but didn't see her. Then I felt a warm hand on my shoulder. I turned and faced Melanie. She smiled and said, "Good timing."

"Yeah, I hope we can find a table."

She pointed over in the corner where miraculously a small table sat unoccupied. We made a dash for it. Melanie looked quite sophisticated in her red sleeveless chemise and matching coat. I helped her out of her coat and folded it neatly on the spare chair. She smiled graciously and took a seat. I sat and said, "So, what do you usually drink? Let me guess. Gin and tonic?"

"How did you know?"

"Whenever I tend bar at a party that's what half the women want."

"I didn't know that."

I waved to the barmaid, and she came over and took our order.

"So, what did you find out?"

She hesitated a moment and then said, "Well, after you left the other day I carefully examined the pottery and checked its authenticity."

"And?"

"The pieces appear to have come from the Moche civilization in Peru. There has been an archeological excavation going on there for twenty years and these pieces resemble many of the artifacts found there."

"Really?"

"So, tell me about the missionary who gave these to you."

"His name was Melvin, I think. I didn't know him very well. He was tall, blond hair and blue eyes—mid-thirties. He seemed intelligent and well-educated. I never expected him to be a deadbeat. He wore conservative clothing and was very outgoing—the typical preacher type."

The barmaid came with our two drinks and placed them in front of us. I smiled and gave her a ten dollar bill. She left and we both took a drink. Then Melanie continued her story.

"Well, he was more than a preacher."

"He was? What do you mean?"

"Did you ever examine the pottery closely?"

"No, I just stuck them up on top of my bookcase as decoration and forgot about them. Why?"

"Well, while I was studying the big ceramic vessel, I noticed a discoloration inside on the bottom. I thought perhaps something had been stored in the bowl which had stained it. But upon running my fingers over it I discovered it was soft and had a different texture than the rest of the bowl."

"Okay. So what does that mean?"

"It meant to me that this substance was placed in the bowl after it had been discovered. . . . So I decided to scrape it off and that's when I realized your missionary was more than a preacher."

"Okay. What did you find?"

"Diamonds."

"Diamonds? . . . You're kidding?"

"I hope you appreciate my honesty. I could have taken them and you wouldn't have known the difference."

"That's true. I'm impressed. Honesty isn't a trait you find in people too often. . . . So tell me more about these diamonds."

"Between all the pieces I found 21 which varied in size from one to three carats. I talked to several dealers and the best offer is $21,100 for the pottery and $315,000 for the diamonds."

My body suddenly became numb. This turn of events

was difficult to fathom. Melanie looked at me expectantly. Somehow I couldn't get excited. Easy money usually meant trouble. I took a deep breath. My mind was racing trying to figure this one out.

"So, Melvin was a diamond smuggler, huh?' I said.

"It appears so."

"Gee. I wonder why he gave me the pottery."

"Maybe he just needed a safe place to stash it."

"True. He knew I wouldn't know what to do with it."

"He probably planned to come back and buy it back from you. You would have been thrilled had he showed up with some cash."

"You got that right. I wonder what went wrong?"

"I don't know," Melanie said. "But it's his loss and your gain."

I looked at her thoughtfully. "Maybe, maybe not. You said you were honest, right?"

"True."

"Well, I've got that same problem. I couldn't do anything with these diamonds until I was sure they didn't belong to someone else."

"You're going to give them back to Melvin?"

"Oh, no. If they really belonged to Melvin I don't have a problem. He gave them to me in payment of a bill so now they belong to me. But if Melvin didn't own them, then I do have a problem."

"So how will you solve that mystery?"

I shrugged. "Your guess is as good as mine."

Melanie leaned forward and said, "Well, my guess is your friend Melvin is long gone and you'll never solve that mystery. So why bother trying? Let's just celebrate our good fortune."

"Our good fortune?"

She smiled, "Yes, my cut is $50,415."

I laughed. "Hmm. I guess you're right. *Our* good fortune."

Melanie waved to the barmaid and she came back over to our table. "Another round of drinks, please," she said. I was already a little light-headed from the two drinks I had already consumed, but there was no stopping Melanie now. She was excited about her good fortune and she wanted to party.

It was eight-thirty when I finally got loose of Melanie. I couldn't go home because I was half drunk, so I went back to the office and made coffee. After I felt a little better I called Rebekah—not to tell her the news for that was too delicate a subject—but to explain my disappearance.

"Where have you been? I've been worried sick."

"I'm still at the office. I've been buried in these real estate contracts. They're going to close tomorrow and I have to make sure there isn't anything too egregious in them."

"You're at the office? I called there at seven but there was no answer."

"I went over to Subway and grabbed a sandwich."

"Hmm. Why didn't you call?"

"I'm sorry, honey. I just got wrapped up in this stuff."

"Well are you planning on coming home?"

"I'm about to leave. I'll see you in a half hour."

"Okay, I miss you."

"Me too. Bye."

*****

The next morning on the way to work I drove into the Dallas Auto Impound and parked in front of the administrative office. I need to take some pictures of Richard Banks' car. I went inside and walked up to the counter. A young man in jeans and a t-shirt came up and said, "What can I do for you?"

"I need to see the Porsche that killed Anant Ravi a few weeks ago. The police said you'd have it."

"What was the name of the driver?"

"Richard Banks."

The clerk looked through a bin full of tickets and finally

pulled one out. "Okay, here it is. You want to pick it up?"

"No, I just need to look at it."

"All right, I'll take you to it. It's in slot R27."

We took a golf cart to the space where the vehicle was stored. As I inspected the vehicle I knew something was wrong. I said, "This isn't a 1982 Porsche. Are you sure this is the right car?"

The man looked a the paperwork he had brought with him and replied, "It's a '72 Porsche just like it's supposed to be."

My stomach began to twist into knots. I couldn't believe what was happening to me. How could the newspaper have made a ten year mistake when they reported on the accident? I shook my head in disbelief.

"But the police report and the newspaper stories said it was a '82 Porsche. How could there be such a discrepancy?"

"Somebody made a mistake on the initial identification of the vehicle and everybody just copied it, I guess. It happens all the time."

I put my hands on my hips, gazed at the beat-up Porsche and said, "Wonderful?"

After getting over my initial shock and disappointment over this new revelation, I told myself the situation might not be all that grim after all. Even if Banks was driving an older car it still was a classic and he probably had it well insured.

CHAPTER THIRTEEN

Poetry

The next morning I went to a Dallas Bar Association breakfast meeting on ethics. It lasted until about eleven. When I returned to my office there was a pile of phone messages waiting for me. I looked at each one, placed the important ones in a pile, and then began returning them. An hour went by before I hung up the phone after making my last call. I turned to the stack of new mail Jodie had placed in my in-box. Feeling tired I sunk back into my chair. I had been at the office early to prepare for a hearing and my eyes were getting heavy. I was about to tackle the mail when I was informed I had a call from Don. I picked up the phone.

"Stan, I'm sorry to bother you, but I got this strange letter from my insurance company."

"What's so strange about it?"

"It says we need to hire an attorney because they're tendering the full face amount of the policy into the registry of the court. They're not going to defend us anymore."

"Oh, shit. They're tendering their limits?"

"So what in the hell does that mean?"

"Well, apparently the insurance company has decided that there is no question that you and Jennifer are liable for what happened. Since the doctor was killed, his damages, in their estimation, are going to exceed the policy limits of $300,000. Since they figure they are going to lose anyway, they decided just to pay the policy limits so they don't have to bear the legal expense of defending you."

"Can they do that?"

"Yes, I'm afraid so. You've got ten days to substitute in a new attorney."

"Can you handle it?"

"Sure, but I must warn you it's liable to get expensive."

"How expensive?"

"Anywhere from $15,000 to $50,000."

"What? I don't have that kind of money. This is ridiculous!"

"You don't have to come up with it all at once. I only need $5,000 right now."

Don was silent. I could hear him breathing heavily.

"Is there any other alternative?"

"Well, the cheapest way out, of course, is bankruptcy."

"Bankruptcy? I can't file bankruptcy. Do you know how humiliating that would be?"

"I know, but you could get out of this thing for about a thousand dollars versus possibly $50,000."

"Bankruptcy is out of the question, there's got to be another way."

"Okay, drop a check in the mail for $5,000 and I'll prepare the papers to substitute in as counsel. You guys haven't actually paid me anything yet, and I'm starting to run up a lot of hours."

"I know. I appreciate you not gouging us. I wish I could send you $10,000, but you know our financial situation."

I felt bad about having to ask for a retainer from a good friend, but I had no choice. I couldn't very well continue to practice law without some cash flow coming in. While I was continuing to feel guilty, Jodie advised me that Rob Blaylock was waiting to go downtown for his docket call. I picked up his file, threw it into my briefcase, and went into the reception room. We shook hands, then left the office, and walked to the elevators.

"So, how have you been?" I asked.

"Oh, okay, I guess."

"You guess?"

"Well, actually I've been kind of depressed."
"Ha. Join the club," I said.
"What?"
"Oh, you know—everyone gets depressed from time to time—even the sharks."

Rob frowned, not comprehending my dismal attempt at humor. A bell rang, and the elevator door opened. We got in. The door creaked as it began to close, then it paused half open and half closed. I pushed the close button, and it jerked a little and finally closed. We waited what seemed like an eternity for the elevator to start to descend.

"This elevator may solve both of our problems," I said.

Rob shrugged but had no clue what I was talking about. Clients don't realize attorneys have problems too. They think all attorneys are rich and have life by the balls. But that's rarely the case. That's why most attorneys are alcoholics. They have thick skins, so no one notices they are being killed slowly from the inside out.

Rob continued. "Yeah, I can't sleep. I can't concentrate at school. It's really becoming a problem."

"Really? So what do you think is causing it—your criminal case?"

I suspected that the source of Rob's sleep problems was the fact that he had discovered Luther's body the night of the murder. I didn't know if Jennifer had told him that she had confessed to me or not. It seemed logical that she would have, but I decided not to bring up that issue in case she hadn't.

"That . . . and Jennifer."
"What about Jennifer?"
"I don't know. She's just hard to figure out sometimes."
"I know. But that's a problem with most women."

We arrived at the bottom floor with a jolt, gratefully got out of the elevator and walked into the parking garage. Once on the road, we continued our conversation.

"I just can't get over the fact that she's pregnant."

"Yeah, you should have seen the look on your face when you found out."

He laughed. "I know. It was definitely the biggest shock of my life."

"And your life will never be the same. That's for sure."

"I know. Everything is just so complicated now."

I shook my head wishing I could say something to console him. Nothing magical came to mind, so I decided just to listen. A friendly ear is always good therapy.

"So, have you and Jennifer talked about any of this?"

"We hadn't been able to until last night. My father grounded me after the arrest. He wouldn't even let me call Jennifer. Finally, last night he let me go see her."

"What happened?"

"I was a little nervous, so I waited a moment to gather my thoughts before I went up to the front door. Before I could knock, the door flew open and Jennifer, as beautiful as always, stood before me smiling. She ran into my arms and we embraced.

"She was so excited. She told me how much she had missed me and how rotten it was for my father to have grounded me. Her mother doesn't believe in grounding—she prefers a whack on the ass."

"I'm with Mrs. Rich," I said. "Quick, immediate punishment is the best. Dragging it out over hours or days just causes too much anxiety and bitterness. It just exacerbates the problem. My gym teacher in high school used a ping pong paddle—very effective. Nobody messed with Coach Brewer."

Rob nodded. "Anyway, then she noticed my car had been fixed. She told me what a great job the body shop had done on it. She felt terrible about wrecking it. I told her it wasn't her fault. There was little she could have done after the Chrysler pulled out in front of her.

He continued. "Then we got in the car and drove to

Town East Mall to get coffee. We relaxed at a table overlooking a tropical waterfall. I wanted to talk about the baby. We had to make some decisions. Some difficult decisions.

"I hadn't been able to sleep much thinking about the baby. I didn't want Jennifer to have an abortion even though that would have been the easy way out. I wanted to know how she got pregnant. She had told me she was on the pill. So I pressed her on that issue and she admitted she had lied to me.

"She said she hadn't used birth control. Apparently her mother wouldn't let her take the pill. She said it would lead to promiscuity.

"I couldn't believe I had misjudged her so. She had always struck me as being so smart and in control. I couldn't believe she had let herself get pregnant. I would have used a condom if I had known she couldn't take the pill.

"She said she didn't plan to have sex with me. I laughed at that. She said she just wasn't ready to go home and couldn't think of anything else to make me stay. This totally blew my mind. I couldn't imagine someone being so irresponsible, but then I realized I had been the same way.

"I was such an idiot," Rob blurted out.

"Don't beat yourself up," I said. "We all make mistakes. Your mistake was not having some protection with you when you went out on the date. A beautiful woman can unleash a powerful spell over a man that few can resist. Believe me, I know."

Rob grinned and looked at me expectantly.

I continued. "I could tell you a few personal stories, but now isn't the time. Suffice it to say, this won't be your last encounter with a determined woman."

"What do you mean determined?"

"If a woman really wants something from a man she usually will get it. It's a fact of nature. . . . Remember, you told me that Jennifer wouldn't give you the time of day, and then suddenly overnight she became your lover."

"Right."

"Did it occur to you that she was using you—that maybe she was already pregnant when she invited you to her bed?"

"What?"

"I may be wrong, but I think you were chosen to be the father of her child."

Rob just stared at me in disbelief.

I continued, "What I'm saying is you may want to have some testing done before you accept responsibility for this child."

Rob swallowed hard. "You think so?"

I shrugged. "That would be my legal advice, but I sense that maybe you want to be the child's father?"

He nodded. "I was getting used to the idea."

"So you love Jennifer?"

He smiled. "Yes, and she says she loves me."

"Do you believe her?"

"I don't know. I want to."

"Are you going to get married?"

"Yes, that's our plan, but my parents will be against it. Dad wants me to become a major league baseball player and Mom wants me to go to college. Marriage and a baby will probably kill any chance of either one of those ever happening."

"Not necessarily. I went through law school with a wife and four kids. If you really want to be a baseball player, having a wife and a child shouldn't stop you."

Rob raised his eyebrows. "Was it hard going through law school with a family?"

"It wasn't easy, but I guarantee it gives you a lot of motivation when you have mouths to feed. . . . And it actually helps you focus, because you understand how important it is to be successful. If I were you I'd go to college and play baseball there for now. If you are good enough the scouts will notice you and you'll get drafted. Then you'll probably get a signing bonus and that will help you make it financially. Jennifer can go to college too. I remember at UCLA there were a lot of women bringing babies to class. It was no big deal."

"Jennifer's mom said we could live with her until we graduate from high school."

"Oh, good. So you've got everything worked out."

"Except for breaking the news to my parents."

"Ummm. I wish I could help you out there, but it would probably be best if you and Jennifer told them in person."

"I can't wait," Rob muttered.

"I think they will be pleased actually. . . . They may not show it at first, but I think they will be happy that you two came to such a responsible decision."

We arrived at the courthouse and went inside. The courtroom was empty so we sat down in the gallery to wait.

As we were talking, the Assistant DA, Paula Waters, walked into the courtroom. A blond with deep blue eyes and the whitest teeth I'd ever seen, she was definitely a looker. She wore a smart grey suit with a white ruffled blouse. Paula had been a casual friend during law school but at the time I was working full time so I didn't have much time to get to know my classmates. She and I would talk before and after class, study together occasionally, and even have lunch once in a while, but that was the extent of our relationship. She motioned for me to come into the jury room where she had set up a temporary office. I told Rob to wait and I followed her in and sat down. We exchanged greetings.

"I haven't seen you around here before," she said.

"No, I don't do that much criminal law."

"Just a murder case here and there?" she noted nonchalantly.

I looked at her and laughed. "You heard about that?"

She rolled her eyes. "You know, I was really pissed you got that trial."

"Why?"

"You didn't even take *clinic*."

She was referring to criminal law clinic at SMU. It was a great place to get courtroom experience while attending law school. Working full time, I hadn't had the time to take the class and had regretted it.

I laughed. "You know, I was so over my head in that trial, I don't know how I ever got through it."

"I thought it was so unfair for Judge Brooks to make you serve jail time."

The judge gave me thirty days for ignoring his ruling not to put my client under hypnosis while she was testifying. I had done it anyway as it was my only chance at proving her innocent. It had worked, but the judge didn't care about that.

I shrugged. "He had to do it, I guess. . . . It wasn't so bad."

She smiled again and gazed into my eyes. I felt a little uncomfortable and looked away. Then she took a deep breath and opened Rob's file.

"So, what are we going to do with Mr. Blaylock?"

"It's his first offense. His girlfriend begged him to take her out. He wanted to stay home and watch a Ranger game but she was a Yankee fan and wasn't interested."

"Right, it's always someone else's fault," she noted.

"No, that's not it. I'm just trying to say Rob is a good kid. He's got a chance at making it into the major league. He never gets in trouble. He's a good student and actually does respect authority—which is rare these days."

"He just doesn't obey laws. What if he had killed somebody?"

I sighed. "Believe me. He realizes what he did was stupid. Haven't you ever done something stupid to impress a guy?"

She cracked a smile and said, "Not more than once or twice a week."

"Exactly. We all have. It's human nature."

"Okay, if he pleads guilty I'll recommend probation."

I frowned. "How about deferred adjudication? He's never even had a traffic ticket for godsakes."

She took a deep breath. "There's going to have to be some community service. I want him to have a lot of time to think about what might have happened had the policeman not stopped him before he got out on the road."

"I agree. Absolutely. Community service would be good for him."

"Okay, then. We'll announce our agreement to the court, do the paperwork and present it to the court next week."

"Great, thanks."

We shook hands. She didn't let go, but pulled me up close and we embraced. She sighed. "It's been too long, Stan. Let's get together soon, okay?"

"Okay," I said enjoying her friendly embrace.

She finally let go and I turned to leave. Rob was at the door with a smile on his face. I walked over to him.

"I like your negotiation technique," he said.

"Yeah, it was your lucky day. Paula's an old friend."

"Not a determined one, I hope."

I smiled and then related to him what had transpired. I informed him of the DA's offer and recommended he take it. He agreed. When the judge called our case we announced it to the judge and that was that. Rob had been lucky this time, but this was only the first of many battles to come. We left the courtroom and drove back to my office. As I was cleaning out my briefcase I found a small linen envelope with "Stan" typed on the front. Inside there was a small piece of matching notepaper with what appeared to be the beginning of a poem. The envelope had a faint scent of perfume. *Where did this come from?* I opened it and read the contents.

Alone
The clock is my worst enemy

> It ticks with chilling regularity
> You should be next to me, annexed to me
> I long for your touch, the warmth of your body
> But I'm alone. Always, always alone

I stared at it in amazement—turning it over and over trying to fathom its significance. *Where did this come from? Rebekah? It looked kind of like the stationery she used... Rebekah is writing me poetry? Boy, I must really be neglecting her.* "Oh, my God." Tears began to well in my eyes. What was I going to do? Everybody was dumping their problems on me—I could scarcely breathe—and now I had a crisis at home. *Damn it!* I closed my briefcase and headed for the parking garage. On the way home I stopped at a florist shop and bought a dozen roses. *What ever possessed me to become an attorney? There's got to be a easier way to make a living. Poor Rebekah. I bet she regrets marrying me. Her life has been so difficult. I've let her down so many times.*

When I got home Rebekah was in the den reading a magazine. I walked in holding the flowers behind my back. When she saw me, she looked at her watch.

"Wow. You're home and I haven't even started supper yet."

"Good. We're going out. Just you and me. Your mom can watch the kids."

I showed her the flowers and she smiled. "What's the occasion? It's not my birthday and our anniversary is months away."

"The occasion is that... well... I've been neglecting you lately and I wanted to say, I'm sorry. I'm so, so sorry. I love you."

She sprang up and we embraced. "Gee, I don't know what brought this on, but I like it."

"Good. Because it's going to happen a lot more. I promise."

She began to cry. "Oh, Stan. I worry so much about

you. I don't know what I would do without you."

"You don't need to worry. I'll always be here."

That night we dined at Old San Francisco, Rebekah's favorite restaurant. She wore a pretty black party dress and the pearls that I had given her as a wedding present. She was as beautiful as the day I married her. She asked how the Luther Bell investigation was going.

"Well, I'm starting to get a picture of Mr. Bell. He was friendly and likeable—a good salesman. He had great potential but for some reason could never quite get it together. Eventually, he became frustrated and angry and decided he would do whatever it took to get what he wanted. Unfortunately, that's when the Blaylocks got in the picture."

"Mmm, poor Pam and Don," Rebekah moaned. "So do you think one of them killed him?"

"I don't know yet. There are a lot of possibilities—of course Pam, Don, and Jim are at the top of the list. Then there are his girlfriends, his ex-wife, and Rob."

"Rob? But he's only 16 years old."

I hadn't told Rebekah about Jennifer's confession yet, so I filled her in.

"Oh, my God. What does Rob have to say about what happened?"

"I don't know. I haven't discussed it with him yet. I guess I should have but the timing never seemed right."

"You better talk to him about it."

"I know. There is just so much to do and I don't have a lot of time since I have a few other clients, you know."

"I know," Rebekah replied. "Can't you hire a private investigator?"

"I could, but I like to question everyone myself. You can't really read a person from a report and usually one question will lead to another. So a stock set of questions won't work. Plus I learn a lot just listening to people."

She nodded. "So you can't afford one?"

"That too," I admitted, "and my clients can't afford to pay me much less a private investigator."

"When do you think the police will charge someone?"

"I don't know. It's early yet. Only time will tell."

The next day there was a message from Melanie on my desk when I got back from lunch a little after two. I picked up the telephone and dialed the number. It must have been her direct line because she picked up immediately. After a little small talk she got to the point.

"So what are you going to do?" she asked.

"I don't know yet. I've been so wrapped up in this murder investigation, I haven't had time to think about it."

"I don't want to rush you, but I'm worried about these diamonds lying around. I don't want someone to steal them."

"Okay, why don't I come get them and put them in my safety deposit box so they will be safe?"

"Good idea."

"It's almost two-thirty. The bank closes at four. If I tried to get down to Fair Park and back right now I might not make it. Why don't you get the diamonds and meet me at Valley View Bank. You ought to be able to get there by three-thirty."

"All right. I'll see you at three-thirty."

The more I thought about the diamonds, the more I knew I really had to do some serious investigation before I dared sell them. If they were hot and I was caught selling them, it would be assumed I was in cahoots with Melvin, whoever he really was.

I decided to hire International Tracing Services to find Melvin. They would do it on a contingent fee basis. If they found him it would cost me a couple hundred bucks, if not, it wouldn't cost me a dime. After Jodie found the file I called them and got the ball rolling. Melvin's last name turned out to be Schwartz.

At three-thirty I pulled up in front of Valley View Bank. Melanie was already inside waiting. She looked stunning in her charcoal suede pants with long matching coat and blue blouse. I complimented her on her outfit.

We went downstairs to the safety deposit vault and signed in. A clerk took us to the box and opened it for us. I pulled it out and took it to a private booth. Melanie pulled a small velvet bag from her coat pocket. She removed the rubber band and then poured the diamonds into her hand. Seeing them took my breath away. It was hard to belief she could be holding $315,000 in one hand.

After counting them, she put them back in the bag and then asked, "Where did that rubber band go?"

We looked around but couldn't find it. I said, "Wait a minute and I'll go get one from the receptionist."

When I got back she secured the bag with the rubber band, dropped it into the box and closed it. She waited in the booth while I put the box back in its slot and secured the lock. After leaving the bank we went over to Valley View Mall to walk and talk about our predicament.

"I've got a search going on for Melvin Schwartz," I said.

"Good. How long will it take to find him?"

"Not too long."

"What will you do if you *do* find him?" Melanie asked.

"I don't think I will."

"Why not?"

"Because he should have already been back to pick up the pottery. The fact that he hasn't means he can't come back or he doesn't know the diamonds were hidden there. . . . So, if I do find him, I'll tell him I was getting ready to sell the pottery and wanted to give him an opportunity to buy it first. I would almost bet he'll have no interest in buying it back."

"But how could he not know about the diamonds?" Melanie asked.

"I don't know."

"Will you call me if you find him?"

I stopped and turned to Melanie. "You know I will. If

you didn't trust me you wouldn't have told me about the diamonds. In fact, I'm still a bit mystified as to why you did tell me. I know what you said about being honest, but I'm not totally buying that."

She took a deep breath. "Okay, you want to know the truth?"

"Yes, that would be nice."

"I was afraid to sell them myself. If it turned out they were hot and someone came after me, the police or a pissed-off gangster, I wouldn't have a chance. If I were just a broker though, nobody would blame me for doing my job. They'd come looking for the seller."

"Oh, good. Lay all the heat on me."

She smiled. "You're a smart attorney. I figured if anybody could figure out a way to keep the diamonds, you could do it."

"I don't know. This may be out of both of our leagues."

She took my hand in hers, pulled me close and looked me in the eyes. "Come on, Stan. You can pull this off. I know you can."

Her touch was exhilarating. We were so close now I could smell the sweet scent of her body. I could scarcely breathe as she squeezed my hand and smiled, confident that I would do her bidding. I broke away.

"Okay, I'll do my best. I've got to get back to the office. I'll call you if I hear anything."

She nodded and we went our separate ways.

****

At five o'clock I was back at my desk and still hadn't tackled the day's mail. Reluctantly I began going through it. I tossed out a couple pieces of junk mail and then came upon a letter from the Dallas Police Department. I ripped it open and began studying it. It was the police report on Anant Ravi's death. I read it.

"Shit . . . Damn it!" I said and threw the report on my desk. Jodie, hearing me swear, got up and came in to see what was the matter.

"What's wrong, Stan?"

"I just got the police report on the Ravi auto accident and it says Richard Banks didn't have any insurance!"

"Oh my God, you're kidding?!"

"I wish I were . . . damn it! I can't believe he didn't have any insurance! Jesus."

I got up, went over to the window and stared at the flood of office workers fleeing the building as the day came to a close. If the glass hadn't been there I might have jumped.

"Now what?" Jodie asked.

"I don't know. I can't believe this shit."

"Maybe it's just a mistake?"

"God, I hope so but somehow I doubt it."

"What happens if he didn't have insurance?"

"We've got to hope he owns some assets or was on the job when the accident happened."

"If he was on the job, we can go after his employer?"

"Right."

"But, what if he wasn't on the job, and he doesn't have any property?"

"Then the best we can do is get his driver's license revoked."

"Huh? You mean he would get off scot free?"

"Yeah. That's about the size of it."

Depression quickly consumed me. As usual nothing ever went right when it came to money. It seemed I was destined to struggle for every dime and every dollar. Fortunately, I didn't have time to dwell too much on the accident report. I had more pressing concerns, namely finding Luther Bell's killer.

To find him or her, I was going to have to really get to know the people around Luther. I decided to start with his girlfriend, Margie. She was the closest person to Luther and would know everyone else in his life. If there was anyone out there who hated him enough to kill him, she would likely know who it was. I called her to see if she would talk to me. She didn't make a definite commitment but agreed to talk about it the next morning at ten. When I got to the condo, Luther's Cadillac was parked out front. After knocking on the door, I waited.

Margie opened the door and I introduced myself. She folded her arms beneath her breasts and looked at me warily. She was pretty with her long brown hair falling lazily across one shoulder. Her brown eyes were narrow and her nose a little too broad but only a slight blemish to her overall beauty. She wore a dusty lilac top with a cardigan to match and khaki pants.

"Why should I talk to you?" Margie asked. "One of your clients is a murderer."

"Maybe, maybe not. I'm just trying to sort this thing out. I could use your help."

She looked at me thoughtfully for a moment and then stepped back and opened the door. I walked in and looked around. The condo was nicely decorated–white leather sofa and love seat, glass coffee and end tables, crystal lamps–very nice.

"Have a seat," Margie said. "Would you like some coffee?"

"If you have some made. Don't make a pot just for me."

"I just made some. Be right back."

She left, giving me a chance to scope the place out a bit. Luther obviously liked to live well. The condo couldn't have been cheap. I guessed it must have cost two hundred grand—another twenty-five to decorate it. A promoter-type, though, could get a place like this for five percent down easy—less than twenty thousand in hard dollars. But that's the way it worked with them. You think they are rich the way they live, but a balance sheet always gives them away—lots of assets, tons of liabilities and no cash. Margie came back with two coffees.

"Thank you," I said taking one of them from her.

"You're welcome," Margie said as she sat next to me on the sofa and placed her coffee next to mine. She looked up and smiled. "So, how can I help you?"

"First of all, I'd like to say I'm very sorry for your loss. I understand you and Luther were to be married."

She lowered her head and took a deep breath. "Thank you. It's been very hard. I loved him very much."

I nodded. "If it isn't too painful, I'd like to go back to the first time this Golden Dragon partnership came up. I'm trying to understand what was going on. You're probably the only person who can tell me the story from Luther's perspective. There are always two sides to a story and it's important I know Luther's side."

Margie thought a moment, biting her fingernail nervously, then she took a deep breath and began telling me how they met.

CHAPTER FOURTEEN

Margie's Recollections

Had Luther not been distracted by the Golden Dragon franchise and been in trouble at work, we probably wouldn't have met. Luther was worried and depressed. Usually when he got depressed he went to the Rendezvous Club or a strip club called the Sunset Strip. He hated to be alone so he was always looking for companionship. I was at the Rendezvous Club after work one evening for the same reason.

I was at a table drinking a margarita when Luther walked in and took a seat at the bar. He ordered a beer and then started looking around, studying every female in the place one by one. When he looked my way, our eyes met. We studied each other for a moment and then he got up, grabbed his drink and came over to my table. I smiled at him, and that was enough to break the ice. He sat down and we started talking.

"Just get off from work?" Luther asked.

"Uh huh," I said.

"So did I. I'm an insurance salesman—well, we like to call ourselves *financial planners*, you know, it sounds better, more impressive. What do you do?"

"I work at Gateway National Bank. I'm a teller."

"Ah, it must be fun to be around money all the time," he said.

"It was at first, but now it's just dirty paper."

"Oh really? Well you can pass some dirty paper my way anytime, honey!" Luther laughed.

"What I mean is, it's the bank's money and they don't give it away, so it's no big deal being around it."

"Right. . . . Hey, I'm Luther Bell. What's your name?"

"Margie Mason."

"Nice to meet you Miss Mason. Yeah, I reckon they don't pay bank tellers too well."

"You got that right."

"I haven't made a lot of money selling insurance either but, you know, I am on the verge of making some serious money."

"You are?"

"Yeah, franchising is the way to make it big nowadays. You know if you buy a franchise you're buying a business that is tried and true. The people who sell it to you already have figured out what to do and what not to do. You just slide into the business, follow their instructions and then start counting your money."

"What kind of business?"

"It doesn't matter. Whatever it is, it's been test marketed and all you have to do is find a suitable place to set it up. Most franchisors will even help you find a good location."

"So, are you going to buy a franchise?"

"Maybe, I need some investors though, some silent partners who won't get in the way but have lots of cash and need tax write-offs."

"I see. Do you have any candidates in mind?"

"Not yet, but that's my next project once I get my boss off my back."

"What's his problem?"

"He's under a lot of pressure from his nagging wife and he's taking it out on me."

"Wonderful."

"You know I sold a big million-dollar policy to a guy in the oil business. This guy is loaded. The last time I was there he had a tailor in his office fitting him for custom suits. You know, his office looks like it could be in the White House, right? So I write him a big twenty-pay life, a twelve thousand dollar annual premium, the biggest policy I've written all year. This puts me way over my quota for the year so I figure I can relax now and work on this franchise idea."

"So . . . what happened?"

"The jerk lets his policy lapse and now I'm twenty-five days from being on straight commission."

"Is that bad?"

"Yeah, it's really bad."

"I'm sorry."

"Can I buy you another drink?"

"Sure, a margarita please."

"You're a mighty fine-looking lady. You're not married are you?"

"Divorced."

"Ain't that a coincidence, so am I . . . or I guess I should say, almost divorced. We have a few issues yet to resolve."

"Are you happy about the divorce?"

Luther gave the question some thought and then replied, "Well, yeah. I reckon. It just didn't work out. It's for the best, I guess."

"You still love her, huh?"

"It's hard to stop loving someone just because they quit loving you."

"I know. . . . My husband took off with another woman after I put him through dental school. I could have killed the little bastard."

"What! You've got to be kidding. He must have been some kind of idiot to dump a beautiful thing like you."

Margie smiled and replied, "Oh, thank you. She was a slut who became a dental hygienist just so she could get her grubby little hands on a rich dentist."

"Well, he obviously didn't deserve you."

"You're very kind, but you don't really know me well enough to make a judgment like that."

"I feel like I've known you for years."

Margie smiled and replied, "Do you? I kind of feel that way too. Isn't it funny how you can sit down with a perfect stranger and suddenly feel so at ease."

"You hungry? I know a good Italian place up the street. Why don't you let me buy you dinner . . . then, you know . . . we'll play it by ear after that."

"Well, I don't know. I was supposed to meet my girlfriend for dinner."

"She'll understand. Go call her and tell her something's come up. I really want to talk with you some more. We have a lot in common."

"Okay, I'll be back in a minute."

I got up and went to the restroom where several phones were located. Luther finished off his drink and prepared to leave. After dinner he took me back to his condo just off Northwest Highway near North Park. It was an old apartment complex that had been recently converted to condominiums. I found out later Luther had picked it up for a song at a foreclosure sale. Of course, he would have never told me that then. He always liked to impress people—particularly women.

"This is really nice. It must have cost you a fortune to decorate," I said.

"Yeah, it wasn't cheap. . . . Have a seat."

I sat down and Luther sat next to me. He had succeeded. I *was* impressed with his not-so-humble abode.

"It doesn't appear you do that badly selling insurance?" I remarked.

"Oh, I do okay, but I don't really like doing it. Most people don't want to think about dying, and whenever you bring up life insurance they feel uneasy and don't want to talk about it. It's much easier to sell something concrete and positive like real estate or stocks, you know what I mean?"

"Sure, so what kind of franchise do you think you'll get into first?"

"Oh, I'm looking at a restaurant deal right now in Greenville."

"A restaurant? Aren't they pretty risky?"

"Not if you get a proven franchise, like the *Golden Dragon.*"

"*Golden Dragon?* I've never heard of that."

"It's really big out in California. I've talked to the Texas sales representative and he says they're going to open up twenty-seven locations in Texas this year. All I need is about a hundred and fifty-thousand dollars. A hundred thousand for fixtures and equipment, twenty-five for finish-out and twenty-five for inventory."

"I'm sure you won't have any trouble lining up the money, if that's what you really want to do, but why Greenville? Why not Dallas?"

"Someone already has the Dallas franchises, so Greenville is the closest I could get."

"Well, I wish you the best of luck."

"Thank you. Can I get you a drink?"

"Some wine, maybe."

Luther stepped into the dining room and pulled a bottle of Chablis out the wine rack. Then he found an ice bucket under the sink, set the bottle of wine inside and then packed ice around it.

"It will just be a few minutes. How about some music? What do you like?"

"Something soft and relaxing."

"A little jazz maybe?"

"Sure."

Luther turned on his stereo and then walked over to the sofa and sat down next to me. For just a moment he didn't say a word but only gazed into my eyes. Then he blinked and said, "I'm sure glad I met you. I hate to be alone. Will you stay the night?"

I stiffened, shocked a little by his abrupt manner. He was amused by my reaction.

"Well, I don't know. My roommate will wonder what happened to me."

"You can call her and tell her you're okay and not to worry. I've got a phone."

Luther put his arm around me and drew my lips to his. I resisted a little, for show, but I wanted him too. I wrapped my hands around his neck and kissed him passionately. After a minute though, I felt a pang of remorse and pushed him away. I said, "Let's not do anything we'll regret."

"There's nothing we could do *I'd* regret," Luther replied.

"Let's just take it a little slower, okay?"

"Fine, I'm sorry . . . but I just feel so comfortable around you it just seemed natural to—"

"I know, but that's just infatuation. It would be easy for me to jump in bed with you too, but then tomorrow I'd feel like a tramp."

"I'd never consider you a tramp. It's obvious to me you are an intelligent, sophisticated woman. I bet you haven't made love to anyone since your divorce, have you?"

"Well. . . . I did once."

"Who was it?" Luther asked seemingly very interested. I hesitated, wondering if I should be sharing secrets with this man.

"Come on. Tell me," he persisted.

"Well . . . it was my trainer at the health club. I had let myself go a little while I was married so I joined President's. Roy was my trainer—what a hunk! We dated a few times and I thought I had fallen in love with him. One night he brought me home to his place and things got out of control. The next morning I realized he and I could never be permanent. Sure enough I was right. He had the club assign me a new trainer and would barely look at me when our paths crossed. I'd like to go back to his apartment and see if there's a notch in his bed for our night together."

Luther laughed and said, "You can inspect my bed anytime. There aren't any notches, I promise. I'm looking for a long-term relationship, someone to share my life with and I think tonight I've found her."

I looked Luther in the eye and smiled at him wondering if I could believe him. He inched over toward me and finally pressed his lips to mine one more time. I felt the warmth of his breath and the caress of his soft lips. Luther slipped his arm around my waist and pulled my body next to his. I knew I should resist him but my body wouldn't obey. Our love making went on for over an hour until Luther collapsed in complete exhaustion. Feeling a little uncomfortable, I put my blouse back on without a bra and sat silently on the sofa. Luther went into the bedroom and got a robe.

"How about that wine now?" Luther said. "It should be cold."

I forced a smiled and replied, "Yes, that would be good."

Luther went into the kitchen, poured two glasses and returned.

"God, you were fantastic," Luther said. "I hope you enjoyed that as much as I did."

"It was good. . . . It's been a long time for me. I'd forgotten how good it can be."

"Well, I won't ever let that happen again," Luther laughed.

After we had killed the bottle of wine we went to bed. The next morning I got up before Luther, left the condo, and went home. The next night we were to meet again at the Rendezvous Club at five thirty. I was late. When I walked in he got up immediately and went over to me. He was visibly upset.

"Margie, what happened? I was worried sick about you."

"I'm sorry, I was out of balance and I couldn't leave until I figured out why I had $292 more than I was supposed to have."

"Huh, well, I'm glad you're here. What do you want to drink?"

"A margarita, please."

"Bartender! We need a margarita over here," Luther yelled. "So, other than being out of balance how was your day?"

"Fine, we were busy today. It was payday and everyone was in either cashing or depositing their payroll checks."

"I had a hectic day myself."

"Really, what did you do?"

"The franchise papers came in from California. I had to go over them with a fine-tooth comb and work up some financial projections."

"How did they look?"

"Not very good until I made a few adjustments."

"What kind of adjustments?"

"Well, since I'm going to manage the restaurants I made sure I will be well compensated for my trouble."

"Can you do that?"

"Sure, it's my deal, isn't it? I'm the one who has busted my ass to put it together."

"How many investors do you have?"

"Two or three. . . . Maybe more."

"That's good. When will you start?"

"Just as quick as I can put everything together. I went and picked out a couple potential locations today, one downtown and another near the freeway. Tomorrow I've got to go see my banker to see what kind of financing we can get."

"It sounds so exciting. Are there any Golden Dragon restaurants opened yet in Dallas? I'd like to go see one."

"The closest one is in San Antonio. It opened last month and is doing quite well."

"How do you know it's doing well?"

"Ah. Well. I heard it from someone at the Golden

Dragon home office."

"Hmm. What about the Dallas franchises? When will they start up?"

"I don't know, pretty soon I would imagine."

"What does your lawyer think?"

"What lawyer? I never use a lawyer. I wouldn't trust one of those sleazy bastards. That's why I took business law at Penn State so I wouldn't have to depend on a lawyer. There's really nothing to a franchise, that's the beauty of it. Anyone who can read and follow instructions will do just fine. Besides most lawyers are deal-killers. They'd just scare away the investors with a lot of negative talk."

I didn't necessarily agree with Luther on that point, but I didn't feel like arguing—particularly an argument I couldn't win.

"I suppose you're right."

"Believe me, I know what I'm talking about. I've been through it with lawyers before. You wouldn't believe how many of my insurance deals lawyers have shot down."

"Really? I wonder why?"

"They are control freaks. Unless something is their idea it's no good, you know what I mean?"

"Uh huh. So what do you want to do tonight?" she asked.

"Why don't we go back to my place and watch some TV?" Luther replied.

"I was thinking about last night. Maybe we started off a little too fast. Why don't we go to a movie?"

"A movie?"

"Yeah, my roommate saw *My Bodyguard* and said it was hysterical."

Luther was obviously disappointed, but he didn't argue too much. After the movie he wanted to take me back to his condo but I made him take me home. As soon as I had driven away, however, I regretted it. We didn't see each other the next day. I called him to apologize but just got his answering machine. The following morning I decided to pay him a surprise visit. I was in an amorous mood and was planning to give him some morning delight. I rang the doorbell. After a minute, he answered.

"Margie. Ah. . . . Hi. How are you?"

"I'm fine. I thought I'd come over and maybe we could talk."

"Ah. . . . Well. . . . It's not a real good time."

I knew something was wrong from the tone of his voice. Men are rarely good liars. "What's that I smell, fresh coffee? I could sure use a cup," I said, and then stepped inside.

"Uh. . . . Margie can we take a rain check on this. I'll call you later and we can plan to do something together."

Anger welled inside me. "Do you have someone in there?"

"No, I'm just tired. I got drunk last night and I've got a terrible hangover."

"Yeah, right," I said as I pushed my way past Luther and headed for the kitchen. I stopped dead in my tracks when I saw a woman standing there, naked from the waist up, holding a spatula. She put her hand up to her mouth and said, "Oh my God!" I shook my head in disgust, turned and made a hasty retreat glaring at Luther as I left the condo. He followed me out the door.

"Margie, let me explain!" Luther pleaded.

"Explain what?! Obviously our relationship isn't worth shit!"

"It's not like that," Luther shouted as I jumped into my car and slammed the door.

It was several weeks before I saw Luther again. He called one afternoon and pleaded with me to meet him to talk things out. I resisted at first, but finally gave in. He said to meet him at the bar at Anthony's, a restaurant in North Dallas. The partners were having a party to celebrate their new venture and he wanted me to meet him after it was over, around nine. I was still mad and had no intention of making up that night, so I was less than excited when he walked in at ten after nine.

"Hi, Margie," he said like nothing had happened.

I glanced over at him but said nothing.

"I'm so glad you came. I was worried I wouldn't ever be able to explain what happened the other day. I know what it must have looked like, but it really wasn't."

"Luther Bell, you are so full of shit!" I said. "If you're going to expect me to believe that the naked girl in your room was your sister, forget it."

"No, she wasn't my sister. She was a dancer."

"A dancer? A topless dancer?"

"Right."

"Oh, Jesus, I'm out of here," I said as I grabbed my purse and prepared to leave.

"Wait! I didn't invite her to my place, she drove me home because I was too drunk to drive. When I woke up I was shocked to see her, believe me."

I shook my head. "I'd like to believe you, but somehow I can't imagine her coming to your place without an invitation."

"It was the night I quit."

"You quit?"

"Yes, and I was so depressed I stopped at the Sunset Strip to try to forget what had happened. I drank a little too much and when I went to drive home—well it was obvious to her that I shouldn't be driving. She may have saved my life. At the very least she kept me from going to jail for DWI. I couldn't very well be—you know—abrupt with her."

I laughed and said, "Luther, you are one hell of a bullshit artist. It must have been so painful for you to look at her naked breasts while she cooked breakfast for you."

"Okay, laugh at me, but it's the truth. I didn't invite her home. The only person I'm interested in right now is you. That's why I wanted to try to explain what happened. Give me another chance, I've really missed you."

"Have you really?"

"Yes, I really enjoyed the time we spent together and I want to spend more time with you, a lot of time."

I looked deep into Luther's eyes. He gave me a hopeful smile. "I don't know. I'm just not sure I can trust you."

He took my hand and gave me a wounded-puppy-dog look. "You can, I promise I won't even look at another woman as long as we are seeing each other."

"Are you sure that's a promise you can keep?"

"Yes," he said as he pulled me close to him.

I sighed. "Okay, I'll give you another chance, but this isn't a baseball game. You don't get three strikes. Two strikes and you're out."

"Fine," Luther said as he wrapped his arms around me and gave me a passionate kiss.

The other patrons at the bar watched us with interest as we made out in front of them. Finally the bartender came over and suggested we might want to take our passion elsewhere. Luther paid the tab, and we left Anthony's and headed to Luther's condo. On the way home I asked Luther about the big party.

"So what was the occasion tonight? It looked like that was some shindig you were having."

"Do you remember that franchise deal I told you about?"

"Sure."

"Well, it finally came to pass. We closed the deal today."

"Oh, that's wonderful. So how long will it take you to get your restaurant opened?"

"Hopefully just a couple of months. It's going to be really important to get it finished out quickly, so we can get the cash flow started. We're kind of thinly capitalized."

"Really?"

"Yeah, we only have $50,000 available and I've already

spent nearly thirty thousand. Next week I've got to pay the first and last months on our lease which will be about $7,500. That only leaves me $15,000 for inventory, supplies, advertising, and operating capital."

"What happens if you run out of money?"

Luther thought a moment. "Well, if I run out of money, then I'll have to make a cash call."

"A cash call? What's that?"

"That's a request to all of the partners for additional capital contributions. Once I make the call they have to come up with the cash or they can forfeit their interests."

"Do they know that?"

"It's right there in black and white in the partnership agreement. Jim asked about it, so I know they are aware that it's there."

"Hmm. I don't think I would invest in your deal."

Luther laughed. "Thanks a lot. I'm not planning to make any cash calls. If we can just get the place opened with the cash we have, then the cash flow should take care of itself."

I gave Luther a skeptical look. "I hope you're right."

"I know I'm right. I've done all the projections. Everything is going to be fine."

"But you said you altered the projections."

Luther took a deep breath. "Yeah, but even so there should still should be a good profit."

"What if you should have to make a cash call? Will they be okay with it?"

"No, they will be pissed as hell, but they will just have to cough up the dough. They won't have a choice in the matter. Life's a bitch."

I liked Luther, but I felt sorry for the Golden Dragon Partners. He was obviously taking advantage of them, but what could I do about it? It wasn't any of my business, so I decided to stay out of it. Unfortunately, that didn't turn out to be a good strategy. Luther ran out of money right away and had to make several cash calls. The partners got angrier and angrier until finally one night at a partner's meeting they fired him. That really knocked the wind out of him. I had never seen him so mad.

"What's wrong?" I asked. "You look like someone who just got mugged."

"That's what I feel like. You ready? Let's get out of here."

"Sure, let's go."

We left and headed for the Rendezvous Club. Luther said he needed a few drinks before dinner. We went inside and found a table off in a corner. The barmaid brought me a margarita and a scotch and water for Luther.

"Okay, when are you going to tell me what you're so steamed about?" I asked.

Luther looked at me and said, "Those bastards fired me. Can you believe that?"

"Fired you? Why?"

"They're blaming the embezzlement on me."

"Can they do that? I mean, fire you."

"No! I've got a contract. They'd have to prove I participated in the embezzlement or was negligent in letting it happen."

"Can they prove that?"

"Of course not! How was I to know that Carl would embezzle from us? If anybody was grossly negligent, it was Abe Dumas."

"Who's he?"

"Our peg-legged accountant."

"Excuse me?"

"Yeah, he lost a leg in a car wreck. He wears a patch over his eye and looks kind of like a pirate."

"And he was your accountant?" I said, trying not to laugh.

"Yeah, I met him in a bar near the restaurant. He was handy. He should have seen the duplicate payments and questioned all those voided receipts."

"So what are you going to do?"

"I'm going to make them wish they were never born. If they think they have trouble now, just wait until I tear them a new asshole."

"Why do you hate them so much?"

"Because they think they know so much about business, but they don't know shit. They're going to let Don's little bitch, Pam, run the restaurant. She's in for a rude awakening. I just wish I were there to see her fall flat on her face."

"Why do you think she'll fall flat on her face?"

"Because she knows nothing about running a business, let alone a restaurant."

"You didn't know anything about running a restaurant when you started."

"That's different, I went to franchise school and I've been operating my insurance business for years."

"Why don't you just leave them alone? They've already lost a lot of money."

Luther glared at me and said, "Whose side are you on anyway?"

"I'm on your side, I just don't want any trouble. We don't need any trouble."

"Oh baby. There's going to be lots of trouble, but it won't be *our* trouble. They can't touch me. This is Texas, we live in debtor's heaven, did you know that, honey?"

"No, I didn't."

"Yep, only the rich and the insured are accountable. The rest of us citizens can do whatever we please, because we've got nothing to lose."

"That doesn't seem right."

"Yeah, Abe told me that Texas was first settled by a bunch of deadbeats who had been thrown out of Tennessee and Kentucky. When Texas became a republic they made sure the laws protected their kind."

"That's not true, is it?" Margie asked.

"I don't know, Abe's pretty knowledgeable."

"I don't think I would believe anything a one-legged pirate told me."

"He's not a pirate, he just looks like one."

"Most accountants are just collection agents for the IRS, that makes them pirates in my book," I said.

"Hmm, you may be right. I hadn't thought of that."

After a few more drinks Luther started feeling better so we went to dinner. By the time we were finished it was nearly ten, so we went straight home. I wanted sex but Luther had drunk too much and fell asleep on the sofa. I threw a blanket over him and went to bed.

The following morning before anyone arrived at the Golden Dragon, Luther was there cleaning out his desk and making copies of papers and documents that he thought might be useful to him in the future. He went through the unopened mail and noticed some certified items from the Internal Revenue Service, the landlord and the State Comptroller. He grabbed them up and threw them in his briefcase. Then he wrote one last check. That night he couldn't wait to tell me what he had done.

"But you're not the manager anymore," I protested.

"That's what they think. As far as I'm concerned I'm still the manager. In fact, I went to the post office and had all the mail forwarded here to the house."

"But how are they going to run the business without getting any mail?"

"It should be interesting," Luther said.

"Luther, I don't think you should be interfering with them. Sue them if you want, but don't try to undermine their business."

"Suing them would be a waste of time. Besides I don't want to make any damn attorney rich. No, my way is better. Much better."

The following Friday Luther had picked up his mail

and brought it home. He sat down at the kitchen table and started going through it. I was busy cooking lunch. Suddenly he began to laugh.

"Oh, this is fabulous," Luther said. "The IRS is about to levy the Golden Dragon's bank account."

"How do you know?" I asked.

"I've got the *Notice of Intent to Levy* right here."

"Luther, you're not going to keep all the Golden Dragon's mail are you?"

"Of course I am. The IRS is going to seize their bank account and they won't even know about it until it's too late."

"They're going to be very mad at you, Luther."

"Do I give a shit? I've got more good news."

"What?"

"Pam Blaylock bounced three checks."

"What?"

"She must not have realized I paid myself my October management fee. Oh, no! Did I forget to record that check in the register? Oops!" Luther laughed.

"Luther, you're terrible."

"Hey, I warned them not to fire me. I told them they would regret it. I just didn't realize how quickly I'd get such sweet revenge."

That night Jim Cochran came by the condo. Luther was there but he didn't want to talk to him. He told me to get rid of him, so I told him Luther wasn't home yet. The next day Luther did turn loose of the post office box. He said he'd accomplished what he needed already.

After listening to Margie for two hours, I understood why the Golden Dragon partners hated him so much. He was selfish, arrogant, and obviously lacked any kind of a conscience. You would have thought the son of a preacher would have some deference for truth and honesty. You'd think he'd have a little compassion for his fellow man. But that wasn't the case with Luther Bell.

Now that I understood why he was murdered, I

needed to focus more on the night of the murder and who had an opportunity to kill him. Since Margie had discovered the body, she was the logical place to start. "When Jim arrived that day, was he driving the Lincoln?"

"Uh huh."

"Where did he park it?"

"On the curb in front of the building."

"When you went out that Wednesday night before Luther was killed, did you see Jim's car at all?"

"No."

"You didn't see a Lincoln driving around?"

"No."

"I understand you found the body around 10:15?"

"Yes, I had just got home from the Rendezvous Club. Lucy Patterson and I had gone out for the evening. We went to dinner and a movie before we stopped at the club."

"Did you see Jim's Lincoln when you came back to the condo?"

"No."

"Walk me through everything that happened when you came home that night."

"Well, the condo has a two-car garage, so I had been parking my Accord next to Luther's Cadillac. When I got close to the house, I pushed the garage door opener and was shocked to see the door closing. It apparently had been opened when I got there. I pushed it twice to get it back up. As I started to drive into the garage I noticed Luther lying on the ground. I slammed on my brakes, got out immediately, and ran up to him—but he was dead."

"How did you know he was dead?"

"His eyes were wide open, he wasn't breathing, and his body was stiff."

"So what did you do then?"

"I just stood there a minute in shock and then I ran into the condo and called the police."

"Did you see the murder weapon?"

"Yes, the tire iron was on the ground about three or four feet away from Luther's body. It was covered with blood. Between the smell of Luther's body and the sight of blood, I almost vomited. If I hadn't been so upset I probably would have."

"I understand Luther's wallet and watch were stolen?"

"Yes, they were missing. "

"Did Luther carry a lot of cash?"

"Yes, he usually had two or three hundred dollars along with six or eight credit cards."

"How valuable was his watch?"

"It was a diamond Rolex. I think it was worth about $5,000."

"Have you or any of your neighbors had any problem with theft or burglary in the past?"

"I only know of one other case this year."

"What was stolen?"

"Jewelry, a VCR, and a TV."

"Hmm."

I couldn't think of any more questions, so I put away my yellow pad and closed my briefcase. Margie had been very open and honest with me, which was more than I had expected. She appeared to be a decent person who was genuinely in love with Luther Bell. But I didn't understand how she could have stood by and watched Luther maliciously attack the Golden Dragon partners. Was that the kind of man she was prepared to spend the rest of her life with? I put my yellow pad in my briefcase and closed it up.

I looked at her and smiled. "Well, thank you very much. I know you didn't have to talk to me. You've been a tremendous help."

She returned the smile and replied, "Actually, I'm kind of glad you stopped by. It's been pretty lonely around here since Luther died. It felt good to talk to someone about all that has happened."

"Yeah, I know what you mean. It's not good to keep

your feelings inside. . . . Listen, if you ever need . . . or just want to talk, call me. I'm a good listener."

She gave me a surprised look and replied, "Thank you. I just might have to take you up on that offer."

We said our goodbyes, and I left.

CHAPTER FIFTEEN

Richard Banks

The next morning I stopped by the Dallas Police Department. I was there to interview the officer who had arrested Richard Banks. I went up to the information desk and advised the dispatcher that I had an appointment with Officer Wentworth. She said she would page her. I sat down next to a mother holding a cranky baby and waited. After a few minutes Officer Wentworth walked up to the dispatcher. I got up and walked toward the officer.

"Hi . . . Officer Wentworth?"

"Yes, you must be Stan Turner."

"Correct, thank you for meeting with me."

"No problem, come on back, and we'll find an empty office."

"Thank you."

I followed her into a small, sparsely furnished office. She sat down at a small round table.

"Have a seat."

"Thanks."

"So, how can I help you?" she asked.

"I need to ask you about the Richard Banks' arrest."

"Banks? . . . Why? It's all in my report."

"Well, true. I wanted to see if you might explain what happened in a little more detail. Your testimony could be very important. Why don't you just tell me again what you remember."

"Well, I was on patrol when I got a call about an accident on Lemmon Avenue near Wycliff. I immediately went to the scene."

"Were you the first officer there?"

"Yes. When I arrived I noticed Mr. Banks sitting in his car. The victim was lying face down near the median of the highway. I called for an ambulance and then went over to the victim to see if he was alive. He was breathing but was unconscious. A Care-flight helicopter arrived almost immediately and Mr. Ravi was taken away."

"So, then what did you do?"

"I took Mr. Banks' statement."

"Did you notice anything unusual?"

"Yes, while he was talking I noticed his speech was slurred and I smelled liquor on his breath. He said he was traveling eastbound on Lemmon Avenue about forty-five miles per hour when Mr. Ravi suddenly appeared out of nowhere and ran out in front of him. He said he didn't have time to apply his brakes because it all happened so fast. He said after he hit him, he then slammed on his brakes and skidded completely around so he was facing on-coming traffic."

"So, what happened next?"

"I went over to the car and noticed an empty bottle of scotch on the floor in the back seat. I decided I now had probable cause to do a field sobriety test."

"How did he do?"

"He failed the test completely, so I arrested him on a charge of DWI. When we got him back to the station we found out Mr. Ravi had died, so we charged him with involuntary manslaughter and transferred him to the county jail."

"Did they video tape him at the station?"

"Yes, they did, and I viewed the tape later. He acted belligerent, uncooperative, and appeared very drunk."

"What about a blood test?"

"There was a blood test, but I haven't seen the results. The DA is handling it now."

"So, what's the status of his case? Do you know?"

"The grand jury has it. I was told they should come down with an indictment pretty soon."

"Good. . . . Well, I really appreciate you talking to me. I'm sure we're going to have to take your deposition and I know we'll need your testimony at the time of trial."

"You'll need to serve me a subpoena. I can't voluntarily be a witness."

"I understand. Thanks again."

When I got back to the office, I decided to check on Mr. Bank's indictment. I didn't understand what was taking so long. The problem was grand jury deliberations were secret and there wasn't any official way I could check on what was transpiring. Then I thought of Paula. I'd call her. She might be able to check into it for me.

"Sure, what was his name?" Paula asked.

"Banks—Richard Banks."

"Okay, I'll ask around and let you know."

"Thank you. I really appreciate your help. I owe you one."

"You can buy me lunch—or better yet, dinner."

"Yeah, Okay, I'll do that."

"Call me."

"Okay."

"Soon."

"Sure. . . . Bye."

*****

While I was trying to solve Luther's murder, I still had to do what I could to help the Golden Dragon partners defend themselves from the vultures who were trying to pick the Golden Dragon carcass clean. I arrived at the IRS collections office at 10:35 a.m. I checked my Daytimer and saw that the meeting was on the 8th floor. An attractive young black lady was waiting at the elevator. When the door opened she got in, and punched eleven. I followed her in and hit eight.

"Oh . . . the dreaded eighth floor," she said.

I smiled and replied, "Yeah, I'm afraid so."

"Hmm . . . you don't look scared enough to be a taxpayer," she said, "and you don't look mean enough to be a revenue agent."

I laughed and said, "You're very observant. I'm a lawyer."

She shook her head and said, "That figures. Mr. Cool, huh?"

The elevator stopped on the eighth floor and the door opened. The lady smiled and said, "Have a nice day."

I shook my head, half smiled and replied, "Right."

I stepped out and observed an office to my right with a sign that read *Internal Revenue Service, Collections Branch*. I entered and looked around. It was a cold, sterile office decorated with cheap, artificial plants and brightly colored plastic chairs. A large bulletin board was strategically placed by the doorway so it wouldn't be missed. Attached to it were ominous notices of seizures, levies, and asset auctions, obviously designed to intimidate the taxpayers who had been summed to go one on one with a revenue agent. I spotted Don and Jim seated in the reception area and walked over to them.

"Hi, gentlemen," I said. "Have you checked in?"

"No," Don replied. "We thought we better wait for you."

"Okay, let me go tell them that we're here. I'll be right back.

I walked over and got in line at the reception window. After waiting about five minutes, I advised the clerk that we had an appointment with Agent Clyde Richmond. I was told to take a seat, and that Mr. Richmond would be with us shortly.

"How's Pam?" I asked.

"I don't know," Don said. "She won't leave the house. She's afraid she might see someone she knows. I'm really worried about her."

"She'll be okay in a few days, I bet. It must have been

an incredible shock for her to suddenly be confronted by a cop ready to drag her away like a common criminal—especially with her friends there."

"It was humiliating. I'm not sure she'll ever get over it," Don said dejectedly.

Twenty minutes later Agent Richmond had yet to come out, so I went back to the reception desk and inquired as to whether Mr. Richmond was going to meet with us or not. The clerk said Mr. Richmond was out but was due back any minute.

"Can you believe this, Stan? We made an appointment with this guy yesterday. You'd think he would have the decency to show up."

"He'll be here. He just wants to make us sweat a little."

"Are you serious?" Don said.

"Uh huh. It's a negotiation technique."

"Do you think this guy will cut us any slack, Stan?" Jim asked.

"Don't hold your breath," I replied. "This is the IRS, remember."

The door flung open and a tall, slim man about thirty-five years old appeared. He was nearly bald and wore steel framed glasses.

"Mr. Turner?" he said in a loud voice.

I raised my hand and said, "Yes, right over here."

"Come with me please," he said.

We followed him into a room partitioned into twenty or thirty meeting cubicles. He pointed to a cubicle and said, "Take a seat right there. I'll grab another chair."

Soon Agent Richmond came back with another orange plastic chair. He put it down and everyone took a seat. I opened my briefcase and pulled out a file folder.

"All right," he said. "You wanted to talk about the levy on your bank account?"

"Yes," I said. "The partners were very surprised by the levy. They did not receive a notice of it."

Agent Richmond looked in his file and said, "I've got a green card right here, signed by a . . . Luther Bell."

"Yes, Mr. Bell was the manager until he was fired recently. Without the authority of the other partners, he changed the address of the partnership with the post office. They didn't get any mail for over a week. Mr. Bell did not notify them of the IRS Notice of Intent to Levy."

"Well, I guess the ultimate question is what are we going to do with these outstanding tax liabilities. Are you going to write me a check?" Agent Richmond asked.

"Unfortunately my clients don't have the funds to pay the full amount due at this time. Their manager embezzled a lot of money from them, which left them low on cash. We would like to work out an installment payout arrangement if we could."

"If you think we're going to release the levy, forget it. Whatever we've captured belongs to us now. We can talk about an installment payout of the balance due, but frankly with so many of you financially responsible for this debt, I doubt if it would be taken very seriously."

"What do you show the balance due to be?" I asked.

"$32,231.22 as of the date of the levy."

"I thought it was only around $25,000," Jim said.

"That may have been the initial amount on the return, but we've assessed some penalties and interest."

"What kind of penalties?" Jim asked.

"There's a 10% penalty for filing the return late, another 10% for not remitting the tax with the return, plus interest at the statutory rate."

"Do you know how much you got in the levy?" I asked.

Agent Richmond looked in his file and said, "$18,250. That leaves a balance of $13,981.22."

"Can you give them some time to pay that off?" I asked.

"Perhaps. I'll have to get them to fill out a financial statement, but let me warn you if the financial statement shows they have the ability to pay, then I won't be able to give them any additional time."

"Okay, give me a minute with my clients so we can make a decision how to proceed."

Agent Richmond stood up and said, "All right, I'll be back in a couple minutes."

I turned to Don and Jim and said, "Well, gentlemen, what do you want to do? I'm not sure you want to give them a financial statement. No telling what they will do once they know where all your assets are."

"I sure as hell don't want them to know I've got stock options," Jim said.

"Damn, I hate to cough up another four grand. This deal is really draining me," Don said. "Pam is going to have a stroke."

"You don't have much of a choice, really," I said. "They can garnish your wages if you don't pay the tax."

"Oh, that would be lovely if my boss got a notice of garnishment from the IRS. I'd probably lose my job," Don said.

"You could file a chapter 13," I suggested.

"My wife's at home right now, too embarrassed to leave the house because of her arrest. Can you imagine how she would feel if her friends read about her bankruptcy in the newspaper?"

"We could file in Dallas. There are so many bankruptcies there the paper doesn't bother to publish them anymore."

"I don't think so. Let's just pay the money and get the hell out of here," Don said.

"I guess we don't have any other choice," Jim concurred.

I saw Agent Richmond in the distance talking to another revenue officer and motioned for him to come back. He held up his hand, briefly acknowledging the summons, finished his conversation, and then strolled back to the cubicle.

"So what's it gonna be?" Agent Richmond asked.

"They're going to write you a check. There are five investors so each will pay twenty percent."

"Where are the others?"

"I'll get their checks this afternoon and bring them to you in the morning," Jim said.

"Very good. Once I get all the checks I'll release the levy and the tax lien against the partnership."

We left the IRS office on Alpha Road and met at a coffee shop a few blocks away. I needed to talk to Don since I had been contacted by Detective Besch. He wanted to talk to Pam and Don, so I suggested he come by my office the following day. I hadn't had an opportunity to advise Don of the meeting so I took this opportunity to do it.

"Tomorrow?" Don said.

"Right. He wanted to do it today, but I told him it was a bad time with the IRS and everything. He'll be in my office tomorrow morning at nine. Why don't you and Pam come in at eight-thirty so we can go over a few things before the interview."

"All right, but is it critical that Pam come? I don't think she's ready for this type of trauma."

"I know. I asked him the same question but he's adamant he speak to both of you."

"Wonderful. I wish I *had* killed Luther Bell. The asshole has ruined my life."

"I know things look pretty dismal right now, but you've got to try to focus on the positive things in your life."

"Like what?" Don asked.

"Like you still have a great wife and a wonderful family. You have a good job, and everybody is in good health. That's a lot to be thankful for."

"Yeah, but how long is that going to last?"

"What do you mean?" I asked.

"Hell, they may whisk me away tomorrow and throw me in jail. Then I won't have a damn thing."

****

The next day it was cold and rainy in Austin. I had been taking a deposition in a wrongful termination case downtown. The depositions ended as scheduled at 1:30 p.m. but unfortunately, on the way to the airport, my taxi got a flat. By the time a new cab was dispatched I had lost twenty minutes and ended up missing my flight. I was able to get on the next flight and still would have made it back for my six o'clock meeting except that fog had socked-in Love Field and the plane couldn't land.

The flight returned to Austin, refueled and at 6:30 touched down again in Dallas. It was 7:15 when I finally walked into my office. Key was sitting reading a magazine and Amit was pacing nervously. Jodie smiled when she saw me arrive.

"We'd almost given up on you," Jodie said.

"I'm so sorry. I've never been through such an ordeal." I explained what happened.

"Sounds like you've had a difficult day, Mr. Turner," Amit said.

"Yes, and I'm so sorry you had to wait. I know you're leaving tomorrow for India."

"Correct. We have a 10:00 a.m. flight."

"Well, we'll try to make this meeting as short as possible. Come on into my office."

Amit and Key followed me into my office and we all sat down.

"Okay, the last time we met we didn't really have time for you to tell me about your relationship with your father, Key. I need to know how you two got along. What you did together. What impact your father's death will have on you. This is all important in determining damages. We've got to show, hopefully, the devastation you felt when your father died."

"Well, since my father was killed, I won't be able to get to know him."

"What do you mean? Were you planning to spend more time with him to get to know him better?"

"No, I was planning to find him and get to know him."

"Huh? What do you mean find him?"

"What he's trying to tell you Mr. Turner," Amit said, "is that he never knew his father. He had never met him. Anant and his mother got a divorce when Key was only two years old. He disappeared after that. None of us knew where he was until we were contacted about his death."

I leaned back and put my hands over my eyes. The cold chill of disappointment gripped me. How could my luck be so bad? In nine hundred ninety-nine cases out of a thousand when a son lost his father he would have suffered immeasurable damages—mental anguish, loss of support, loss of consortium—but with no relationship whatsoever with his father, never even having seen him or talked to him, there were *no* damages, none, nothing. I struggled to keep my composure.

"I suppose Anant didn't visit or talk to his father in India either?"

"No. . . . Well, he did send him a letter once just to let him know he was alive."

"Great."

After Amit and Key had left I went home. Rebekah was watching TV and didn't smile when I walked in. "Where have you been? It's nearly eight o'clock. The kids have been terrible. I've been trying to help Reggi with his poetry assignment, and Marcia's been a pest—hanging on me like a little monkey."

"Don't even start," I said. "You don't know the kind of day I've had."

Rebekah glared at me for a minute and finally said, "So what happened to you?"

I told her the tragic news.

"He didn't even know him?"

"No. Not at all."

"So what does that mean?"

"It means we don't have any damages. The case isn't worth shit!"

Rebekah stiffened. "You mean . . . you mean, we won't be able to recover anything?"

"That's about the size of it."

She shook her head and grimaced. "That's just our luck. I knew this was too good to be true. Damn it!"

"I'm sorry, honey. I thought maybe this was real, but—"

Rebekah looked at me, her eyes pleading. "Isn't there anything you can do?"

I smiled faintly. "Our only hope is that the grand jury indicts Richard Banks. Then I should be able to prove gross negligence. If I can do that, all I have to do is show my client has one dollar of actual damages."

"So what's one dollar going to do for us?"

"A lot. If I prove one dollar of actual damages then I can ask for a million dollars of punitive damages."

"You can do that?"

I forced a confident smile. "I sure as hell can. So don't give up quite yet."

"When's the grand jury going to indict him?"

"Soon, I hope."

"So, all isn't lost then?"

"No, it won't be easy, but I know a pretty creative psychiatrist who can probably find some damages even without a relationship between Key and Anant. I'll have to call him."

"Good, we need that money, Stan. I was really counting on it."

"I thought you weren't going to count on it?"

"Well, you got my hopes up. You sounded so sure about this."

It would have been a good time to tell her about the Peruvian pottery and the diamonds Melanie had found but I just couldn't bring myself to do it. Another disappointment would be unbearable.

"I know. I'm sorry. I should have kept my mouth shut about it. It just looked so promising, and it might still work out."

"No it won't. It's just our luck," Rebekah said as she began crying. "It's just my luck. I've always been unlucky. Just when I see the light at the end of the tunnel, there's a damn earthquake and I get buried alive! There is a dark cloud hanging over me. There always has been."

I grabbed Rebekah by the shoulders and looked her in the eyes. "Hey, we've survived, right? It hasn't been so bad. We have wonderful children who never give us any kind of trouble. We live in one of the nicest communities in the world, everybody's healthy and we have each other. So I don't think we should be feeling sorry for ourselves."

Rebekah stared at me for a moment and then wiped the tears from her eyes. "You have such a knack for putting things in perspective, don't you."

"I'm an attorney. I have to keep things in perspective or I would go crazy."

"Hmm," Rebekah said, giving me a wry smile. "A girl can't even feel sorry for herself around you. You're no fun."

"If you want to have some fun, I've got some ideas."

"Yeah, I bet you do. You think sex is the solution to all our problems."

"Isn't it?" I said with a smile.

"We've got kids running around the house, in case you didn't notice."

"Isn't it their bedtime?'

Rebekah looked at her watch. "It's only eight o'clock. Sorry."

I shrugged. "The kids are busy upstairs."

"What if they come down?"

"Just don't moan too loud, and they'll never know what we're doing."

Rebekah laughed and smiled at me. "Okay, wise guy. Let's do it." She unbuttoned the back of her dress, shook her head, then gave her shoulders a little twist. The dress fell to the floor leaving her standing in her bra and panties. I went to her and we began kissing excitedly. Just then Reggi walked in the kitchen.

"Mom and Dad! Gee whiz. What are you doing?"

"Ooops!" Rebekah laughed. "Dad and I are just—"

"Messing around," I said. "Get the hell out of here, and leave us alone!"

Reggi covered his eyes and turned away. "Okay," he said and quickly left the room.

"I think we better take this to the bedroom," I said.

Rebekah nodded and we walked quickly down the hall, went into our room and shut the door. We looked at each other and suddenly burst out laughing.

"Did you see Reggi's face? Rebekah said hardly able to contain herself.

"Yes, the poor kid. We shocked the hell out of him."

Rebekah took a deep breath. "Oh God. I really needed a good laugh."

"Me too."

She looked into my eyes and smiled tenderly. "I love you, Stan Turner."

******

Detective Besch arrived at my office at nine sharp. Jodie showed him into the conference room overlooking Central Expressway where we were waiting for him. It was a clear day and bright sunlight flooded the room. Jodie went over to the windows and drew the blinds.

"Would you like some coffee or a cold drink?" she asked.

"A cold drink would hit the spot," he replied.

Jodie nodded and left the room. I introduced Detective Besch to Don and Pam. Everyone took a seat and waited in awkward silence. After Jodie returned with the drinks the interrogation began.

"All right, my clients have agreed to talk with you," I said to Besch. "However, Mrs. Blaylock has not been well, so if we could make this as brief as possible we would appreciate it," I said.

"Sure, I'm sorry folks. I hate to have to bother you, but I've got my job to do. I'm sure you understand."

"Yes, how can we help you?" Don asked.

"Well, to expedite things, let me tell you that I'm familiar with your restaurant venture and how Luther Bell ran the place into the ground. Margie Mason has confirmed that Luther set Mrs. Blaylock up to write the hot checks for which she was arrested. I guess what I want to explore is where everyone was on Wednesday night, the night of the murder. Obviously, all of the partners are suspects simply because of the strong motive each had to kill Mr. Bell. We're not accusing you of anything, but *somebody* did beat him to death."

"We understand," I said. "You've got your investigation to do and we want to cooperate as much as possible. My clients are innocent and they have nothing to hide."

"Good, then Mr. Blaylock, let's start with your whereabouts the night of the murder."

"That's simple. We were at home watching TV."

"Is that right? Didn't you go over to Jim Cochran's house that night?"

"Yes, and I came back about seven-thirty. Jim just lives up the street. Pam was in her room the entire night. I watched TV after I came home."

"What did you watch?"

Don thought a moment. "Knight Rider or maybe Magnum P.I., I don't remember. We weren't in a really good mood since we had been locked out of the restaurant that day."

"Did anyone come over?"

"No."

"Did anyone call?"

"Pam's mother called to see how Pam was holding up. Pam talked to her for awhile."

"What time was this?"

"About nine, I think."

"Mrs. Blaylock, did you stay in your room the whole evening?"

"Yes."

"Do you know what Jim and his wife did after the meeting?"

"No," Don replied. "They were at their house when I left."

"Did they say they were going out?"

"No."

"What about your son Rob?"

"He's not a partner," Don said.

"I know, but he probably wasn't too happy about the way Luther treated his mother."

"He was out running around with his girlfriend. They came and went a couple times during the evening."

"Do you know where they were?"

"I think they went to dinner and then to the library."

"So, that's all you can tell me about everybody's whereabouts on the night of the murder?"

"Yes, sir," Don said.

"Well, frankly that wasn't much help. None of you appear to have anything close to an alibi so that's going to make my job tough. I'm going to have to take each of your lives apart until I find the murderer.

I said, "I'll discuss it some more with them. Maybe we can come up with something to nail down their alibi. I'll let you know."

"Okay, I'll need both of you to come over to the station to give us fingerprints, and hair samples. Will you allow me to search your house, or do I need to get a warrant?"

Don looked at me. He seemed alarmed. "Is that really necessary?" he asked.

"Yes," Detective Besch said. "Since you have no alibi, I've got to search for evidence."

He shrugged. "Go ahead. You won't find anything."

"Thank you. I appreciate your cooperation."

"Why the hair samples?" I asked.

"Several different types of hair were found in the front seat of the Cadillac and in the pool of blood from Luther's head."

Detective Besch stood up. "I guess that will do it for now. Oh, Don. . . . One more thing. I'm going to need to talk to your sons, Rob and Greg. Do you know how I can reach them?"

"What? Can't you leave them out of this? They had nothing to do with any of this," Don replied.

"Rob is my client too," I said. "If you'd like to meet with him I can arrange that for you. I guess he can bring along his brother too, if it's really necessary."

"This is a murder investigation," Besch noted. "Of course it's necessary. How about tomorrow about this time?"

"They go to school. Could they do it later in the day, like say . . . four o'clock?" Don said.

"That'll be fine. I'll be here at four," Detective Besch replied, and then left.

Don and Pam stayed awhile to try to figure out how to prove they were home on the night of the murder. I suggested they get a detailed phone record from Southwestern Bell showing calls, both in and out. We knew there had been at least one telephone call from Pam's mother. That would add credence to Pam's claim that she was home in her bedroom. I was hopeful an inspection of the phone bill might indicate that someone else had called that night—someone Don and Pam had forgotten about.

After the Blaylocks had left, I went back into my office and looked around, wondering what I should do next. It occurred to me I needed to talk to Jim Cochran or someone who knew him well. He was an unknown to me. I was pretty certain that neither Don or Pam were killers. Cochran, on the other hand, did have a bad temper. Even after meeting him just one time I got the feeling he didn't let people push him around. In order to understand him better I decided to talk to his wife, Wanda. She hadn't been at the meeting, so that gave me the reason I needed to go visit her the next morning.

Wanda got up and took a coffee cake out of the oven. It was nine-thirty and she graciously offered me a piece. Having skipped breakfast, I accepted.

"Hmm. This is good," I said. "Rebekah had to take the kids to school early today so she didn't have time to make breakfast."

"Well this was good timing then."

"You bet."

"So, what can I do for you, Mr. Turner?"

"Oh, you can call me Stan."

"Okay, Jim said you wanted to talk about Luther Bell."

"Yes, I need to get your perspective on what happened. I'm expecting the police to try to pin the murder on one of the partners—you know, since you all had good reasons to kill Luther."

Wanda said, "Pam especially—after he got her arrested and all. I'd have probably been in the funny farm by now, had it been me."

"Yes, that was pretty traumatic."

"Which one of us do you think the police will try to pin it on?"

Wanda gave me a half smile and then looked down at the floor. I felt her discomfort. "I don't know. What do you think?"

"Oh. There's probably nothing to worry about, but . . . well, after Don came over on the night of the murder—"

"Yeah."

"Jim didn't stay home. He went out."

"Oh really? Where did he go?"

"I told him to stay home, but he was very upset and

said he needed to get out and get some fresh air. I begged him to stay home, because he has kind of a hot temper, you know?"

"Right, I heard that.."

"Well, he wouldn't listen to me. He left about eight o'clock and didn't come home until after midnight."

"Do you have any reason to think—"

Wanda's voice began to crack, "I can't imagine him killing someone. I don't think he would have done it."

As tears flooded from Wanda's eyes, I wondered if she knew more than what she was telling me.

"I'm sure he didn't kill Luther, Wanda. Did you ask him where he went?"

"Yes, he said he just drove around. I asked him if he drove by Luther's place, and he didn't answer me. He just changed the subject."

"Really," I said. "Did you look at his clothes? Was there any blood or anything?"

"Yes, after he left for work the next day I checked his shirt and his suit. There was no blood but they smelled of smoke and there was a faint odor of perfume."

"Perfume?"

"Cheap perfume."

"Was he drunk when he came home?" I asked.

"No, but I could tell he had been drinking. His breath smelled of liquor."

"Does he go out by himself at night very often?"

"Sometimes. But I'm not worried about him being faithful. We've been married twenty years, and he's never given me reason not to trust him. I'm just worried that he might have killed Luther. He was so upset when he left."

"Well, don't jump to conclusions. It's not likely he did it. Let's assume he didn't do it."

Wanda blew her nose. "Okay."

"Who else are you worried might have done it?"

This was a cruel question to ask of Wanda. She

certainly wouldn't want to point the finger at any of her friends, but I believe in women's intuition, and I wanted to know what Wanda thought.

"You know, I'm kind of worried about Rob."

"Rob? Why?"

"Pam said he was out running around Wednesday night too. He was very upset about what Luther had done to his mother. He told Don he was going to 'beat the crap out of him.'"

"Hmm."

"Do you think this mess will ever be over?" Wanda asked.

"Not any time soon, I'm afraid."

"If Jim did kill Luther, being in prison would drive him crazy. I know him. He couldn't stand the confinement. He'd probably lose his temper and kill a guard or another inmate—if he didn't get killed himself."

"Don't even think like that. I'm sure everything will work out okay in the end."

"I wish I could convince myself of that."

"I should be going," I said. "I appreciate you talking with me."

Wanda pushed her chair out and stood up. I got up and followed her as she slowly made her way to the door. Although I didn't acknowledge it to her, I shared her fear about Jim. After his little confrontation with Margie Mason and with no alibi, he was sure to be the DA's number one suspect.

"If the police stop by, don't talk to them," I cautioned her. "Call me, okay?"

"I will."

"Thanks for the coffee cake. It was delicious."

"You're welcome."

She forced a smile as I gave her one last glance. When I got to my office Jodie reminded me I had a full slate of appointments all day culminating with Detective Besch's interview of Rob and Greg at four.

At three forty-five, Rob Blaylock arrived. Jodie escorted him immediately into the conference room. I needed to get his version of what had happened on the night of Luther's death. We had to make a decision whether to tell Detective Besch the truth or abort the interview and tell him nothing.

"Hi, Rob. How have you been?"

"Okay."

"We don't have much time, so let's get down to business."

"Yes, sir."

"Jennifer told me what happened the night of the murder but I need hear it from you."

Rob related his version of the discovery of Luther's body. His story closely matched Jennifer's rendition. After discussing the options with Rob, we decided to tell Detective Besch what happened as he was bound to find out anyway.

When Detective Besch arrived, I let Rob speak freely.

He said, "I'm glad you told me about this. At least for now I'll give you the benefit of the doubt. Your story is a little hard to believe though."

"It's the truth," Rob said.

"What time was it when you found Luther?" Detective Besch asked.

"A little after ten."

"Did you see anybody when you pulled up into the driveway?"

"No. Jennifer and I were arguing so I wasn't paying a lot of attention."

"Was the light on in the garage?"

"No, it was dark. As we drove into the driveway, we realized the garage door was up. We didn't see Luther's body until we were almost on top of it."

"Did you touch anything?"

"No, we just got the hell out of there."

"Why didn't you call the police?"

"We were scared. If they knew we had been at the scene of the crime, they might accuse us of the murder."

"Okay. . . .One last question. Had Luther still been alive, would you have killed him?"

Rob gave the detective a hard stare and then replied, "I don't know."

Detective Besch smiled. "Well, maybe you *are* telling me the truth. I certainly hope so, for your sake."

Later that night I discussed my progress on the investigation with Rebekah.

"What did Rob have to say?" Rebekah asked.

I told her what had transpired. "He convinced me. I don't think he killed Luther."

"Really? Are you sure?"

"Yeah. I just can't see him ruthlessly beating Luther the way the killer did," I said. "He'd hit him hard once or twice and then leave. I think the killer was scared to death that Luther might somehow survive the attack and strike back. You know, like when you run across a snake or a scorpion. You get a shovel and beat the sucker repeatedly until you are damn sure it's dead and won't bite you. It's my gut feeling the assailant was smaller and weaker than Luther and felt compelled to repeatedly strike him to be sure he was dead."

"That could be, but what if it was a crime of passion. The assailant really hated Luther and when he or she began to hit him, it felt so good they couldn't stop."

"Perhaps. . . . I just wonder where Jim was all night."

"You said he smelled of perfume." Rebekah noted.

"Right."

"Maybe he went to a club and found a drinking companion."

"Possibly. I guess it's time to talk to him and find out."

"I would think so."

"I've got to be careful though. He's not technically my client. I work for Don. If he tells me anything incriminating he may not be able to invoke the attorney-client privilege," I said.

"Oh. So what are you going to do?"

"Tell him up front not to talk to me if he's guilty. If he keeps talking I've got to assume he's innocent and treat him simply as a witness."

"If he is innocent, then that leaves—" Rebekah asked.

"His ex-wife, Laura Bell, and his girlfriend, Margie Mason."

"I can see an ex-wife doing it."

"Particularly if there was insurance," I said. "Being an insurance agent, Luther probably had a big policy. The question"

"What about Margie?"

"The problem with her is she had no obvious motive. She probably wasn't a beneficiary of his insurance, they wasn't married yet so she wouldn't inherit anything, and she was living with him—apparently quite happily."

"You're right. It wouldn't make sense for her to kill Luther."

"Unless we're missing something."

"I don't know what it would be."

"I don't either."

CHAPTER SIXTEEN

The Alibis

The next day while I was going through the mail Jodie handed me of a phone message from Herb Winters of Prime Lending Bank. I crumpled up the note in disgust. I knew why he was calling—more bad news for the Golden Dragon partners. I wondered how much more adversity they could stand before they just gave up. Giving up was the worst thing they could do because then their adversaries could walk right over them. But the human spirit can only take so much. I dialed the number. Herb got right to the point.

"We've been advised that your client shut down the restaurant. We were really shocked to hear it. I knew they had that embezzlement, but I had thought the partners had covered that loss," Herb said.

"We thought so too, but Luther apparently wasn't doing such a great job managing the place. They've been losing money from the get go and didn't even know it. The landlord finally locked them out."

"Well, I'm sorry to hear that. I really thought they had a gold mine. Anyway, we need to talk about their loan. I would have called them directly, but I knew you were representing them so I figured I better call you."

"Well, we haven't figured out yet how to deal with the bank's loan. The lockout has stopped the cash flow, so things are looking pretty grim."

"We either need to get the loan paid off, or arrange to pick up the collateral."

"What's the balance due?"

"$105,500 as of September 30th."

"What do you think you can get for the collateral?"

"Not more than twenty to thirty cents on the dollar, so you're still looking at a $70-80,000 deficiency."

"If the partners get hit with a $20,000 cash call we're going to have to have paramedics on standby to resuscitate them from heart failure."

"I'm sorry Stan, but we've got the bank examiners in next week and we've got to move on this problem quickly. They'll be all over us if we're lackadaisical about this."

"Okay, let me talk to the partners and see what they want to do."

"Fine, call me tomorrow," Herb said.

I wasn't anxious to call Don or Jim to tell them the bank's position. No telling what another jolt like this would do to them. Unfortunately, I had no choice in the matter. Jodie got Don on the line for me. I told him about the call from Herb Winters.

"Oh, shit," he moaned as Pam picked up another extension.

"What's wrong?" she asked.

Don said, "We've got to pay our note—$105,000."

"What note?" Pam moaned.

"The equipment loan. If we don't pay it we have to surrender the collateral, and they will still sue us for the deficiency."

I could hear Pam's muffled crying. She must have been holding the phone up to her chest. My heart went out to her. She had suffered so much.

"So, that's about $20,000 each?" Don asked.

"Right," I said.

"Oh Jesus! We don't have $20,000. We just can't pay it. Let them sue us!" Pam screamed.

I waited a moment and then said, "If you don't come up with the money then they can sue you for the entire $80,000. You're all jointly and severally liable."

"We could lose everything if we don't stick together and all take care of this obligation," Don said.

"Is there ever going to be an end to this?" Pam moaned. "Why don't we call all our creditors and just invite them over to the house and they can take everything?! Damn it! I can't believe this!"

"I'm sorry, honey. I know it was a big mistake getting into this franchise, but it's history now. We've just got to survive this ordeal somehow."

"I don't know if I can take any more," Pam said. "This is just too much to handle. I just can't sit around and watch our life disintegrate. It's much too painful."

Pam hung up the phone.

"I'm sorry, Stan. I've got to go. I'll talk to Jim and we'll get back to you. Right now I've got to talk to Pam. She's been threatening to take Donna and go to her parent's place in Seattle."

"Oh, no!" I said. "Go ahead. Go talk to her. If I can do anything let me know, okay?"

"I will. Thanks."

I felt sick inside and helpless. I hadn't been able to do much to help Don and Pam. If only they had come to see me *before* they got into the Golden Dragon venture. The following day, Jim called me early in the morning. By the tone of his voice I could tell he hadn't taken the news well either. I had never seen anyone fall on hard times so fast. I wanted so badly to figure out a way to save them, but I couldn't think of a damn thing other than a chapter 11. Unfortunately, they wouldn't ever consider bankruptcy, so there was nothing I could do but watch their lives crumble.

"I'm sorry about the bank, Jim," I said.

"We'd like you to contact them and arrange to let them have the collateral so they can liquidate it. Then when they know what the deficiency is we'll each send you our share and you can pay it."

"You know, if they sell the collateral they'll get next to

nothing for it. We might want to find a buyer ourselves. I bet we could get fifty cents on the dollar instead of ten or twenty."

"How would we do that?"

"We can contact GD Enterprises in California. They might know of some franchises that are going in where the equipment could be used. It's damn near brand new equipment."

"That's a good idea," Jim said. "Will you do that for us?"

"Sure. If we find a buyer, then I'll arrange to sell it to them and get a release from the bank. I think you'll save quite a bit of money doing it this way."

"Okay, good idea. Thanks for the tip."

"No problem," I said. "Keep your fingers crossed. I'll call you if I get a buyer."

"Great."

There was silence on the line. I sensed Jim had something else to tell me.

"Everything else okay?" I said.

"No, the police came by last night."

"Detective Besch?"

"Yeah. I told him I didn't want to talk without you present but he asked a bunch of questions anyway."

"Like what?"

"Like what I was doing the night Luther was murdered."

"You didn't talk to him, did you?"

"No."

"What *were* you doing the night of the murder? Wanda wasn't sure where you went that night. "

"I hung out at a strip club, the Sunset Strip."

"Well, good. Hopefully someone saw you there."

"At least one of the girls should remember me."

"Which one?"

"Julie. I've been there a few times before. She likes

me."

"Hmm. Well, I'll pay a visit to the club and see if I can talk to her."

"Yes, talk to her. I'm sure she'll verify that I was there when Luther was killed."

"Good. . . . Is Besch going to call me to set up an interview?"

"Yes. That's what he said he'd do. . . . He also said you had a conflict of interest. What did he mean by that?"

"Well, if you are charged with Luther's murder I couldn't represent you because that might require me to try to prove Don was the murderer. Obviously I couldn't do that since he is a client. . . . But as long as nobody has been charged, I can investigate Luther's murder as a part of my representation of the Golden Dragon Partnership in its claim against Luther's estate."

"Oh. Well, I'd just as soon you represent everybody. The last thing we need is a dozen lawyers sucking us dry."

"I'll call you if I hear from Detective Besch."

"Thanks, Stan."

I immediately called GD Enterprises in California but Howard Hurst was out of the office. His secretary said she'd have him call just as soon as he returned. A few hours later he called and said he would check and see if any of the other franchisees needed additional equipment. He seemed positive.

The next day, Don called me to let me know Detective Besch had been questioning his neighbors. I told him he was just confirming his alibi. He wanted to be sure they were at home on the night of the murder. I told him not to worry about it and then decided to do my own alibi checking. Margie had told me she went to the Rendezvous Club and a movie on the night of the murder. I wondered if she had been telling the truth, so I decided to go over there and see if anyone remembered her. It was early and the happy hour crowd was just beginning to wander in. I started with the bartender. I introduced myself and gave him a card.

"I wonder if you might answer a few questions?"

"It depends on the questions."

I pulled out a photograph of Margie I had clipped from the newspaper and handed it to the bartender. "Last Wednesday night this young lady claims to have been in here between nine and ten. She would have been with a girlfriend. Were you on duty that night?"

"Yes."

"Do you remember seeing them?"

The bartender looked at the photos very carefully moving them around to get a better light on them. I stared at the bartender waiting for his response but nothing happened. Then I realized this was the moment I was supposed to pull out my wallet and start offering cash. I sighed, then pulled out a twenty dollar bill and laid it on the counter.

"Oh yeah, I remember now, they came in about nine and were picked up by couple of cowboys. They had a few drinks, danced a little bit, and then left about nine thirty or ten."

"You can't pin the time down a little closer?"

"Hey, I don't make the customers punch a time clock. That's the best I can do."

"Okay. Did they leave alone or were they with the cowboys?"

"I'm not sure, they just left."

"All right, thanks. I appreciate your cooperation."

The thirty minutes between nine thirty and ten were critical. If they left at nine thirty, Margie would have had time to go home and kill Luther, but if she had left any later she probably wouldn't have. The bartender's testimony wasn't a big help except that he did verify that Margie and her friend were at the bar just like she said. I wondered if Jim's alibi would hold up as well. I decided to pay a visit to the Sunset Strip while I was out.

It was noon and businessmen were pouring into the club for the free lunch buffet. After leaving my Corvette with the parking attendant, I paid the cover charge, handed my card to the doorman and asked to see the manager. He asked me to get a table, and he would have the manager come out to talk to me. As I was waiting, a tall brunette came over and began to dance for me. At first I tried to ignore her, but she got her breasts up so close to my face I couldn't move. Finally, I pulled out a five dollar bill and stuck it in her g-string, hoping she'd move on to the next table. She didn't. Instead she began circling me with one hand on my shoulder. Then she started rubbing my shoulders and nibbling at my neck. I closed my eyes about to succumb to her charm, when I heard someone say, "You wanted to speak with me?"

I opened my eyes and saw a tall man hovering over me. I stood up and the dancer moved on. "Oh, hi. Are you the manager?"

"Yes. I understand you wanted to speak with me."

"Right. I'm Stan Turner. I'm an attorney. I wonder if I could ask a few questions of you and your girls."

"All of them?"

"Well, if you don't mind. I'm investigating a homicide. A couple of my clients are suspects in a murder and I need to know if anybody in your club saw a certain person here last Wednesday night. It's very important."

"Does he have a name?"

"Jim Cochran."

"I don't know him, but I suppose you can talk to the girls during their breaks."

"Okay, How often are they?"

"Each girl has a ten minute break every hour. Just go on ahead into their dressing room and catch them while they're getting dressed."

I gave him a double take. "They won't mind that?"

"Are you kidding? They love to have men watch them. That's why they're dancers."

"Hmm. All right," I said as I stood. I thanked him and made my way to the dressing room door. I hesitated, swallowed hard, then opened the door and walked in. Naked women were scurrying about all around me. They didn't seem to notice my presence. For a moment I just stood there mesmerized, then I went up to the first dancer I saw and said, "Hi miss, Sorry to disturb you, my name is Stan Turner." I noticed a sign on the mirror that read *Ruby*.

She gave me a wry smile. "Couldn't get a good enough view from your table, huh?" Ruby said.

I chuckled. "No, the view at the table was fine. That's not why I'm here. I'd like to ask you a few questions, if you don't mind?"

"Who the hell did you say you were?"

"Stan Turner. I'm an attorney investigating a murder. My client, Jim Cochran, claims to have been here last Wednesday night. I just wondered if you might remember seeing him."

She stood up straight. I couldn't help but gaze at her fine breasts. She seemed amused. She asked, "What does he look like?"

I looked up and smiled. "Oh," I said, and then reached for a photograph of Jim which I had put in my shirt pocket. I handed it to her. She studied it a minute, looked up and said, "He looks familiar. I think he *was* here. Let me ask Candy. She'd know."

Ruby led me to the other end of the dressing room. I smiled at all the pretty women putting on makeup and putting on their costumes. Ruby stopped in front of a red-headed dancer who was putting on a long silver cocktail dress.

Ruby sat on a stool next to her and held Jim's picture out where she could see it. "Do you remember this guy?"

She nodded. "Yeah, I hope he comes back soon. He's a big spender. He dropped a fifty on me for a two-minute lap dance."

"When was that?" I asked."

Candy thought a moment and then replied, "Last Wednesday night, if my recollection serves me right."

"When did he arrive?"

"I'm not sure, I gave him the lap dance a little after eight, just before my break."

"When did he leave?"

"Oh gee . . . I don't know, maybe nine thirty . . . or ten. I really don't know for sure."

"Did he talk to you?"

"Not much, he was just mainly watching the girls. We didn't say much to each other, just small talk, you know."

"Did he talk to any of the other girls?"

"Sure, I think Julie, Julie Iverson. She spent some time with him. She's out with the flu today, or I'd go find her for you."

"Oh, she is?"

"Yeah. She said she'd be back in a few days. She didn't want to infect any of the rest of us."

"Oh . . . makes sense. I'll have to come back next week then, I guess."

"I guess so. Unless you want to stop by her apartment. It's just down the street."

I thought about that for a moment but dismissed the idea as being imprudent. It would be better to meet her in a public place for obvious reasons. Besides, I didn't want to get the flu. I could wait a few days.

"Well, that's okay. I'll wait. Thanks for your help."

"Our pleasure."

I turned and walked slowly toward the door savoring the last few seconds of my visit to the Sunset Strip dressing room. After leaving the club, I got into my car and, as I drove away, I was already looking forward to my return visit.

*****

When I got back to the office, a message from Rob was

waiting for me. I dialed the number and he picked up immediately.

"Hi, Mr. Turner. I'm sorry to bother you, but you said to call if anything came up."

"Right. No problem. What's up?"

"I just wanted to let you know the meeting with my parents didn't go so well."

"Oh, no. What happened?"

"I told my parents that Jennifer and I needed to talk to them. So we went over there last night and told them that we had decided to get married and keep the baby. Well, they went ballistic. Dad said I was throwing my baseball career out the window and Mom was worried about college. Why couldn't they be more understanding—like you were when I told you our plans?"

"They are under a tremendous amount of stress right now. Their lives are falling apart and they aren't thinking straight. You just need to be patient with them."

"I know. But I'm worried. They both seem to be getting more and more depressed each day. Mom spends most of the day in her room and Dad stares at the TV but has no clue what's on."

"Hmm. We may need to get them some therapy. I would certainly need it if I were in their shoes."

"I'm worried about Donna too. Greg is old enough to handle it, but Donna doesn't understand what's happening. Mom is pretty much ignoring her and Dad yells at her all the time. I wish she could come live with Jennifer and me, so we could watch out for her. She's the only one who is excited about the baby and having Jennifer as a sister."

"Well, you can't take Donna away. Pam would definitely go crazy if you did that. . . . Do you go to church? Is there a minister you can call?"

"No, my parents aren't very religious. They go to church occasionally, but I wouldn't know who to call."

"Okay, I'll talk to them and see if they will get some

counseling. There's a therapist who works in my building who is pretty good."

"Thank you, Stan. I know this isn't a legal matter, but I didn't know who else to talk to."

"No problem. Just keep your head up and let me know if I can help in any way."

Rob hung up and I called Don. I didn't tell him that Rob had called. I asked him how he and Pam were holding up. He said they were okay. I told him about the therapist I knew. He said he would talk to Pam and maybe they would go see her. Somehow I knew that would never happen. Clients too often don't seek help until it was too late.

As I was getting ready to leave I went through the mail. There was a letter from International Tracing Service.

Dear Mr. Turner,

> We are pleased to advise you we have found Melvin Schwartz. In checking social security records we located his last employer, the First Baptist Church of McAllen, Texas. They advised us he no longer worked for them but were able to give us the address and telephone number of a next of kin, Bridget Schwartz-Christopher of Fort Worth, Texas. Upon contacting her we were able to locate the subject. He is now residing in the New Hope Cemetery in Boerne, Texas. We are enclosing a death certificate as proof that we have found the subject. An invoice for our services is enclosed for your convenience. It has been a pleasure doing business with you.
> Sincerely,
>
> Margaret Weller
> Account Manager

The letter didn't surprise me. But the death certificate did. The cause of death was a gunshot wound to the head. Melvin Schwartz had been murdered. I immediately called Melanie to tell her the news.

"Murdered?"

"Yes, that's why he never came back for the diamonds."

"So, since he's dead there's no way anyone can trace the diamonds to you. We can sell them and collect the cash, right?"

"I suppose so, but I'm still worried."

"Why?"

"I don't know. It's just a feeling that somebody is out there searching for those diamonds."

"That's more reason to get rid of them."

"Maybe. But let's hold off a little while. I don't want to make a mistake and end up dead."

"Okay. You're probably right. Let me know when you're ready."

"I will. Thanks for your patience, Melanie."

"No problem."

CHAPTER SEVENTEEN

Mid-America Life

It was a cold rainy Saturday. I hadn't slept well because I couldn't keep my mind off of Don and Pam. I was racking my brain for solutions to their growing array of problems. I had finally made contact with Margie's friend, Lucy Patterson, and arranged to meet her for a cup of coffee at Denny's. Lucy was a short blond with pretty blue eyes and a cute smile.

"So, Ms. Mason tells me she was with you Wednesday night, is that right?"

"Uh huh."

"Where did you go?"

"We went to dinner and a movie."

"Oh. Where did you go for dinner?"

"Chili's."

"What time did you get there?"

"About 6:15, I think."

"When did you leave?"

"About an hour later. We went to a movie."

"Where?"

"AMC Park Central."

"Why would you go to movie on a Wednesday night? Isn't that a little odd?"

"No, we go out when we get in the mood. Margie was bored. Luther wasn't going to be home so she called and said let's go to dinner and a movie. Brad, my husband, was away at a sales meeting so I was glad when Margie called."

"Did you go home right after the movie?"

Lucy swallowed, hesitated slightly, and then said, "No, we went to a club after the movie. The Rendezvous Club."

"What time did you get there?"

"About 9:15, I think."

"Did you see anybody there that you knew?"

Lucy smiled and replied, "No, but we had a drink with a couple of guys."

"Do you know their names?"

"No, never saw them before and probably will never see them again."

"Was Ms. Mason with you the entire evening?"

"Uh huh."

"When did you leave?"

"About 10:00 or 10:15, I don't remember exactly, too many margaritas, I guess."

"Did you actually see Margie get into her car?"

"No, we weren't parked close together. We went our separate ways. I didn't see her actually get into her car."

"Well, okay. . . . I appreciate your cooperation."

"You're welcome. I hope you find Luther's killer. I kind of liked him myself."

I smiled, raised my eyebrows and said, "Well, you're the first person I've heard about who didn't hate him—except for Margie, of course. I guess I can take you off the suspect list."

"Most definitely, I promise you I didn't do it," she said with a smile.

After listening to Lucy Patterson verify Margie Mason's alibi, I went to see Clifford Walsh again. I had neglected to ask him a few questions that now seemed pretty important. Since Margie had an alibi, that only left Laura Bell on my list of favorite suspects. Walsh would have the information on her most obvious motive. Walsh's secretary escorted me into his office where I was invited to sit down.

"Sorry to bother you again, but I forgot to ask you

about Luther's insurance."

"Oh, right."

"I know most agents carry a good amount of insurance."

"Yes, to be a good salesman you have to believe in your product. How can you ask someone to buy life insurance if you think so little of it that you don't have any yourself?"

"Good point. So, how much insurance did Luther have on his life?"

"Well, I'll have to pull his personnel file." Walsh picked up the telephone and got his secretary on the intercom. "Get me Luther Bell's personnel file."

After a minute Walsh's secretary came in and handed a file to him. He searched through it and said, "Okay, he had $50,000 group term, $300,000 supplemental term and $400,000 variable life."

"So if he died how much would his beneficiary receive?"

"Seven hundred fifty thousand unless he died accidentally, then it would be $1.5 million."

"And who is the beneficiary?"

Walsh flipped through the file when suddenly his eyes widened and he said, "Well I'll be damned. Luther forgot to remove Laura as beneficiary. She gets everything. That was one of Luther's problems—details— you've got pay attention to details."

"Does Laura Bell know she's still the beneficiary?"

"I wouldn't know. Claims are handled out of New York."

"Would you check and see if she has filed a death claim yet?"

"Sure. Give me a minute. I'll call the claims department."

Walsh asked his secretary to get the claims department on the line. After talking to them for several minutes he hung up the phone.

"No, there hasn't been a claim filed yet."

"Well, thank you for your help, Mr. Walsh."

"No problem, if I can be of any further assistance, just let me know."

I knew better than to jump to conclusions too early in a case. Sure, three quarters of a million dollars was plenty motive for murder, but not everyone was greedy enough to beat someone to death with a tire iron, even for that kind of money. This new revelation, however, had to kick Laura Bell to the front of the long line of suspects. It was obviously time to pay her a visit.

The following morning, Rob and I met Assistant DA Paula Waters at the criminal courts building to prove-up our plea agreement. Rob waited in the courtroom while Paula and I went over the paperwork. I set my briefcase down on the table and rummaged through it to find the paperwork I had prepared.

"Here it is," I said.

"Good. Let me look it over. The judge will be on the bench in a couple minutes."

She took the papers and began to read them. Then she looked up and smiled.

"You remember the first week of contracts?"

She was talking about the first week of law school. It wasn't one of my favorite topics. Law school was very hard for Rebekah and I with four kids and both of us having to work full time. I thought a moment.

"Yeah, vaguely."

"Remember the big pillars in the back of the room. It was so funny. You always sat behind them so Professor Mobley wouldn't call on you."

I blushed and said, "You noticed that?"

She laughed. "Yes, I thought it was so clever."

I smiled. "I had to get to class early. Those seats were prime real estate." I gave Paula a good look. "Yeah, I remember now. You were always raising your hand. You always had the answer."

"It was just a ploy. You see I had a strategy too. The first few days I studied really hard and volunteered a lot in class. Pretty soon Professor Mobley wouldn't call on me anymore so I didn't have to worry about being prepared for class after that. Every once in a while I'd stick up my hand but he'd never call on me."

"We were pretty resourceful, weren't we?"

She nodded. "I just wish we could have spent more time together."

I sighed. "I'm sorry I wasn't more sociable but, you know, working full time and trying to spend a little time with the family didn't leave me much spare time."

"I bet. I don't know how you did it."

"I don't either."

"Don't forget you owe me dinner."

I looked at Paula. I felt guilty—selfish. She knew all about me, what I had been doing—she obviously cared about me but I knew nothing about her. I barely knew she existed. There just wasn't enough time to get to know people. I often regretted not making more friends in law school. It would have been nice to know a few attorneys on a social basis. I said. "I'm looking forward to it. You can fill me in on what you've been doing the last few years."

Her eyes lit up. "Yes, I'd like that."

Our eyes locked for a minute. Finally she looked down at the paperwork and said, "This looks fine."

"Okay, I'll get Rob and we'll wait around for the judge."

The prove-up went well, and Rob was very much relieved to have it behind him. I went back to the office to prepare for Detective Besch's interrogation of Jim Cochran, which was set for 10:00 a.m.

*****

Jim and I had talked a few minutes before the detective arrived and were ready. I cautioned Jim not to volunteer information, but just answer the questions. Jodie served coffee and after a little chit-chat, Detective Besch began the interrogation.

"I guess you heard about Luther Bell?" Detective Besch said.

"Yes, it was terrible."

"I understand you and he were partners?"

"Yes, along with some other folks. It was a restaurant, a Chinese restaurant—the Golden Dragon."

"Margie Mason says you came by her house the other night and threatened Luther, is that right?"

"Well, I was pissed off. You know what that S.O.B. did?"

"No, why don't you tell me."

"We fired him as our manager for gross mismanagement of the partnership business . . . but that's another long story. Anyway, after he had been fired, he changed the partnership address and diverted all of our mail to himself! Can you believe that? Sure, I was pissed. I went over to give him a piece of my mind, but I don't kill people. I'm not a murderer. I'm a businessman. I get mad—sure—but I know how to control my temper."

"Where were you on Wednesday night?"

"At home talking with Don and some of the other partners about how to deal with our deteriorating financial situation."

"When was that?"

"Ah . . . well, let's see. It started about 6:15 or 6:30 and ended maybe an hour later."

"Where did you go when it was over?"

"I was pretty upset, so I drove around awhile."

"So how long is *awhile*?"

"Probably about forty-five minutes. Then I stopped at a club called the Sunset Strip. It wasn't very crowded on Wednesday night so I got lots of attention from the staff, if you know what I mean."

"How long were you there?"

"I don't know. I kind of lost track of time, you know, after a few beers and all those beautiful women."

"Can you give me any names?"

"Sure. Julie. I spent most of the time with a girl named Julie. She'll remember me."

"Do you go to the Sunset Strip often?"

"On occasion."

"Was your wife up when you got home?"

"No, she was in bed. She's a volunteer at the hospital and has to get to work early."

"Your wife doesn't mind you being out late during the week?"

"I'm a workaholic. She doesn't look for me much before nine or ten. She gave up worrying about me years ago."

"So, did you go anywhere after the Sunset Strip?"

"Nope, straight home."

"What time did you get home?"

"I don't know, 10:00 or 10:30. I'm not really sure."

"How long is it from your house to the Sunset Strip?"

"Twenty minutes if there is no traffic."

"Do you know who killed Luther Bell?"

"No. Absolutely not. I'm sure a lot of people would have liked to."

"What about Don Blaylock? Didn't he threaten Luther too?"

"Well, yes, and he had good reason."

"On account of Luther causing his wife to go to jail?"

Jim shook his head affirmatively. "But I've known Don for years and I guarantee you he didn't kill anyone."

"Oh really, he was with you Wednesday night?"

"No."

"Then you can't guarantee anything, can you?"

"I mean, he's not a killer."

Detective Besch raised his eyebrows and said, "Everyone's a killer, Mr. Cochran—given the right circumstances. And from what I've heard, Luther Bell pushed Don Blaylock to the limit."

Jim looked at me then back at Detective Besch.

Detective Besch continued. "He said Luther was going to pay for what he had done to Pam, didn't he?"

Jim didn't answer.

"I'm going to need your fingerprints, a blood sample and a lock of your hair," he said. "I've got someone waiting outside to get it from you."

Jim shrugged.

"Thank you, Mr. Cochran. Don't leave town. I'm pretty sure either you or Don Blaylock murdered Luther Bell, and I promise it won't be long before I know which one of you did it. I'll be in touch."

Jim stood up. "I know you think you've got it all figured out, but you're wrong. We didn't do it."

"Right," Detective Besch said.

I stood up and showed Jim to the door. I whispered, "I want to talk to Detective Besch a minute so I'll call you later, okay?"

"Sure. See you later," he replied.

I went back into my office, closed the door and sat back in my seat. "So, you don't have enough to arrest anybody?" I asked.

"No, I can't figure out which one of your clients did it yet. They all hated Luther, I'm sure."

I smiled. "What about the ex-wife? I heard she pulled a gun on Luther earlier this year."

Detective Besch looked surprised. "Where did you hear that?"

"Walsh—Luther's boss told me about it. The day they split up I guess Luther didn't leave quick enough."

"Funny. Laura Bell didn't mention that to me when I talked to her."

"Funny thing. . . . Did you know she's still the beneficiary on Luther's insurance?"

"I would have thought Luther would have changed that considering the pending divorce," Detective Besch replied.

"According to Walsh he didn't. Three-quarters of a million dollars is a pretty good motive for murder, don't you think?"

Detective Besch shrugged. "Like I said, we're still investigating. We haven't reached any conclusions yet."

"I'm not so sure about Margie Mason either," I said. "I know she has an alibi but going out to a movie on a Wednesday night with a girlfriend and then to a bar seems kind of strange. Why wasn't she with Luther or at home waiting for him?"

"Like you said, she's got an alibi and so far the alibi checks out. Besides, what's her motive? We've established that she's not a beneficiary of the insurance and Luther and she were in love and planned to get married. You don't kill someone you love."

"That kind of blows my mind too."

"What?"

"That anyone could love someone as evil as Luther Bell. How could she stand by and watch Luther do the things he did to Pam and the other investors? She can't be a good person."

Walsh nodded, then stood up. "She may be as evil as Luther but as long as her alibi holds up she's not a suspect. . . . I'm afraid I've got to go. I'm due to testify to the Grand Jury in 20 minutes."

"Just one last question, Detective," I said. "Did you find anything at the crime scene to implicate any of my clients?"

Detective Besch gave me a long stare. Finally he said, "No, not yet."

I stood up and escorted Detective Besch to the door. We shook hands and agreed to let each other know if we turned up anything important.

When Detective Besch had gone I sat back and contemplated our conversation. It was a relief that Detective Besch didn't have any direct evidence to prove any of my clients were at the crime scene. I thanked God for that. After a few minutes I started going through my mail. Midway through the stack I came across a type-written note addressed to me. It looked like a thank you note so I opened it and read it.

Alone
The clock is my worst enemy
It ticks with chilling regularity
You should be next to me, annexed to me
I long for your touch, the warmth of your body
But I'm alone. Always, always alone

The long days without you drain me
I feel weary and subdued
Depression is my only companion
You should be with me, to cheer me
But I"m alone, always, always alone
Your Love

"Oh, my God," I said. "Not another depressing poem from Rebekah." I guessed dinner and flowers the other night had only been a short term fix. I wondered what I could do to let her know how much I really loved her and wanted to be with her every minute. After careful thought I realized I hadn't bought her much jewelry. Money had always been tight so trips to the jewelry store were infrequent. After checking my credit limit on a new VISA card I had acquired, I decided I could spend about $500 for something really nice. On the way home I stopped at Sterling Jewelers hoping to get her a nice tennis bracelet. A friendly clerk showed me everything they had and I ended up spending $628 and some change. It was after eight when I got home.

"Well, look what the cat brought in," Rebekah said.

"I'm sorry, but I had an important errand to run."

"I hope it was worth missing supper."

I knew she was kidding. She liked to complain when I was late, but her mission in life had always been to take good care of me and the kids. She would never let me go hungry.

"It was. . . . I got something for you."

She looked at me suspiciously.

"What is it?"

I handed her the blue velvet box my gift came in.

She smiled. "What's with you? You got a girlfriend or something?"

I laughed. "Yeah, sure. I have so much spare time."

She opened the box. Her eyes widened. "Stanley Turner. My God. Did you win the Irish Sweepstakes?"

"No, I charged it."

She gave me a dirty look. "What possessed you to do that?"

"You should know."

She frowned. "It's so beautiful. All my friends are going to be jealous. But, how do you plan to pay for it?"

"A few bucks at a time."

She shook her head. "Hmm. Put it on me, would you?"

"Sure." I took it out of the box and fastened it around her wrist. She smiled and then embraced me. We kissed. I was about to ease her toward the bedroom when Marcia wandered in.

"Daddy! There you are. Did you get lost?"

"No, sweetpea. I didn't. I bought Mommy a present."

Rebekah stuck out her wrist.

"Oh, it's so pretty, Mommy. It's the prettiest bracelet I've ever seen. How much did it cost, Daddy?"

"Marcia, you are not supposed to ask that question," Rebekah said.

She squinted. "Why not?"

"The price doesn't matter. It's the thought that counts," Rebekah said.

"I bet it cost a million dollars," Marcia exclaimed.

We both laughed and soon the rest of the family gathered to look at Rebekah's new bracelet. The kids were duly impressed and Rebekah seemed to be thoroughly enjoying the attention she was getting. I wondered where in the hell she had got the idea to write me poetry. I figured she must have run across a magazine article—*Rekindling the Romance in Your Marriage* or *How to Lay A Guilt Trip on Your Man*. Most of the ladies' magazines seemed to be full of those types of stories. Or maybe she got the idea while helping Reggi with his poetry assignments from school. Anyway, whatever the source, it was working like a charm.

* * * * *

The following day, Rob brought Jennifer to my office so the attorney for the Estate of Dr. Windsor could take her deposition. Don was already there reading a magazine in the reception room. Jodie greeted them and asked if she could get them anything. They declined so she showed all of them into the conference room. When Jodie told me everyone was there, I joined them. We exchanged greetings.

"Thanks for coming by early," I said. "I wanted to fill you in on my progress on the investigation and find out how everyone is coping with all that's been going on. I guess my first question is: How's Pam?"

Don closed his eyes. Jennifer looked away.

Rob said, "Not well, after Friday night."

"Oh, no. What happened now?"

Rob shook his head and then began telling the story.

CHAPTER EIGHTEEN

The Wedding

Jennifer and Rob had stopped by to see Pam and Don early Friday night. When they walked in the kitchen, Pam and Don were sitting at the table arguing. The conversation was so intense, neither noticed Rob and Jennifer enter the room. The argument was about Pam's refusal to leave the house. Even though it had been nearly two weeks since her arrest, Pam was only just beginning to venture out of the bedroom. Don was trying to coax her out to dinner and a movie, which was their usual Friday night routine.

"'What's hiding out in the house going to accomplish?'" Don asked.

"'If they don't see me, maybe they won't think about what happened. I couldn't bear to look into Melinda's eyes after what she witnessed. You don't know how women talk. . . . Maybe we should move.'"

"'Move! We just bought this house less than two years ago. I love my job and the kids love it here.'"

"'We could move to Garland or Plano.'"

"'Honey, I think you underestimate your friends. They'll understand that you were the victim here. They won't hold it against you.'"

"'Oh sure, they'll tell me how sorry they are, and what a terrible mistake it was, but when I'm not around, they'll laugh at me and wonder if I'm guilty. . . . I'm resigning as president of Junior League.'"

"'Oh honey. You've worked so hard to get that job, and you love being Junior League president. You can't resign.'"

"'I already did. I sent a letter to the secretary this morning.'"

"'That will just make them think that you *are* guilty.'"

"'It doesn't matter if I'm guilty or not, the damage has been done. I'm ruined.'"

"'I think you're really overreacting here, honey. It's not the end of the world.'"

Rob coughed. Don looked over at him. "'Hi, Dad,'"Rob said.

Don, trying to smile, replied, "'Hi, guys."

"'Hello, Mrs. Blaylock,'" Jennifer said. "'Are you feeling any better at all?'"

"'A little,'" Pam replied, obviously embarrassed that they'd caught them quarreling.

"'Well, we came by to tell you the good news,'" Rob said.

Don smiled."'Good news? We could use some good news. What is it?'"

Rob put his arm around Jennifer and gave her a squeeze. "'We got married.'"

Don frowned. "'Married?'"

"'We probably should have told you, but with all that was going on we just decided to do it. We just came from the Justice of the Peace.'"

Pam, with a look of horror on her face, said, "'Why didn't you tell us? I can't believe I missed my son's wedding!'"

"'With all the problems with the restaurant and everything, we didn't want you to have to spend money on a wedding,'"Rob said.

"'You have to get married in the church, it's not right to just go to a JP,'"Pam scolded. "'I can't believe this! . . . I might as well jump off a bridge. What's the use of living?'"Pam burst into tears.

Jennifer began to cry too. She said,"'I knew we should have told them, Rob.'"

"'It's my fault, Mom. Jennifer wanted to tell you guys and at least have a small wedding, but I talked her out of it. I just didn't want to be a burden right now. We can have a big wedding later, after all this mess is over.'"

"'Okay, everybody calm down,'" Don said. "'We're happy you are married. It just wasn't the way we had planned it. Your mother is just disappointed. You know how women live for weddings.'"

Pam suddenly turned and looked Don straight in the eye. "'Look what you've done! You've ruined my life. Why did you have to make that God damned investment! We didn't need it. We were doing just fine. Damn it, Don! Why did you do it? I just want to die.'"

Pam stormed off toward the bedroom. They heard the door slam shut. Don yelled, "'You can't blame this entire fiasco on me!'" He glared at Rob. "'I'm not the only one around here who screwed up!'" Jennifer and Rob stood silently, dumbfounded at what was happening. Don got up abruptly knocking over his chair. "'I don't need this shit!'" he said, and then stormed out the back door, slamming it behind him.

CHAPTER NINETEEN

Deposition

They all looked at me across the conference table with solemn faces. It was time for me to try to pick them up, but I didn't know if I could. It seemed no matter how hard they tried to make things right, the situation only got worse. Don and Pam were on the verge of self-destruction and none of us seemed to know how to stop it.

"I am so sorry all of this is happening to you." I said. "I wish I could do more to relieve your pain. There's just no simple solution for all of your problems."

"I know you are doing all you can, Stan," Don said.

The court reporter walked in and started setting up at the head of the table. We watched in silence as a video camera was placed across from the witnesses chair. Jodie brought in coffee and refreshments and set them on a small table. She asked if anyone needed anything and then left.

After another long moment of silence Jodie brought in Mr. Schultz and Dr. Windsor's young widow. When everyone had been introduced, the court reporter asked for the correct spelling of everyone's name.

"All right, I guess everybody's ready, huh?" I asked.

"Yes, I believe so," Schultz replied.

"Okay, do you want to go with Jennifer first?"

"Yes, that would be fine."

"Jennifer, if you'll sit across from the court reporter we'll get started," I said, turning to Schultz. "The usual agreements—reserve objections until the time of trial except the form of the question and responsiveness?" I asked.

Attorneys in Texas usually agreed to waive objections to the time of trial in order to expedite the taking of the deposition. If the deposition was taken subject to the rules of evidence, it could take days to complete and if disputes arose there would be no judge available to settle them. There would then have to be a hearing and possibly another session to complete the deposition.

"Okay," Schultz replied and then began his questioning of the witness. The most significant portions of the testimony were as follows:

"Page 1
Q. Please state your name for the record?
A. Jennifer Blaylock.
Q. Blaylock? I'm sorry I thought it was *Rich*?
A. It was, I was recently married to Mr. Blaylock's son, Rob.
Q. Oh, I see. Where are you residing?
A. The same address. Rob moved into my mom's house.

Page 28
Q. While you were in the warehouse how many drinks did you have?
Mr. Turner. Objection, assumes facts not in evidence, ambiguous as to what *drinks* means.
Q. I'll rephrase. While you were in the warehouse did you drink any alcoholic beverages?"
A. Yes
Q. What did you drink?
A. Beer.
Q. How many did you have?
A. One.
Q. Just one?
Mr. Turner: Objection. Asked and answered.

A. One.
Q. Earlier in the evening did you have any beer or other alcoholic beverages?
A. Yes, I had a beer at Rob's house.
Q. Just one?
A. Just one.

Page 57
Q. Okay, so after the police left with Rob and his friend, what did you do?
A. We went home.
Q. What route did you take?
A. We went south on Central Expressway to I-30 and then went toward Mesquite . . . ah . . . east I guess that would be.
Q. How fast were you going?
A. I don't remember. I was just going along with the flow of traffic.
Q. Do you know what the speed limit was?
A. Ah . . . well, I presume it was 55.
Q. You presume, but you don't know for sure?
A. I wouldn't swear to what it was . . . but I'm pretty sure it was fifty-five.
Q. So you went along with the flow of traffic, right?
A. Yes.
Q. So, if the traffic was going 55 then you would have been going 55.
A. Right.
Q. And, if the traffic had been going 75, you would have been going 75.
A. I don't think I was going 75.
Q. Objection, non responsive. You said you were going with the traffic flow, right?
A. Yes.
Q. Then if the traffic was going 75 you would have been going 75, right?

Mr. Turner. Objection. Calls for speculation.
A. I guess.
Q. So you were speeding.
Mr. Turner. Objection! Calls for a legal conclusion, improper question, mischaracterization of the testimony. I instruct the witness not to answer the question.
Q. So if the traffic was speeding then you were speeding?
Mr. Turner. Objection. Calls for speculation. I instruct the witness not to answer the question.

Page 88
Q. Why did you veer into the left lane in front of Dr. Windsor's car?
A. Because suddenly, out of nowhere, there was a red convertible in front of me. It must've come up the on-ramp. I came up on it so fast I had to turn to avoid hitting it.
Q. So you took your eyes off the road for a minute?
A. Not a minute. Just a second or two.
Q. So you took your eyes off the road for a second or two and when you looked back at the road in front of you there was a red convertible which you were about to hit?
A. Exactly. There was nothing else to do but to swerve to the left to avoid the collision.
Q. Did you look to your left before you swerved?
A. No, there wasn't time.
Q. Did you look in your rear view mirror or side mirror to see if anyone was in the lane next to you?
A. No, I told you there was no time.
Q. So without looking or even considering the consequences of swerving into the left lane you did it anyway?
A. I didn't have time. I told you, I didn't have time!
Q. Objection. Non-responsive. Please answer yes or no.
A. What's the question again?
Q. So without looking or even considering the

consequences of swerving into the left lane you did it anyway?
A. I guess . . . yes.
Q. And what happened when you swerved into the left lane without regard to who or what was there?
A. I hit his . . . I hit the doctor's car.
Q. And he died as a result of your carelessness, isn't that right Ms. Blaylock?
Mr. Turner. Objection. Calls for a legal conclusion. I'm instructing the witness not to answer the question.

At the conclusion of Jennifer's deposition I took Don, Rob and Jennifer to lunch at my favorite Italian restaurant, Carelli's. Jennifer was very happy to have her deposition over and was feeling pretty good. Don, on the other hand, looked a little pale.

"So Mr. Turner, I hope I didn't hurt our case," Jennifer said.

"No, you did okay. I don't think there's much else you could have said. The facts are the facts. Unfortunately, we don't know who was driving the convertible. That's the person who ought to be paying for Dr. Windsor's death."

"How do you think it looks, Stan?" Don asked.

"Well, without proof of the red convertible, it doesn't look too good . . . for Jennifer anyway. As for you, they've got a tough burden to prove you were negligent and responsible for Jennifer getting into the accident."

"What happens if they get a judgment against Jennifer?" Rob asked.

"Well, you kids don't have anything so it will be a worthless piece of paper. This is Texas, where you can own a house and considerable personal property and no creditor can touch it. All they can do is abstract the judgment and hope sometime you'll be foolish enough to buy some non-exempt real estate in Dallas County where the judgment would be filed."

"That wouldn't ever happen," Don laughed.

"True, they're really after *you*, Don. You know we might be able to put an end to this whole thing right now if you'll give me permission to tell them a little lie?" I said.

"Tell them a lie?"

"I know you and Pam would never file bankruptcy. You've both made that perfectly clear but—"

"But what?"

"Well, they don't know that. If I just lay the cards on the table they might pack their bags and go home."

Don looked at me and frowned. "Pam would never go for it. She'd kill me if I let you represent to someone that we were going to file bankruptcy."

I took a deep breath and replied, "Well if I don't actually say you're going to file bankruptcy would it be okay? If I just implied it?"

Don raised his eyebrows and replied, "I guess it can't hurt. Just be sure you don't say we're going to file. If she ever thought I had allowed you to say that, she'd kill me."

"Don't worry, I won't." I smiled and looked at Rob and Jennifer and said, "You two okay with this?"

Rob looked at Jennifer and she nodded affirmatively. Rob shrugged and said, "I guess pride is not important at a time like this."

"No, it's not. The important thing is to get this thing over with so you all can go on with your lives."

After lunch I asked to have a private conference with Mr. Schultz. I took him into my office and closed the door.

"Okay, Bob. Do you mind if I call you Bob?"

"No, that's fine."

"You and I both know litigation is expensive," I said. "God knows how much you've already spent prosecuting this case. Now for some reason the insurance company saw fit to deposit three hundred grand into the registry of the court. I don't know why they did it. Frankly, I don't think your case is that good."

"They must have thought it was pretty good," Schultz replied.

"Apparently they did, and it's done. There's nothing I can do about it. I know you and your client are feeling pretty good right now. You're on a roll and you'd like to get what . . . another two or three hundred thousand? I don't think you're naive enough to think you're going to get $2.5 million."

"You never know."

"True, but I just wanted to point out a few things to you. There are a few facts you probably don't know, but you need to know, to properly analyze your position here. . . . Jennifer Blaylock is just a kid. She's pregnant and may never get a high school diploma. She has no money. Her mother is divorced and is barely surviving. If you go ahead with this lawsuit I'm going to slap her into bankruptcy so fast your judgment won't be worth much more than the envelope it comes in."

Schultz shook his head and smiled, "You think I'm stupid or something? Why do you think we sued the owner of the car?"

"Exactly. I understood your thinking. . . . Don Blaylock is a successful businessman. He's got some assets you can get to. You probably think he's good for the two or three hundred thousand dollars, right? . . . Ha!" I laughed. "I'm afraid not."

I got up, gazed out the window for a moment and then continued, "This would ordinarily be attorney-client privileged information, but my client very reluctantly has authorized me to tell you this."

I turned around and looked Schultz in the eye. . . . "He's broke! Flat ass broke! You've probably heard about Luther Bell's murder, right?"

"Yes, I've read about it in the newspaper."

"Well, he got Mr. Blaylock into a franchise deal that went sour. Don's lost everything. Between the IRS, the comptroller, and the bank there ain't nothing left. So, if you get a judgment against him, guess what?"

Schultz frowned and replied, "Bankruptcy. . . . I get the picture."

I nodded. "So, as I see it right now your firm has made out like a bandit. You've got . . . what . . . fifty hours in this case so far? Let me see, your one-third is one hundred thousand dollars divided by fifty . . . ah, $2,000 an hour. Wow! Don't you love this profession?!"

"We've actually got over sixty hours in the case."

"But if you continue this case, before you know it you'll have what— two, three hundred hours? Oh . . . and those expert witness fees, investigators, court reporters . . . Jesus! How much do you think they will run? How do you think your client will like paying all those expenses?"

Schultz got up and walked over to the window and stared at the cars traveling down Central Expressway.

"Oh," I continued. "I forgot. Don's a prime suspect in the Luther Bell murder."

Schultz turned and glared at me.

"Well, I just mean he may be in prison. You're not going to be able to collect anything from him if he's in prison, are you?"

Schultz threw up his hands and said, "Okay. . . . You made your point. I need to talk to my client."

"Please do. I think it would be a very wise thing to do."

After a brief discussion with his client, Schultz indicated they would settle for what had been tendered. We shook hands and they left. I called everyone in and gave them the good news. "Well, it's over. They're going to accept the $300,000 as a complete and final settlement of the case. Our little deception worked like a charm."

"You didn't tell him we were going to file bankruptcy, did you?" Don asked.

"No, I told him you were the prime suspect in Luther Bell's murder. You should have seen his face."

Don thought for moment and then burst out laughing.

"That's right . . . I'm damn good with a tire iron."

Feeling a little better with one more problem resolved, I went home early and took the family out to dinner. It was Thursday, our bowling night, so we headed over to Triangle Bowling alley when we were done. Reggi, Mark, and I were in a church league. None of us were great bowlers, but we always had a lot of fun. Rebekah usually came with Peter and Marcia to watch. In between turns, I brainstormed with Rebekah about Luther's murder.

"I just can't see a man repeatedly hitting Luther the way the killer did. Luther's murder had the mark of a woman. It was a crime of passion or fear, or both.

"So, who do you think did it?" Rebekah asked.

"Well, the obvious list includes Pam, Wanda, Margie and Laura Bell.

"Dad, you're up," Reggi said. I looked over at him and smiled. "Okay, I'm coming."

After retrieving my ball, I took center stage. All eyes were on me. Having never taken bowling lessons, I was a straight shooter. This meant even if I hit the pocket I still was likely to leave a couple pins and if I missed the pocket and hit the first pin, I'd get a split. My unprofessional approach to resolving this problem was to get way over to one side or the other and try to hit the pocket at an angle. Sometimes this would work but more often than not, it wouldn't. I took a deep breath, took a few strides toward the pins, and let it go. The ball went straight for the pocket. All the pins scattered except one which stood like a rock in a raging surf.

"Damn," I said.

"It's okay, Dad. You'll get the spare," Reggi said.

Rebekah said, "You don't think Pam did it, do you?"

"I don't know. She seems extremely traumatized by all that's been happening. I wouldn't be shocked if it turned out she did do it. I hope she didn't, but—"

"I know she didn't do it. I know her. It wouldn't even cross her mind. . . . But if it had been *me* . . . yes, I would have definitely killed the bastard!"

I didn't laugh. She was telling the truth. Rebekah would have had no tolerance for someone messing with her life the way Luther had done. Although generally sweet and kind, if you threatened her family she'd become your worst enemy and your worst nightmare. Few people knew this about her as this dark part of her personality rarely surfaced, but I knew it only too well. I still wondered if she had killed Sheila Logan, the lonely wife of one of my clients who had lured me into a cabin for sensual pleasures. Nothing happened, but it might have had I not knocked over a kerosene lamp and set the cabin ablaze. Later that night, after being in a car wreck and ending up in the emergency ward at the hospital where Rebekah was working, Sheila mysteriously died. When I had pressed Rebekah on the issue after the murder charges against her were dropped, she refused to flatly deny it. She just shrugged and gave me a wry smile.

I said, "I'm going to focus on Margie and Laura. They are the most likely ones to have killed him."

"What about Wanda?" Rebekah asked.

"I can't see Wanda doing it. She is so quiet, gentle, and loving. It would be totally out of character."

Rebekah raised her eyebrows. "It's the quiet ones you have to watch out for."

I laughed. "Right, I know."

CHAPTER TWENTY

Laura Bell

The next morning, I stopped by Laura Bell's apartment. She was my best suspect. She had a motive and had shown a propensity for violence in the past. I prayed she didn't have an alibi. Her house was located in a lower middle class neighborhood in Balch Springs. I climbed the stairs to the second floor, found apartment number 221 and rang the doorbell. After a minute, the door opened and a pretty dishwater blond, about twenty-five years of age, greeted me with a warm smile. I introduced myself and told her why I was there. She invited me in.

I entered the room and looked around. The apartment was immaculate, which surprised me a little. A little girl was playing in the corner with a Fisher Price gas station. She looked up at me curiously.

"Would you like some coffee?" Laura asked.

"Sure, I could use a cup."

Laura went into the kitchen and fixed some coffee. She returned shortly and handed me a Texas A&M mug and then sat down.

"Did you go to Texas A&M?"

"No, one of my brothers did. I wanted to go, but Luther and I got married instead."

"When did you hear about Luther's murder?"

"It was on the news in San Antonio. Friday, I think."

"You were in San Antonio when the murder took place?"

"Yes, that's where I'm from. My family is still there."

A shroud of disappointment fell over me. *She has an*

alibi, damn it. "How long had you been down there?"

"About ten days."

"Ten days?"

"Yeah. . . . One of my sisters got married."

"Oh. Was it a big wedding?"

"Pretty big. There were about three hundred and fifty guests. We've got a big family and the groom was from San Antonio, too."

"When was it?"

"Saturday night. I stayed down there since there wasn't really much I could do up here. I didn't see any reason to miss the wedding. Luther's parents were arranging the funeral so there wasn't really anything for me to do anyway. We flew back Monday afternoon and went straight to the funeral home. We didn't get back here until late last night."

"Where were you Wednesday evening?"

"At the rehearsal dinner. The groom's parents had a dinner for everyone at the Marriott Hotel on the Riverwalk. It was so romantic. I hope my sister's marriage works out better than mine did."

"So, what happened to you and Luther?"

"He had a lot of great ideas, but he could never put anything together right. He wasn't good with the follow-through, you know. First he wanted to be a minister, then he sold cars, then it was the stock market, commodities, and finally life insurance. He never was very good at anything, and he always blamed someone else for his problems. I just got tired of his empty promises."

"So, you decided to divorce him?"

Laura took a deep breath and replied, "Yes, we weren't getting anywhere. He blamed a lot of his failures on me. One day I woke up and realized it was never going to work. I'd be living in a dingy little apartment like this for the rest of my life, if I stayed with Luther."

What about for better or for worse? I didn't say it but Laura Bell apparently could read my mind.

"Well actually that wasn't the reason I left him. It was the broken promises, lies, deception, and adultery."

"He cheated on you?"

"Huh," Laura laughed. "He'd come home late at night smelling of perfume. His favorite line was: 'Oh, well I was sitting next to some broad who had taken a bath in her perfume.' Can you believe I'm supposed to swallow that shit?! The kicker though was when I found the bite mark on his shoulder. I hadn't had sex with him in weeks so I knew I hadn't left the mark. It was the proof I needed. There was no doubt in my mind when I saw that bite that he had been unfaithful."

"What about your child?"

"Betsy and I do just fine. Someday I'll get her a nice father, someone who can love her and take care of her the way a father should."

"Are you dating anyone now?"

I wanted to take that question back. It was none of my business but Laura Bell didn't bat an eye.

"No. I haven't found anyone I really like yet. But I will, just give me time."

"All right. Well, I'm sorry I had to bother you."

"No bother, I enjoyed talking to you. Good luck with the investigation."

"Oh, one more thing. How are you going to get by without Luther's child support?"

Laura shrugged. "I don't know, I was going to ask his parents if they might help out. They really love little Betsy. They're good people. You know Luther's father is a preacher, right?"

"Yeah, I heard that. . . . What about Luther's insurance?"

"Insurance? Well, I don't know if he still had any. After he quit Mid-America Life I doubt if he kept up the payments. The premiums were pretty high and Luther was short on cash," Laura said. "If he did have any I suspect he changed the beneficiary to his parents, or maybe even Margie."

"What if I told you he kept up all his insurance and you were still the beneficiary? Since your divorce was never finalized, the insurance proceeds will still go to you."

Laura gave me a puzzled look, "Are you serious?"

"Yes, you're the beneficiary of three policies with a face amount of $750,000."

Laura put her hand up to her mouth and said, "Oh my God! I can't believe it. I just figured the insurance was history. This is the first promise Luther ever kept."

"What do you mean?"

"He always said if he died I wouldn't have to worry about money."

"Huh. Well, don't spend the money yet, the insurance company won't pay the claim until the murderer is apprehended."

"Oh really?"

"Uh huh, they've got to be careful they don't give the money to the murderer. By law the murderer cannot collect on the policy."

"They don't think *I* did it, do they?"

"No. It's not up to them to make that determination. Insurance companies just don't take chances, particularly if it gives them a good excuse to hang onto their money."

After talking to Laura, I called Detective Besch. I wanted to see if he had developed any evidence yet against my clients. I used my meeting with Laura Bell as an excuse to call him.

"Laura seemed genuinely surprised when I told her she was still the beneficiary on Luther's insurance," I said.

"Really? Maybe she was," Detective Besch replied.

"I don't know, but she does appear to have a good alibi."

"The wedding?"

"Right. You've talked to her."

"Another detective did. He told me about the alibi,"

Detective Besch said.

"So what about Jim's alibi? Have you checked it out?"

"Yes. It was very interesting. Jim was there Wednesday night, but I'm not sure how long. Some of the girls think he left around nine or so."

"Really?" I said. "When I talked to them they were talking more like nine-thirty or ten. That wouldn't give him time to get to Luther's house before the murder took place."

"Well, I understand your client laid a lot of cash on the dancers so I'm sure they would love to provide him an alibi. But that doesn't mean a jury will buy it."

"I agree. I still have one more witness to interview. She is supposed to know Jim better than anyone and might be able to pin down to the precise time of departure. I clocked it from the Sunset Strip to Luther's house and it took about thirty-seven minutes without traffic. So he would have had to leave the club before nine," I added.

"More or less. The time of death is only an approximation."

"Right.... What about the Rendezvous Club? Have you checked out Margie's alibi?"

"Yes, there seems to be some question as to when the girls left and who they left with."

"That's my reading too," I said. "Margie and Lucy said they left about ten, but the bartender remembers nine-thirty. Of course, that was after I gave him $20 to refresh his memory."

"You can go broke paying for information, Stan."

"Hell, I'm already there. . . . So, how long does it take to get from the Rendezvous Club to Luther's condo?"

"Seventeen minutes," Detective Besch replied.

"How sure are you about the time of death?"

"The coroner's 9:30 p.m. estimate is based on a bacteria study."

"Bacteria study?"

"Yeah, the body decomposes at a certain rate

depending on the temperature, humidity, et cetera. By examining the bacteria that have appeared and developed, they can interpolate the time of death."

"Okay. So they might be off a few minutes?"

"I would think the margin of error could be ten or fifteen minutes."

"Well, I'll let you know if I dig up anything new."

"Do that," Detective Besch said.

I hung up feeling pretty good. It still didn't seem the police had come up with any evidence against my clients. That was good news. Then, just when I thought the Blaylock's fortunes had taken a turn for the better, Rob called.

"Dad just tried to commit suicide! I don't know what to do."

"I'm on my way," I said, and hung up the phone.

CHAPTER TWENTY-ONE

The Last Straw

I arrived twenty minutes later. Rob and Don were sitting on the sofa. Jennifer was biting her fingernails as she gazed out the window. Don looked like he hadn't slept all night. He was sweaty and unshaven. His shirt was half untucked and he smelled like booze. A gun lay on the coffee table. I swallowed hard.

"What happened, Don? You look terrible," I said.

He looked up at me with pain in his eyes. "Oh, Stan. She's gone. Pam is gone!"

"I'm so sorry, Don. What happened?"

Over the next hour Don, Rob and Jennifer explained what had happened. They told me Don had been optimistic about the future after our last meeting, and that he had felt better than he had for months. He couldn't wait to get home and tell Pam the good news. I could visualize the scene in my mind's eye. After parking his car in the driveway, Don hurried inside.

"Pam, guess what? . . . Pam . . . Where are you?" he called.

Don searched the house for Pam, but she wasn't there. *Damn it, where are you?* He looked in the back yard but only saw Rip pacing back and forth at the back door wanting to get in to see him. Then he noticed a note on the kitchen table. He picked it up and read it.

Dear Don,

Donna, Greg and I have gone to my mother's. Like I told you, I just can't sit around here and watch our lives fall apart. I need some time to breathe. All the stress and turmoil isn't good for Donna and Greg either. Please don't be mad at me. I don't blame you for what happened, it doesn't matter who's at fault. I guess we had the good life and never really appreciated it.

Maybe God is punishing us for taking for granted all the wonderful things He has given us. We had such a great life, didn't we? It seems now to be just a distant memory. Whatever happens to us I want you to know that I love you and if I die tomorrow, I'll die in peace because I had so many wonderful years with you.

Love, Pam

He crumpled up the paper and threw it into the trash can, "Shit! Damn it! Why didn't she wait one more day?"

He went to the phone and called Pam's mother's house. The phone rang and rang but nobody answered. After twenty or thirty rings he gave up and slammed the phone down. Then he just collapsed into a chair in despair.

After awhile he got up and called American Airlines. *I'm not going to let my family slip through my fingers. The worst is over, life will be back to normal soon. I'll tell her how Stan talked Mrs. Windsor's attorney into dropping the wrongful death suit. I'll convince her to come home, I know she'll listen.*

He rushed into his bedroom and threw some clothes

into a suitcase. He forced it closed and headed for the front door. Before he reached it, the doorbell rang. He stopped. *What now?* He put down his suitcase and opened the door.

A deputy constable stood at the door holding some papers. "Don Blaylock?" he asked.

"What is it!" he screamed. "What do you want?"

He gave him a startled look and said sternly,"You've been sued."

"Who the hell this time!?"

The deputy looked at the paper and replied, "It says Venture Management Co."

"Oh Jesus! The landlord. How much blood does he want?"

"I don't know. Read it yourself. I'm sure it will say."

The deputy handed him the papers and then turned and left. He slammed the door and ripped the papers opened and began reading them. *Two hundred and eighty-five thousand dollars.* "This is bullshit! God damn it!"

He couldn't believe it. He threw down the paper and kicked over a coffee table. His face was getting hot, and his head felt like it was going to explode.

"I can't believe this!" He screamed. He dropped to his knees and began to cry uncontrollably. "What did I do to deserve this?"

Suddenly he remembered his gun."I'll show Pam who's had enough." He walked quickly into the bedroom and opened the drawer to the night stand. The Colt .38 revolver was under some t-shirts. He pulled them off and gave the gun a hard stare. His hands trembled as he slowly lifted it toward his mouth. He was sweating profusely as his lips felt the cold steel barrel. He closed his eyes and tried to pull the trigger, but his strength was gone. He opened his eyes and took a deep breath. *I don't want to live without Pam.* He closed his eyes again and summoned every once of strength he could and with one last rush of adrenalin, squeezed the trigger. *Click.*

Two hours later Jennifer and Rob came by the house to check on Don. The house was dark. They turned on a lamp and looked around.

"Dad! . . . Mom! Is anybody home?" Rob yelled.

Rob began to search the house as Jennifer stood by the front door. He went into the kitchen and saw the crumpled note on the floor. He picked it up and read it quickly. Panic overcame him as he feared the worst. He rushed back into the living room. Jennifer was holding the citation with a distressed look on her face.

"What is it?" he asked.

"It's another lawsuit . . . two hundred and eighty-five thousand dollars."

"What?" he said, and continued his frantic search of the house. He went in the bedroom and turned on the light. Don was lying face down on the carpet with the Colt .38 next to him.

"Oh my God! Dad . . . Dad . . . What have you done?!"

Jennifer came running in and screamed, "Oh, Rob. No!"

He picked him up and held him in his arms and cried, "Dad . . . dad . . . no . . . no."

"Is he dead?" Jennifer asked.

"I don't know, call an ambulance!"

Suddenly he began to stir. "Pam? . . . Pam?" he moaned.

"It's all right, Dad. Just relax. Everything's going to be okay."

His eyes began to focus and his memory began to slowly return. Then he mumbled. "Shit! It wasn't loaded was it? Damn it! I always keep it loaded."

"Dad, why would you try to kill yourself? I don't understand this."

"Your mom left me. My life is over. . . . Why fight it?"

CHAPTER TWENTY-TWO

Reluctant Witness

It was 11:55 a.m., and I was camped out in the lobby of One Main Place. I looked nervously at my watch. Marilyn Watson, an eye witness to the killing of Anant Ravi was supposed to meet me. She had resisted this meeting, canceling several times for one reason or another. I wasn't sure what her problem was, but I needed her testimony desperately. I watched load after load of humanity pop out of each elevator, anxious for an hour of relief from the day's toil.

At 12:15 I was about to give up when I spotted a well-dressed young lady lingering in the lobby. Not knowing exactly what Marilyn Watson looked like, I walked over to the woman and said, "Mrs. Watson?"

"Yes, are you Stan Turner?"

"Right. . . . I'm so glad we finally were able to get together."

"I'm sorry I had to cancel last time, but my daughter was sick."

"I understand. Let's go get some lunch. How much time do you have?"

"I've got an hour."

"Good. This is your turf, where do you suggest we eat?"

"There's a deli downstairs in the basement."

"Good. Lead the way."

We made our way down the escalator to the underground mall and walked a few blocks until we came to a place called Max's Deli. We went inside and found a table. After ordering lunch, I began to question her.

"So, you have a daughter. How old is she?"

"Eight."

"Are you married?"

"No, divorced."

"It must be tough bringing up a daughter alone."

"We get along okay."

"I've got an eight-year-old daughter myself. She's sweet, but she's got three older brothers watching out for her. I pity anyone who tries to date her."

"Four kids! I don't know how anyone could keep up with four kids."

"Luckily, my wife takes care of them. I don't have to worry about them until I get home at night."

"I wish all I had to do was stay home and watch my baby."

"That would be nice. . . . So tell me, where were you going on the day Anant Ravi was killed?"

"I was on my way to Texas Commerce Bank. I had been paid and needed to deposit my check."

"Where were you when you first saw Mr. Ravi?"

"I was on traveling northbound on Wycliff Avenue. I stopped for the light signal at Lemmon Avenue. Mr. Ravi was crossing the street just off to my right."

"Why don't you tell me what you saw."

"Like I said, I had pulled up to the traffic signal when I noticed a well-dressed man waiting to cross the street. The light changed and I started to go across the intersection when I noticed this brown car barreling down on the intersection apparently trying to beat the light. I delayed to let him clear, but I noticed the man had started to walk across the intersection, oblivious to what was happening. I knew almost immediately that he was going to get hit because he was walking quickly across the street looking straight ahead."

Marilyn began to cry and continued, "It was horrible, the brown car hit the man and he flew straight up into the air. Then he came down on the car's front window smashing it."

"Oh God. What happened next?"

"The body kind of rolled along the top of the car and fell to the pavement. The man in the brown car finally slammed on his brakes, and the car spun completely around and came to a stop."

"Did the driver try to stop before he hit Mr. Ravi?"

"No."

"Did he try to swerve out of the way or evade him in any manner?"

"No, he just hit him head on without even slowing down."

"How fast was he going?"

"I'm not sure."

"Well, was he going about as fast as the other traffic?"

"No, faster."

"Well, how fast do you think?"

"Fifty-five, maybe sixty."

"When the car came to a halt, what did the driver do?"

"He just sat in his car."

"He didn't get out at all?"

"No, several bystanders went over to see if they could do anything for the victim. I found a pay phone and called the police, but the driver just sat there until the police came. They should throw the book at him. It was a horrible thing he did."

"That's what we're hoping will happen. Did you give a statement to the police?"

"Yes, I told them what I saw, and they said they would be in touch. A private investigator called me too."

"Really?"

"Yeah, he said he worked for some lawyer."

"Right. That would be the driver's criminal attorney,

I'm sure. . . . Well, I'm going to need your testimony at trial. It probably won't be for a year or two."

She frowned. "I can't testify."

"What?"

"I don't want to get involved. I've already told everybody what happened. The investigator said I didn't have to testify if I didn't want to."

"Well, that's not true. You can be subpoenaed, but I don't want to do that. You said it was horrible seeing Mr. Ravi killed. Don't you want to see Mr. Banks brought to justice?"

"He'll get off anyway. It doesn't really matter if I testify or not."

"That's not true. If he was speeding, then he was negligent as a matter of law, and Mr. Ravi's family can recover damages against him. Your testimony will be critical."

"The investigator said I could be in serious trouble if my testimony wasn't one hundred percent accurate. I can't afford to get into trouble. I've got my daughter to think of."

I shook my head. "Believe me. You can't get into trouble by testifying. Mr. Banks' investigator is just trying to scare you because he knows your testimony will hurt his client."

"Maybe so, but I can't afford to take any chances."

"Listen, the only way you can get into trouble is if you don't testify when subpoenaed, or if you are untruthful. Just get up there and tell the truth, and everything will be fine, okay?"

"We'll see."

You'll see?! I glared at her. I was shaken by her attitude. Her testimony was just what we needed to nail Richard Banks and get a big judgment, but now I had to worry about whether she would show up or, if she did show up, whether she'd have a lapse of memory.

*****

That night after dinner I went to my study to work on some wills that I had brought home to finish. The clients were coming in to sign them the next morning, and I still had a few corrections to make. When I opened a drawer, I saw Jim's gun. I had brought it home with me after Don had tried to commit suicide.

"Why do you have a gun?"

"It's Don's. I figured I better hang on to it until he gets better. There aren't any bullets, so it's harmless."

She frowned. "I don't care. I don't like having it in the house."

"I'll lock it up in the drawer to my desk. Only you and I have a key, so it should be safe to keep it there."

She looked at me skeptically, then turned, and left the room. My thoughts turned back to Don. I wondered how anyone could be depressed enough that he'd put a gun in his mouth. Then I remembered the Marine Corps when I was so depressed about my court martial and the possibility of losing Rebekah, that I had considered downing a bottle of pain pills. Luckily, I hadn't done it, but I did understand, to some extent, what Don was going through.

CHAPTER TWENTY-THREE

The Lineup

Jodie brought me the list of the occupants of the Lakeside Village Condominiums that she had gotten from the manager. My plan for the evening was to question everyone who lived in the condominiums to see if any of them had seen anything on the night of the murder. I hoped somebody had seen something, because so far I still had no idea who had killed Luther Bell. Fortunately, I had represented some homeowners' associations in the past and understood the politics involved in their operation.

I drove over to the condominiums and went to the manager's office where most of the unit owners were supposed to be gathered for a homeowner's meeting. It was after seven o'clock and almost dark. The manager, an elderly woman with beautiful white hair and pale blue eyes, got up and greeted me when I entered the office.

"You must be Stan Turner?" she said.

"And you're Mrs. Field, I presume?" I replied.

"Yes, it's so nice to meet you. I've told all the members that you were coming. We're all anxious to help."

"Good. Thank you."

"None of us knew Luther very well. He kept to himself and didn't introduce us to any of his lady friends."

"Is that right? How many lady friends did he have?"

"Well, he had his wife, Laura, who came around a lot. Then there was Margie Mason. She's a bank clerk, I understand."

"Yes, I've met both of them."

"Then there's that prostitute."

"Prostitute?"

"Yes, I don't know her name, but she and Margie got into it one morning. Margie came over, it was before they were living together, and she caught him with her. I saw it from my patio."

"Right. Margie Mason told me about that. A topless dancer, I think."

"I wouldn't know. I try to mind my own business."

I smiled and turned to address the members who were seated on two sofas and three rows of folding chairs.

"I want to thank all of you for giving me a few minutes of your time tonight. You've all heard about Luther Bell's brutal murder right here in the Lakeside community. Many of you have probably already talked to the police. I represent several of Mr. Bell's partners who are suspects in the case. My clients are innocent but until the killer is found they are suspects and their lives are in turmoil. This is why I need your help. Now, I'm particularly interested in the night of the murder. I was hoping one of you might have seen something . . . something unusual maybe."

An elderly man raised his hand and replied, "He played his stereo mighty loud, kept my wife and I up half the night many times. The first time I complained to him about it he apologized and said he would keep it down in the future. But he didn't, it only got worse. When I complained again he said I ought to learn to enjoy it or buy some ear plugs."

"Is that right?" I laughed. "We all know he liked to party and entertain women. But on the night of the murder did anybody see anything?"

A middle aged lady in a grey suit spoke up, "I don't know if this is important, but I was coming home from visiting my daughter about seven-thirty Wednesday night and a car drove by very slowly. I didn't think anything about it until I saw it again about seven forty-five."

"What kind of car was it?"

"A black Lincoln Towncar.... I know it was a Towncar because my brother-in-law has one just like it. I thought maybe he and my sister were coming for a visit, but it wasn't them."

"Could you tell who was in it?"

"I'm pretty sure there was just one person in the car, a middle-aged man."

"Did he stop and get out?"

"No, after I saw him the second time I went out to ask if he needed directions or something, but when he saw me he took off."

"Could you identify the man if you saw him again?"

"I think so. It was dark but there's a streetlight right in front of my apartment. He looked right at me so I got a good look at him."

I rummaged through my briefcase and retrieved photos of Don, Rob, and Jim. I showed her Don's picture first. She shook her head negatively. It was the same for Rob. Then I showed her Jim's picture.

"That's him. That's the man I saw driving by slowly, looking at Luther's apartment."

"Did you tell the police about this?"

"Yes, but they didn't have a picture. . . . Is he your client?"

"Yes, I'm afraid so."

I continued to ask them questions. Nobody saw Luther come home, the garage door go up or anyone lingering around Luther's garage between nine and ten. I wondered if anyone had seen Rob and Jennifer there that night. If there *were* a witness I needed to see if Rob and Jennifer were telling the truth. I said, "Did any of you see a car drive up into the driveway around ten that night—before the body was discovered?"

There was silence as everyone looked around at each other. Mrs. Field said, "Everyone was probably in the recreation room playing bridge or watching TV."

I nodded. Mrs. Field continued, "We didn't notice anything until the police came. Then I went right over to see what was going on. I told them I was the manager, so one of the detectives asked me some questions like you've done tonight."

"Did you see the body?"

"Yes, Luther was on his side, his eyes were opened, and a pool of blood was coming from his skull. His hands were bloody too. I guess he had been trying to defend himself from the attacker. There was also glass all over the floor from where the killer had broken the light bulb so Luther couldn't see."

"Did you see Margie?"

"Yes, she was in the back of a squad car. Someone was with her so I couldn't talk to her. She was crying and looked pretty upset. I felt so badly for the poor child."

"While you were at the crime scene, did you hear or see anything else that you remember?" I asked.

She thought a moment. "Well, did I mention they found a lighter by Luther's body. I guess since it was so dark he must have used it to see where he was going."

After a few more questions, I thanked the homeowners and went home. The next day at my office I was thinking about what I had learned the previous night. I was angry that Jim hadn't leveled with me. It made me wonder if he wasn't Luther's killer. I was about to call him to confront him with this revelation when Jodie told me Detective Besch was on the line. I took the call and was advised that I needed to bring Jim, Rob, and Don down to the police station to participate in a lineup.

I called them and arranged for them to appear at eleven-thirty that morning. When I arrived at the station, I was taken to a room with a one-way window. The witness from the Lakeside Condominiums stood behind it, along with Detective Besch and myself. Eight men entered the room including Don, Rob, and Jim. They stood facing the glass as the witness quickly scanned them. I already knew she'd pick out Jim. Detective Besch looked at the witness and said, "Well, do you see him?"

The witness squinted and then said, "Yes, I believe it is the third one from the left."

Detective Besch smiled and said, "Are you sure?"

"Positive. He's the man that was in the Lincoln Towncar."

I took a deep breath and left the room. I found Don, Rob, and Jim and took them into a conference room.

"I'm sorry, Jim, but the witness picked you out of the lineup. She says you drove by Luther's house on the night of the murder around 7:00 p.m. I think it would be wise for you to retain a criminal attorney."

"But I thought you were my lawyer?"

"I am for the civil actions we have going on, but this is different. This is murder, you need a criminal expert and one that is totally independent. I've got several potential conflicts of interest here."

"Damn it! I can't believe this. Where am I going to get the money for a criminal attorney? I didn't kill Luther, Stan, I want you to know that. I may have driven by his place but I didn't stop."

"I believe you, but I'm afraid the police are close to getting enough evidence to arrest you. You better retain someone quick. I can give you a referral if you like."

"Good, because I sure as hell don't know any criminal attorneys."

"Why were you driving by Luther's place?" Don asked.

"Don't answer that," I said. "Don't discuss your case with anybody but your attorney. If you talk to Don or anybody else, the state can make that person disclose what was said. So keep your mouth shut."

"I'm sorry," Don said. "I didn't realize—"

"It's okay," I said. "You guys just need to be really careful from now on."

After the lineup, I went by Detective Besch's office to find out where he was on the investigation and to see if they were going to arrest Jim. He offered me a cup of coffee and a stale donut. I declined. He poured himself a cup and then sat on the edge of his desk.

"So, it looks like Mr. Cochran was at the scene of the crime, Stan," he said.

"Right, but way before the murder. It doesn't prove he killed anybody."

"No, but he was obviously stalking Luther. He had motive and now we know he had opportunity."

"So, you think that's enough to arrest him?"

"We didn't arrest him, did we?"

"No, but are you going to anytime soon?"

"We're getting close, but we don't want to do anything premature. If we do though, are you going to represent him?"

"No, I advised him to get a criminal lawyer. I was Don's lawyer first, so if I have to make a choice it would be him."

"Makes sense," he said.

"So, what about your other suspects. Any breakthroughs?" I asked.

"No, everybody has an alibi," Detective Besch said. "I'm afraid it's looking more and more like Cochran's our man."

"I really don't think he did it. What would he gain by it? It's not going to make any of his problems go away. It just doesn't make any sense."

"Murder doesn't always make sense," Detective Besch pointed out. "It's impulsive and usually driven by extreme emotion. Jim was angry at Luther Bell and for a lot of good reasons. Perhaps he killed out of anger and frustration or maybe he just wanted revenge. The only thing he had to gain was the satisfaction of seeing the person responsible for his problems punished."

"I still don't buy it. I know Jim, he's not a killer."

"Anyone can become a killer if they are adequately provoked. Luther's little games were about to destroy Jim, his family and his friends in the Golden Dragon partnership. He was agitated and upset and he decided to teach Luther a lesson. Or maybe he just wanted to scare him and got carried away."

After leaving Detective Besch's office I ran into Paula Waters. It was nearly lunch time so I suggested we go to Sonny Bryan's for some barbeque. She accepted the invitation with alacrity. We took my car.

"You know, this isn't going to get you off the hook for dinner," she said.

I laughed. "I know. But I'm glad we ran into each other. We can get a head start on catching up."

She nodded. "So, how are you?"

"I've been better. One of my clients just got picked out of a lineup."

She shook her head sympathetically "Oh, God . . . Well, I've got some more good news for you."

"Really?'

"Yeah, on your wrongful death case. It looks like the grand jury is going to *no bill* your defendant Banks."

"What?"

"Yeah, his blood alcohol level came up a little short on proving he was drunk, so the DA recommended a *no bill.*"

"You're kidding! I can't believe it. The police report said he failed the field sobriety test and they found an empty bottle of scotch in his car."

"Well, the problem may have been that the blood test wasn't taken until several hours after the arrest. By that time he no doubt sobered up quite a bit."

"Oh my God! How stupid. Why—"

"Hey, this isn't my case. I'm just reporting what I was told."

I looked at her and smiled. "I know, I'm sorry. I'm just disappointed. This was my first wrongful death case. It started out so great and now it's falling apart."

"Don't worry. There will be others."

"I suppose."

"So, why aren't you cashing in on all your notoriety from the Sarah Winters case? Your co-counsel, what's his name? Harry Hertel. He's got two or three high-profile murder cases going."

"I'm not a criminal attorney. I've got a general practice. The only time I take on a criminal case is if one of my clients gets in trouble or somebody twists my arm pretty hard."

"That's a shame. I would give anything to get a good murder trial, and you're turning them down left and right. Maybe someday I can be your second chair."

I laughed. "Sure, I usually need all the help I can get. . . . Too bad you're working for the DA. I'd be happy to refer Jim Cochran to you. I can't handle his case since I have a conflict."

"Shoot. I would love that. Maybe I should resign. This might be my chance to start my own practice."

I looked at her very much surprised. "Are you serious?"

"Yes, you got any extra office space?"

"Well, I do have an empty office."

"That would be great. When the case is over, we could be partners."

"I don't know. I never thought about having a partner. I can barely support myself."

She laughed. "I seriously doubt that. I'll carry my weight. I promise. I'm a great litigator."

Paula's sudden interest in joining me in law practice was a complete shock. It *was* lonely practicing by myself—overwhelming sometimes. The thought of having Paula as a partner was exciting. But I knew how Rebekah would feel about me having a woman as a partner—particularly an attractive one like Paula. It just wouldn't work.

"Ah. I don't know. Everything is so hectic right now,

it's not a good time."

"It's a perfect time. Sounds like you need me more than ever."

After lunch, I dropped Paula off at her car. I told her that I would think about her proposal and get back with her. I should have just torpedoed the idea right then, but the thought of being with her and working together was tempting.

But of more concern to me at that moment was the *no bill*. My mind began to race as I considered the implications. *How could they no bill that drunken piece of slime! Drinking a bottle of scotch and then racing down Lemmon Avenue going 65 mph. What does it take to get an indictment? . . . Maybe it was because Anant is from India . . . Oh, my God. I bet that was it!*

*****

Later that day, I stopped by Margie Mason's place. I couldn't bring myself to believe that Jim was a murderer. But unless I kept pushing to find the truth, Detective Besch would find a way to pin it on him. I had a few more questions for Margie since there was a discrepancy between her story and the bartender's recollection of her activities on the night of the murder. I knocked, waited a minute, and knocked again. Finally the door opened and she appeared in her nightgown, her eyes half open. She obviously had been sleeping and I had awakened her.

"Oh. Mr. Turner. Yes. What do you want?"

"I have a few more questions for you if you have a minute."

"Well, I was asleep actually."

"I'm sorry, it will only take a minute or two. It's really important."

"Okay, let me get some clothes on."

Margie closed the door for a minute. When she opened it again she invited me inside.

"I'm really sorry to bother you, but I was talking to the

bartender and there are some discrepancies between what you and Lucy told me and what he remembers."

"Really?"

"Yeah. It revolves around the time you left and other things."

"What other things?"

"Well, he says that you and Lucy picked up some cowboys and left with them around 9:30 or 10:00."

Margie frowned and replied, "I didn't leave with anybody. I was alone. Lucy might have taken one of those gigolos home with her, but I wouldn't think of it."

"So you left the bar alone?"

"Yes."

"Are you sure it was 10:00 p.m.?"

"Or a little later, the bartender must be mistaken."

"Do you know the names of the men you met at the bar?"

"No, I'd never seen them before."

"Can you describe them?"

"One was 6' 2" maybe, had short black hair, blue eyes, a mustache and lots of muscles. He was a good looking guy, but I don't pay for sex."

"Is that the one Lucy took home?"

"I don't know if she took anyone home, I just said she might have."

"What about the other one?"

"Around five foot seven, long brown hair, brown eyes," she recited thoughtfully, "a chain smoker—big ego. I didn't like him very much."

"How long were you with them?"

"I'm not sure, an hour maybe."

"Well, very good, I just wanted to double check my notes. I appreciate you talking with me."

"No problem, but if you don't mind I'm going back to bed."

"Oh, one other question. How were you and Luther

getting along—you know, with all the problems he was having with the Golden Dragon investors?"

"Just fine."

"No problems at all?"

"Well, I was a little upset when Luther would go to a bar instead of coming home. I worried about him."

"So, how did you resolve that problem?"

"We didn't. It was something I just had to live with."

"I see. . . . Well, thanks for your help. I guess I'll let you get back to sleep. Sorry for the intrusion."

Even after talking with Margie I was still troubled by the thirty-minute discrepancy. I needed to find a way to pin down her departure from the Rendezvous Club precisely. Unfortunately, I didn't know how I could do that. I wanted so badly for the murderer to be someone other than one of my clients. For now, I decided there wasn't anything I could do so I turned my attention to Jim's alibi.

I decided to try to find Julie at the Sunset Strip. As I was getting into my car, Margie's door opened and she waved at me to come back in. I shut the door and went back up the steps to her front door.

"Your secretary is on the line. She's says it's an emergency."

I rushed inside and took the phone.

"Stan, they've arrested Jim. Wanda just called and said Detective Besch just picked him up."

"Oh great," I said, shaking my head. "Okay. I'll call Wanda."

I asked Margie if I could make a phone call. She said I could, so I dialed Wanda's number.

"Hello, Wanda?"

"Stan, they just arrested Jim! They've taken him away. They say he killed Luther Bell."

"I'm sorry, Wanda. I was afraid they were going to do that."

"Can you get him out? You can't let him go to jail."

"Listen Wanda, I gave Jim the name of a couple good criminal attorneys. Didn't he contact either one of them?"

"Yes, but they both wanted a $20,000 retainer. We don't have any more money. We spent every dime we had on cash calls. You've got to help him, Stan."

"All right, I'll go down and see what's going on. I can't promise anything. I've got a potential conflict since several of my clients are suspects. I'll need a waiver."

"A waiver from who?"

"All of the Blaylocks."

"Don't worry about it. I'll get it from them. Just go take care of Jim, okay? . . . please."

"Okay, I'm on my way. I'll call you later after I learn something."

I made one more call to Detective Besch's office and found out that Jim was at the Mesquite Police and Courts Building. I thanked Margie, got in my car and drove there immediately. Once inside, I went directly to the front desk. A young lady was busy typing a report.

"Hello, miss."

"Yes?"

"You wouldn't know where they hold prisoners would you?"

"Down the hall to the next corridor and take a right, second door on the left."

"Thank you."

I followed her instructions and quickly found the police detention room. I opened the door and went inside. I identified myself and asked the receptionist about Jim Cochran. She said to take a seat and she'd notify the appropriate party of my arrival.

After a minute, one of the inside doors opened and Detective Besch appeared. He raised his eyebrows when he saw me and said, "What are you doing here? I thought you weren't going to represent Jim Cochran."

"He ran out of money and couldn't come up with the

retainer to give the attorney I had recommended to him."

"So, you work for free?"

"No, but I'll let him pay me out. Hopefully you guys will cut us some slack here on bail, so he can keep working and I can get paid as we go along."

He laughed. "We'd like to help you out here, Stan, but we can't let murderers out on the street. We've got to protect innocent citizens."

"Jim's no threat, and your case is pretty weak unless you've come up with something more than you had the last time we talked."

"We've got enough. The DA wouldn't have let us arrest him unless they were sure we could convict him."

"What about Jim's alibi? Did you talk to Julie at the Sunset Strip?"

"Yeah, I know Julie confirms his alibi, but she's a topless dancer for godsakes. She might even be a hooker and we know he dropped a lot of money on her. Nobody's going to believe her. The DA thinks we can bust the alibi wide open."

"Really? What about Margie? You haven't ruled her out have you?"

"Her alibi is a little shaky but she's got no motive. She doesn't get a dime from Luther's estate or any of the insurance. As far as I know she was in love with him and was devastated by his death."

"What about Laura Bell?"

"What about her? You're know she was out of town at a wedding when the murder took place."

"Yeah, but it's only a four hour drive to San Antonio. Did you verify that she was actually down there when the murder took place?"

"Yes, we did. Forget Laura Bell. She didn't do it. Sure she had a motive—she's gonna pick up a nice check one of these days for $750,000—but she couldn't have killed Luther Bell. She was 300 miles away when Luther was killed."

I sighed. "Okay, what else did you find on Jim to justify his arrest?"

"I'm not at liberty to say right now but—" He flexed his fingers in front of me.

"Fingerprints?"

Detective Besch shrugged. Then he ran his fingers through his hair."

"Hair fibers too?" I said shocked by this revelation. *Damn it. Jim's been lying to me. Jesus!*

"I didn't say a thing. I'm sure the assistant DA assigned to the case will fill you in when the time is right."

Later that day, Jim was transferred to the Dallas County Jail and bond was set at $250,000. It only took Wanda a few hours to find a bail bondsman to put up the bond. Apparently Jim's boss didn't want him missing any work so he put up the collateral required by the bondsman. I talked to the Blaylocks, and they consented to my representation of Jim and waived any conflict of interest. Much to my dismay, I was now facing a murder trial. I couldn't wait to tell Rebekah. She was going to be thrilled.

Before Jim went back to the county jail, I confronted him about the evidence Besch had found at the scene of the crime.

"Okay, I did get out of my car. . . . I wanted to see if Luther was home so I went up to the garage and peeked inside."

"Did you touch anything?"

"Well, I guess I might have touched the glass trying to get a good look inside."

"Okay, that explains the fingerprints but what about your hair?"

"I got a haircut that morning and there were hair trimmings all over me. I must have dislodged a few when I was straining to see into Luther's garage."

I shook my head and said, "Wonderful."

After leaving Jim, I headed back to the office. Then I

thought of Paula. Everything had happened so fast I had forgotten about her. She was going to be pissed that I hadn't referred Jim to her. I thought about asking her to be second chair, but I knew she would have to quit her job to do that. That would be a big commitment for her now, and for me later if she pushed the issue of becoming my partner. At any rate, I had promised her I would consider her proposal and get back to her. I hated to do it, but I had to call and tell her something. After I got back to the office I called her.

"I was wondering if you were going to call."

"Listen, I got roped into taking Jim's murder case."

"Roped?"

"Well, I was going to refer him to you but he confessed to me that he had no money to pay an attorney. I didn't figure you wanted to work for nothing."

"He has no money?"

"No, this Golden Dragon deal wiped him out."

"Shoot. So how are you going to get paid?"

"He's going to pay me out. It will take years, I'm sure."

"Well, I could still be second chair."

"But, I'd have to pay you and I don't have enough money right now."

"I don't need a big salary. Just match what I'm getting now."

I sighed. "Paula, it's not going to work right now. Maybe when I get more stabilized financially. Anyway, you should know, I'm not the greatest businessman."

"If you had the money, would you hire me?"

"Absolutely, I'd love to have you as a partner, but—"

There was silence. "I'll put up some capital."

"What?"

"I don't expect a free ride. I've saved up some money and I am a good business manager. My major in college was finance.'"

"Really?"

"Yes. You didn't think I was just another dumb blond,

did you?"

"No, of course not."

"Anyway, it sounds like you need me."

I laughed. "Yeah, maybe so. . . . I guess we should talk some more."

"Definitely."

I hung up the phone feeling pretty good about the prospect of having Paula as a partner. It would be wonderful not to have to deal with the management side of a law practice. But I still had the problem of talking Rebekah into it. She wouldn't like the idea. I knew it.

At the end of the day, I called Rebekah and told her I had to interview witnesses and wouldn't be home for dinner. I started to mention Paula's proposal to her but then thought better of it. This was a subject I had to breach carefully. I hung up and turned my thoughts back to Luther Bell. If Margie had left the Rendezvous Club at 9:30, then conceivably she could have been at Luther's place in time to kill him. I needed to talk to Lucy one more time. Since I only had a few questions, I called her.

"I've told you everything I know," Lucy said.

"Are you sure?"

"Of course, I'm sure."

"Well, the bartender says you two left with the cowboys. Is that true?"

There was silence.

"Listen, I'm married and I love my husband. But he travels a lot and I get lonely."

"So that's a yes?"

"Listen, my personal life is none of your business."

"I don't care about your personal life. All I need to know is when Margie left the Rendezvous Club."

"I told you—10:00 or 10:15 p.m."

I could see talking to Lucy wasn't going to change anything. She was sticking by her story, but with an illicit affair going on her credibility had taken a dive. After I hung up, I called the Sunset Strip to see if I could set up a meeting with Julie.

"Hello," Julie said.

"Hi, this is Stan Turner. You don't know me, but I'm an attorney and I need to talk to you for a few minutes. I was wondering if I could meet you somewhere and we could talk. I'll buy you dinner if you don't have plans."

"What do you want to talk about?"

"I have a client who desperately needs your help."

"This isn't a lame attempt to get a date is it?"

"No, I just need to ask you a few questions. It won't take long."

"Okay, pick me up outside the club at 5:30. I only have an hour for dinner, so you *will* have to feed me."

"No problem. It will be my pleasure."

I drove to the club arriving at 5:25 p.m. I parked out in front and waited. Right at 5:30 the tall, slender blond came walking out of the club. I waved at her and she nodded and walked over to my car and got in.

"Hi," Julie said.

"Hello. Thank you so much for meeting me," I said, as I handed her one of my cards. "Just wanted you to know I was for real."

"Oh, I could tell you were for real by the way you talked to me."

"Really?"

"Yes, I hear so much bullshit all night at the club it's nice to talk to someone who is polite and professional."

We drove down Walnut Hill Lane toward restaurant row. As we approached the area, I smiled at Julie and asked, "What do you feel like for dinner?"

She smiled back and replied, "Would you mind taking me to Pelican's Wharf? I love seafood."

"I do, too. Let's go."

We drove to Pelican's Wharf and went inside. We were seated immediately. The waitress served us drinks and then we ordered.

"So, who's your client that needs my help?"

"Jim Cochran. He was in the club a month or so ago, and I understand he spent a lot of time with you."

"Different guys like different types of women. When they find someone they really like, they can't get enough of them. It's not unusual."

"Well, I can see why Jim liked you. You certainly are beautiful."

Julie smiled and said, "Thank you."

"I'm defending Jim. He's been accused of murder."

"I figured. The cop who came to see me a few days ago was from homicide."

"Yeah, that must have been Detective Besch. Did he give you a hard time?"

"No, not really. He just didn't like what I had to say."

"What did you say that upset him?"

"I told him that Jim was at the club until at least ten o'clock."

"That *would* upset him, because if that's true then Jim couldn't be Luther Bell's killer."

"Luther Bell?!"

"Right."

"Huh . . . I didn't realize he was the victim. Gee, I can't believe he's dead."

"You knew him?"

"Yeah, really well. He came to the club a lot. He had a thing for me too."

"Is that right?"

"Yeah, he got too drunk one night to drive home. I don't know why, but I felt sorry for him and took him home."

"To his condo?"

"Right. I was tired so I stayed the night. His girlfriend was really pissed off when she found me with him the next day."

"I heard about that. So that was you?"

"Yeah, there were fireworks, believe me."

"Did you and Luther. . .did Luther and you ever . . . ever—"

"Have sex? . . . Yeah, one night he offered me a lot of money to go out with him. I'm not really a prostitute. I don't have sex with men for money too often, but I kind of liked Luther so I just considered it a date with a fringe benefit."

"I see."

"Where did you go this second time?"

"A motel somewhere. The Red Roof . . . no . . . no, the Blue Ribbon Motel."

"I see. When did that happen?"

"A few days before he was murdered."

"Did Margie know?"

"I didn't tell her."

"Could she have seen you?"

"I doubt it. It was pretty late—well early in the morning."

"Hmm. Was that the only other time?"

"Yes."

"Did you ever go to his condo again?"

"No."

"Huh. . . . Well, that's very interesting. You didn't tell Detective Besch about this?"

"No, he didn't ask. He wouldn't even tell me what he was investigating."

"He thinks he can discredit you because you are a dancer. You're certain of the time Jim left?"

"Uh huh."

"It's not that I doubt you, but I'm curious how you are so certain he was at the club until ten?"

"I don't know. It's just when I started thinking about it. I just remembered ten o'clock was about the time he left."

"Do you have a watch on when you dance?"

"No," Julie laughed.

"Is there a clock in the dressing room?"

"No, but I keep my watch in my purse."

"Could you have looked at it?"

"I doubt it."

"Do these shows start at any particular time so you might have deduced the time by when a show started?"

"No, the DJ announces them. They're every ten minutes but you couldn't set your watch by them."

"Did Jim mention the time, maybe?"

"No, I don't think so."

"Were you just trying to help Jim out by telling Detective Besch what he didn't want to hear?"

Julie gave me a big smile and laughed, "He was very generous, but I don't think that's it. I definitely would have remembered that."

During dinner, I learned a lot about Julie. She was going to college at El Centro and someday wanted to be a fashion designer. She was a stripper because the money was good and the hours fit in with her school schedule. Besides that, she liked to dance and enjoyed entertaining. She was proud of her body and didn't mind showing it off.

After dinner, I took Julie back to the club. Before I got out of the car I pulled another card out of my pocket and handed it to her. "If you think of anything that might help prove the time Jim left the Sunset Strip, anything at all, please call me."

"I've already got one of these, but I'll keep it. One of the girls is bound to need a nice lawyer."

"A nice lawyer? Not a good lawyer?"

"Yeah, a nice lawyer. It's hard to find a good lawyer but damn near impossible to find a nice one."

I laughed, "Okay, if you think of anything let me know."

"Okay. . . . Wait, I remember now why I knew it was ten o'clock."

"You do? What was it?"

"One of the girls in the club, Lindsay, had been caught with a big-named minister in a motel. We were told she was going to be on the ten o'clock news. The news was on in the dressing room. I remember going back there right after Jim left. The news had already begun and the story about Lindsay was just starting."

"The ten o'clock news. Damn, that's good, Julie! I can verify that with the TV studio. . . . Oh, I'm so glad you remembered that," I said. "You're a lifesaver. I owe you one."

"I'm glad I could help. Thank you for dinner, I really enjoyed talking to you."

"Me too. . . . I'm sure Jim will be by to thank you personally."

"Good. See you later," she said and then ran across the street and disappeared into the club.

CHAPTER TWENTY-FOUR

The Miracle

After Don's attempted suicide, Rob and Jennifer moved into the Blaylock house to keep an eye on him. His depression had gotten so bad he had difficulty eating and sleeping. He tried to go to work, but he was so distracted that his boss finally made him take a week of vacation to try to pull himself together.

Near the end of that first week, Rob called and scheduled an appointment to see me. He said he needed to talk to me to discuss Don's condition and get a status report on all the legal matters involving the Golden Dragon. At the appointed time Jodie advised me he was waiting in the outer office. I told her to show him in. I got up and shook his hand.

"Hi, Rob. How's your dad?"
"He's a little better. He's starting to eat some."
"Well, that's good. How's Jennifer?"
"She's fine. She's starting to show a little."
"I bet. When's the baby due?"
"April third."
"That soon? Wow. . . . Have you talked to your mother yet?'
"I called her and told her what happened," he said dejectedly. "I expected her to jump on a plane and rush home, but she didn't. She seemed cool and detached, which isn't like her. It was really scary. Do you think they might get a divorce?"
"God, I hope not."

"A lot of my friends parents have gone through divorces. I always felt lucky that Mom and Dad loved each other and got along so well. You wouldn't believe the horrible stories I've heard from my friends. I'm not so concerned about myself. I'm almost seventeen. It's Donna—she is so young and has her entire childhood in front of her. I can't stand the thought of her being tossed back and forth between Mom and Dad with no stability in her life. There has to be something I can do to bring them back together."

"God, I hope you figure out what it is."

"I've got an idea."

"Really?"

"Yes. Jennifer's mom is pretty smart. She's been through a lot of counseling, you know, for her own divorces."

I laughed. "Right."

"She says we have to get Mom and Dad back together immediately. The longer they are apart the more likely they will actually go through with the divorce."

"Did you ask your mom to come home?"

"Yes, but she said no."

"Hmm."

"Anyway, Mrs. Rich says that when a husband and wife have money problems they're usually too embarrassed to talk about it to anyone but each other. Consequently, when they are together that's all they talk about. After a while, every time they look at each other they are reminded of these problems. Eventually the mere sight of a each other causes negative feelings and emotions. These negative feelings can destroy the love that they once had. So the problem is they have to learn not to discuss their problems every time they are together. They need to find someone else to talk to when things go wrong."

"Like who?"

"Like a counselor, a priest, or maybe an attorney like yourself."

"Well, you know I really like your parents, and I'd do

anything to help them, but some things are beyond my expertise. Many people, like Mrs. Rich, think I'm some kind of omnipotent magician who can solve any problem they bring to me, but I assure you, that is not the case."

Rob shifted uncomfortably in his chair, his face suddenly becoming quite serious. I smiled, trying to break the tension. I said, "But don't give up just yet, I've had few near miracles."

Rob managed another forced smile and replied, "I know, and I appreciate what you've done. I just needed to get updated on everything. Since my dad is sick, I figured I better keep on top of things until he's better."

"Well, I'm sure he'll appreciate that when he recovers. . . . Okay, let me see. . . . I answered the breach of lease suit you brought me the other day, so there's nothing imminent coming from that front. Eventually, though, they're going to get a judgment against all of the partners."

"Don't we have any defenses?"

"Ordinarily the landlord would be able to re-let the premises and that would take the partners off the hook for any future loss of revenue. Unfortunately, since this is the second restaurant failure at this location, it's not likely the landlord will be able to find a new tenant. Consequently, he is likely to get a judgment for the full balance left on the lease."

"Crap! You mean we have no defense at all?"

"Oh, I can dream up some defenses which will delay the case six months or a year, but eventually we'll lose. It's just a question of whether it's worth a bunch of attorney's fees just to postpone the inevitable."

"How much would the attorney's fees be?"

"Oh, I don't know, probably five or ten thousand. It just depends on how hard they fight me."

"Are there any other lawsuits going on?"

"No, they paid the IRS, the state comptroller, and the bank. None of the vendors have sued yet."

"What should we do?"

"I know your parents don't like the idea, but I'm afraid bankruptcy is the only realistic solution. If they try to fight the suit it will cost them a bundle in attorney fees, and if they don't fight it and let the landlord take a judgment, then they'll have that hanging over their heads indefinitely. I just don't see any other choice."

"I'll do whatever I can to help you convince them to file. I agree it's the only option."

"At least once they file bankruptcy they'll be debt free and they can start rebuilding their lives."

"If we can get them back together. Right now Mom doesn't seem to care about the relationship."

"She does. She's still in shock. Your parents had the perfect life and then all of a sudden everything around them began to crumble. She's confused and angry, and I don't blame her."

"She's angry at Dad, but it's not his fault."

"No, it's not."

"Do you think there is any way you can get Mom back here so we can talk some sense into her?"

"What do you mean? You want me to ask her to come back to Texas so we can figure out how to save her marriage?"

"Something like that."

"Well, that's not really part of a lawyer's job."

"Aren't you a counselor too?"

"True, a counselor at law, but—"

"Divorce is legal, right?"

"Well, yeah, but—"

"So, make Mom come back and we'll convince her to quit blaming everything on Dad, file bankruptcy, and start rebuilding their lives together."

"You've got it all figured out, huh?"

"We have to try. I want Donna to have the same happy childhood that I had. I don't want her to have to deal with a divorce. It's not right. No kid should have to go through that."

"All right, I'll get her back here, but then it's up to you to get her to stay."

"Don't worry. I'll make sure she stays. I'm not letting her leave again."

I smiled as Rob got up to leave. He was a great kid and I just wished Pam and Don would open their eyes and see how important it was to keep the family together. Rob certainly understood this, and I was proud of him. I prayed I could get Pam back to Texas.

Later that day Jodie entered my office with a letter she had just opened and said, "Here's the response to your demand letter to Richard Banks from his attorney."

When I was first retained to handle the case for Keyur Ravi I had sent a demand letter to Richard Banks. He had turned it over to his attorney who was just now getting around to responding to the letter. She handed it to me.

"Dear Mr. Turner,

This firm has been retained by Richard Banks to respond to your wrongful death claim recently asserted against him by your client, Keyur Ravi. Please direct all further communication in this regard to this office.

In evaluating your demand we wanted to point out several factors which might influence your client's decision whether to sue on this claim. First, you may have been misled by the newspaper reports about the accident. Mr. Banks is a grocery clerk making $6.64 per hour. He has no assets and he never will. His parents have set up a spendthrift trust, which will be the beneficiary of his inheritance. As you know, your client will never be able to touch the corpus of that trust no matter how big a judgment they might get.

> Rather than spending thousands of dollars in litigation expenses, my client has arranged an advance of $20,000 which he proposes to pay your client for a full and complete release of their claim. This is an amount equal to the minimum insurance requirements of the State of Texas under the financial responsibility statutes. Accordingly, by accepting this offer, your client would be no worse off than if my client had been properly insured.
>
> Please have your clients consider this offer. We firmly believe that a settlement along these lines would be to everyone's best interest. Should you require further verification of Mr. Banks' precarious financial condition, we will be happy to provide it.
>
> Sincerely,
>
> Paul Byrom

Jodie looked at me and said, "Can you believe that? They're only offering $20,000."

"Well, under the circumstances its probably a generous offer. If Mr. Byrom knew that Key had never met his father, he wouldn't have offered squat."

"So what are you going to do?"

"It's just a first offer. If they are willing to pay $20,000 then they must be worried about something. If we can figure out what it is, maybe we can get them to pay more."

"Hmm," Jodie said. "So what do you think it is?"

"I don't know. It could be they just want to avoid the cost and hassle of a trial. But most defense firms like to run the meter awhile before they settle a case for nuisance value. For his parents to offer money they must be concerned about something."

"What could it be?"

"It might be that mom and dad don't want their son to lose his drivers license. Yeah, I bet that's it. Normally it wouldn't be any big deal because he could just file bankruptcy, discharge the judgment, and get his license back in four or five months. But since there was liquor involved, the judgment isn't dischargeable, so he would have to pay the judgment to reinstate his license." I laughed. "I wonder how much a drivers license is worth?"

"Can't he get a hardship license?"

"Maybe. Maybe not. But even so, that would only allow him to drive back and forth to work. It would still be a pain in the ass for him."

"I couldn't imagine not being able to drive. I'd go nuts."

"Would you pay, say . . . a hundred thousand?"

"If I had that kind of money. Obviously, I don't."

"Let's send them a counter offer."

"Okay."

Jodie went and got a notepad and I dictated the following letter:

Dear Mr. Byrom,

We are in receipt of your recent offer of settlement and regret to inform you that we must reject your offer. As you must realize $20,000 wouldn't even begin to compensate my client for the extensive damages he has suffered on account of your client's negligent and reckless conduct. In fact, the offer is an insult and has only strengthened our client's resolve to prosecute this action to the fullest extent of the law. Be advised that once judgment is rendered in favor of our client he has instructed us to conduct an exhaustive examination of your client's financial affairs.

Also, you might remind your client of the Texas Fraudulent Conveyance statutes and how they might affect any attempt on his part to transfer or conceal assets. Finally, since a judgment in this matter will not be dischargeable in bankruptcy, we will continue to monitor your client's financial situation on a quarterly basis.

Our client does realizes that there may be a limit to what he can recover from your client. He knows he will never be able to get what he justly deserves, but $20,000 isn't much incentive for him to settle. If Mr. Banks really wants to get rid of this case, our client would reluctantly accept $250,000. Please communicate this offer to your client immediately. It will expire in ten days at which time no further offers less than the full amount of our client's damages will be considered.

Sincerely,
Stan Turner

Jodie closed her pad and said, "That ought to shake them up a bit."

"I hope so. It's our only chance to salvage anything out of this pitiful case."

*****

The following week, Pam and Don Blaylock came to my office purportedly for a meeting to discuss the several lawsuits against them. Pam resisted the meeting at first but finally agreed when I stressed the urgency of the situation. Don had just picked Pam up at the airport and when they arrived they appeared to be cordial. Pam looked even thinner and paler than when I had seen her last. Don was very nervous and concerned for Pam's comfort. I thought how things had changed from the first time I had met them at the Little League game a year earlier. I knew this meeting might be their last chance to ever restore life as they once knew it. It was time for a miracle.

"Hi, Pam. How have you been?" I asked.

"Okay. I'm a little tired from the flight."

"Thank you so much for coming. I know it was a lot to ask of you, but it's absolutely imperative that we respond to the discovery requests that we just received from the attorneys for the landlord."

"What kind of discovery?" Don asked.

"Well, we've got interrogatories, requests for admission, and requests for production. It will probably take us several hours to go through all of this and then you'll have to go see if you can find all of the records they're looking for."

Pam stiffened up, looked me in the eye and said, "Couldn't Don have done this by himself? Why do you need me?"

"You need to approve and sign all of this discovery since you're a named party."

She took a deep breath and sunk back in her chair.

"Before we get to the discovery, though, I wanted to talk to you about something else."

"What's that?" Pam said.

"You know about the time I met you two I got an incredible break. . . . At least it seemed like one at the time. An old client referred a wrongful death case to me. You may not realize it, but a good wrongful death case for any attorney is like winning the lottery. I was elated. I was so excited I canceled all my appointments, went home, and took Rebekah and the family out to celebrate. You probably think I'm rich, right? Most people think all lawyers are rich. Well, that's not the case. I started my practice on a shoestring four years ago, and since then I've spent 110% of what I've earned. Finally, I thought, I'd have a few bucks in the bank and, maybe even a little financial security for a change. It was just a matter of time.

"Anyway," I continued. "The case was great. The newspaper reports said that our client's father was hit by the son of a rich Oklahoma oil man who was driving a 1982 Porsche. To top it all off, the driver was arrested for DWI and involuntary manslaughter. It was a dream case, I knew I was going to be an instant millionaire. I even promised Jodie a new BMW, if you can believe that."

"Unfortunately, my dream quickly turned into a nightmare. The 1982 Porsche turned out to be a 1972 Porsche. The driver, it seems, was estranged from his family and was penniless—so broke, in fact, that he didn't even have insurance. Then I discovered my client had never met his father and the extent of his damages were that he wouldn't be able to look his father up some day!"

"So, my last hope is that this guy gets indicted for DWI and manslaughter. At least that would insure that I could get a big punitive damage award which would at least enhance my reputation and perhaps lead to some better wrongful death cases in the future. Ha! What a joke. The grand jury *no bills* the driver because his blood test isn't quite incriminating enough. So, now I've got nothing. Actually, less than nothing. Now I've got court costs, expert witness fees, investigation bills and court reporters to pay. If the case has to be tried it could cost me twenty-five grand. But that's not the worst. A wrongful death case could take hundreds of hours away from my practice. I could lose another thirty to fifty thousand easy in billable hours. Suddenly the price tag for this little fiasco is fifty to a hundred thousand bucks!"

I got up and went over to the window and looked out at the Dallas skyline. Don shook his head and gave me a sympathetic smile. Pam shifted slightly in her chair but said nothing. "So," I continued. "What I'm trying to tell you is, I really screwed up. I should have investigated the facts thoroughly before I ever took the case, but I didn't. I got greedy and now I'm paying for it. So I just want you to realize *everyone* makes mistakes for one reason or another. We're all just human beings struggling to survive. If we didn't have some bad times, how could we ever appreciate the good times, right?"

I came back to my desk, sat down and leaned toward Pam and Don, and said, "You know, several years ago I had a client who came to me about a business venture. He wanted my advice about whether to do the deal or not. I looked over the material that he gave me, talked to the principals involved, and even flew to the location of the business to inspect it. When I was done I concluded that the deal *stunk* and I advised my client to forget it.

"Unfortunately," I continued, "he was sold on the deal and didn't take my advice. In fact, he got mad at me for telling him it was a bad deal! I tried to reason with him and point out why the deal was bad but he didn't listen. In fact, he ended up firing me.

"Just a few months ago he called me up and wanted a meeting. I consented, and we met at a bar and had a drink together. He told me the deal was a disaster. Everything that I had told him that would happen did happen. Not only had he lost his investment but he was sued and lost his entire business as well. He concluded by saying that he blamed *me* for everything that happened to him.

"Of course, I was flabbergasted by his statement and asked him how he figured I was to blame. He said I should have whacked him over the head and made him take my advice. I should have flat forbidden him to do the deal!

"Of course, I've given what he said a lot of thought, and, you know, he might be right to a degree. Sometimes maybe I'm not getting across to my clients what they should do, particularly when the choice is clear. . . . And this is particularly the case with you two.

"I know neither of you like the idea, you've told me you'd never do it and I know you don't want to hear this, but . . . you need to file bankruptcy! It doesn't matter what anyone thinks. It doesn't matter what it will do to your credit. It doesn't matter how humiliated you might feel. It's the *only* thing you can do considering the desperate circumstance you find yourself in."

"Is this why you brought me all the way from Seattle?" Pam asked. "You thought you were going to convince me to file bankruptcy?"

"No, I brought you here at the request of your son who has been devastated by what's happened to both of you. We brought you back here to take one last stab at saving your marriage."

"What? Are you a marriage counselor now?" Pam said.

"No, but I do a lot of bankruptcy and a fair amount of divorces and one thing I've observed is that financial stress is devastating to a marriage. You know it's been almost a year ago that Rebekah and I first met you two. Since then we've gotten to know you pretty well. We always admired both of you and your wonderful family. I don't think I've ever known anyone happier than you two were when we met you. . . . Now the only thing that has happened in the last year is you've lost a lot of money and you've incurred a lot of debt. So what?! It's not anybody's fault. It's just money. You still have the most important thing in life, each other's love and the love of your children. Don't throw the most precious things in your life away!"

I paused a moment and then continued, "So I'm telling you now *file bankruptcy*! Get on with your life. Once your debts are all forgiven the stress in your life will vanish and the healing process will begin."

When I was finished neither Pam nor Don said a word. I thought of my old days when I sold life insurance. Once you've made your pitch, the first person to talk loses. After a minute Pam took a deep breath and said, "Do I have to go in front of a judge?"

I smiled and replied, "No, just ten minutes in front of a trustee and I'll be right there at your side."

Don looked longingly at Pam and before long they were in each other arms. I got up and left the room to give them a little privacy.

When I got home and told Rebekah the news she was elated. "It's too bad they have to file bankruptcy, but I'm so glad they are back together. When you see a family as strong as the Blaylocks in trouble, you wonder if the same thing could happen to you."

I looked into Rebekah's eyes and said, "It would never happen to us. Our family will always be together. I promise."

We embraced.

Rebekah said, "Now all you have to do is get Jim off and everything will be back to normal."

I sighed. "Yeah, wouldn't that be sweet. Unfortunately, Margie and Laura Bell both have alibis. Margie's is a little shaky but she has no motive unless—"

"Unless what?"

"Unless she caught Luther cheating on her."

I let Rebekah go and walked a few feet away.

"You think he was two-timing Margie?"

"Yeah—with a stripper named Julie. If Margie somehow found out about it, she might have been pissed off enough to want to kill him," I replied.

Rebekah thought for a moment. "But why kill him? They weren't married. Why not just leave him?"

"Good question. She had nothing to gain by killing him."

Margie's lack of a motive baffled me. She had to be the killer. If she wasn't, then Jim or Rob had killed Luther. I couldn't accept that. Racking my brain for an answer and only coming up with a headache, I decided I needed to probe Margie's life a little deeper. There were two obvious places to start—her employer and her ex-husband. I opted for the ex-husband since he would be more likely to give me dirt on Margie than her current employer. He agreed to see me after he closed up his office at five. We met at Denny's a few blocks from his dental clinic.

"I've talked to Margie, and she's told me some things about you two that I'd like to verify. I know there are two sides to every story."

"What does our relationship have to do with your murder investigation?"

"Well, it doesn't directly. I'm more concerned with Margie's veracity than anything else. Have you ever known her to lie?"

"No, she was always pretty honest."

"She says you got a divorce because she caught you with your dental hygienist?"

He shrugged. "Yes, I'm afraid that's true. She dropped in my office just after work, and Mary and I were letting off a little steam. You should have seen her face. Oh, was she pissed."

"What did she do?"

"Oh, God. While we were getting dressed she trashed my dental office."

"Really? She has a hot temper?"

"Oh, yes. You don't want to be in her path when she erupts."

"Do you think she would be capable of murder given sufficient provocation?"

He thought for a moment and then replied, "I couldn't rule out the possibility."

Now that I knew about Margie's temper, I pretty much had the scenario figured out. Unfortunately, I needed evidence if I was going to get a jury to believe it. I didn't have to prove my theory completely, just create reasonable doubt in the minds of the jury.

CHAPTER TWENTY-FIVE

Docket Call

Several weeks after Jim Cochran was arrested, we were scheduled for a docket call. Judge Martin Wingate of the 555th Criminal District Court had been assigned the case. Judge Wingate was a no-nonsense judge known for moving his docket quickly. When I called my old law professor Harry Hertel to ask him about Wingate, he told me the judge would probably sign a scheduling order to push the case along quickly. This concerned me because my investigation was far from complete, and I needed as much time as possible to get ready for trial.

The press mobbed me as I walked out of the elevator on the sixth Floor of the Dallas County Courthouse.

"Mr. Turner. How does it feel to be trying another murder case?" a reporter asked.

I tried to make my way through the crowd of reporters but quickly realized I was pinned in. It was apparent I was going to have to answer a few questions before they would let me in the courtroom. I replied, "Sobering to say the least. . . . I just hope I get my client a fair trial."

"Is it true Mr. Cochran threatened to kill Luther Bell a few days before the murder?" a second reporter asked.

I chuckled. "Believe it or not, a lot of people threatened to kill Luther the week before he was killed, but obviously they all didn't do it."

A narrow crack in the wall of reporters developed so I quickly slipped through it and forced my way into the courtroom. Much to my surprise, Paula was there. I walked over to her.

"Hi," I said.

"I thought you might need some moral support."

"Thanks."

"They've assigned Will Thornton to prosecute this case. He's a world class asshole. I don't know a single person who likes him."

"Oh, wonderful."

"You better watch your back because he'll do anything to win. The word ethics isn't in his dictionary."

"So, what are his weaknesses?"

"His ego. He's often over-confident and thinks his evidence is better than it really is. If you out-hustle him you can win. Just don't let his cocky, know-it-all attitude intimidate you."

"Thanks. I appreciate the heads-up."

She gave me a frustrated look. "I wish you'd let me be second chair. I could really be a valuable asset."

"I know. Maybe I will. Just give me a little time with—"

"With?"

"My wife, Rebekah. She won't be crazy about me having a woman as a partner."

"Oh, so that's the problem."

I nodded. "But, it's not an insurmountable one if I handle it right. Just give me a little time."

"Okay. I've got to run. I just wanted to warn you about Will."

After Paula left, I went up and introduced myself to Will Thornton. He was very cool and didn't seem interested in talking to me right then so I took a seat and waited. After a few minutes Jim Cochran walked in the courtroom. I went right over to him.

"Hi, Jim. How are you doing?"

He shrugged. "I've had better days."

"Well, not much is going to happen today. The judge will ask for your plea and then he'll set the case for trial. The DA has assigned Will Thornton to prosecute your case. I understand he's a prick so this isn't going to be a fun trial."

"Oh, just my luck."

The court reporter's door opened and she quickly took her chair. The bailiff stood and said, "All rise!" The judge entered the courtroom and took the bench. He shuffled through some papers and then looked up.

"The State versus Michaels."

An assistant DA approached the bench along with a short, bald attorney. They talked with the judge for a few moments and then left. Several other cases were called and then the judge said, "The State of Texas verses Jim Cochran."

Thornton and I approached the bench and stood in front of the judge. He opened the file, studied it a minute, and then looked at us. "Well, gentlemen, I want to get a few things straight before we start. Mr. Thornton you will present yourself in this courtroom with dignity and respect. Do you understand?"

Thornton glared at the judge without saying a word. "Do you understand, Mr. Thornton?" he repeated.

Thornton took a deep breath and said, "Yes, Your Honor."

"Good," the judge said, and then turned to me with his piercing glare. "And Mr. Turner, if you disobey an order of this court I'll throw you in jail for contempt without hesitation. And I won't wait until after the trial. . . . Do you understand?"

I swallowed hard. "Yes, Your Honor."

"Then with that out of the way, is your client ready to make his plea, Mr. Turner?"

"Yes, sir. He is."

The judge looked at Jim and asked, "Mr. Cochran you are charged with first degree murder. How do you plead?"

Jim stood up straight and confidently said, "Not guilty, Your Honor."

The judge nodded and said, "Very well, I'm going to

set this case for trial on February 13, 1984 at nine. My clerk will forward a scheduling order which will be followed to the letter without exception. Understood?"

We both replied, "Yes, Your Honor."

"Then that will be all. You're dismissed."

Thornton bolted out of the courtroom. Jim and I followed close behind. As we walked toward the elevators, we talked.

"I guess the judge wanted us to know who's boss," I said.

"It sure looked that way. . . . Who stuck a pole up his ass?"

I laughed. "I don't know, but I can tell my stomach is going to be in a knot for the next few months. Not only do I have to deal with an asshole prosecutor but now I get to look forward to a judge who'd love to throw me in jail."

"I'm glad you're the attorney and not me."

"You want to trade places?" I said.

"I don't know. I'd have to give that some thought."

After I had briefed Jim on where I was with my investigation, I went back to the office. My adrenalin level was so high I could barely sit still. I brought Jodie up to date on everything that had happened and then she left me alone. When I had calmed down a little bit, I looked around to see what task was begging the hardest for my attention. There was always a lot more to do than any human being could possibly accomplish. Before I got it figured out, Jodie advised me I had a call from Paul Byrom. My pulse quickened.

"Paul?"

"Hi, Stan. Okay, this is the best I can do. $50,000 and not a dime more."

"Come on. That's pocket change for your client's daddy."

"Maybe so, but that's all he's willing to cough up. He's fed up with bailing Richard out of trouble and is thinking about revoking the trust and cutting him out of his will."

"Hmm. Sounds like he's pissed."

"To say the least."

"Well, let me run it by my client. I can't promise anything."

"Tell him to take it, Stan. I promise it's the most blood he's going to get out of this turnip."

I laughed. "Okay. I understand."

I called Ravi and explained the situation. He wasn't happy but reluctantly agreed to settle when I told him in rather strong terms that this was the best he was going to get and if he didn't settle, he might get nothing. Jodie walked in when I hung up the phone.

"So much for my BMW."

"Oh well, twelve grand is better than a stick in the eye," I said.

"Eight grand after expenses," she reminded me.

"Eight, ten . . . whatever. It's just money."

She shook her head, turned around and walked out. As I looked out the window at the Dallas skyline, a great sense of relief washed over me. I had really been stupid in the way I had jumped on the Ravi case without thoroughly checking it out. It could have turned out worse had I been forced to try the case. It had been a tough lesson, but one I wouldn't soon forget.

As I was packing up my briefcase to go home I noticed another linen envelope in my briefcase. *Oh, come on, Rebekah! I don't need this today.* I reluctantly picked it up, opened it, and read its contents.

Alone

The clock is my worst enemy
It ticks with chilling regularity
You should be next to me, annexed to me
I long for your touch, the warmth of your body
But I'm alone. Always, always alone

> The long days without you drain me
> I feel weary and subdued
> Depression is my only companion
> You should be with me, to cheer me
> But I'm alone, always, always alone
>
> The long nights are the bleakest hours
> As I yearn for the sound of your voice
> We should be together, hand in hand
> But I am alone, always, utterly alone
>
> *Your Love*

A chill darted down my spine. *Okay, my love. This is getting creepy. I got the message. What we need is a little time together.* I put the letter back in its envelope and stuck it with the others in the first slot in my briefcase. I was saving them as a keepsake. I didn't know why. I wanted to rip them apart and burn them. Could Rebekah's life be *that* horrible? When I got home Rebekah was full of questions on all that had transpired during the day. I went over everything in great detail. Then I gathered the family together to make an announcement.

"Since I have been neglecting all of you lately, I want to make it up to you. So, I thought we'd go to lake Texoma for a week. We'll bring the boat and do lots of fishing, relax and have a great time."

"Yippee!" Marcia explained.

"Oh, cool, Dad." Reggi said. "Maybe we'll come across another school of bass."

"Don't forget to buy a Texoma license," Peter said.

Reggi and Mark glared at Peter. "Oh, I mean. Don't forget to get Mom one."

Rebekah frowned. "Don't bother. I'm not doing any fishing and I hope you're planning to get a place in the lodge.

Camping is not a vacation for me."

I smiled. "Sure, we'll get a room in the lodge. You and Marcia can hang out at the pool while we are fishing."

"I want to go fishing. You promised me I could go fishing," Marcia complained.

Rebekah shook her head. I smiled. "I'll tell you what, Princess. We'll go out once, just you and me. We'll see if we can find a crappie hole somewhere."

"Stan," Rebekah protested.

"If it's just Marcia and I, it will be safe. I'll take good care of my little girl, don't worry."

"Hmm. I'm not crazy about this."

"Don't worry. The crappie are the only ones who need to be worrying, huh, Marcia?"

She jumped up and down with excitement. "Uh huh. We're going to catch a *million* of them."

Mark shook his head. "No, you won't. You probably won't catch any."

"Yes, I will," Marcia yelled.

"No you—"

I said, "Okay, cool it. You kids go play now. I need to talk to your mother." Everyone got up and scattered. I looked over at Rebekah and raised my eyebrows.

"So, when do we leave? I'm ready," she said.

I laughed. "Is tomorrow soon enough?"

She nodded. "Play your cards right and we can enjoy some other recreational activities besides fishing."

"Oh really," I said. "Do I have to wait until tomorrow?"

She winked at me. "Maybe, maybe not."

I took her hand and pulled her to me. We kissed and then held each other for a long minute. Everything in my life was perfect. I prayed nothing would happen to our family like what had happened to the Blaylocks. We let each other go and smiled.

"I better call the lodge and see if they have any rooms this week," Rebekah said. "Do you have their number?"

"Yes, I stopped by AAA on the way home and got a brochure. I'll get it for you."

"No, you go relax and watch TV. You must be exhausted after all you've been through today. Just tell me where it is and I'll get it."

"Okay," I replied. "It's in my briefcase."

She nodded and went into the study. I closed my eyes and was almost asleep when I heard a crashing sound. I jumped up and ran into the study. Rebekah had kicked by briefcase and knocked everything in it all over the floor. Then I saw the linen notes in her hand.

"You dirty bastard! Who is *my love?*"

"You, of course."

"Bullshit! I didn't write these poems."

"You didn't?"

"Don't bullshit me, Stan. Who is she? I want to know so I can rip her head off."

"Calm down. I don't know *who* wrote them. I assumed it was you. That's why I've been showering you with gifts and trying to spend more time with you. I thought you were sending me a message."

"You expect me to believe you don't know who sent these notes?"

"Right, because it's the truth."

"I am so pissed to think some woman is out there trying to get her grubby little hands on you. Ohhhhh! I could scream."

"Okay, okay. I'm going to get to the bottom of this. Just calm down."

"You better—and fast."

Rebekah left the room. The kids, who had gathered around to see what all the ruckus was about, retreated without a word. I collapsed into my chair. My head was pounding. It never occurred to me that the letters were from someone other than Rebekah. *Who would be sending me love letters? I can't believe this.* After downing three aspirin and waiting for my head to clear, I began to think about the women in my life. Who might possibly have a crush on me without me realizing it? The woman I was closest to and saw nearly everyday was Jodie.

I liked Jodie a lot, and she liked me, but she was ten years younger, and I had been careful not to flirt or get too close to her. She was a great secretary and I didn't want to spoil that relationship. It was true she had broken up with her boyfriend and hadn't found a new one yet. I considered this. Then I remembered how concerned she was about my finances. I thought it was because her job depended on the viability of my law practice, but was it more? Did she love me? My feelings for her were strong and if it weren't for the fact that I was married and had a family, our relationship could certainly could become closer. Then I remembered the abortion. Could she be trying to—"Shit!" I was getting nowhere and my headache was intensifying. "It can't be Jodie. Who the hell is it?"

I ran through all the other women I saw on a regular basis. Pam Blaylock—I *was* attracted to her before she self-destructed, but was she attracted to me? She never did anything to indicate she had any interest in me. Maybe she wanted to punish Don for all the grief he had caused her? "No." I dismissed that idea. Then I remembered Paula. She popped in out of nowhere and suddenly was moving in on me like a black bear on a beehive. I wanted to kick myself. It was so obvious.

Not wanting to let Rebekah stew too long, I went into the living room. The kids were all gathered around Rebekah like new born puppies. All eyes were on me.

"It's time for bed, kids," I said. "Mom and I have to talk."

Without a word the children calmly disappeared. They were scared and I felt badly that they were having to go through this. I sighed.

"I figured it out."

"Who is it?" Rebekah asked.

I told her.

"So what are you going to do?"

"Have a little chat with her."

Rebekah shook her head. "That's not going to work. You don't know women the way I do. She won't give up that easy."

"She has to give up. There is nothing else she can do, for godsakes. She can't force me to be her lover."

"Don't be so sure."

"Well, what do you suggest?"

"I'll talk to her."

"No, you'll just get into a brawl with her, and you might get hurt."

"Oh, don't worry about me. I can take care of myself."

"Forget it," I said. "I'll handle it. Just give me a day or two."

"What about our trip?"

"Well, do you want me to wait until we get back?"

"No. Take care of it now. I won't sleep until that bitch is out of our lives."

******

The next day, when I should have been cruising with my boys on Lake Texoma, I was sitting in my office trying to determine how I should handle the situation with Paula. It was going to be a very delicate matter since there were obviously some personal dynamics involved that I couldn't begin to understand. Dealing with women wasn't my strong suit anyway. I loved, respected, and trusted women in general and consequently they often ran right over me. Should I take Paula to lunch? Meet her somewhere? Bring security? I needed a woman's advice. Rebekah was out of the question, so I decided to ask Jodie. After I filled her in on the situation she shook her head.

"Gee, Stan. I don't know. What a psycho."

"How should I tell her discreetly to buzz off?"
"You could write her a poem."
We laughed.
"Come on, seriously. What should I do?"
"Meet her somewhere public. Just tell her the truth—that you love Rebekah and your family, and you'll never do anything to jeopardize that relationship."
"Okay, I'll call her and suggest we meet at the cafeteria in the basement of the courthouse."

Jodie gave me a few more words of encouragement then went back to work. A minute later she was on the intercom. "Forget the meeting. Reggi just called to tell you Rebekah is on her way to have lunch with Paula right now!"
"Oh, shit! Where are they going?"
"The Highland Park Cafeteria."
"And he said she had a gun."
"What!?"

I rushed out of the office to the parking garage and jumped into my Corvette. I was only fifteen minutes away so I thought I had a chance of beating Rebekah to the restaurant. *She must have taken Don's gun. Damn. Why did I bring it home? Thank God it isn't loaded.* As I drove I imagined the scene at the restaurant.

Rebekah and Paula are sitting across from each other. Rebekah stands up abruptly, slips her hand into her purse and pulls out the big .38. Paula freezes. A lady sitting next to them screams. Everyone scrambles for the exits. Rebekah points the gun at Paula. She says, "This gun isn't loaded but if you mess with Stan, next time it will be."

Two policeman cautiously enter the restaurant. "Put the gun down!" one of them says. Rebekah turns inadvertently pointing the gun toward them.

She says, "It isn't—"

Both officers fire striking her in the shoulder and the chest. She falls to the ground.

Oh God, noooo!

I pressed down the accelerator and passed two cars, barely darting back into my lane before hitting one that was coming straight at me. When I got to the cafeteria, everything seemed normal. Relief swept over me like I had plunged into a cool lake on a hot summer day. I straightened my tie and walked into the restaurant. Scanning the room, I didn't see Paula or Rebekah. Then I heard Rebekah laughing. I turned and saw them sitting at a table in a corner. They were smiling and laughing like sorority sisters. For a moment I just sat there is shock, then Rebekah noticed me.

"Stan," she yelled. "Over here."

I went over to them smiling. "Hey. What's going on over here? I didn't know you two knew each other."

Rebekah frowned. "We don't . . . or we didn't. Paula asked me to lunch. What are you doing here?"

"Ah . . . well I was just passing by, and I saw your car so I wondered what you were—"

"Oh, checking up on me, huh?"

I blushed. "No, just surprised to see you in this part of town. I figured you must be out with Marcia."

"No, my mother is watching her."

I looked at Paula. "So, lunch . . . what's the occasion."

Paula replied, "I'm sorry, Stan. It was probably presumptuous but I wanted to meet Rebekah and get to know her since I'm going to be your partner."

"But I hadn't—"

"Yeah, when were you going to tell me the good news?" Rebekah asked.

I blushed again. *The good news?* "Ah, well I was—"

Rebekah laughed. "Oh, it's all right. Paula has been telling me all about it. What a load off your back it will be when Paula takes over administration of the firm. Maybe now you'll be able to get home in time for dinner and you won't have to bring work home, huh?"

Rebekah was beaming. Paula knew exactly how to handle her. It was a unbelievable. I looked at her and shook by head in amazement. She winked. Then it struck me. What about the letters? There wasn't any way to discreetly ask how they'd overcome that complication. Then Rebekah answered the question.

"Paula says she's going to keep an eye on you for me too, since you obviously have a woman with her sights on you."

"Huh?" I said, shocked to hear that Paula wasn't the author of the poetry. I didn't blush this time, I turned beet red. "Oh, God . . . I just—"

"It's okay, Stan," Paula said. "I like you a lot, but I wasn't looking for a romantic relationship. My interest in you is your propensity for attracting thugs and murderers."

We all laughed. "That's right, you did say that. . . . But now I'm really perplexed. Who's writing me poetry?"

Paula and Rebekah shrugged. "Now I'm completely baffled."

Rebekah said, "Well, when you do figure who it is, let me know and I'll take care of her. Paula's going to teach me how to use that gun you brought home so I can protect our homestead from your clients and wannabe girlfriends."

Paula looked at me and laughed. "Your wife's a hoot. I love her already."

"I didn't know the DA's office trained you in handling weapons," I said.

"They don't, but the sheriff does. It helps when we are prosecuting cases if we know something about the weapons criminals use. Plus, in this day and age, it can be dangerous being a prosecutor."

I nodded.

"Wonderful, now I'll be coming home to an armed wife."

"Yeah," Rebekah said, in her best John Wayne imitation. "So don't even think about coming home late again. . . . *Comprendez?*"

CHAPTER TWENTY-SIX

Turner & Waters, L.L.P.

Jodie looked at me with a blank stare when I told her Paula Waters was going to be my new partner. I hadn't even thought about talking to her about the idea of bringing Paula in the firm because it had been just talk. Paula's sudden friendship with Rebekah had changed everything. Now it was a most fortuitous event with a big murder trial lurking in the near future and my bank account so low. Jodie sat down slowly in a side chair across the desk from me.

"This is so sudden. I didn't know you two were even talking about a partnership."

"Frankly I didn't think it would ever happen, but Paula really wanted to do it, and Rebekah seems comfortable with the idea."

Jodie gave me a concerned look and said, "Will I have to do work for her?"

"Just for a little while. She'll get her own secretary soon. . . . Nothing will change between you and I."

"I hope not. I love my job, and I'd hate for someone to come in and spoil it."

"Don't worry. Everything will work out fine. Just try to be helpful to Paula until she gets settled."

"Of course," Jodie said, and then got up and left.

Just after lunch Paula arrived, and I showed her to her new office. She didn't have much in the way of furnishings as her office with the DA was small. Jodie was civil with her, but I could see she wasn't at all thrilled with another woman invading her territory—particularly one who was her superior.

After Paula was settled in I briefed her on the Jim Cochran case, and we began to develop a strategy for getting an acquittal.

"You know we are taking a big risk here just assuming none of the Blaylocks killed Luther," Paula said.

"I know and I explained that to Jim when he hired me. He is confident that none of them did it and doesn't want us to turn the investigation in their direction even if it might help him win at trial."

"Okay, so our strategy will be—?"

"My theory is that Margie killed Luther. Her alibi is weak and I think we can poke holes through it at trial."

"But she has no motive," Paula reminded me.

"Maybe. Maybe not. . . . Don't you think it is strange that she's still living in Luther's condo?"

"Why is that strange?"

"Because it now belongs to Laura Bell."

"It does?"

"Yes, the divorce wasn't final and Laura Bell gets everything. . . . I keep asking myself why hasn't Laura Bell kicked Margie out?"

"Good point."

"She's also still driving Luther's Cadillac even though she owns her own car."

"Is there a probate yet?"

"I don't know. Probably not. But Laura Bell is the executrix under Luther's will, so if she wanted the condo and the car, she could file the will for probate and be in control of everything within two weeks. The fact that she hasn't done that leads me to believe Margie and she may have a deal."

"What kind of deal?"

"In exchange for Margie killing Luther, she gets the condo, Cadillac and a cut of the insurance money."

"But you said you thought Margie loved Luther. Why

would she kill him?"

"Margie's ex-husband told me she has a very violent temper. When she gets mad, she'll do just about anything. Remember the stripper, Julie?"

"Yes."

"On the Monday night before Luther was murdered he took her to a motel where they drank and had sex. That night Margie was sitting at home stewing because Luther hadn't come home. She knew about Luther's history with Julie so she went to the club where Julie worked to see if Luther was there. When she found his Cadillac in the parking lot she waited for Luther to come out. When he finally did come out, Julie was with him so she followed them to the motel. That's when I think she concocted the idea to kill Luther."

"Go on."

"She was in a rage. She wanted to kill Luther for betraying her, but if she did she'd be left with nothing. So I would guess that night or the next day she went straight to Laura Bell's place. I can almost picture the scene. Laura Bell opening the door and shocked to see Margie there. Curious as the purpose of the visit she lets her in. Margie then tells her of Luther's treachery and what a perfect opportunity it was for them both to get revenge and come out with seven hundred and fifty thousand dollars in their pockets."

"Wow. That's great. Too bad you can't prove it," Paula said.

"Well, I don't have to prove it. All I have to do is create reasonable doubt. Don't you think a jury will buy it?"

"Only if you come up with evidence of the conspiracy. It doesn't have to be much. Maybe someone saw Margie visit Laura Bell that night or we can prove they called each other," Paula said.

"Good idea. I'll subpoena Margie and Paula's phone records. Why don't you check with the neighbors and see if anyone saw Margie's car there that night," I said.

"Okay. I think I'll go tell Will I'm second chair now and

find out exactly what evidence they have against Jim Cochran. We've got to be able to poke some serious holes in his case if our strategy is to work."

"Be my guest. I doubt he'd give me the time of day."

"Don't worry. I know how to handle Will Thornton."

It was great working with Paula. She was so confident and obviously loved what she was doing. As a sole practitioner I often felt lonely, isolated, and overwhelmed by the tasks that confronted me. But now with Paula at my side I felt a surge of confidence that I had never known before. I thanked God for sending her to me.

The next afternoon Paula and I discussed what we had both found out since we had last spoken. Paula had checked the neighbors and nobody could confirm seeing Margie or her car there the night of the murder. I advised her the subpoenas were out to the phone companies, but it would be at least thirty days before they came back. Then she told me about her conference with Will.

"Okay, here's what they've got. Jim's verbal threats to kill Luther were heard by numerous persons. Margie's testimony that Jim visited the condo a few days before the murder and threatened Luther again. Then they have Jim's fingerprints on the window of the garage as well as hair fibers on the ground. Finally they have an eyewitness who saw Jim driving by the condo a few hours before the murder," Paula noted.

"So a lot will be resting on Julie's testimony that Jim was with her," I said. "Nothing they have right now puts Jim at the scene of the crime between nine-thirty and ten.

"Right. I asked Will about that and he laughed. He said by the time he gets through with Julie on cross exam, we'll wish we had never called her."

"What does he mean by that?" I said.

"I don't know, but he's almost daring us to put her on the stand. He obviously knows something that we don't."

"Or he wants us to think he does, so we won't call

her," I said. "I think he's bluffing."

"I don't think so. He's got something up his sleeve. I could feel it."

"Well, we don't have a choice in the matter. Julie is our only hope."

"We've got an awful lot riding on her," Paula said. "For Jim's sake, I hope she comes through."

After Paula and I were done, I noticed a call slip from Melanie. *Shit! That's all I need now.* The diamonds in the vault scared me. Every time I thought of selling them I imagined dire consequences. *Maybe I'm just paranoid.*

I picked up the phone and called Melanie.

"Hi, I'm sorry I haven't called you. It's just been so hectic with the trial and everything."

"I can imagine. I wouldn't have bothered you except that the buyers are getting anxious. I'm afraid we might lose them if we don't act soon."

"Okay, contact them and we'll do it."

"Great. I'll be in touch."

A chill darted down my spine as I hung up the phone. Adrenalin began flooding my system. I couldn't imagine getting a quarter million dollars. *Won't Rebekah be shocked.* I was glad my dealings with Melanie would soon be over. She was a dangerous woman for me to be around. If I wasn't careful she could ruin my life in a flash. It occurred to me the time might be right to tell Rebekah about the diamonds. *But what if something happened and I didn't get the money. She'd be devastated again.* I didn't want to chance more disappointment, so I decided to keep my mouth shut until I had the money in the bank. I wondered how long that would be.

CHAPTER TWENTY-SEVEN

State vs. Cochran

The phone records didn't turn up any calls between Margie and Laura Bell, so our defense strategy was shaky at best. Our only hope was that we could trip them up during cross examination. Many times catching a witness in a lie would lead to the revelation of other truths or at least lessen their credibility with the jury. After careful analysis, we decided our best shot would be with Laura Bell since she was just a player and not the mastermind behind the scheme.

It took a day and a half to pick the jury, so testimony started Tuesday afternoon with the prosecution putting on various witnesses to establish the crime scene, cause of death, and murder weapon. It was the afternoon of Wednesday, February 15, 1984, when Margie Mason took the stand. Thornton led her through the events from Cochran's appearance at her front door to her discovery of the body when she came home from the Rendezvous Club. Her testimony was quite convincing, and the jury gave me a hard look when I took her on cross.

"Ms. Mason. You testified that you and Lucy Patterson went to the Rendezvous Club after the movie and had a few drinks before going home," I asked.

"That's right."

"Did you drink alone?"

"No. A couple of guys joined us."

"Can you tell us who they were?"

"No."

"You testified that you arrived at the club at nine, right?"

"Yes."

"So, how long did you drink with the two men?"

"Forty-five minutes to an hour?"

"So you left between nine forty-five and ten?"

"Yes."

"Were you alone when you left?"

"Yes."

"Was Lucy alone when she left?"

"I don't know. I didn't follow her."

"Did you ask her about it later?"

Margie hesitated. "No. . . . I mean—I might have. I don't remember."

"Isn't it true that you called her the next day and she admitted to you that she took one of the men home with her?"

"I'm not sure. She might have but it's none of my business so I wouldn't have pressed it."

"Lucy Patterson is a married woman, isn't she?"

"Yes."

I picked up one of Margie Mason's telephone bills that we had subpoenaed and handed it to her. She picked it up and studied it. "Now I've just handed you what's marked as Defendant's Exhibit 7, and I would ask you to identify it."

"It's one of my telephone bills."

"In fact it is the Southwestern Bell Telephone statement for October 1983, isn't it."

"Yes."

"Now, would you look at the highlighted call on October 20, 1983."

"Yes."

"Do you recognize the number?"

Margie began to squirm in her chair. She looked at the jury and then took a deep breath. Finally, she said, "So what if I called Lucy."

"So, that entry does show a call from you to Lucy Patterson?"

"Yes."

"And that call was made a 5:32 AM, isn't that right?" I asked.

"I guess."

"So what was so important you had to call Lucy at that time of day?"

"I didn't sleep that night. Luther had been killed. I probably didn't realize it was so early."

"Or did you call her to make sure she could provide an alibi?"

"No. No way."

"You threatened her, didn't you? If she didn't provide an alibi you would tell her husband about her infidelity, right?"

"Objection!" Thornton yelled. "Argumentative."

"Overruled," the judge said.

"Do you know a woman by the name of Julie Iverson?"

Margie thought for a moment. "I'm not sure."

"She works at the Sunset Strip."

"Oh, *that* Julie. Yes, I'm afraid so."

I ran her through her first confrontation with Julie. She didn't deny any of it. Then I asked if she ever saw Luther and Julie together after that day."

"No, I don't go to strip clubs."

"You didn't go to the Sunset Strip on Monday, October 20th of last year looking for Luther?"

"No."

"You know Ms. Mason the Sunset Strip has valet parking attendants. I've got one who is prepared to testify that he saw you that night. Do I need to bring him in?"

"Okay. . . . So, maybe I did go looking for Luther. He was depressed with all the shit the Golden Dragon partners were putting him through. I just wanted to be with him to console him."

"But instead of consoling him you found him with Julie Iverson, didn't you."

Margie just stared at me.

"Your Honor. Would you instruct the witness to answer the question?"

"Ms. Mason, you must answer the question."

She sighed. "Yes. He took her to a motel."

"A motel. He took her to a motel. . . . So what did you do?"

"Nothing. I figured he was under a lot of stress and just needed to get away from everything."

"Now, that's not true, is it?"

"Objection!" Thornton yelled. "Argumentative."

"Sustained."

"Weren't you livid?"

"No."

"Don't you have a bad temper?"

"Objection!" Thornton yelled. "Irrelevant."

"Your Honor," I said. "She testified she wasn't upset about seeing Luther take another woman to a motel. I have a right to impeach that testimony."

"Overruled," the judge said.

"Thank you. You have a bad temper, don't you?"

Margie didn't answer.

"I can call your ex-husband to testify if need be. He'd be happy to tell about how you trashed his dental office when you found him screwing his receptionist."

"Objection!" Thornton yelled. "Counsel is testifying."

"I'm sorry. Let me rephrase."

"Ms. Mason—"

"Mr. Turner," the judge said. "In my courtroom when an objection is made, you will wait for a ruling before you proceed. I warned you about disobeying the rules. If there is any further violation of proper courtroom procedure you're going to find yourself behind bars and Ms. Waters will have to try this case."

"I apologize, Your Honor."

The judge nodded and then said, "Objection sustained."

I turned back to Margie and continued, "Ms. Mason. Did you trash your husband's medical office after you found him having intercourse with his secretary?"

"I wouldn't call it trashing. I just kicked over a few things."

"Didn't you react the same way when you found out Luther was cheating on you?"

"I was in my car. There weren't any pots to break."

"No, but it got you thinking about revenge, didn't it?"

"No."

"You didn't go to Laura Bell and tell her about Luther's betrayal?"

"No."

"You didn't offer to kill Luther—"

"Objection, Your Honor. There is no foundation for this line of questioning. Margie Mason is not on trial here."

The judge said, "Mr. Turner. Unless you have some evidence to support this line of questioning I can't let you proceed."

"Withdraw the question," I replied. "No further questions."

The judge said, "All right. We will recess until tomorrow morning at 9AM."

Everyone stood up as the judge left the courtroom. I looked at Jim and shrugged. Paula said, "That went pretty well. She admitted she knew about Julie. She tried to act reasonable and restrained but I don't think the jury bought it. They've got to be wondering about her now."

"I hope so. I just wish we could find someone who saw them together plotting."

"Fat chance," Paula said. "They could have met anyplace. A bar, a restaurant, or even the public library. Who knows?"

"Well, if we can't prove they met before the murder, maybe we can get them together now."

"What do you mean?"

"I've got an idea. We'll need Luther's old boss, Mr. Walsh to help us."

"What are you talking about?"

I explained my plan to Paula. She thought it was worth a shot so we contacted Walsh. He reluctantly agreed if it would help find out who really killed Luther. Since we had to be in court at nine the next morning we had to work fast. I called a client, Monty Dozier, a security guard I had done some work for. He owed me money so I asked him to help us out and said I'd credit his time towards his bill. He agreed, so I asked him to follow Margie and instructed him to take pictures if we were able to get Margie and Laura Bell together. Paula and I briefed Walsh on our plan and gave him a tape recorder and a transmitter to put in his coat pocket. With this setup we could hear and record any conversations between Walsh and Laura Bell.

Thick dark thunderclouds hung overhead as Walsh drove up to Margie's house. It had been raining all day but now a ray of sunlight was shining through a momentary crack in the clouds. Half of a rainbow could be seen in the distance. I wondered if we would find the pot of gold today or just get another drenching from Mother Nature. Walsh got into his car and drove to Laura Bell's apartment. He parked in front, went upstairs and knocked on the door. The door opened quickly. We made ourselves comfortable in Paula's Camry down the street while we listened.

"Hello," Laura Bell said.

"Hi, I'm Clifford Walsh, Mid-America Life Insurance Company."

"Yes, please come in."

"How are you today?" he said.

"As good as can be expected, you know . . . under the

circumstances."

"Yes, it's always difficult when you lose someone you care for."

"Well, Luther and I were getting a divorce, but he was the father of our child, Betsy. We'll miss him."

"At least he had sense enough to buy an adequate amount of insurance to take care of you and little Betsy."

Laura began to weep and said, "Yes, he really loved Betsy and I think he still loved me. He didn't want the divorce. It was me, it was my doing."

"Huh," Walsh said as he pulled an envelope out of his coat pocket and handed it to Laura. "Well, here's a cashier's check for $50,000. This was the group term policy. The supplemental life policy proceeds should be here in a few more days."

"Oh, all right. I sure appreciate you coming out to my place to bring this to me."

"It's no problem. You know at Mid-America we believe good service is important, particularly in time of tragedy like the loss of a loved one."

"Well, thanks again."

Walsh stepped outside. He shook Laura's hand and then walked to his car. He got in and drove off. Paula and I waited and watched down the street. She came out of her house five minutes later and got into her car and drove off. We quickly began to follow her at a safe distance. She drove for awhile and then turned into a branch of Republic Bank. Getting out of her car, she looked around as if concerned about someone tailing her. Not seeing us, she went into the bank. We waited outside.

Laura left the bank ten minutes later, got back into her car and drove to the Granada Theater. She parked in the theater parking lot, bought a ticket and then went inside. Paula and I got out of the car and walked into the theater. Our private investigator was already in the lobby. He told us Margie had gotten there a few minutes earlier and went into the theater. We watched Laura Bell enter the theater. She made her way to the right aisle door, opened it and went inside. She hesitated a moment apparently waiting for her eyes to adjust to the darkness. Then she walked down the aisle, found Margie Mason and sat down. We sat a few rows behind them and the detective took a seat near the door.

"Hi," Margie whispered.

"Hello," Laura replied.

"You got the package?"

"Uh huh, no problem."

"Good, I really need it. I'm totally broke."

Laura pulled an envelope out of her purse, handed it to Margie and said, "Mr. Walsh said he'd have the rest in a few days."

"Good."

Suddenly there was a flash of light, then another and another. Margie and Laura Bell jumped up and bolted for the exit but not before the private detective got a couple good shots of them leaving.

Before we went home, we asked the private detective to keep an eye on Laura Bell until we could put her on the stand later in the week. If she really had conspired with Margie to kill Luther, she might just think about running. We couldn't let that happen now that she was critical to Jim's defense.

On Thursday the prosecution called Jim and Pam Blaylock to explain to the jury Jim's motive for allegedly killing Luther. Thornton artfully led them through all of the pain and tragedy of the Golden Dragon Partnership. He even had Pam in tears a couple of times recalling Luther's dirty tricks. I didn't do much on cross as Jim's motive was clear, and denying it would have looked foolish. At noon on Friday, Thornton finished putting on his case.

I thought the judge would recess the case until Monday, but he didn't. He told us to proceed. We called our private detective. Paula took him on direct exam.

"Please state your name?"

"Monty Dozier," he said.

"Mr. Dozier. Did you have an occasion to—"

"Objection, Your Honor. This witness is not on the witness list."

"Your honor," Paula said. "Mr. Dozier is a rebuttal witness. He was just retained a few days ago. His testimony will establish a relationship between Margie Mason and Laura Bell."

The gallery stirred. Thornton glared at Paula.

"All right," the judge said. "Objection overruled. Proceed."

"How are you employed, Mr. Dozier?" Paula asked.

"I'm a private detective."

"And were you hired to follow Margie Mason on Wednesday night?"

"Yes, I was."

"And did she go anywhere that night?'

"Yes, she went to the Granada Theater."

"Did she meet anyone there?"

"Yes, she met Laura Bell."

The crowd erupted in conversation. The judge banged his gavel and said, "There will be no conversation during examination of witnesses. Bailiff, if anyone can't keep quiet escort them out of the courtroom. The bailiff nodded.

"I'm going to show you Defendant's Exhibits 8-13," Paula said and handed a stack of photos to the witness. "Can you identify these photos?"

"Yes, I took these Wednesday night at the Granada Theater. They show Margie Mason meeting with Laura Bell."

Paula took the photos and showed them to Thornton. Then she said, "Your Honor, we request that Defendant's Exhibits 8-13 be admitted.

Thornton looked up and said, "Objection," Your Honor. These are irrelevant. Margie Mason and Laura Bell are not on trial here.

"Overruled."

"Pass the witness," Paula said.

Thornton jumped up. "And how is it, sir, that you just happened to be at the Granada Theater on Wednesday night?"

"Stan Turner hired me to follow Margie Mason and take pictures if she met up with Laura Bell."

"I see. How do you suppose Mr. Turner knew Margie Mason would be meeting Laura Bell?" Thornton asked.

"Objection." Paula snarled. "That's irrelevant."

"Overruled, I would like to hear the answer to that question," the judge said.

"I don't know. He didn't tell me that."

Thornton gave the witness a puzzled look. The judge said, "Any further questions, Mr. Thornton?"

"No, Your Honor."

"Redirect," the judge asked.

"No further questions," Paula replied.

"Very well," the judge said. "Call your next witness."

I stood up and said, "The defense calls Laura Bell."

The Bailiff escorted Laura Bell into the courtroom. She looked scared as she quickly made her way to the witness stand.

"Do you promise to tell the truth, the whole truth and nothing but the truth?" the judge asked.

"Yes," she said.

I started out slowly with Laura asking her simple questions about her background, her marriage to Luther, their child and the onset of their marital difficulties. Then I asked her about the night they broke up.

"Tell us about your last night with Luther?"

"What do you mean?"

"You had an argument, right?"

"Yes, I discovered he had been unfaithful again."

"So you were angry?"

"Yes, of course I was. I told him to get out."

"Did he leave?"

"Eventually."

"After you pulled a gun on him?"

The crowd stirred. The judge sat up straight and glared at the gallery. Laura Bell lowered her head.

"I wasn't going to use it. I just wanted to scare him."

"So you pulled a gun on him and told him to get out, is that right?"

"Yes, and had he not left, would you have killed him?"

"Objection!" Thornton yelled. "Calls for speculation."

"Sustained."

"Your husband was in the insurance business, right?"

"Yes."

"Did he carry a lot of insurance?"

"Well, I don't know if you would call it a lot."

"Seven hundred and fifty thousand dollars, right?"

"I believe so."

I laughed. "I think that would qualify as a lot."

"Objection!"

"Withdrawn."

"Mrs. Bell. You testified your divorce was never finalized, right?"

"Yes."

"So, were you still the beneficiary of the insurance?"

"Yes, I was really surprised to learn that, but I guess I was."

"Have you already received some of that insurance money?"

Laura Bell's face turned stone grey. She squirmed in her chair. The gallery waited for her response. She finally said weakly, "Yes."

"And when did you receive that money?"

"A few days ago."

"Wednesday to be exact, right?"

"I guess."

"Did you give any of that insurance money to Margie

Mason?"

"No. Why would I do that?"

"Your Honor," I said. "May I approach the witness."

The judge nodded. I took the photos up and handed them to Laura Bell. She took a quick glance at them and then looked up.

"Is that you sitting next to Margie Mason?"

She nodded.

"You'll have to answer out loud so the jury can hear you and the court reporter can take down your answer."

"Yes. That's me with Margie Mason."

"And was that taken Wednesday night?"

"Yes, we were going to see a movie. Is that a crime?"

"No, of course not. But I'm curious how you and Margie became so close."

"Well, we're not that close."

"She's staying in your condo isn't she?"

"Huh?"

"Doesn't the condo belong to you now that Luther died?"

"Well, technically, but I couldn't kick Margie out when she's still mourning."

"Oh, so is that why you let her keep the Cadillac and gave her part of the insurance proceeds?"

"Objection, assumes facts not in evidence," Thornton said.

"I'll rephrase."

"Did you give part of the insurance proceeds to Margie Mason? And I'll remind you, you're under oath."

"It was just a loan. She was broke. I felt sorry for her."

"Was that it or was it her cut for murdering Luther Bell?"

There were several gasps of shock from the gallery. Everyone started talking. Several newsmen jumped up and scampered out of the courtroom. The judge banged his gavel. The bailiff stood up and glared at the gallery.

"Objection!" Thornton screamed.

"Overruled." The noise in the gallery hadn't subsided. "Silence!" the judge screamed. Finally the room became quiet again. Thornton nodded to Laura Bell to answer the question.

"No. I just felt sorry for Margie. I understood how betrayed she must have felt after Luther left her with nothing."

"Betrayed? Did she tell you she caught Luther at a motel with a stripper a few nights before he was murdered?"

Laura Bell was breathing heavy now. She looked at the judge and then back at me. "No, I don't recall that."

"Are you going to be loaning more money to Margie when the rest of your insurance proceeds come in?"

"Oh, no. She's got enough." Laura blurted out and then froze. I looked at the jury hoping they were focusing on Laura Bell. Her expression was her confession and I prayed the jury had read it the way I did. Thornton didn't bother to cross examine Laura Bell. He probably figured it might make matters worse, as Laura Bell was shaking badly when she finally left the stand.

Fortunately, the judge recessed the case and told us to return at ten on Monday morning. I was glad to get a break, as it had been an exhausting week.

When we got back to the office, Jodie jumped up and said, "I'm glad you're back. You've got to go to Parkland Hospital right away."

"Parkland Hospital? Why?'

"Melanie Dixon's has been beat up pretty badly. They found your card in her purse and called here. I told them you were in trial but would get over there just as soon as possible."

"Who beat her up?"
"I don't know."
"How badly is she hurt?
"Pretty bad. She's in ICU."

"Oh, my God!" I said, and rushed out the door. It took me about thirty minutes to get to Parkland. On the way I couldn't help but think Melanie's attackers were connected to the diamonds. A police detective was in the waiting room when I got there. I introduced myself.

"Who do you think did it?"

"Professionals. They were looking for information."

"Information? What kind of information?"

"I don't know. I thought maybe you might help us out there."

"Well, I wouldn't know. Melanie was just selling some Peruvian pottery for me. I can't imagine why anyone would beat her up. Is she going to be okay?"

"I think so. They've moved her into a room. It looks like she's out of danger."

"Thank God. Do you think they will let me see her?"

"Sure, I just left her a minute ago. She's coherent."

The detective gave me his card and said, "If you think of anything or learn anything from Ms. Dixon, please give me a call."

"I will. Thanks."

After checking in at the nurse's station to find out Melanie's room number, I walked in. Her eyes were closed so I just watched her for a moment. After a minute she coughed and opened her eyes.

"Stan," she said. "I'm so glad to see you."

I walked over to her and sat on the side of her bed. She smiled up at me weakly.

"What happened?" I asked.

"When I came back from lunch today, two men grabbed me and pulled me behind our building. They said they knew I had the diamonds and they wanted them."

"Oh, God. What did you tell them?"

"I told them I didn't know what they were talking about. They said they knew Melvin dumped them somewhere in Dallas, and when I started shopping for a buyer they put two and two together."

"Shit!"

"I told them I didn't have them—that I was just a broker. That's when they started beating me."

"Are you in a lot of pain," I said, feeling very guilty that I had gotten her into this mess.

"They've given me medication. I'm okay."

"So, then what happened?"

"They wanted to know who *did* have them. I wouldn't tell them so they beat me some more."

"Oh, you poor girl. I'm so sorry. You should have just told them. I guess it's time I go to the police."

"But I thought you couldn't do that? They might think you were part of the smuggling operation."

"I know, but I don't want you to get hurt. They might come back, and *this* time they might kill you."

"I'll go away until this all blows over. They won't find me again."

"But where will you go?"

"I have a sister I can visit. She uses her married name so they'll never be able to find her. I'll call you when I get there so you'll know I'm okay."

"But what about your job?"

"I've got some vacation time coming. It won't be a problem."

"Good. It may take a little time, but I'll figure out a way out of this mess," I said.

"Be careful," Melanie said with a genuine concern in her voice. "If they figure out you have the diamonds they'll come after you to get them."

I nodded. "I know. So much for sleeping at night."

Monty Dozier was surprised when I called him with another job. He agreed to make sure that when Melanie left the hospital, she got to her sisters house okay. I told him an old boyfriend was stalking her. He seemed to buy the explanation.

CHAPTER TWENTY-EIGHT

A Low Blow

When my alarm went off on Monday morning, I didn't want to get up. It was a pivotal day and I was scared to death it wouldn't go well. We were putting Julie Iverson on the stand and I knew Thornton would be ready to rip her apart. I wondered how she would hold up against a ruthless prosecutor like Will Thornton. If she didn't convince the jury that Jim was with her when Luther was killed, Jim would likely be convicted. I lingered in the shower a little too long, so Rebekah came looking for me.

"Don't you have to get to court?"

"Yeah," I said and turned off the water.

"Will you finish today?"

"Probably."

"What do you think?"

"It's a toss up. We could win or lose."

"I think I'll leave the kids with my mother and come watch. Is that okay?"

"I guess. I won't have time to entertain you."

"I know. You won't even know I'm there."

I shrugged. "Okay."

Paula and Jim Cochran were sitting at the defense table when I walked in at 8:58 a.m. Paula exhaled when she saw me. "Where have you been? I was afraid I'd have to take Julie on direct exam."

"I'm sorry. I overslept."

Paula shook her head in dismay. "How can you oversleep when you've got a murder trial going on?"

The court reporter came in the room, and the bailiff stood. "All rise!" The judge came in and quickly took his seat. He shuffled a few papers and then looked at the bailiff.

"Bring in the jury."

After the jury was seated, the judge looked at me and said, "Mr. Turner. Call your next witness."

"Yes, Your Honor. The defense calls Julie Iverson."

All eyes immediately focused on Julie as she strolled down the aisle toward the witness stand. She was elegantly dressed in a black knit dress, silver earrings with matching bracelets, and a big diamond ring. She winked at me as she walked by. After she was seated, the judge administered the oath, and I got up to take her on direct examination. I couldn't help but feel sorry for Wanda who was sitting in the first row, as I knew this line of questioning was going to be painful for her.

"Miss Iverson. Will you tell us where you are employed?"

"Yes, I'm a dancer at the Sunset Strip."

"I would like to direct your attention to the defendant who has been sitting next to me. Do you know him?"

"Yes, that's Jim Cochran."

"How do you know him?"

"He's a customer at the Sunset Strip."

"And what is the Sunset Strip?"

"It's a men's club."

"I see. And did you have an occasion to see Mr. Cochran on the night of October 19, 1983?"

"Yes, he came into the club, and I spent most of the evening entertaining him."

"When did he arrive?"

"About eight."

"And when did he leave?"

"At ten. I remember because it was just before the ten o'clock news came on. Everybody was in the dressing room watching because Lindsay, one of the girls, had been caught with a minister, and it was gonna be on TV."

"So there is no doubt in your mind that Jim Cochran was in the Sunset Strip between eight and ten that evening?"

"No, sir."

"Did you know the victim, Luther Bell?"

"Yes, he was a customer too."

"Now, I am sorry to have to ask you about this, but did you and Luther ever have sex?"

"Objection!" Thornton yelled. "Your Honor, this is totally irrelevant and calculated to prejudice the jury!"

I replied, "Your honor, if I may continue I will show Miss Iverson's sexual encounter with the decedent to be very relevant."

"Mr. Turner alluded to this earlier in the week. I'm relieved to find out it wasn't pure fabrication. Proceed, counsel. I'll give you a little latitude but get to the point. Objection overruled."

I turned back to Julie and said, "Miss Iverson, did you ever have sex with the decedent?"

"Yes, one time."

"And when was that?"

"He took me to the Blue Ribbon motel a couple days before he was murdered. October 17, 1983, I believe. We partied awhile and then had sex."

"When did he leave?"

"About eleven fifteen"

"Do you know Luther's girlfriend, Margie Mason?"

"Yes, we had met on a previous occasion."

"And on that occasion what happened?"

"Margie caught us together. I was cooking breakfast and didn't have any clothes on."

"How did Margie react to that?"

"She was livid. She stormed out of the house and told him their relationship was over."

"Did Margie see you and Luther the night you went to the Blue Ribbon Motel?"

"I don't know."

"But she might have?"

"Objection! Speculation."

"Sustained."

"If she had seen you together do you think she would have been angry enough to kill Luther?"

"Objection! Move to strike! Calls for speculation! Inflammatory. Again, Margie Mason is not on trial here."

"Your honor. She testified that Margie was livid the last time she caught them together."

"Objection sustained. You haven't established that Margie Mason saw them that night. The jury is instructed to disregard the question."

"No further questions."

"Mr. Thornton, your witness," the judge said.

"Miss Iverson. Do your customers pay you?" Thornton asked.

"Yes, most of them do."

"And on the night in question, did Mr. Cochran pay you?"

"Yes."

"How much?"

"Two or three hundred dollars."

"And was he a regular customer?"

"Yes."

"So if Mr. Cochran is convicted, you stand to lose a lot of money, isn't that right?"

"I suppose so."

"So you'd do anything to make sure Mr. Cochran wasn't convicted, isn't that right?"

"No, I've told the truth. I wouldn't lie under oath."

"You sell your body for money, but not your honesty. Is that what you're saying?"

"Objection! Argumentative," I said.

"Sustained."

"Miss Iverson, When you walked up to the stand, I noticed you winked at Mr. Turner."

Adrenalin began flooding my system. I stood up but couldn't think of what to say.

"I beg your pardon?" Julie said.

"Have you ever had sex with Mr. Turner?"

"Objection!" I said as I gave Thornton a scathing look. The gallery erupted in excited conversation. Rebekah gasped. I looked over at her in dismay. "You son of a bitch," I said to Thornton.

The judge said, "Order! Approach the bench."

We both walked up and stood before the judge. I felt like choking Thornton to death in open court.

"What are you doing, Mr. Thornton! I warned you about this type of behavior. I may have to declare a mistrial."

"Your Honor," Thornton said. "I've got photographs of Mr. Turner with the witness."

I replied, "Well the only photographs you could have would be of me meeting her for lunch to discuss this case."

The judge looked at Thornton. He replied. "Well, she obviously has a thing for Mr. Turner. You saw her wink at him!"

"Step back!" the judge yelled.

"Objection, sustained. Ladies and gentlemen of the jury. I apologize for Mr. Thornton's outrageous conduct. You are instructed to disregard his question and the insinuation that Mr. Turner has any kind of relationship with this witness. I hesitate to declare a mistrial because of the tremendous expense that would cause the taxpayers, but if any of you do not feel you can disregard what just happened then I must do so. So if any one of you think you will be unable to disregard what Mr. Thornton said and render a fair and impartial verdict, please raise your hand.

The jurors looked at each other, but nobody raised a hand.

"Good," the judge said. "Mr. Thornton, do have any further questions?"

"No," Your Honor.

"Mr. Turner?"

"Your Honor, may I have a moment to confer with my co-counsel?"

"Yes. Take a minute."

I whispered to Paula. "What do think I should do?"

"Leave it alone. It's a trap. If you try to rebut the innuendo that you had sex with Julie, you may open the door for the topic to come up again."

"But if I don't, the jury may think I *did* have sex with her."

"Leave it alone. I'm telling you."

I addressed the court. "Your Honor, no further questions."

"Thank you, Mr. Turner. The witness is excused."

Julie stood up and walked quickly out of the courtroom. As she stepped into the hall, a reporter yelled, "Miss Iverson, Did you have sex with defense counsel?"
I cringed when I heard it. Thornton looked at me with a big smile on his face. Paula shook her head. I looked in the gallery for Rebekah but she was gone.

We called several more witnesses that day and on Tuesday the case went to the jury. By five o'clock the jury hadn't rendered a verdict so the judge sent them home. That night when we were alone Rebekah said she understood that Thornton's accusations were nothing but a dirty trick. But she obviously had been humiliated by it. It didn't help that it was mentioned prominently on the ten o'clock news.

"Why did you have to take this case?"she moaned. "You promised me you'd never take another murder case. I hate being in a glass bowl! How am I going to face my friends? What are my parents going to think?" she said, and then began crying.

"I'm so sorry, honey. Paula said Thornton was a

bastard, but I never dreamed he would stoop so low. I'm going to file a grievance against him with the bar association."

"No!" Rebekah said jumping to her feet. "Then it will be all over the papers again. Just forget it! I don't want to ever hear about it again." She stormed off. I heard the bedroom door slam. I closed my eyes and prayed tomorrow would be a better day.

CHAPTER TWENTY-NINE

The Verdict

It rained hard on the way to work on Wednesday. It had rained all night, and I wondered when it would let up. I couldn't believe the jury was still out. I didn't sleep well with Jim Cochran's fate still on the line and Rebekah so upset with me. I just prayed Jim would get acquitted so life would get back to normal. I hadn't been at my desk for more than ten minutes when Paula called. She said the jury was coming back with a verdict. When I got to the courthouse, Paula was sitting on a bench outside the courtroom.

She smiled and said, "Hi. Wonderful weather, huh?"

"For sure. . . . So what's happening?"

"The bailiff is getting ready to bring them into the courtroom. Jim and Wanda are already inside. We better go on in."

We went inside and took our seats at the defense table. The gallery was nearly full and I could feel the excitement and tension in the air. Thornton gave me a hard look and I stared right back at him. He finally turned and started to talk to an associate. The court reporter's door opened and she took her place. Then the bailiff rose and said, "All rise!"

The judge entered the room and said, "Be seated." He looked over at the bailiff and said, "Bring in the jury."

The bailiff got up and went into the jury room. A moment later members of the jury began filing out. When they had all been seated, the judge said, "Ladies and gentlemen of the jury, have you reached a verdict?"

The foreman rose and said, "Yes, Your Honor, we

have."

The foreman handed a piece of paper to the bailiff and he took it to the judge. The judge read it and handed it back to the bailiff. The judge said, "How do you find?"

The foreman said, "On the charge of murder in the first degree, we find the defendant *not guilty.*"

The gallery erupted into excited conversation. Paula turned and smiled gleefully. I shook Jim's hand and then looked over at Thornton. He was shaking his head in disbelief. I shrugged.

The judge said, "The defendant is free to go. Ladies and gentlemen of the jury, thank you for your jury service. You are dismissed. This court is adjourned."

Relief quickly engulfed me. I felt like I was going to float away as the weight of so much adversity had finally been shed. Paula was as high as a satellite. Her dreams of being a big time criminal attorney had finally come true. I deferred the press to her as I was anxious to get home and tell Rebekah the good news.

On the way back I decided to stop by the office to leave my briefcase and check for important messages before I went home. As I drove in the parking garage an ominous feeling came over me. I looked around but saw nothing, so I cut the engine and got out of my car. I opened the trunk and grabbed my briefcase. As I was closing the trunk I saw movement in my peripheral vision. I looked in that direction but saw nothing. As I was walking toward my building, a tall man jumped out from behind a car. He grabbed me from behind, thrust me hard up against a pillar, and stuck a gun in my back.

He said, "Do exactly what I say and you won't get hurt."

"What do you want?!" I moaned as he dug the gun deeper into my back. Fear swept through me.

"We're going for a little ride," he said.

I heard a car approaching fast. The car came to a

screeching stop and the man forced me into the back seat He gagged me and tied a blindfold over my eyes. The car sped off. We traveled in silence for ten or fifteen minutes and then the car stopped. I heard a garage door go up and we drove inside and stopped the engine. The garage door closed, then my door opened and someone grabbed my arm and yanked me out of the car. I hit my shoulder on the door and pain shot through me like an arrow.

Once inside they sat me on a chair, removed my gag, and tied my hands behind my back. A door slammed. I didn't know if I was alone or if someone was still there with me. Then I heard the faint sound of someone breathing.

"What do you want with me?" I said.

"Shut up! You'll find out soon enough," a male voice said. He had a Massachusetts accent just like Rebekah. I wondered if he were a member of the mob. A few minutes later the door opened. It sounded like several people entered the room.

"Mr. Turner. It seems you have some property that belongs to us."

"What property is that?"

"Don't play coy with us. You know what I'm talking about."

"Why don't you just tell what it is, and if I have it I'll tell you."

"Diamonds."

"Oh, that. Those belong to you?"

"Yes, and you're going to return them aren't you?"

"Sure, no problem. How did you know I had them?"

"You made the mistake of going to visit Melanie in the hospital. We didn't kill her because we figured whoever had the diamonds would contact her."

"Listen. I knew nothing about the diamonds. A client just gave me some pottery in exchange for legal services. He didn't tell me about the diamonds. Melanie just found them by accident when she was trying to sell the pottery."

"You expect me to believe that?"

"Yes, it's the truth. I don't know anything about what you guys are into, and I don't care. The diamonds are in a safety deposit box at Valley View Bank. We can go get them right now."

"That's exactly what we're going to do."

"Good. I don't want the diamonds. I knew they were trouble the first time I heard about them."

They led me back to the car and threw me in the back seat. We drove another twenty minutes before the car stopped. I figured we were at the Valley View Bank because I could hear the traffic on LBJ Freeway.

"All right, Mr. Turner. I'm going into the bank with you. You're going to take me to the safety deposit box and get me the diamonds. Then we are going to come back to the car. Once we are at a safe distance I'll let you go."

"No way. I don't want to see who you are. If I see your face you'll have to kill me. Untie me and then disappear. When you're gone, I'll take off the mask and go into the bank and get the diamonds. I'll bring them back here and leave them in the car. I'll go back into the bank and wait ten minutes before I come out."

"Do you think I'm an idiot or something? As soon as you get inside you'll call the police or notify security. I can't risk two million dollars."

"Two million dollars?"

"Yes, why do you think we've kept searching for six months? Schwartz was supposed to deliver them to us but he betrayed us."

Melanie had lied to me. She must have planned to cheat me. It suddenly dawned on me she hadn't called once she got to her sisters. I was confused and angry. I said, "You know who I am. You know I have a family. If I betrayed you it would be suicide. Believe me this is the best way to handle it for your sake and for mine. If you go in there with a gun in my back someone might get suspicious and then it will be all over. It's too dangerous. Trust me. My way is best."

"All right. But believe me I *will* kill you and your family if I don't get the diamonds."

"I know. You'll get them. Don't worry."

They untied my hands, and I heard each of the car doors slam. I waited several minutes to be sure they were gone and took off the blindfold. I glanced around, it appeared everything was normal. I opened the car door and walked slowly into the bank. The thought of running to a security guard crossed my mind, but I knew that was too risky. I didn't really know who I was up against. If it were the mob, the police couldn't protect me or my family. I headed for the elevator and went downstairs to the vault.

The receptionist smiled as I walked up to her.

"I need to get into my box."

"Okay," she said and pointed to the log book. I signed in and she got up and led me into the vault. We both put in our keys and opened it. She carried the box into a private stall and set it down. I thanked her, and she left. I opened the box and lifted the felt bag.

It was too light. Panic ripped through me like a chain saw. The bag was empty. *Oh my God! Melanie must have switched bags on me. . . . The rubber band. She sent me for a rubber band to give her time to make the switch. Oh God! No!*

I fell back hard against the side of the cubicle. I heard a voice. "Are you all right in there?"

"Yes, I'm fine," I said as I tried to figure out why she had taken them. She must have planned it all along. Make the mobsters think I have the diamonds, and she gets away clean. Brilliant, but what a cold heartless woman.

My mind began to spin out of control. I thought of Rebekah and my children being mowed down by machine guns. Blood was gushing from their wounds. I could hear them wailing. *What should I do? Oh, my God! Help me. Okay, get hold of yourself. Think.*

I knew if went outside without the diamonds they

would kill me on the spot. I had no choice now but to notify a security guard of the situation. I got up and headed for the receptionist. There was a man with her who was signing in the log book.

"Ma'am. I need to talk to a security officer," I whispered.

She looked at me with fear in her eyes. "What's wrong?"

"I don't have time to explain. Just get a security officer down here immediately."

The receptionist picked up the phone but before she could punch in the extension, the man signing in pulled a gun and pointed it at us. She screamed. We both raised our hands. "Get inside and get me those diamonds," he said.

He pushed us back into the vault and stuck the gun in my face. "Get the diamonds now!"

I rushed into the cubicle and picked up the safety deposit box. I knew he'd probably kill me just as soon as he found out I didn't have the diamonds. I came out of the cubicle and ran straight at him like a linebacker after a quarterback. He fired at me and I felt the box slam into my chest. I fell to the ground, the wind knocked out of me. There was more gunfire—a lot of gunfire. I looked up and saw a security guard shooting at the man. He went down, blood gushing from his wounds. I tried to breathe and regain control of my body. The man fell next to me, reeling from the sting of the bullet. I lunged for his gun. He fought me, but he was weak and gave up the battle quickly as his body went limp.

Then there were sirens and security guards swarming around. I sat up against the wall and tried to regain my breath. Some policemen came down the stairs and asked the security guards what had happened. Then a detective showed up. He came over to me. He stopped and squinted.

"You look familiar. Do I know you?"

"I don't know. I'm Stan Turner."

"Right. You were on TV today. Didn't you win a big murder trial?"

"Yeah. You'd think that would be enough excitement for one day."

He laughed. "So what was all this about?"

I told him the story. He shook his head. "You're lucky you are alive."

"I know."

It was nearly seven o'clock before the police released me. Rebekah came to the station to pick me up. She had been frantic with worry all day since she had expected me to come home after the trial. I explained everything to her on the way home. She cried.

"You should have just given the diamonds to the police."

"I know. But I thought maybe the diamonds fell into my lap for a reason. Maybe we were supposed to have them. I wondered if Melvin Schwartz even knew they were there."

"Oh, God, Stan. I almost lost you today," Rebekah moaned. "Promise you won't ever get involved in anything like this again."

"God, I hope not. I've had enough excitement for a lifetime."

"You don't think they'll come after you again, do you?"

"No. They probably think the police have the diamonds now. Melanie was a pretty smart girl. She had me completely fooled."

Losing the money didn't bother me too much. I never really believed it would be mine. What did piss me off was Melanie putting me and my family at risk. I wondered if she'd have given a damn if we'd all been killed. I thought about trying to track her down, but I had a family to protect and a law practice to run. I couldn't be gallivanting all over the country chasing diamonds. Besides, Melanie was probably long gone—particularly now that the Mob knew she had their diamonds.

CHAPTER THIRTY

A Million Fish

One of the great things about Texas is that in the dead of winter the weather can suddenly turn warm. Although it was still February, the temperature was a pleasant seventy-three degrees, and it had been that way all week. It was late Saturday afternoon and we were near the end of our vacation. The boys and I had been fishing all day and were tired when we pulled into the busy marina. Once the boat was securely moored, we headed back to our room where Rebekah and Marcia were waiting to go to dinner. There was restaurant in Pottsboro known for its great catfish where we planned to eat. Then it was off to a movie in Dennison. *Chariots of Fire* was playing, and although it had been out for quite awhile we hadn't seen it. On the way back to the resort we discussed the dreaded but inevitable return home.

"We should leave by noon so it's not too late when we get home," Rebekah remarked.

"Just as long as I can sleep in. This week has been fun, but I'm totally exhausted from everything we've done."

"Tell me about it. I don't usually swim or play tennis everyday."

Marcia, who had been half-asleep in the back seat, piped up. "Daddy, when are you going to take me fishing?"

"Hmm," I said, then looked at Rebekah. She gave me a dirty look.

"I'll tell you what. After we get up tomorrow and have breakfast I'll take you out for a couple hours, okay?"

"Yippeee!" Marcia yelled. "I'm gonna catch a million

fish."

Rebekah shook her head and looked away.

I said, "I hope not. I wouldn't want to clean that many fish."

"Don't worry," Mark said. "She won't catch anything."

"Yes I will," Marcia replied indignantly.

"Okay, no fighting. Mark, you went fishing twice this week so don't be a bad sport."

Mark let out a grunt and went back to sleep.

The next morning we had a big breakfast at a little diner down the road, and then Marcia and I headed for the marina. Rebekah reluctantly let her baby go, after reminding me of a half dozen common sense safety tips. I patiently listened and then assured her everything would be fine.

It was a glorious day out on the lake. There was a gentle southerly breeze and a bright blue sky with big, fluffy cumulus clouds dancing overhead. Fishing for crappie was entirely different than fishing for striper. Crappie were usually found around trees and cover, not in the open waters where striper usually schooled. After cruising along the bank for awhile, I spotted a little cove with a lot of tree trunks protruding from the water. There were several fishermen already in the cove, which indicated to me that this might be a good spot to stop.

"How about over there?" I said.

"Yeah, yeah. That looks like a good spot, Daddy," Marcia replied.

I slowed the engine and glided into the cove trying not to disturb the other fisherman. Then I cut the engine and tied the boat to a tree trunk. Marcia was jumping around, full of excitement. She watched me intently as I prepared her pole for action. After I had attached a minnow to the hook, she grabbed the pole and started to cast it.

"No, just drop it over the side and let it sink," I said.

"Okay," she said as she took a seat near the edge of the boat and dropped her line.

Once her line was in the water I fixed up my rig and got it in next to hers. Then we waited.

"How long will it take, Daddy?" she asked.

"You never know. Sometimes just a couple minutes and sometimes a couple hours."

"A couple hours?"

"Sometimes."

She wiggled around on the hard wooden seat. I figured it wouldn't be long before she was ready to go home. Then the big red bobber disappeared under the water.

"Daddy. I lost my bobber."

"No, you didn't. You've got a fish."

Just then the reel let out a deafening whine as the big crappie took the hook. Marcia was jerked toward the edge of the boat and nearly fell overboard. I grabbed her shirt and held on.

"Daddy. It's a giant one. It's gonna get me."

"Reel it in slowly. I've got you. Don't worry."

She reeled the fish in as fast as she could, but it was stronger that she was. I secured my pole and then got behind her and helped her reel it in. It was a nice three-pounder which jumped up and wiggled around in the bottom of the boat. I stepped on it lightly for a moment so I could remove the hook. Marcia took her pole and rushed over to the minnow bucket. Much to my surprise she deftly netted a minnow and tried to grab it so she could bait her hook. After watching her with great amusement for a minute I pitched in and we got the minnow on the hook.

"I told you I was gonna catch a million fish," she said.

I laughed. "Your brothers are going to be so mad."

After a couple of hours, we had caught eleven fish. That was way more than we needed or could possibly eat so I suggested we call it a day.

"Nooo, Daddy! I haven't caught a million yet."

"I know, but you've got plenty. Mom wants to leave early so it isn't too late when we get home. Your brothers have school tomorrow." Marcia pouted a little and then reluctantly began helping me secure the poles so we could leave. As we were throwing the fish into the cooler, I noticed for the first time the other boats had left. Then I took a look around and saw that it had become overcast and the south wind out on the lake had picked up quite a bit.

"We better get a move on. The weather looks like it's fixin' to get bad."

Marcia looked around warily but didn't say anything. I checked both our life jackets and then settled in my seat and cranked the engine. It sputtered a little but then roared to life. As we were pulling out of the cove it began to rain. I figured it was about twenty minutes under normal circumstances to the marina. Unfortunately as the waves got larger and larger from the strong southerly wind, I had to slow down to avoid capsizing. Soon the rain turned into a torrential downpour and I could hardly see where I was going. The waves grew in size and ferocity. Marcia got seasick and started to vomit. I cut the engine and held her over the side of the boat. She began to cry.

"Come on baby. You're gonna be all right. We'll be back at the marina soon."

"Daddy, I feel terrible. Please take me home."

"I am, honey. It won't be long now."

I got the engine going again and started moving but the visibility was so bad I couldn't see where I was going. The wind had turned us around too and I really didn't know which direction to go. Realizing that travel under these circumstances was futile, I started searching for land. I figured we could beach the boat and wait for better weather.

"Daddy, take me home," Marcia whined.

"I will, honey. Just be patient."

After a few minutes I thought I saw land so I turned the boat and headed straight toward it. After we had the boat securely tied to a tree stump. We scampered under a rock protrusion from the cliffs above. We cuddled to keep warm since our clothes were soaked.

"When will it stop, Daddy? I want to go home."

"These storms usually blow over in a hour or so. It shouldn't be long now."

"I don't want to go back in the boat. It might turn over. Can't we walk home?"

"I don't know, honey. It might be kind of hard."

"Please daddy? I don't want to go in the boat. Take me home."

I looked around and saw a small cabin in the distance. When the rain let up we took off toward it. There was smoke coming out of the chimney so I figured someone was there and they might let us use their phone. We climbed up the stairs to the front porch and knocked on the door. The door opened and a middle aged lady appeared.

"Hi, ma'am. I wonder if we can use your phone. We got caught in the storm and—"

"Come right in. You'll catch a death of cold out there," she said, looking at our drenched clothing. "Go get over there in front of the fire and dry off. I'll get you the phone."

While I was on the phone the lady poured a cup of hot soup and gave it to Marcia. When they finally connected me to Rebekah she was frantic. I assured her we were fine, but I could tell she wouldn't believe it until she saw us face to face. I relayed to her directions to come get us.

"My word. I thought I saw a tornado earlier. It's a wonder you weren't swept away and killed," the lady said.

"Oh, no. I think it was just a thunderstorm."

Marcia said, "I saw a tornado and it was heading straight for us. Then it went up in the clouds."

"Honey," I said. "I didn't see that."

"You were busy driving the boat, Daddy. But I was watching and I saw the big green tornado."

"I think she's right, sir. I saw that eerie green sky too. You know how it looks just before a tornado strikes."

I cringed just thinking of Rebekah's reaction if she

found out we had narrowly missed death at the hands of a tornado. She'd never let us fish again or, if she did, we'd have to clear every outing with the National Weather Service. About twenty minutes later I heard Rebekah's car pull up and Mark, Peter, and Reggi run up the stairs. I went to the door and opened it.

"Daddy, Daddy. Are you okay?" Mark asked. Peter hugged me like I had been gone six months. Rebekah stood at the door.

"Come on in," the lady said.

"Oh, thank you," Rebekah replied, looking embarrassed over our intrusion into the poor woman's cottage. Marcia came running over, and Rebekah picked her up.

"Honey, are you okay?"

"I threw up. It was rocky and terrible."

"I know, honey." Rebekah glared at me.

"Well, we better go," I said, as my kids were making themselves at home. I smiled at the lady. "You have been so nice. Thank you so much. . . . Listen, I'm an attorney and if you need any legal services, please let me know. It will be on me." I looked over at Rebekah. "Honey, give her one of my cards, would you?"

Rebekah put Marcia down and fumbled through her purse for a card. She found one and handed it to the lady. "Yes, thank you so much for everything."

As we were walking to the car I suddenly remembered my boat. "Oh, honey. I'll have to drive the boat back to the marina. You take the kids to the resort and I'll meet you there in about an hour."

Reggi said, "Dad, I'll go with you."

"No, you won't. I'm not crazy about your Dad taking out the boat today, let alone you."

Reggi frowned and headed for the car. I started down to the beach toward where we had left the boat. My stomach tightened as I scanned the beach for *Christine* but didn't see her. I looked back and saw Rebekah about to get into the car and leave. "Rebekah!" I yelled. "Wait."

When I got down to the beach the boat was gone. I bent down and picked up the rope where it had snapped. "Damn it!" I heard voices and looked up and saw the boys running toward me. I turned and walked back and we met half way back to the car.

"What happened?" Rebekah asked.

"She's gone?" I said as tears began to well up. "The wind must have been so strong it broke the rope and she drifted out into the middle of the lake. I'll have to hire someone to take me out and look for her."

Rebekah frowned. "No, just forget about it. You don't need a boat. They're too dangerous. Look what—"

"Daddy, Daddy!" Reggi screamed pointing at the cliffs. We turned and looked where Reggi was pointing. It was *Christine*. She was two hundred yards away, smashed up against the cliffs.

"Oh, my God!" Rebekah said. "How did it—"

I said, "There *was* a tornado. Holy smoke! Marcia was right."

CHAPTER THIRTY-ONE

A Perfect Snow

Growing up in Southern California, I never woke up to a white landscape. It didn't happen often in Texas either, but once or twice a year we got lucky. It was such a day in early March when I woke up and saw the lawn and trees covered with snow. Some kids were already up making a snowman across the cul de sac. It was a perfect snow because the temperature was hovering just above freezing so there was no accumulation of snow on the roads.

It had only been a few weeks since the Cochran trial and we had already picked up a new murder case. I let Paula take the lead on this one as I needed a rest. Jodie was relieved when we hired a secretary for Paula. His name was Stewart. He was a big, muscular guy who used to be her personal trainer. Paula called him Stew and obviously enjoyed bossing him around all day, and I enjoyed kidding her about him.

When I got to the office, there was a message from Jodie that her driveway was iced in so she wouldn't be coming to work. She lived in McKinney and apparently the storm had been worse up there. Paula showed up thirty minutes later and she too had a message from Stewart with a similar excuse as to why he wouldn't be in.

"Boy, any excuse to stay home, huh?" Paula said.

"Oh, well. It should be a quiet day. We should get a lot of work done."

"You want some coffee?" she said.

"Sure, if you're making it."

"I am. I'll bring it to your office in a minute."

"Okay."

Several minutes later she strolled into my office with two cups of coffee. She came around behind me and set mine down in front of me and then started drinking hers directly behind me.

Paula took a deep breath and sighed. "Isn't it wonderful. We finally are together. We've just won our first big trial."

I swung my seat around and looked up at her. "Yes, this is working out quite nicely."

She put her coffee down and gave me a tender smile. "I've got something for you."

"What?"

She pulled a piece of note paper out of her pocket and handed it to me. I took it, opened it and began reading.

Alone

The clock is my worst enemy
It ticks with chilling regularity
You should be next to me, annexed to me
I long for your touch, the warmth of your body
But I'm alone. Always, always alone

The long days without you drain me
I feel weary and subdued
Depression is my only companion
You should be with me, to cheer me
But I"m alone, always, always alone

The long nights are the bleakest hours
As I yearn for the sound of your voice
We should be together, hand in hand
But I am alone, always, utterly alone

At last you are with me, next to me
Joy has filled my heart and soul
You are my love and we are one
I will never again be alone, never ever alone.

Your Love

I looked up at her and said, "But you said you didn't write the poetry?"

She shrugged. "So, I lied. What did you expect? Did you think I'd admit to your wife I was out to seduce you?"

I shook my head and said, "Rob was right?"

She frowned, "What?"

"Nothing."

She smiled again and then leaned over and gave me a kiss. As she fell into my lap I got a glimpse of a picture on my credenza of Rebekah and the kids getting ready to go swimming at the community pool. Guilt overcame me. I pushed Paula away. "Stop it! This isn't going to work."

Paula stood up. "What do you mean? I found us a nice condo down the street. Whenever we feel like it we can take a break and go make love."

I stood up and said firmly, "No. We've got a good thing going here with the new partnership. If we're lovers, the first time we have a lover's spat or Rebekah figures out what's going on, the firm will be in jeopardy. . . . Come on, Paula. You're a big-time criminal attorney now. Do you want to screw that up?"

Paula took a deep breath and gave me a disappointed look. "I've wanted you since the first day I met you in law school."

"I know. I'm sorry. But I'd probably only disappoint you anyway."

She laughed. "How do you figure?"

"You got a thing for the big, burly brutes."

She grinned and said, "Go to Hell, Turner." Then she sauntered out of my office shaking her head. When she was gone I fell back into my chair and let out a huge sigh of relief. I knew that probably wasn't the last time she'd try to lure me to her new condo, but I hoped and prayed if it happened again I'd have the strength to resist her one more time. It was a dangerous way to live but I had gotten used to living on the edge.

Other Stan Turner Mysteries

Undaunted
Book I

Trade Paperback List Price $14.95 ISBN 0-9666366-0-0

As a youngster Stan Turner is determined to become an attorney. He is mysteriously forewarned that the path to his dream will be difficult and fraught with danger. At every turn Stan is confronted with seemingly insurmountable obstacles, yet he pushes forward, undaunted by the unknown forces that seek to derail him.

Forced into the U.S. Marines by a vicious twist of fate, he leaves his family and reports for duty. On his first day he unwittingly befriends a serial killer and soon finds himself charged with the murder of his drill sergeant.

Brash Endeavor
Book II

Trade Paperback, $12.95 ISBN 1-884570-89-5

Step into the shoes of Dallas attorney, Stan Turner as he begins the practice of law in Dallas in the late 70's. Broke but determined to start practice he begins with a two thousand dollars cash advance on his credit card. Then hang on for the ride of your life as Stan immediately steps into a rattlesnake's nest and has to do some fancy two-steppin' to avoid a lethal strike from his own clients.

When Stan's wife, Rebekah, is arrested for murder and a client turns out to be a ghost, Stan turns in his legal pad for a detective's notebook and goes to work to solve these most perplexing mysteries.

Sex, greed and a lust for power drive this most extraordinary novel to a stunning conclusion.

Second Chair
Book III
A Stan Turner Mystery
Top Publications $14.95   ISBN 0-9666366-9-4
Trade Paperback

It's 1981 in Dallas and Stan decides to throw a Christmas party at his home as a way of saying thanks to the clients who have sustained him during his first tumultuous year in the practice of law. As Stan's luck would have it, a client is killed and Stan is blamed for his death. While trying to shield himself from the wrath of the grieving widow, he's asked to defend a young college student charged with murdering her newborn child. Knowing he lacks the experience for such an undertaking, he enlists his former criminal law professor to be "Second Chair." What he doesn't know is the professor, who everyone calls "Snake" is a drunk and a womanizer. When Snake fails to show up for the last few days of trial, Stan is devastated.

OTHER NOVELS BY

WILLIAM MANCHEE

Twice Tempted

Death Pact

Trouble In Trinidad

For other Top Publications' novels visit the Top Publications' website at

http://toppub.com

Or visit Manchee at his website

http://williammanchee.com

About the Author

William Manchee grew up during the 50's and 60's in the seacoast town of Ventura, California. At an early age he became interested in politics and was a congressional intern for his local congressman. He loved nature and the outdoors and traveled extensively in the western United States with his family.

At age fifteen he met his wife, the then Janet Mello. He was married in 1967 while at UCLA getting his undergraduate degree in political science. He and his wife both worked to support themselves and their four children while Manchee attended SMU Law School in Dallas in the early 70's. He received his Juris Doctor in 1975 and immediately started his own practice. Recently his son, James, and daughter, Maryanna, have joined the firm.

Manchee first began writing part time in 1995 after the last of his four children went off to college. With time on his hands, for the first time in twenty years, he began to look for something fun to do at night and on the weekends. Writing had always interested him and once he got serious about it, he was hooked. *Ca$h Call* is his seventh novel.